Cecil County Public Library
301 Newark Ave.

JUN 2 2 2011

D0562361

ROYAL
SISTERS

JUN 2 2 2011

ROYAL SISTERS

a Novel of the Stuarts

JEAN PLAIDY

BROADWAY PAPERBACKS   NEW YORK

This is a work of fiction. Names, characters, places, and incidents either are the product
of the author's imagination or are used fictitiously. Any resemblance to actual persons,
living or dead, events, or locales is entirely coincidental.

Copyright © 1966 by Jean Plaidy, copyright renewed 1994 by Mark Hamilton

Excerpt from *Courting Her Highness* copyright © 1966 by Jean Plaidy, copyright renewed
1994 by Mark Hamilton

All rights reserved.
Published in the United States by Broadway Paperbacks, an imprint of the
Crown Publishing Group, a division of Random House, Inc., New York.
www.crownpublishing.com

Broadway Paperbacks and its logo, a letter B bisected on the diagonal, are trademarks of
Random House, Inc.

Originally published in hardcover in slightly different form as *The Haunted Sisters* in
Great Britain by Robert Hale Limited, London, in 1966, and in hardcover in the
United States by G. P. Putnam's Sons, New York, in 1977.

This book contains an excerpt from the forthcoming Broadway Paperbacks reprint of
Courting Her Highness by Jean Plaidy, which was originally published as *The Queen's Favourites*
by Robert Hale Limited, London, in 1966. This excerpt has been set for this edition
only and may not reflect the final content of the forthcoming edition.

Library of Congress Cataloging-in-Publication Data
Plaidy, Jean, 1906–1993.
[Haunted sisters]
Royal sisters : a novel of the Stuarts / Jean Plaidy.
p. cm.
1. Mary II, Queen of England, 1662–1694—Fiction. 2. Anne, Queen of Great
Britain, 1665–1714—Fiction. 3. Queens—Great Britain—Fiction. I. Title.
PR6015.I3H3 2011
823'.914—dc22
2011000643

ISBN 978-0-307-71952-2
eISBN 978-0-307-72084-9

Printed in the United States of America

Book design by Maria Elias
Cover design by Laura Duffy
Cover photography by Richard Jenkins

10 9 8 7 6 5 4 3 2 1

First Broadway Paperbacks Edition

A HUSBAND

FOR ANNE

*T*he Princess Anne, walking slowly through the tapestry room in St. James's Palace—for it was a lifetime's habit never to hurry—smiled dreamily at the silken pictures representing the love of Venus and Mars which had been recently made for her uncle, the King. Tucked inside the bodice of her gown was a note; she had read it several times; and now she was taking it to her private apartments to read it again.

Venus and Mars! she thought, Goddess and God, and great lovers. But she was certain that there had never been lovers like Anne of York and John Sheffield, Earl of Mulgrave, Princess and Poet.

Her lips moved as she repeated the words he had written.

> *Of all mankind I loved the best*
> *A nymph so far above the rest*
> *That we outshine the Blest above*
> *In beauty she, as I in love.*

No one could have written more beautifully of Venus than John Sheffield had written of her.

What had happened to Venus and Mars? she wondered idly. She had never paid attention to her lessons; it had been so easy to complain that her eyes hurt or she had a headache when she was expected to study. Mary—dear Mary!—had warned her that she would be sorry she was so lazy, but she had not been sorry yet, always preferring ignorance to effort; everyone had indulged her, far more than they had poor Mary who had been forced to marry that hateful Prince of Orange. Anne felt miserable remembering Mary's face swollen from so many tears. Dear sister Mary, who had always learned her lessons and been the good girl; and what had been her reward? Banishment from her own country, sent away from her family, and married to that horrid little man, the Orange, as they called him—or more often Caliban, the Dutch Monster.

The exquisitely sculptured Tudor arch over the fireplace commemorated two more lovers whose entwined initials were H and A. Henry the VIII and Anne Boleyn had not remained constant lovers. That was indeed a gloomy thought and the Princess Anne made a habit of shrugging aside what was not pleasant.

She turned from the tapestry room and went to her own apartments. Delighted to find none of her women there, she sat in the window seat and took out the paper.

Soon, the whole Court would be reading the poem, but they would not know that those words were written for her. They would say: "Mulgrave writes a pretty verse." And only she would know.

But it was not always going to be so. Why should they hide their passion?

Her father had always been indulgent, and she preferred to believe he would continue so. Her uncle too, but state policy could come into this—as it had with Mary.

Anne was suddenly frightened, remembering that terrifying day when Mary had come to her, bewildered, like a sleepwalker. "Anne, they are forcing me to marry our cousin Orange."

Matters of state! A Princess's duty! Those words which meant that the free and easy life was over. An indulgent father and a kind uncle were yet Duke of York and King of England; and matters of state must take precedence over family feeling.

Anne refused to consider failure. It was a trait in her character which had often exasperated Mary. Anne believed what she wanted to believe, so now she believed she would be allowed to marry Mulgrave.

Reaching her apartment she went at once to the window and, as she had expected, she saw him in the courtyard below, where he had been walking backward and forward hoping for a glimpse of her.

They smiled at each other. He was not only the most handsome man in her uncle's Court, thought Anne, but in the world.

"Wait!" Her lips formed the words; he could not hear, of course, but with the extra sense of a lover, he understood.

She turned from the window, picked up a cloak, wrapped it round her and pulled the hood over her head. It would help to conceal her identity. Unhurriedly she went down to the courtyard.

He ran to her and took both her hands.

"We must not stay here," she said.

"But we must talk."

She nodded and drew him to an alcove in the stone wall; here they could remain hidden from anyone crossing the courtyard.

"My poem . . ." he began.

"It was beautiful."

"Did you understand what the lines meant?"

"I think I understand," she said.

He quoted:

> "And therefore They who could not bear
>   To be outdone by mortals here,
>   Among themselves have placed her now.
>   And left me wretched here below."

"It sounds as though she's dead," said Anne.

"It is symbolic. I daren't tell the truth. You *are* so far above me . . . a Princess. What hope have I . . ."

"You should always hope."

"You cannot mean . . ."

"I think they want me to be happy."

"And you would be happy?"

Anne never troubled to hide her feelings; she was always frankly herself.

"I want to marry you," she said.

Mulgrave caught his breath with joy, and surprise.

Marriage with the Princess Anne! That thought had entered his head, of course, but he scarcely dared hope. Why, if Charles had no legitimate child—and it seemed unlikely that he would—and James had no son, which also seemed a possibility, and Mary remained childless, well then it would be the Princess Anne's turn. The prospect was dazzling. Married to the Queen of England! She was not an arrogant woman; one only had to look into that fresh-colored face, those eyes which, owing to some opthalmic trouble which had been with her since childhood, gave her a helpless look, at that body which was already showing signs of indulgence at the table, to realize that her air of placidity was an absolute expression of her true nature. She would be easy going, lazy—a comfortable wife even though she were a Queen.

No wonder he was in love with Anne.

He shook his head. "They would never allow it."

She smiled at him fondly. "If I begged and pleaded . . ."

"You would do that?"

"For you," she told him.

He drew her toward him and kissed her almost wonderingly. She was delightful—gentle, yielding, frankly adoring, and a Princess! He, of course, was a very ambitious man, but this seemed too much good fortune. He must not let her delude him into the belief that it would be easy to marry her.

It was a pleasant state of affairs when ambition and pleasure were so admirably linked. Ever since he had become Gentleman of the Bedchamber to Anne's father he had observed the royal family at close quarters and consequently knew a great deal about their weaknesses. No one in the country could help being aware of James's position at this time for already his brother the King had thought it wise to send him into exile on more than one occasion and the Bill, the object of which was to exclude

James from the succession, was being discussed not only in Parliament but in every town and village.

Mulgrave had served with the fleet against the Dutch and been appointed captain of a troop of horse. The Duke of York was inclined to favor him; but what would his reactions be when he knew he aspired to marry his daughter?

Looking into the eager face of seventeen-year-old Anne he believed she was too simple—or too determined to have her way—to see the enormous difficulties which lay before them.

He caught her hands. "We must be careful," he said.

"Oh, yes. We must be careful."

"This must be our secret . . . for a while."

She understood that.

"It would not do for His Majesty to know what is in our minds."

"He has always been so kind to me," she told him.

Kind, yes. Kindness was second nature to the King. He would smile at Anne, pat her hand, tell her he was delighted she had a lover; and immediately begin to arrange a marriage of state for her. In one respect Anne was a little like her uncle. There was a laziness in both natures which made them long for a peaceful existence and capable of doing almost anything to achieve it.

Charles was not very pleased with the Earl of Mulgrave at this time because he knew that Mulgrave had helped to increase the strife which existed between James and Charles's illegitimate son, the Duke of Monmouth. It had become difficult for Charles to banish his brother and not send Monmouth away also; so Monmouth had been exiled too. Charles had seen the necessity, but he remembered that Mulgrave had helped to exacerbate relations between the two Dukes and when he knew of this greatest ambition of all, he might decide he had been too lenient.

Mulgrave wondered how to impress on Anne the need to be very cautious while not letting her believe that marriage between them was quite out of the question. Gentle and yielding as she was to him, so would she be to others; and if it were pointed out to her that she must take a foreign Prince as a husband, would she placidly smile and accept her fate?

"But you understand, my Princess, that we must be very, very careful . . ."

He stopped and gave a little gasp, for someone had stepped into the alcove.

A rather shrill voice said: "Ah, Madam, I have searched and searched for you."

Mulgrave was horrified. Here he was, caught with the Princess Anne in his arms; but Anne merely laughed.

"It's only Sarah," she said. "My *dearest* Sarah how you frightened me!"

"Apologies, Madam. But I thought I should warn you. You are being somewhat indiscreet."

"We thought no one would see us here."

"*I* saw you."

"Oh, but Sarah, you are the one who sees all." Anne was smiling at her lover. "John," she went on, gently, "all is well. It is only my dearest friend who would never bring me anything but good. Sarah, you, who are happily married yourself, will understand."

"I understand, Madam, but at the same time I tremble."

"Tremble! You, Sarah! When did you ever tremble?"

"For myself, never. For you, Madam . . . often."

"You see, John, what a good friend she is to me? I am fortunate indeed to have two such . . . friends. John has been telling me, Sarah, that we have to be very careful not to betray ourselves. What say you?"

"I should say he is right," said Sarah. "And the best way, Madam, if you will excuse my saying so, is *not* to embrace in the courtyards."

"We were well hidden from sight."

"H'm," said Sarah sharply. She peered up at Mulgrave. "You are silent, my lord."

"My dear lady, you seem well equipped to keep the conversation alive."

Anne smiled fondly from one to the other. "You must know that I want you two to be friends."

"Anyone who is Madam's friend is my friend," said Sarah.

Mulgrave put in: "That is a great relief."

"And now," went on Sarah, "I think, Madam, that I should conduct you to your apartments. I will keep watch while you say your farewells."

With that she turned her back on them and for a moment they clung to each other.

"John," whispered Anne, "what shall we do?"

"Nothing . . . as yet," he told her. "We must think of a way."

"Yes, John. You think of a way . . . but think quickly."

"I have only one desire in my life."

"And I."

Sarah said without turning her head: "I think I hear footsteps approaching. It would be well to go now."

The lovers looked longingly at each other for a few more seconds; then John dropped Anne's hand and she went to Sarah.

Mulgrave watched the two young women walk into the palace.

In the Princess's apartments Anne was telling Sarah about her love for Mulgrave. Sarah was displeased; she had learned of this through her own indefatigable efforts as she would always discover any intrigue; but it was disturbing that Anne had not confided in her, for it was unlike the Princess to exclude her from her secrets.

Although Sarah was lady-in-waiting to the Duchess of York, she was constantly in the company of the Princess Anne; and before Mulgrave had enchanted the Princess, Sarah had been more important to her than anyone. Sarah was piqued, but she did not show it. Arrogant and overbearing as she invariably was to others, she was careful in her approach to Anne.

Little fool! thought Sarah. Her sister Mary has a husband, and I have a husband; therefore *she* must have one. She always had to imitate, not having a mind of her own.

So she had chosen to fall in love with the Earl of Mulgrave—an ambitious young man, if ever Sarah saw one; and she was not going to tolerate ambitious people about the Princess, particularly those who would have more influence than Sarah Churchill.

She did not tell her this now; instead she pretended to be pleased.

Anne was explaining how she had loved him from the first moment she had seen him. "And the fact that his name was John . . . like your dear husband's . . . endeared him to me, Sarah."

"Ah, Madam, you always wish to do as I do."

"Mary used to say I imitated her. Alas, I can no longer imitate my dear sister."

"Nor should you wish to, Madam, seeing that the Princess of Orange spends a great deal of her time in tears."

"Poor, poor Mary, married to that hateful creature."

"Caliban!" said Sarah venomously.

"I pity Mary," said Anne, her lips trembling.

"Pity can do her no good, Madam. Let us hope that *you* never have to make a marriage of state."

"It will not be necessary," said Anne complacently. "Mary has done that. I believe I can persuade my father to let me marry for love."

"It will not rest with your father," Sarah reminded her grimly. "Remember the position he is in."

"Poor Papa!"

Poor Papa, indeed! thought Sarah. His future was not very certain. If this Bill succeeded and he was excluded from the throne, unless he had a son it would be the turn of Mary. And after that . . . Anne.

Sarah was a woman who had to make her way in the world by means of her own wits, and she constantly thanked God that they were sharp ones. She had to fight for herself and her John and she was going to find such a niche for them that would be the envy of the country. Both she and John had come to their present hopeful positions by great good luck; they must work hard to keep them.

John had been wise to choose her for his wife; and she had also chosen wisely. She would make him the greatest soldier in the world; yes, and have the world recognize him as such.

But that meant playing the game of life very carefully; knowing your luck for what it was and exploiting it.

Sarah had been a little shocked when she realized how far the Mulgrave affair had gone; not that she was alarmed; she was certain it could not go much farther. For one thing, she, Sarah Churchill, would not allow it.

"However," went on Sarah, "the King is kind to lovers."

"Oh, Sarah," laughed Anne, "how right you are! And so he should be."

"But," went on Sarah sternly, "for the time, you must be careful. This must go no farther than letters and an occasional meeting with another present."

"You, Sarah, of course."

"There is no one else you can trust."

"Oh, Sarah, how wonderful to have you to look after me! All will be well, I am sure. When you think they might have married me to that hateful George who, to my mind, was as bad—or almost—as poor Mary's Orange."

Prince George of Hanover! thought Sarah. She had been alarmed when that possibility had arisen. She had not liked the little German, who could not speak a word of English and gave the impression that he was not going to try. He was small of stature and uncouth in manners.

Ugh! shivered Sarah. And what place would there have been for John and Sarah Churchill at Hanover? She was glad *that* had come to nothing.

"A most distasteful man!" she muttered.

Then she remembered that Anne had been complacent enough. Of course Mulgrave had not appeared on the scene at that time; but Anne had shown no qualms, although the creature was so repulsive and would have carried her off to Hanover.

Anne was adaptable. That was why she was such an excellent mistress for an ambitious woman to serve. Serve! Proud Sarah was not one to serve. She wanted to guide her mistress into giving all that was best to Sarah Churchill, that Sarah might make use of it for John, and this clever couple become the most powerful people in the world.

She was not even in the service of Anne, but that of Mary of Modena, Duchess of York, so she would not have accompanied the Princess to Hanover. Nor had she had any intention of going—although with the Duke and Duchess so unpopular that they must periodically be banished from England, she could not see clearly ahead. If the Duke of York were King it would be good to be in the service of his wife; and to be in the service of Anne might mean that one were sent anywhere in the world if she made a foreign marriage—as the Princess Mary had been sent to Holland.

To play this game now was like walking a tightrope, but Sarah knew she was capable of coming safely across.

"Write your love letters," said Sarah. "I will see that they are delivered. Then . . . in time . . . we must think of a plan."

Anne threw herself into her friend's arms.

"I am thinking of all I owe you, Sarah," said Anne.

Sarah was thinking: She grows fatter than ever.

As soon as Sarah was alone she asked herself how best she could put an end to this unfortunate romance. In the first place she did not care to see Anne more enamored of another person than she was of Sarah herself; and there was no doubt that she was positively besotted about Mulgrave.

The marriage is most unsuitable! Sarah said to herself. Anyone but my foolish Anne would know it. As for Mulgrave, he, poor fool, is prepared to make a bid for power. So with one blinded by ambition and another by love, they might be prepared to put up a fight for what they call their love.

"Love!" said Sarah aloud. "Fiddle-faddle!" And when had Anne ever put up a fight for anything? No, Anne would be guided by her strongest adviser—and Sarah had no doubt who that was.

She looked back over her career with great satisfaction—and, she reminded herself, it was only beginning.

When she and her sister Frances were young it had seemed that they had had little hope of ever reaching Court. And now here she was, firmly established, a close friend of the Princess Anne who might one day (and Sarah was determined that this should be) become Queen of England.

But if the foolish fat creature began romancing with the first handsome man who came along, who could say in what trouble that might not land her? And if Anne made the wrong marriage what effect was this going to have on Sarah Churchill?

It was not often that the daughter of a humble squire obtained service in the royal apartments. But both she and Frances had. They were born lucky, their mother was apt to tell them; but Sarah would always respond sharply that what others called luck was really the result of hard work and clever planning by the brilliant ones who achieved it.

Looking back, Sarah decided she was predestined to greatness. She had been born at the time of Charles II's return to England. She often smiled to think of all the gaiety in the streets, all the garlands strewn on the cobbles; the bells ringing, the bonfires blazing, the processions; the joy because the long Puritan reign was over and England was going to be merry again. All that in the streets, and in a little house at Holywell, not far from St. Albans, Sarah Jennings was being born.

Sarah liked to think that all the bells were ringing for her; all the rejoicing was because Sarah had come into the world. Foolish thoughts—but the people had been greeting a ruler and it was not always those who wore crowns that ruled.

It seemed incredible that she and Frances should have come to Court. Their father was dead and their mother had disgraced herself by telling fortunes and setting herself up as a seer, but the Jennings' had been wealthy during the Civil War and had lost their fortune in fighting for the royalist cause; therefore some recompense was due to them and a simple way of repaying the service was to find two places at Court for the girls of the family.

Frances came to Court with her mother as her chaperon, and there the Duke of York immediately fell in love with the girl who had always been the beauty of the family, but Frances had no intention of succumbing, and had created a scandal by allowing some of the Duke's love letters to fall at the feet of his jealous Duchess. After that the Duke left her in peace.

While Frances and her mother were enjoying Court life, Sarah was left to the care of servants in the house at St. Albans. It was not considered necessary to give her a good education; and in any case Sarah had decided she did not need one. Books did not interest her; and she believed that she was capable of learning all she needed without help. She was determined to rule that household, which she did when her mother, who was of a similar temperament, was not there to be in conflict with her.

Frances made the most of her opportunities, married and became Lady Hamilton; in time it was Sarah's turn and she came to Court to be a maid of honor in the household of Mary Beatrice of Modena who, on the death of the first Duchess of York, had become the second.

It was not long before Sarah and her mother were quarreling. Sarah said that if her mother remained at Court, she would leave it and as a result Mrs. Jennings was asked to leave; but her retort had been that if she went she would take Sarah with her. Sarah, quickly realizing that there was a danger of the troublesome Jennings' being sent from Court, quickly became reconciled to her mother and both remained there.

She was fortunate to be in the service of Mary Beatrice of Modena who had recently become the second wife of the Duke of York.

The first Duchess had been a woman whom Sarah must admire, for she had, in spite of great odds, married the Duke of York who was heir presumptive to the crown. And she a commoner! But she had been too fond of food and priests, and had consequently become too fat and too religious; and when that religion was Catholicism this was clearly not helpful in a Protestant land. Her luck had changed, for she had a malignant growth in her breast and after giving the Duke of York his two daughters, Mary and Anne—and sundry other children who did not live—she died. The Princesses were brought up at Richmond with Lady Frances Villiers who watched over them, her own brood of daughters, and a few other young girls who had been selected to share their childhood. Sarah became one of these.

What great good fortune! Sarah had chosen Anne as her friend understanding immediately that she would never have made the same success with Mary, who was quite different from lazy, easygoing Anne. Mary was a sentimental little girl, dreaming idly through the days, so that the biggest shock of her life had been when at fifteen she was told she was to marry the Prince of Orange.

Sarah had very soon become an important member of the royal nurseries, although Elizabeth Villiers—the eldest Villiers girl—was very sly and the only one, Sarah saw, who had to be watched. And how right she had been, for if rumors were correct, Elizabeth Villiers had already found her way into Caliban's bed, and when one considered the Dutch Monster was cold and might be near-impotent, as many said he was, Elizabeth's achievement was considerable.

Then John Churchill had fallen in love with Sarah. Sarah was handsome enough, her features were well defined and her glorious golden hair had a touch of red in it—but her domineering ways had frightened off most young men. All to the good, Sarah thought grimly. She wanted no partnership with a man who was easily frightened, nor with one who might attempt to underrate her. John, however, had been attracted by her character.

John, like Sarah, was an adventurer; they were both aware of this and the knowledge strengthened the attraction between them. He was the son of a Sir Winston Churchill, a country gentleman who, like so many, had lost his fortune fighting the royalist cause. There had seemed little hope of retrieving that fortune until Sir Winston's daughter Arabella, who was no beauty, fell from her horse when in the company of the Duke of York and his suite. Arabella's limbs were beautifully white and well formed and the Duke of York happened to catch a glimpse of them as she lay on the ground. With Arabella's fall the Churchills' fortunes began to rise, for she needed little persuasion to become the Duke's mistress; and because she was more astute than the ladies James usually chose, she soon began to reap great benefits not only for herself but for other members of her family. Among these was a commission for John in the army. This was a beginning. John soon became the Master of the Robes in the Duke's household.

John, who was something of a rake, attracted the attention of the King's mistress, Barbara Villiers, Countess of Castlemaine, and there was a story in circulation which was often repeated. The King, it was said, had surprised Churchill with his mistress and Churchill had had to leap naked from her bed to make a hasty exit through the window into the courtyard; Charles, reaching the window in time to see who he was, shouted after him that he need have no fear; he was forgiven for he did what he did for his bread. It was true that John did accept five thousand pounds from Barbara. He was a man who, having been short of money, was very careful with it, and bought himself an annuity of five hundred pounds a year which he was able to do with four thousand five hundred.

He was ten years older than Sarah, but as soon as they met he fell deeply in love with her. His emotion was clearly genuine, for Sarah was poor. As for Sarah, she had imagined herself making a grand marriage; but the immediate attraction could not be overcome and they knew at once that they would never be happy without each other. Sarah was aware of John's reputation, but she had no doubt of her ability to make him forsake his lechery and become a virtuous husband, because Sarah had never doubted her ability to do anything. Therefore she dismissed all the stories of the scandalous life he led. There would be no amatory adventures *after* the marriage, she was determined. But although she was seriously considering marrying John she showed no sign of eagerness, and when she heard that Sir Winston was set against his son's marriage to this penniless Jennings girl, she declared that she certainly did not count it such an honor to marry into the Churchill family, who although they had come far, she was ready to admit, had done so solely because of John's sister Arabella's illicit relationship with the Duke of York. Her own sister, Frances, whom she preferred to call the Countess of Hamilton, was in Paris with her husband, and in order to escape John's courtship and relieve the Churchills, who appeared to have such a mighty opinion of themselves, she had decided to ask leave of the Duchess of York to join Frances.

John, frantic at the thought of losing her, told her he was ready to defy his family and begged her to marry him—in secret. This Sarah considered and, deciding that once the marriage was an accomplished fact the Churchills would have to accept it, agreed.

So she became Mrs. John Churchill when she was eighteen and John twenty-eight. She had gone at once to the Italian Duchess of York and confessed to her what she had done, finding there, as she had expected, nothing but sympathy. Thus the marriage remained a secret for some months, but then the Duchess spoke to the Churchills who, since such an important lady was supporting her lady-in-waiting, could no longer keep up their objections. They received Sarah, accepting the marriage, thankful that, because of it, their son had been brought to the further notice of the Duke and Duchess of York, who, taking a personal interest in the young couple, were inclined to favor them.

The young Duchess of York, who was on very good terms with her stepchildren, listened to Anne's eulogies on her beloved Sarah; and Sarah told Anne of the virtues of John, which were in turn passed on to the Duke and the Duchess.

It was all very satisfactory, but since the Duke of York was growing so unpopular and had, on occasions, been sent out of England on what could only be called exiles, Sarah was uncertain as to whether she had attached herself to the right faction. The Duke's interest in Catholicism was going to ruin him if he were not careful. Anne was the Princess to whom she must adhere. The Duke's folly was an example of how a once popular Prince could become unpopular. Sarah must be on the winning side.

Sarah's interests had been slightly diverted from Court for a while when her daughter Henrietta had been born; and recently there had been another daughter whom Sarah had had the foresight to christen Anne. She left the children in the care of nurses, for with a husband and children to plan for, quite clearly she must act with care, and that meant remaining at Court. She had always known that the Princess was as capable of folly as her father and this affair with Mulgrave was proving that. If it were discovered that she, Sarah, had helped in that intrigue, she would be decidedly out of favor with such important people as the Duke and Duchess of York—worse still, with the King.

It was matters like this which could ruin years of careful planning; she must think very carefully of how she must act.

The King of England was the most approachable of monarchs. He encouraged his subjects to talk to him and never doubted his ability to be able to please them; and in fact was always ready to grant the requests they made; if it was difficult to fulfill them he could always blame the failure to do so on his ministers.

When Rochester had made his famous quip pointing out that he never said a foolish thing and never did a wise one, Charles had retorted with customary wit that his words were his own, his actions his ministers'. He was grateful to Rake Rochester for pointing this out; he reckoned that once this was generally understood he had the perfect excuse.

It was typical of him that he should find a way for himself out of any difficulty that arose. He often wished that his brother James were a little more like himself, because he saw trouble accumulating for James when his turn came to wear the crown.

He was sitting watching the card play, two of his favorite mistresses, Louise de Kéroualle—Duchess of Portsmouth—and Nell Gwyn, beside him. These two never failed to divert him, and together they were more amusing than apart. Louise played the great lady never so arrogantly as when in Nelly's company and Nelly played the gutter-brat never so bawdily as when with Louise.

With great affection he regarded them; they had pleased him for many years and he hoped would continue to do so for many more; though lately he had begun to feel his vigor passing. A sad state, he thought, for a man to find his senses flagging when his greatest pleasure has been the gratification of those senses.

A pity. He had never been a great eater, drinker, or gambler. No, for him there was no pleasure like being in love.

It pleased him now to glance from Louise to Nelly and to contemplate with which he should spend the night; he knew that they too were wondering; if it were Nelly she would be boasting throughout the Court tomorrow. She was a mad, wild creature; and Louise could not understand how he tolerated her.

Louise now bent toward him and said: "A young woman was asking for an audience with Your Majesty this day."

The King raised his eyebrows. It was unlike Louise to bring young women to his notice.

"I'll warrant she comes to ask a favor for herself," he murmured.

"Or for Mademoiselle Carwell," added Nelly quietly.

Louise flashed her a look of hatred; nothing could anger her more than to hear the people's version of her name. Kéroualle—Carwell. The King's lips turned up at the corners.

"Come, Nelly," he said, "you ladies know that if you desire aught you have no need to send others to plead for you."

"The best beggars often train others to beg for them, Your Majesty," retorted Nelly. "It's a good trade . . . begging for beggars."

"You should be well aware of such trades," said Louise. "I am afraid I lack your knowledge."

"I'll teach you one fine day," Nelly told her. "Catholic whores should learn to keep up with the Protestants."

Louise shuddered, and the King said: "More of the fair young beggar."

"It was one of the Princess Anne's women, Your Majesty. She would tell me nothing, and said she could tell it to none but Your Majesty. It was Churchill's wife."

The King laughed at the mention of Churchill. He thought of an occasion when he had called on Barbara and caught her with that young man.

"Churchill," he said. "They tell me the fellow has reformed since his marriage."

"I have heard it too, Your Majesty."

"God's fish, he was in need of reformation."

"If all those who were in need of reformation reformed, the Court would be a sadder place," suggested Nelly, looking slyly at the King.

"Now who of us would not be better off if we foresook our evil ways, Nelly?"

"Two ladies—if I may call them by the name—not so far from Your Majesty. For if the biggest rake of them all decided to reform, where should *we* be? I'd perforce return to the boards and Madame here to crying stinking fish in Brittany."

"I refuse to remain in the company of this creature," said Louise.

"Hurrah!" cried Nelly.

Louise had risen and walked haughtily away glancing at the King almost angrily as though commanding him to dismiss Nelly and follow her.

Charles affected not to see her, reflecting: Well, they have decided between them. It shall be Nelly tonight.

He liked having such decisions made for him.

The next day he remembered the scene when he found Sarah Churchill standing before him.

A connoisseur of women he automatically summed her up. Virago, he thought, and wondered whether if he had been a younger man she might have attracted him. Although he was ready to promise almost anything for the sake of peace, he could not help being attracted by viragos. Barbara had been one to outdo all others; Louise was not far off—only she fought with tears. This Sarah Churchill, like Barbara, would never do that. He saw the stamp of ambition on her face and wondered momentarily if she would attempt to become his mistress for the sake of advancing her husband's fortunes. He was so lazy, if she did, he probably would give way.

Her first words showed him how wrong he had been.

"Your Majesty, I feel it my duty to bring a certain matter to your notice. I have given much thought to this and know it now to be my duty. It concerns the Princess Anne. Have I your permission to continue?"

"Pray do," said Charles, thinking: No, I never would. She is too hard, this one. And I am old and more selective than in the days of my youth. Young she is and handsome, but she'd make too many bargains before getting into bed.

"The Earl of Mulgrave seeks to marry the Princess Anne, Your Majesty."

He regarded her sleepily.

"I have proof of his intentions," she went on. "This I have brought to lay before Your Majesty."

He took the paper and read the words written there. She was right. A love letter written by his niece to Mulgrave. It would seem that this affair had gone farther than it should have been allowed to.

"I trust, Your Majesty, I have acted wisely."

"I am certain that Mrs. Churchill will always act wisely," said the King graciously.

"Then Your Majesty is not displeased with me?"

"You did not fear that I should be displeased with you," he said with a smile she did not understand. "It is my niece's displeasure you expect."

"Your Majesty, I beg that this may be kept secret from the Princess Anne."

"Who," put in Charles, "has no notion that you have stolen her little *billet doux?*"

"Only because I considered it my duty to . . . the Princess."

"Readily understood, Mrs. Churchill. Have no fear. And . . . I thank you."

"I thank Your Gracious Majesty."

She curtseyed and retired while he stood looking at the paper in his hand.

Poor little Anne! So she had found there was something as sweet in the world as chocolate. There had been times when he had thought she never would.

He folded the paper carefully and put it into his pocket; then he summoned one of his pages and told him that he wished the Duke of York to be sent to him without delay.

When James arrived Charles held out the note which Sarah had brought him.

James took it gingerly and when he read it he looked up, bewildered, into his brother's face.

"You see," said Charles, "that our little Anne is ripe for marriage."

"But Mulgrave!" cried James.

"I echo your sentiments," Charles told him. "I have fancied that of late my lord had become too hopeful."

"You think Anne is in love with the fellow?"

"Anne loves him as she loves sweetmeats, brother, and the love for a sweetmeat is a passing fancy. There it is . . . ah, delectable, adorable. What flavor! The taste lingers for a while—a very little while. And then it is gone. When we have removed Mulgrave from her greedy little eyes she will be looking round for the next fancy. We must find something very sweet and succulent for her, brother."

"My poor child. I cannot forget Mary."

"Anne is not Mary; and we will try to find her a more attractive bridegroom than the Orange."

"I was never in favor of *that* marriage."

"Your misfortune James is that you have rarely been in favor of what was to your advantage."

Charles gave his brother a melancholy smile. What will become of him when I am gone? he asked himself. There would be trouble. With Monmouth casting sheep's eyes at the crown and William who couldn't cast sheep's eyes if it were a matter of saving his life to do so—still, if the poor fellow could not lech for a woman he could for a throne. William could be as chock-full of passion as Monmouth when it came to the crown of England; and there was James—ineffectual, with a genius for doing the wrong thing at the worst possible moment. Oh, God, thought Charles, never was a man more thankful than I that he'll be out of the way when his inheritance is for sale.

"James," he said, "why cannot you show some sense? Why not let it be known that you've given up this flirtation with popery?"

"Given it up! Flirtation! I like not your levity, brother."

"If you could season *your* seriousness with *my* levity, James, and I could mix a little of your seriousness with my levity—what a pair we would make! Nay, but if I were a betting man, which I'm not, I would wager my levity would carry me farther from trouble than your seriousness. If you would ostentatiously attend the Protestant Church, if you would practice popery in secret...."

"You are asking me to deny my faith."

"You wouldn't be the first."

"More's the pity; but I'd not be proud to join the miserable band."

"Do you call our illustrious grandfather one of a miserable band?"

"Our grandfather! I am tired of hearing how he said Paris was worth a mass."

"If you could learn a lesson from his wisdom, James, you would be a wiser man. Do you want to go a-wandering again? God's fish, man, you have just come back from Scotland. Do not tell me that you enjoyed your exile."

"Enjoyed it! Enjoyed being driven from my own country, forbidden to return to my native land . . . the land which one day—though I trust not for years and years—I could be called upon to rule!"

"There's the trouble, James. They are not going to be eager to call upon you to perform that duty."

"It is my right."

"These people consider that we govern only at their invitation. Take care, James, that that invitation is not withdrawn. I tell you this: I did enough wandering in my youth, and I am of no mind to start again."

"Your Majesty fears the people might send you away."

"Nay, James, never. They would not rid themselves of me to get you!" Charles began to laugh. "No matter what I did they'd still take Charles in place of James. Now, brother, I'm warning you—and I'm forgetting why I sent for you. We must find a bridegroom for Anne . . . without delay. Our little plum is ripe for the picking. She needs a husband. Bless her heart, she shall have one."

"But not the one of her choice," said James sadly. "Whom have you in mind?"

"It is a question I have been pondering ever since I received this note."

"I hear that Louis's wife is ill."

"A French marriage! A Catholic marriage! Are you indeed out of your mind, James?"

"My little girl the Queen of France."

"It would not do. But first there is something which I am sure you will agree must be done without delay. I think we should be together when we receive our ambitious young lover. I will summon him without delay."

"What are you going to do with him?"

"Do not look alarmed, James. You know I never take revenge. Nor do I wish my subjects to be in awe of me. I have no wish to be like some of our ancestors. 'Off with his head. He has offended me!'" Charles grimaced at the arch over the fireplace which was decorated with Tudor roses and the initials H. and A. "I do not wish my subjects to go in fear and trembling. I would have them know that I do not take revenge; when I am harsh there is no personal animosity. It is a case of: 'The situation demands this—therefore the King is forced to do it.'"

Mulgrave, who was in his apartments writing a poem in praise of the Princess Anne was startled when summoned to the King's presence. He could not believe that they were discovered; how could this be? They had been so careful; and Anne would never have told because she had sworn not to do so.

What if the King had singled him out for some honor! His luck was in. Why should it not continue?

In good spirits he presented himself to the King; but he was a little uneasy when he saw that the Duke of York was also present.

"Ah, my Lord Mulgrave," said the King genially.

Mulgrave bowed, first to the King, then to the Duke.

Tears came into the Duke's eyes. A handsome young fellow; his dear Anne was going to be badly hurt. James would never forget Mary's sorrow. He had never seen a girl cry so much as she had on that dreadful day when he had had to tell her she was to marry Orange. He loved his daughters dearly and could not bear that they should suffer. He himself had married their mother for love. Poor Mary! Poor Anne!

"My lord," said Charles, "we have sent for you to tell you how much we appreciate your good services."

Mulgrave found it difficult to hide his relief.

Charles went on: "So much so that we are sending you on a mission to Tangier which we know you will perform with your usual talent."

"Your Majesty . . ." gasped Mulgrave.

"Do not waste time in thanks," said Charles, waving a hand. "You will sail in the morning."

Mulgrave did not remember how he left the apartment; all he remembered was that he was standing outside, muttering: "Someone has betrayed us."

Anne was bewildered. There was no one to whom she could turn for comfort but Sarah. It was Sarah who had brought her the news. She had said: "Dearest Madam, I do not want you to hear of this through anyone else. You must be brave. The King has, through some means, discovered your love for Mulgrave, who is now far away . . . bound for Tangier, I have heard."

"Sarah!"

The round mouth sagged piteously; the pink of the cheeks had turned to scarlet; and the vague shortsighted eyes were filled with tears.

Sarah gathered her mistress into her arms.

"I am here to comfort you. I will never leave you."

"Oh, my dearest Sarah, my beloved friend, what should I do without you?"

Sarah rocked the Princess in her arms. Tenderness did not come readily to her so it seemed doubly precious to Anne.

She wept bitterly; she would not be parted from Sarah day or night; they talked constantly of Mulgrave—of his beauty and virtues; and the Princess demanded again and again: "Who could have been so cruel as to have betrayed us?"

"It may be something Your Highness will never discover," murmured Sarah.

Sarah was with Anne when she went along to look at the portrait of Charles King of Sweden. On horseback, the King was quite magnificent. Anne went close to peer at it.

"He is a very handsome man," she said.

Sarah admitted it; and was uneasy. There was an air of authority about the figure. And Sweden! Who wanted to go to Sweden. Not John or Sarah Churchill.

Anne liked the portrait though. Sarah threw an impatient look at her, and said sharply: "It would seem, Madam, that you have already forgotten my Lord Mulgrave."

"No, no, Sarah. I never, *never* shall."

"But you like the look of this fellow?"

Anne began to laugh. How like Sarah to refer to the King of Sweden as "this fellow."

"Sarah," she said, "you'll be the death of me!"

"If I can make my Princess smile I am happy."

"Sarah, Sarah, what should I do without you? When you are there I feel I can endure *anything.*"

Sarah looked imperiously at the portrait. "Arrogant!" she summed up. "I think we could well do without this fellow in our lives!"

She had made Anne laugh again.

Already she had forgotten Mulgrave. But it would not be so easy to prevent the match with Sweden.

Luck was with Sarah. There was one other who was determined to prevent a marriage between Anne and Charles of Sweden; this was William of Orange, who saw no good to Holland coming from a union between Sweden and England. He expressed his disapproval to his uncle

King Charles of England; and as, at that time, Charles wanted William's friendship, he considered his objections.

But, as Charles pointed out to his brother James, there was need of haste. King Christiern of Denmark had a brother George who was marriageable and it seemed to him that this Prince George might be a desirable bridegroom.

"We have been friendly with Denmark for years," he pointed out to James. "After all we have Danish blood through our grandmother. What more natural than that Anne should marry this kinsman?"

"We could have a look at him," agreed James.

"Certainly there can be no harm in looking."

"I do not want to see her unhappy . . . as Mary was."

"Very well. We will invite George over here, have a look at him, and throw the young couple together——"

"As we brought Orange over here? Mary did not stop crying from the moment she knew he was to be her bridegroom to the time she left. If George of Denmark should prove to be another Orange . . ."

"Nonsense, brother, there could only be one Orange in the world."

"Then let us invite him to come, and I trust Anne likes him. I would to God daughters never had to reach a marriageable age."

"Then it's more than they do. The Mulgrave affair should have shown you that, James. Daughters grow up. And remember this: Anne is not like Mary. She seems already to have forgotten Mulgrave."

James admitted this was true. But he loved his daughters dearly and longed to see them happy.

Prince George of Denmark arrived in England on a bright summer's day; he was looking forward with mild pleasure to meeting his bride; but all his emotions were mild, except perhaps his love of food and drink which was excessive; but these indulgences, to whatever excess he carried them, never ruffled his good temper; consequently he was liked, by all who came into contact with him. He was under thirty, already far too plump, but his smile, without which he was rarely seen, was disarming.

Christiern had advised him to do all in his power to bring off the marriage, because it would be excellent for Denmark if ties between the two countries could be strengthened; and George must remember that a Danish princess had married the great grandfather of his prospective bride, so there was even a family connection. Most important of all—there was little for George in Sweden, so it was up to him to seek his fortune overseas.

George knew a great deal about England, through an excellent English friend who would be ready to help him with the language and explain the customs. He had visited England in the company of this friend some years before and had liked what he had seen.

When King Christiern had gone to England to join the celebrations for the Restoration, he had noticed a bright boy of thirteen at the Court and had offered to take him into his service as page. This boy's name was George Churchill, brother of John and Arabella. Like most of his family, George Churchill was ambitious and he had seen more likelihood, of advancement in Sweden than in England; so to Sweden he went, and Christiern had offered the page to his brother George when he had paid his first visit to England.

"George Churchill will act as your interpreter," he said. "More than that he will be at your elbow to explain the English customs."

So useful had George Churchill become that Prince George was eager to keep him in his service.

Thus the two became friends, and when Prince George came to England as suitor to the Princess Anne, it was natural that he should bring George Churchill with him.

Charles smiled at his brother James. "Well, what do you think of our bridegroom? An improvement on the Orange, eh?"

"He is more genial certainly."

"Who could be less genial than our nephew William? This George looks a man of good temper; and think what he will have in common with our Anne. They will be able to discuss the virtues of marzipan versus chocolate which should prove, to them, an absorbing subject."

"I do not want to have to break the news to Anne as I did to Mary."

"Anne is two years older than her sister was when we married her to Orange."

"All the same I should like to warn her that she should look on Prince George as a possible husband."

"Is there need to warn her? The whole Court knows the purpose of his visit, so why shouldn't Anne?"

"I shall tell her," said James firmly.

The King nodded. "And do not look so sad, brother. Why, according to news from Holland, Mary is now devoted to the husband whom she wept so bitterly to accept."

"I shall never believe she truly loves him. He is a monster, that Dutchman. He keeps her almost a prisoner, my friends tell me, and she is afraid to voice an opinion. She dare do nothing but agree with everything he says and pretend to the world that she adores him."

"Our nephew is a man of many parts, brother. We always underrated him. He knows how to rule a wife as well as a country."

"And he keeps a mistress."

"Well, James, it would seem to me that neither you nor I are in a position to complain of such a natural failing. How that man creeps into our conversation! I confess I am a little weary of the Prince of Orange. I find the Prince of Denmark a happier subject. Go and speak to your daughter now, James. Tell her to consider the young man from Denmark. Tell her I favor him—and I have no doubt that she will soon do the same."

The Churchills were a devoted family and as soon as he arrived at the Court, George sought out his brother John, and there was much animated conversation concerning George's adventures in Denmark and John's at home.

With pride John introduced his brother to his wife and George soon realized what an unusual woman he had for a sister-in-law.

"Tell us what sort of man the Prince is," suggested Sarah; "and is he eager for this marriage?"

The Prince of Denmark was genial, George told them; he was easygoing, loving a life of peace, and always affable to those who served him.

"His character is not unlike that of the Princess," commented Sarah. "They should be a good match."

"He would live happily with most people," said George Churchill.

"Easily led," put in Sarah speculatively.

"But I hear he is a man of valor," her husband said.

"That is so," George told them. "If intrepid action is necessary he is capable of it, and when his brother Christiern was taken prisoner by the Swedes he rescued him."

"I have heard of that occasion," said John. "It was during the war between Denmark and Sweden." He turned to Sarah. "Prince George, hearing that his brother was in the hands of the enemy, put himself at the head of some cavalry and broke right through the Swedish lines. They were taken so much by surprise that they allowed him through; he had found his brother and was galloping off with him before they made any attempt to stop him—then it was too late. I call that a brilliant action as well as a brave one."

"Doubtless it happened before he grew quite so plump," commented Sarah.

"Ah, you have noticed that the Prince is getting a little corpulent. The pleasures of the table . . . the pleasures of the vine."

"One would not expect the man to be a saint," said John, smiling at Sarah.

"If he were my husband, I should not expect him to be a fool either," she retorted, "and any man who indulges an appetite is that."

It was a point to remember, thought John. No more pleasant little adventures with the ladies, Sarah was telling him. He wanted to retort: As if I should want to, now that I have my incomparable Sarah.

"It is important that he is accepted here," went on George confidentially. "He has very little in Denmark—only about five thousand crowns and a few barren islands."

"And yet he aspires to the hand of the Princess Anne!" said John.

"Who could," Sarah interrupted, "in certain circumstances become Queen of England."

"Do not forget that he is a royal Prince. They would, however, wish him to live in England which I believe would very likely endear him to the Princess, for what young girl wants to leave her home, particularly one where, if what I hear is correct, she has been greatly indulged by her family."

"So they would live in England," mused Sarah, her eyes alight with pleasure. She looked at her John—so handsome, and possessed of something more than personal charm. If ever I saw latent genius, I see it there, she thought; and she was triumphant in the realization that some women could choose their husbands, while Princesses must have them chosen for them. Prince George of Denmark was the absolute antithesis of John Churchill, and Sarah knew who was going to make the brighter mark in the world.

She turned to George suddenly. "You seem to know a great deal about this Prince. He is friendly toward you?"

"Completely so. He discusses most things with me and so I know his mind on most matters."

Sarah nodded. Then she said slowly: "Thus it is with myself and the Princess. I am her greatest friend. When she marries I shall ask to leave the Duchess of York's household and be taken into that of the Princess Anne. A Churchill with the Princess, and a Churchill with the Prince . . . friends, confidantes. That does not seem such a bad idea."

They understood each other so well. Sarah smiled from her brother-in-law to her husband. She had made up her mind; Anne's marriage to the Prince of Denmark could be a very good thing for the Churchills and therefore a very good thing.

"The Prince is charming!" declared Sarah. "I do believe that if I were not so devoted to my John I could fall in love with him myself."

"Sarah, you really mean it?"

"But do you not agree? Madam, what do you ask of a man? Did you hear how he rescued his brother? What bravery! My John was telling me about it. He said he had rarely heard of such a feat of bravery. And I understand, too, that the Prince is gracious. His servants love him."

"I found him . . . affable," said Anne.

"Madam, dear, you are halfway to being in love with him."

"Sometimes I think of dear Mulgrave!"

"Pah! An adventurer if ever there was one!"

"Oh, no, Sarah, he loved me truly. Those beautiful verses . . ."

"I never thought much of poets. Words mean more to them than deeds. No, I rejoice that in the Prince of Denmark you will have a husband worthy of you. And the more eager you are for the marriage, the more you please your father."

"He was very sad about Mary."

"And who can wonder? When I compare the Prince of Denmark with that . . . monster!"

"Poor, poor Mary! Yet when we were in Holland, Sarah, she seemed happy."

"To see you, to escape from Caliban for a while."

"How sorry I am for her."

"It is no use repining, Madam. Think rather of your joy. You are to have a husband with whom you are already in love . . ."

"But am I, Sarah? I am not sure . . ."

"You cannot deceive Sarah who knows you so well, Madam. If you are not already in love you are halfway there. And who can be surprised at that! This handsome hero has come across the seas to claim you. I am so happy for you, Madam."

"It is going to be a happy marriage, is it not, Sarah?"

"The happiest at Court, Madam. You know I am always right."

That was one thing Anne had learned. Obediently she began to fall in love with her bridegroom, and soon found it difficult to remember what Mulgrave looked like. This was so much more comfortable. George was pleasant, so eager to please; and he was kind, she could see that. Everyone was delighted at the prospect of the marriage. Her uncle wanted it; and so did her father, and when her father took her aside and asked her if she were truly happy and she told him she was, he took her into his embrace and wept over her.

"I thank God, my dearest daughter," he told her, "for I could not have borne to see you unhappy as your sister was."

After that she felt she owed it to them all to be happy. It was not difficult when she considered George.

Cecil County Public Library
301 Newark Ave.
Elkton, MD 21921

There was no reason why the marriage should be delayed. The day chosen was appropriate, being St. Anne's Day, and at ten o'clock at night in St. James's chapel the ceremony took place. The bride was given away by her uncle the King; and afterward there was a brilliant banquet. There was rejoicing in the streets, and the sounds of music and the light from the bonfires penetrated the palace.

Another Protestant marriage! said the people, who had welcomed the Orange marriage for the same reason. James's addiction to Catholicism was always a sore point with those who declared they would have no popery in England. Mary and Anne could well be sovereigns of England and the people had no intention of standing mildly aside while they were made into little Catholics. But there was no danger of that. Wise King Charles—always with an eye on the main chance—had decided. Not only had he taken the education of the Princesses out of their father's hands, but he had found Protestant bridegrooms for them.

The fact that Marie Thérèse, the Queen of France, had just died, made the marriage doubly welcome. Louis, a widower in need of a wife, made a dangerous situation, for all knew that James would have been delighted to see his daughter the wife of the Catholic King of France.

But all was well; she was safely married to Protestant George; so they danced with glee around their bonfires and declared the bride to be beautiful and the bridegroom gallant while Anne and her husband sat side by side, eating heartily.

They had no qualms about each other. They were so much alike; peaceable, comfortable people, who liked to indulge the pleasures of the flesh—eating, drinking, and those yet to be discovered.

What a different bride was Anne from her shuddering sister! When the curtains were drawn about the bed by the royal hand of King Charles of England, when he made his ribald comments on the duties which lay ahead of them, Anne and George turned to each other and embraced.

Everything was natural, simple, pleasantly enjoyable without arousing ecstasy. This was symbolic of the life they would share together.

MRS. MORLEY
AND MRS. FREEMAN

*N*ow that *Anne was a married woman she must* have her separate household. The Duke of York did not wish her to be too far from him, and Charles, delighted with the success of the marriage and to see Anne growing happier every day, for he disliked tears and remembered those of Anne's sister Mary—as indeed who would ever forget them?—had said the happy pair should have the Cockpit.

The Cockpit was close to Whitehall and had been built by Henry VIII as a lodge, set apart from the Palace, where he had indulged his love of cockfighting. It was a pleasant residence and Anne was enchanted with it. Close by was St. James's Palace, where her father was often in residence; and he too was pleased to have his beloved daughter such a near neighbor; for as he said, he had but to walk across the park to visit her.

Sarah was a little disturbed, for she remained in the service of the Duchess of York and although this meant that she could see Anne frequently, now that the Princess was married, she was already on the point of relying more on her husband than on her friend.

Sarah's was a true dilemma. Much good had come to her and John through the Duke of York; and one must not forget that he was the heir presumptive to the throne. The King had been ailing over the last year and although he was still a vigorous man, he was one who took his main pleasure no less zealously now than he had ten years before. James might soon be King of England and how much better it was to be in the service of the Queen of England than in that of a Princess who was not even next in succession.

The Duchess had been kind to Sarah over her marriage; but Anne was ready—or had been before her marriage—to take Sarah's advice in all things.

What to do? Consult with John. John was going to be a brilliant soldier, but Sarah trusted her own diplomacy more than his. She knew that he would say: Stay as you are. We are doing well.

Relinquish Anne? It was unthinkable and yet perhaps in a few years James Duke of York would be king and Mary Beatrice of Modena queen.

When she was disturbed Sarah liked to walk alone, so she slipped on a cloak and left the Palace.

As she crossed the Park she remembered how a short while ago people used to gather there to see His Majesty play pell mell. They had said nobody could drive a ball as he did and the people would applaud when he sent his halfway down the avenue, as though, they said, it were shot from a culverin. He could no longer do that. Perhaps the game bored him; more likely he was too old.

There in the park it occurred to Sarah that momentous events were close. Greatness in people depended on their being a step or two ahead of others, in the right direction, just before it was apparent to everyone else that it *was* the right direction.

She had reached the streets. Very old people who remembered what it was like before the Restoration marveled at the streets of London as they were at this time. There was gaiety everywhere—if one could call painted women gay; they walked with their gallants, arms about each other, blatantly amorous. There was music from the river, drinking and dancing. How many bawdy houses were there along that short stretch of river? This was Restoration London. And how different it must have been under Cromwell and the Puritans! No theaters; no painted women;

sombrely clad men; no fondling in the streets, for singing, dancing, and making love were crimes.

Change! thought Sarah. And all because the King had replaced the Protector.

She passed close to a group of people. A man was waving his arms and shouting: "No popery. Do you know what it means, my friends? You'll smell the fires of Smithfield if we have the papists back."

Sarah paused and listened, watching those grim determined faces.

"No popery!" It was a cry that one heard every day in the streets. The King was ailing. That was why the people so constantly shouted: "No popery!" They meant "No James!" No Catholic Duke of York should be their King.

If only one could peer into the future. It was not possible; one could only guess. But one could guess cleverly and shrewdly.

Already the Duke and his Duchess had been exiled. She thought of her beautiful dark-eyed royal mistress, Mary Beatrice of Modena with her foreign accent. She was clearly an Italian and Italians were papists.

As Sarah turned to the Palace she had made up her mind.

"*Sarah,*" *said Anne,* "you are not happy. Do not tell me you are for I know you too well."

"I see it is no use hiding my fears from you, Madam."

"John has been unfaithful."

"No," said Sarah. "Never."

"He would not dare," suggested Anne mischievously.

"He is too clever not to know what folly that would be."

"Yes, he is very clever, your John; but you are not unhappy about that."

"Oh, it is a matter which will not have occurred to you. But I have seen less of you lately."

Anne's face puckered into dismay. "My dearest Sarah, there has been so much to do. Being Princess of Denmark has meant so many more receptions, so many tiresome people to be received."

"I understand that, and I know it is no fault of yours. But you noticed that I was unhappy and wanted the reason so I give it to you. I have my duties too. I must wait on the Duchess for I am after all attached to her household. How different it would be if I were attached to yours! Then . . . how happy I should be!"

"Sarah. But . . ."

Sarah took Anne's hand and kissed it. "If I were serving you instead of the Duchess, I should always be in attendance . . . never far away. And now that you are reforming your household . . ."

"You must leave the Duchess, Sarah. You must come to me. I will confess that I had thought of it but I did not dare suggest it. For a place with the Duchess, I thought, would mean more to you than one with me."

Sarah was almost angry in her reproaches. "You could think that, Madam! I confess I am surprised. I should have thought you would have known that there is no one I would want to serve save yourself."

"Oh, Sarah, then it must be. I will speak to my father and step-mother. They know of the love between us two; I have no doubt that they will grant me what I ask."

Sarah was certain now that she had acted with her usual wisdom. Every time Anne appeared in the streets the people cheered her. The Protestant marriage had endeared her to them. They were silent for the Duchess of York. Italian papist! Sarah was on the right side.

A few hours later Sarah received a letter from Anne.

"The Duke of York came in just as you were gone, and made no difficulties, but has promised me that I shall have you, which I assure you is a great joy to me. I should say a great deal for your kindness in offering it, but I am not good at compliments. I will only say that I do take it extremely kindly and shall be ready at any time to do you all the service that is in my power . . ."

Sarah folded the letter and put it away. She liked the terms in which it was written; they showed a proper modesty and appreciation.

Sarah swept through the apartments at the Cockpit like a cold wind. All those about the Princess Anne understood that if they wished to prosper they must placate Sarah Churchill because it was clear that, as had been the case for some time, she had more influence with the Princess than any other person. As for the Prince, he was easy enough, being completely contented with his marriage. Here he was, with an affectionate undemanding wife; all he had to do was sleep with her, a pleasant enough occupation, for he was a sensual man, but too lazy to want to hunt for his own quarry; he could eat and drink his fill, chat a little, play cards with his wife; oh, it was a pleasant life. It was true that the King dumbfounded him a little with his witty conversation, but most of this was unintelligible to Prince George and he made no attempt to understand it.

Charles said of him: "God's fish, what have we here? I have tried him drunk and I've tried him sober but can make nothing of him, but the Princess Anne seems satisfied, so it may be she has been more fortunate than I."

And when shortly after the marriage it was announced that the Princess was pregnant, Charles remarked that although his nephew by marriage seemed lacking in wit and political knowledge he had given proof of his abilities as a husband—which was all they need be concerned with.

As for Anne, she was pleased with the marriage; she grew more and more fond of George every day. He never argued with her and never made any demands on her intelligence; he was as excited by food as she was—and there were very few others who were quite so enthusiastic about it. He was teaching her how to improve the dishes by drinking the right wine; and when they went to bed, slightly intoxicated, she found marriage most enjoyable.

She assured herself that she was more sorry than ever for her poor dear Mary, and she wrote very frequently to her sister telling her of affairs in England and how she longed to visit The Hague or that Mary should come to England. Poor Mary, she had had two miscarriages and it did not seem now as though she would be pregnant again. Anne heard distressing reports from various sources in Holland. Caliban was impotent, some said; and yet from other sources came the news that he spent his nights with Elizabeth Villiers. Even so there was no news of Elizabeth's giving birth to a royal bastard, so perhaps he was impotent after all.

Such a matter was not one to be discussed with anyone but Sarah; and as it happened it was a topic Sarah loved.

"I am indiscreet with you, Madam," said Sarah, "though never with anyone else. And I tell you this: Caliban is incapable of begetting children. They say his asthma is terrible. I do not think he will live long. Then we hear these stories of your sister's ague. An ailing sister, an asthmatical Orange—and let me tell you, Madam, that if your sister were to die, *he* would have to take a few steps back. And your father a papist! Madam, I believe that one day I shall have the honor of serving the Queen of England."

"Oh, let be," said Anne, "I am happy enough as I am."

"Those who love you have ambitions for you, Madam."

"I have always said, Sarah, that you are too ambitious."

Sarah was alert suddenly. Was that a warning? Anne did not care to hear criticism of her father, nor did she like references to her sister's death. Anne needed to be molded, thought Sarah.

She smiled, looking down at capable hands—an outward sign of a mind which could dominate a weaker one and was well able to do the molding.

"Not for myself, Madam," she said more quietly than usual, "only for the one I serve with heart and soul."

Sarah would have liked to choose Anne's attendants. That was not possible. She did not really fear people like Lady Fitzharding and Mrs. Danvers. Mrs. Danvers occupied a minor position and was of no great importance. Lady Fitzharding had been Barbara Villiers and was a sister to Elizabeth who, rumor had it, was now the mistress of the Prince of Orange. Sarah thought she might be useful; for, it would be necessary, for the time being, to feign friendship with the Princess of Orange. There was one other, though, who was far too important in the household and this was Anne's aunt, the Countess of Clarendon.

The Countess's husband, Henry Hyde, Earl of Clarendon was the brother of Anne's mother and, because of this relationship Flower, Countess of Clarendon, held a high position in the Princess's household, being the first Lady of the Bedchamber—a post which in Sarah's opinion clearly should belong to her; but because of Lady Clarendon's age and the fact that she had long been close to Anne, she wielded great influence. Something of a scholar she deplored Anne's lack of scholarship and had in fact tried to turn her niece's interest to something other than cards, gossip, and food; this did not endear her to Anne and made Sarah's task of turning the Princess against Lady Clarendon simpler than it might have been.

Just at this time, however, Anne's thoughts were occupied with her pregnancy and Sarah realized that little else interested her except a good game of cards and her food. She grew larger and larger and Sarah was in constant attendance.

She did attempt one or two thrusts at Lady Clarendon.

She was silent one day as she sat with the Princess and, although absorbed as she was with her own concerns, Anne remarked on this—for it was unlike Sarah not to talk incessantly.

"Oh, Madam," said Sarah distantly, "my lot in your service is not always a comfortable one."

Anne was alarmed. "My dearest Sarah, what *do* you mean?"

"Oh . . . it is the Clarendon creature. What airs she gives herself. I know she is your aunt—but your mother's family were remarkably fortunate to be linked with royalty. *She* gives herself airs. And all because she is a Countess and I am plain Mrs. Churchill."

"It seems wrong that that should be," said Anne thoughtfully.

Sarah gave her a sharp look. Would she draw herself from her lethargy sufficiently long to remember?

Anne's father came to visit her at the Cockpit. James had once been handsome, but the events of the last years had been a strain on him and he looked drawn and sallow. He was tall, but not as tall as his brother and although more handsome than Charles, although possessed of a certain dignity of manner, he was singularly lacking in charm.

But as his eyes fell on his daughter his face was lighted by a great affection and he seemed almost young.

"My dearest," he said, "how are you?"

"Very well, dear father," Anne told him. "All goes well, they tell me, and I may expect a fine boy."

"Do not set your hopes on that, my love. Be content with a daughter if a daughter it should be. You have so quickly conceived that I am sure you will have a large family."

"It is what George and I want more than anything."

He kissed her gently on the forehead. "It pleases me to see you so happy. Would I could feel as contented for Mary." His face hardened. "I never wanted that marriage. I feel we have brought a viper into our close family circle."

"Sarah calls him Caliban. I am sure he is a monster. I cannot understand how dear Mary tolerates him. I am sure I never would."

"I fear he is subduing her, making her his creature . . . perhaps trying to turn her against us all. He'll never do that. I know my Mary." He smiled sentimentally at Anne. "I thank God for giving me my dearest daughters. So many children I have had and lost; but I always remind myself that I was allowed to keep two. My dearest Mary; my blessed Anne. We shall always love and cherish each other as long as we shall live."

"Yes, dear father," said Anne, wondering what there would be for dinner.

"And although I am parted from Mary, I know that she continues to love me dearly. It is a secret, daughter, but I do not wish to have secrets from you. Do not mention this to anyone. But if it were in my power to break that Dutch marriage I would do so. And I believe it might be in my power. There is just cause. Mary is childless and he . . . the Dutchman . . . spends his night with another woman."

"Fitzharding's sister, Elizabeth Villiers. It is a well-known scandal."

"A well-known scandal—and my daughter the wife of such a monster! Unfortunately, my dear, your uncle will not have the marriage disturbed. But . . ."

Anne nodded sleepily. Her father very frequently spent *his* nights in the beds of his mistresses. Uncle Charles was not looking so well of late; but each night *he* took one of his mistresses to bed; and it was said that he would not accept his flagging vigor and resorted to artificial means to revive it. Fair enough, whispered his courtiers. Who would not do the like? But what effect was this having on the royal body; and how long could it be expected to stand the strain?

"Well," said James, "that is not for us to discuss now. And my dear daughter is well and everything is progressing as it should. I can scarcely wait for the good news. I shall be near you, dearest, all the time; and if there is anything you want, all you need do is ask for it. You know your father is never happier than when he is pleasing you."

All she need do was ask? It was true. He was the most indulgent of parents.

"Father," she said, "there is one thing I would ask."

His face lit up with pleasure, "My darling daughter, I promise if it is in my power . . ."

"It is not for me, Father, but I have a great friend who has not been as well treated as she should be. I believe you are very pleased with the services Colonel Churchill has rendered you?"

"He is a good man, and I believe a faithful friend to me."

"You need good men and faithful friends, father. Do you think that sometimes we take the goodness of those close to us for granted?"

"It may be so."

"My best friend and the kindest of my women is plain Mrs. while others who are less kind flaunt great titles. It is our duty, is it not, Father, to reward those who serve us?"

He nodded.

"Why, my blessed one, you are asking that the Churchills be honored in some way?"

"A title for the Colonel, so that Sarah may be Lady Churchill to these women of mine and not plain Mrs."

James patted her hand. "That does not seem to me to be an insurmountable difficulty," he said fondly.

Sarah embraced her John. Then she held him at arms' length.

"Well, Baron Churchill?"

"Yes, my lady?"

"Have you a clever wife?"

"The cleverest in the world."

"John, I only had to ask."

"She thinks the world of you, as indeed she should."

Sarah's eyes were dreamy as she looked into the future. "I can see that she will do anything . . . just anything . . . I ask of her. She is in my power . . . absolutely."

"Careful, my love."

She was almost haughty for a moment. "You need not advise me, John Churchill."

He retreated at once. "I know it well."

She softened and put her arms about his neck. He was so handsome, so charming, and he had forsaken his rake's life for her. She saw greatness in him and she was going to build that greatness. He was beginning to understand that now.

They stood looking at each other. This was a partnership. They needed rank, and they had taken the first step toward that, although a barony was not going to be good enough for the Churchills; they wanted wealth (at the moment they were poor, but Sarah would know how to remedy that) and what was more precious than anything to Sarah: Power.

Sarah was as near to loving him as she could love anyone; she saw in him a reflection of herself. He was hers to make and to mold; and she believed she had chosen the finest man in the world on whom to bestow her greatness. She was impatient with a fate which had made her a woman. Had she been a man, she was certain there was no heights to which she would not have arisen; as it was, she would work with John. Together they would stand.

Lord and Lady Churchill—this was the first step.

No wonder they were delighted with each other.

In the Cockpit Lady Churchill was more arrogant than ever; she was, she said, of the frankest nature on earth; but woebetide anyone who tried to be equally frank with her.

With the Princess she was gentle and affectionate—but only to her.

As for Anne, she loved Lady Churchill even more than she had Mrs. Churchill, for it was very comforting to have given so much pleasure to a dear friend.

Anne was sitting alone with her dear friend as she so loved to do.

"Sarah," she said, "you are pleased with your new title."

"You can well imagine what pleasure it gives me to stand on equal terms with some of these *vipers* you have around you, Madam."

"I trust my aunt has not been unpleasant to you."

"She is by nature unpleasant. She looks like a mad woman, that one, for all that she tries to talk like a scholar."

Anne burst into laughter. "Oh, I do see what you mean, Sarah."

"It is pleasant to amuse you, Madam."

"When you call me Madam, Sarah, I feel we are too far apart. You are Lady Churchill now but that is a long way beneath the rank of Princess."

"The rank of Princess," said Sarah coolly, "is one which can only come through inheritance or marriage. It is not to be *earned*."

"When I am with you, dear Sarah, I feel that you are so much more worthy to hold rank than I."

"Why, Madam, we must all accept the injustices of fate."

"I could never bring you up to royal level, Sarah, no matter what I did. So, I have been thinking how pleasant it would be if we could be together as . . . equals."

Sarah was immediately excited. "How so, Madam?"

"When I was a child I loved giving myself names. So did Mary. It was a kind of game with us. Do you remember Frances Apsley?"

Sarah frowned. Indeed she remembered Frances Apsley, that young woman with whom Mary had formed a passionate friendship; and Anne, who always followed Mary in everything had soon been declaring *her* devotion to Frances.

"An insipid creature," said Sarah.

"Compared with you, of course; but Mary and I thought her wonderful. I believe Mary still does. But they have been long separated and

Mary is married to William, and Frances to Benjamin Bathurst now. Frances has a brood of children and poor Mary has none . . . but what was I saying? We all took names for ourselves alone. It was such fun being incognito. Mary was Clorine and Frances was Aurelia—just for themselves—and I was Ziphares and Frances—to me—was Semandra. I should like *us* to have our own names, Sarah. Simple names, so that we could pretend to be two old gossips."

Sarah nodded slowly "But, Madam, I think that is an excellent idea."

"Sarah, I am so pleased. Shall I tell you what names I have chosen— Morley and Freeman. *Mrs.* Morley and *Mrs.* Freeman. Then we are of one rank . . . in fact we are without rank. I think it would give me great pleasure."

"I think so too," said Sarah. "Then I shall feel free to talk to you as I so often wish to. The very fact of your being the Princess does I fear come between us."

"Then Morley and Freeman it shall be. Now we have to decide which is which. You are clever, Sarah, so I am going to make you decide. Who are you going to be, Mrs. Morley or Mrs. Freeman?"

Sarah considered. "Well," she said, "I am of a very frank and free nature so I think Freeman would best suit me."

"You have chosen, Mrs. Freeman. Now sit down and tell me the latest news of Mr. Freeman. Mr. Morley is in great spirits and with me is looking forward to the appearance of Baby Morley which I must confess, dear Mrs. Freeman, still seems to me a long way off."

"You are too impatient, Mrs. Morley. You are like every other mother with a first child. I remember how I was with my Henrietta."

Anne laughed. "Oh, Mrs. Freeman, I think this was an excellent idea of mine. Already I feel you are different toward me."

"I believe it is going to make greater freedom between us, Mrs. Morley."

The Princess Anne was brought to bed of a daughter but almost immediately it became apparent that the child could not survive, and there was scarcely time to baptize the little girl before she died.

Anne was temporarily distressed, but it was easy to comfort her. She was surrounded by loving attention. First there was her husband, plump and genial, to sit by her bed and hold her hand.

"Don't you fret," he said in his quaint English. "As soon as you are well enough, dear wife, we will have others."

There was her father, so anxious on her behalf that it was said he cared for nothing as much as his daughter.

"My poor, dear child," he mourned. "I understand well your disappointment. But you have shown that you are fertile. Why, scarcely were you married than you were pregnant; as soon as you are up and well there'll be another. We all share your disappointment; but, my dearest, I can bear anything as long as my beloved child grows better every day."

"You are the best father a daughter ever had," she told him.

"Who would not be to the best of daughters?" he answered fondly.

Her stepmother came, with the Queen, both of whom had frequently suffered similar disappointments. They condoled with her, but there was one theme of their conversation: there would soon be a baby in the cradle for Anne.

If it were so, she would be perfectly happy, Anne declared. She had experienced motherhood, briefly and tragically, but it had made her realize that she wanted children. This one had been a girl, but there would be boys; and secretly she reminded herself that one of these boys could be King of England.

Anne had never felt so ambitious as she did lying there in her bed surrounded by all the luxuries her father could think of—ambitious for the son she would have.

The King came to visit her—kind, as ever, but looking older. His smile was merry, but there was a tinge of red in the whites of his eyes.

"Don't you fret, niece," he said. "If ever I saw a good stud, it's our friend George. Don't waste too much time being the invalid and, by God's fish, I'll warrant you'll soon begin to swell again!"

It was all very gay and she felt secure and happy, sparing a thought now and then for dear Mary who had suffered miscarriages and must have sadly missed her father, stepmother, uncle, aunt, and most of all the kindness of a husband. Dear, dear George, how different he was from that hateful William, who, so reports from Holland had said, blamed Mary for the loss of her children.

What a good family she had, and how comforting it was to feel oneself cherished!

She was so contented that for some days she forgot the existence of Mrs. Freeman, who, to her disgust, was not allowed the liberty which had been hers before. Lady Clarendon had taken charge of the household and naturally the Duke of York paid more attention to his sister by marriage than to his daughter's favorite woman.

It shall not always be so, thought Sarah, and during Anne's confinement she grew to hate the Duke and Duchess of York.

Papists! she thought. They were nothing more than papists. Madame of Modena had swept through the apartments like a Queen bestowing little attention on Lady Churchill.

Well, Madam, thought Sarah, you will be sorry for that. Lots of people were going to be sorry one day.

But Anne was soon asking for Mrs. Freeman who complained to her bitterly that she had been kept from her Mrs. Morley at the time she was most needed.

"I missed you," Anne told her.

"It was a pity Mrs. Morley did not demand that Mrs. Freeman be brought to her."

Anne yawned faintly and Sarah noticed this. She must curb her frankness with the Princess, who was of course utterly spoiled by those around her and in particular her father.

"Well, we are together now and I shall see personally that my dear Mrs. Morley does not over-tax her strength, for I do believe that it was due to this that we have had this unfortunate tragedy."

"Please, do not let us talk of it. Get the cards, Mrs. Freeman, and call Barbara Fitzharding—and whom shall we have for a fourth?"

Not that old aunt of yours, thought Sarah, hurrying away to summon Mrs. Danvers. And how dared she suggest cards when clearly Sarah wanted to talk.

But John was right, of course. She must go carefully.

So when she returned with the cards and the players she insisted on placing cushions about the Princess and setting a box of sweetmeats beside her.

Anne smiled at her contentedly and the game began.

And very shortly afterward Anne was pregnant.

THE KING IS

DEAD

Great events were about to break over England, but none was aware of them on that February day. It was dusk and enormous fires were blazing in the royal apartments. Anne, now obviously pregnant, sat with her husband and some members of their suites playing basset. The stakes were high and Anne was smiling delightedly. Sarah, in attendance on her mistress, looking on at the game, was shocked because the bank contained at least two thousand pounds in gold. A wanton waste! she grumbled inwardly thinking of what the money would mean to the Churchills. Anne, knowing that she was far from rich, had given her several gifts of money; and these she had gratefully taken. This should continue, she decided; and she must find means of diverting more and more money into the Churchill purse. She would do so with a better conscience after having seen it wasted at the gaming table.

The King was sitting with three of his favorite women—the Duchesses of Portsmouth, Cleveland, and Mazarine. He looked ill and had eaten scarcely anything all day, but he was smiling and chatting with his usual affability; and now and then would caress one of the ladies.

Queen Catherine was not present—she was often absent from these occasions. Doubtless, it was supposed, because she did not care to see her husband with his mistresses; and, although he was kind to her in all other ways, this was one concession he would not grant her. It was the same with his brother the Duke of York; he was married to a beautiful wife, many years younger than himself and although she had hated him when she had first come to England she was now passionately in love with him and deeply resentful of his mistresses—yet he, though ready to do everything else she might ask, was not able to forgo this dalliance with women.

The Duchess of Portsmouth was leaning toward the King telling him that he was tired and she suggested a little supper in her apartments.

Cleveland and Mazarine were scowling at Portsmouth and Charles said that while he ever found supping in her apartments delightful, he had lost his appetite for the day.

Cleveland and Mazarine were smiling triumphantly, but Portsmouth replied: "I have had a special soup made for Your Majesty—very light but nourishing."

Charles smiled and declared that he would taste it. He was anxious to leave the hall for he found the light trying and the noise from the basset table and the singer in the gallery gave him a headache.

In the company of the ladies and a few of his courtiers he left the hall; and no one knew then that it would never be quite the same again.

Charles spent a restless night and then in the morning when he left his bed for his closet his attendants noticed that he walked unsteadily. Later when he talked to them he seemed to forget what he was talking about and his speech was slurred.

It took a long time to dress and as he moved away from his bed he swayed and would have fallen had not his attendants steadied him.

Dr. King, one of his physicians, was in the palace and he came at once to the King's bedside, but Charles was now clearly very ill indeed, for his face was purple and distorted and his power of speech had left him.

There was tension throughout the palace. The King was ill—more ill than he had ever been before.

They were sending for the Duke of York. What now?

The King was still alive, but there was anxiety throughout the kingdom. He had lived for his own pleasure; he had set the tone of immorality not only in the Court but throughout the country; unknown to his ministers he had made treaties with France; and he was said to be a secret Catholic; yet rarely had the English so sincerely mourned the passing of a King.

In the streets they were weeping openly. Many of them remembered his coming back to them twenty-five years ago—the flowers strewn over the cobbles; the music in the streets; the bonfires; wine and dancing and merriment. And if it had not turned out as wonderful as they had believed it was going to, at least it had been gay and lighthearted and different from the gloom of old Noll Cromwell's day.

They loved him; they called him the merry Monarch; they remembered some of his sayings which had often been repeated because they were wise and witty. And now he was dying, and leaving them—James!

Under the sorrow there was low rumbling of "No popery!"

In his bedchamber the King lived on. It seemed he could not die. They had tried all the remedies they knew; they had opened his veins with a penknife; they had put a hot iron on his head; they had purged him; they had placed newly killed pigeons at his feet.

Under all these ministrations he rallied for a time and when the news was spread through the streets, the people shouted in their joy; they made bonfires and all the bells of London were ringing at once. He had been ill before and he was well again. All those who had seen him riding through his capital, sauntering through his parks in the company of his ladies with his spaniels at his heels, all those who had seen him throwing at pell mell were certain that he had the strength of ten men.

But the rejoicings were soon over. He could not live and although as he said—and apologized for it—he was a long time a-dying, he was dying all the same.

James was kneeling at his bedside, weeping, begging him to take the sacrament before he died.

Poor James! he was a sentimental man and they were brothers. Later he would think of what his brother's passing meant to him, but at this time he could remember only the long years of intimacy, of struggle and endeavor, of exile and strife and, at last, the homecoming.

Charles tried to frame the words: "James, best of friends and best of brothers. . . ."

The tears ran down James's cheeks, and Charles begged forgiveness for those exiles which had been a necessity, but he was sorry for them.

The Queen came to the bedside; she was a heartbroken woman; there were others too, women, who followed her into the bedchamber, to remind him that though she was his wife they were the ones who had shared his company.

The Queen was sobbing; she begged him to forgive her if she had ever offended him. "Alas, poor lady," cried Charles, "she begs my pardon! I beg hers, with all my heart."

He could not breathe; there were so many people crowding the apartment and all day and all night they remained.

James came to the bed, his eyes alight with fanaticism; he bent his head and whispered to his brother that since he was at heart a Catholic he should receive the rites of the Catholic church.

"No," said Charles, "you endanger your life, brother."

But when had James thought of danger? He had the chamber cleared and Father Huddleston, who had once saved the King's life at the battle of Worcester, was brought disguised into the death chamber.

"Brother," said James, "I bring you a man who once saved your life; now he comes to save your soul."

The sacrament according to the rites of the church of Rome was given with extreme unction.

Then the doors were thrown open and those who had been shut out were allowed to return.

The next morning Charles II was dead.

LONG LIVE

THE KING

*T*here was a quiet throughout the country. There was a new King on the throne—King James II—and everyone was waiting to see what would happen. The cries of "No popery" were no longer heard, but eyes were alert and there was an air of waiting, an implication that the present era was uneasy and perhaps temporary.

There was one who was in the minds of all, though few mentioned his name: James Duke of Monmouth, at present at The Hague, the guest of the Prince and Princess of Orange. What would he do now? His greatest enemy had been the Duke of York who was now King James II. Monmouth had ostentatiously called himself the Protestant Duke. And what was the Protestant Duke doing now?

Anne, heavily pregnant, was thinking constantly of the child she was to have. She indulged herself more than usual.

"I am determined this time," she told Sarah, "that my child shall live."

"He will be a step nearer to the throne when he is born than when he was conceived," commented Sarah.

Anne wept then for Uncle Charles. "He was always so kind to me.

I cannot believe that I shall never see him again. Of course, dear Mrs. Freeman, there were times when I had no notion of what he meant. He was so witty always, but kind with it, and you know that is a rare gift. Is that why he was so loved, do you think? Oh, how I miss him."

Fat, pink fool! thought Sarah. You could be Queen of England before long and all you think of is crying for Uncle Charles!

Sarah had long talks with John. They were growing closer together; they were more than lovers; they were partners and their ambition burned more brightly than any passion; Sarah was once more pregnant and this time they hoped for a son.

"John, John," she cried, "what does this mean? What *can* this mean?"

"We can only wait and see."

Sarah stamped impatiently. "We must not wait too long."

"But, my dearest, for a while we must wait. I am wondering what is happening now on the Continent."

"Monmouth?"

"And William. Do not forget William, my love."

"Depend upon it Caliban is hatching some plot."

"And forcing his wife to help him, I'll swear."

"She has about as much sense as my dear Mrs. Morley. They are told 'Do this' 'Do that.' And like idiots they do it."

John touched her cheek lightly. "Which is very good for my dear Mrs. Freeman."

"I'm thinking of the other one—Mary. Don't forget she comes first."

"We must not plan too far ahead, my dear. Remember James is still the King."

"But is he going to remain King?"

"He has stepped into his brother's place naturally and easily. I confess I expected trouble. There has been none. It seems he understands his danger for he has been behaving with more good sense than he usually shows."

Sarah clenched her hands. "And Monmouth? What of Monmouth?"

"They'll never accept the bastard."

"The Protestant Duke!" said Sarah with a sneer. "And William? Those two are said to be friends. Rivals, as Charles once said, for the same mistress. And that mistress is the crown which James now wears."

"We'll keep our eyes on The Hague. That's where the next move will come from."

"William and Mary! Do you think they'll make an attempt?"

John shook his head. "Not yet. William's too clever. James will have to commit himself more deeply before it would be wise for anyone to try to oust him from the throne. The English don't want a papist King but you know what they are for fair play. They wouldn't like Mary to take over before her time ... unless it was for a very good reason."

"Mary! They say she does not enjoy good health and William would have no chance without her. And then it would be Queen Morley's turn. John, do you understand that the day my plump Morley mounts the throne *I* can rule this country?"

John smiled at her. "I believe you capable of anything, my love. But we must be patient. We must wait ... alert. We must first see which way the wind is blowing. It would not do for us to get caught in the coming storm."

He was wise, she knew. Sarah had no doubt that when the time came they would be on the winning side.

The preparations for the new King's coronation went smoothly. Anne's great regret was that she would not be able to attend for she was expecting her child to be born any day.

James had found time to visit her at the Cockpit in spite of all his new duties. He embraced her with great tenderness and told her that she should rejoice to have a King for a father.

"Rest assured," he said, "that I shall see benefits flow to my beloved daughter."

That was comforting.

"Dear Father, but look at the size of your daughter! Delighted as I am by my state I am irked that I shall not be able to see you crowned."

James smiled secretly and later Anne learned that he had ordered that a special closed box be erected in the Abbey from which she should watch the ceremony in the company of her husband.

"You do not imagine," he said, "that I could allow my dear daughter to be absent on this great day!"

So Anne was in the box with George while the ceremony took place and afterward Mary Beatrice, the new Queen, made a point of visiting her stepdaughter there.

"What do you think of my dress?" asked Mary Beatrice, her lovely dark eyes shining; she was always happy on such occasions because she liked to see honor bestowed on her husband.

"Worthy of a Queen," declared Anne. "Tell me, how do you feel . . . now that you are a queen?"

Mary Beatrice looked a little sad. "I should feel happier if I were in *your* condition."

"You will be . . . ere long," said Anne.

Ten days later Anne's daughter was born. She seemed healthy and although Anne and her husband had longed for a boy they now declared themselves to be completely delighted.

"Soon she shall have a brother," George promised Anne; and she was sure he would be proved right.

"I shall call her Mary after my dearest sister," said Anne. "Poor Mary. I feel so guilty to be happy here in England while she must remain in Holland with Caliban."

John had returned from a mission to France whither he had gone ostensibly to tell Louis of James's accession, but actually to attempt to obtain further loans from Louis. This he failed to do, but when he returned there was an opportunity of spending a few weeks with Sarah in the house he had built on the site of that old one near St. Albans where Sarah had spent part of her childhood.

Then came the news that Monmouth had landed in England. And John knew he must return to Court without delay.

"So," said Sarah, "you will fight for the Catholic against the Protestant?"

John smiled. "This is the King against the bastard," he said. "Until

James changes the religion of this country he is still the King as far as I am concerned."

Sarah agreed that this must be so.

"We should never bow to Monmouth," she said. "You will defeat him, John."

"Feversham will be in command," John replied sardonically, "and I see that the trouble will be mine but the honor will be his."

"It shall not always be so," declared Sarah firmly.

The defeat of Monmouth was due to Churchill, for when the battle of Sedgemoor began Feversham was in bed, having, with many of his cronies, drunk rather heavily, and the command was left to John Churchill who started a strong offensive and secured victory for the King's men.

Monmouth was discovered in a ditch and brought as prisoner to London. There followed his trial, death on Tower Hill, and the great scandal of Judge Jeffrey's Bloody Assizes.

That affair was ended and James II was firmly on the throne.

Everyone in England seemed aware of the King's unpopularity except himself. Like a true Stuart James had an inherent belief in the Divine Right of Kings and it was inconceivable to him that his throne could be threatened by the people. He had had two enemies in his nephew Monmouth and his son-in-law William; now Monmouth was dead and only William remained. He had always disliked William and had never ceased to deplore the fact that his beloved daughter Mary had married him. He himself had been against that marriage, but Charles had insisted on it, pointing out that because William was a Protestant it was more necessary to James than to anyone else, for if James did not allow his daughter to marry a Protestant, Charles believed that the people would insist on excluding him from the succession.

So there had been this Dutch marriage—but he never trusted his son-in-law and what was so heartbreaking was that he believed William was trying to influence his daughter against him.

Rake and libertine that he could not prevent himself being, James had a great desire for a happy family life to which he could retire for a short rest from his mistresses. He had convinced himself that he had enjoyed this for a time with Anne Hyde, the mother of his daughters, and the two girls themselves. He remembered several occasions when they had sat on the floor and played childish games together. He looked back—sentimentalist that he was—with great yearning to that period.

He sincerely loved his daughters. In her childhood Mary had been the favorite, but she was far away and William's wife, whereas Anne was at hand and he could see her frequently. Moreover he had written to Mary in an endeavor to convert her to Catholicism, and her replies had been cool; she implied that she was firmly Protestant.

William's wife, he thought sadly, scarcely James's daughter now.

So he turned to Anne. He increased her allowance, for the dear creature had no money sense at all and in spite of her enormous revenue she was constantly in debt. He enjoyed those occasions when she sought his help; it was a pleasure to see her woebegone face break into a smile when he told her that she could rely on her father to help her in any difficulty.

"You are the daughter of a King now," he was constantly telling her. "The beloved daughter."

Anne thought what a pleasure it was to be a sovereign. So much homage; so much adulation. Sarah had grown even closer because that year they had both given birth to daughters: Anne's Mary and Sarah's Elizabeth.

Sarah would whisper to her: "And think, dear Mrs. Morley, one day you may be the Queen of England."

"I do not like to think of that, Mrs. Freeman, because my father would have to die first."

"H'm!" retorted Sarah. "He is a papist, you know, and that is not good."

"Alas no." Anne was a staunch Protestant, as she had been brought up to be, for her uncle Charles had taken her education and that of Mary out of their father's hands. "But he is firmly convinced that he is right."

"Mrs. Morley must never allow herself to be converted. That would be dangerous. They would never allow you to be Queen if you became a papist. These papists are a menace."

"I know, I have heard from my sister. . . . She is not very pleased with my father."

"Nor is it to be wondered at. He is under the thumb of his wife. She is the real culprit."

Anne looked puzzled as she thought of her lovely stepmother with whom she had always been on good terms.

"I have never trusted Italians," went on Sarah. She thought of the Queen sweeping through the Cockpit and showing no respect for Lady Churchill. Her influence with the Princess must not be allowed to grow; it was too great already.

"She always seems to be kindly."

"Oh, but so proud, Mrs. Morley. She pretends that she is gracious to all, but have you noticed the change in her since she became Queen?"

"Hush, Mrs. Freeman, your voice carries so. If anyone heard you speak thus of the Queen. . . ."

"We should give her a name, so that no one would know of whom we were speaking."

Anne was very fond of giving people nicknames; she had always done so throughout her life; so she fell in with the suggestion at once.

"It ought to be something like Morley and Freeman," she said. "An ordinary sort of name. I have it. Mansell. My father shall be Mr. Mansell and the Queen, Mansell's wife. How's that?"

"Mrs. Morley, you are a genius! I cannot think of a name that would suit them better."

"Mansell!" said Anne savoring it; then she burst out laughing. "It is absolutely right."

And from then on the King and Queen became Mansell and Mansell's wife; and it was extraordinary how the change robbed them of dignity. Mrs. Freeman could talk more contemptuously of the Mansells; and Anne found that she could listen, and as usual, she began to share Sarah's opinions.

Anne was soon pregnant again and as little Mary was surviving happily, she let herself dream of the large family she would have.

This time, she told George, it should be a son.

They were happy days and Anne was able to indulge herself in all her favorite pastimes, to which one had been added: gossip—more than gossip, intrigue.

Wherever Sarah was, there was drama; and Anne found that her friend's racy conversation and pungent criticisms of almost everyone about them were so diverting. The only people who were good and reasonable were Mr. and Mrs. Morley and Mr. and Mrs. Freeman. Others were perhaps misguided. Anne did not care to hear criticisms of her sister. But there was Caliban to be slandered. As for the King and Queen, Anne was already beginning to dislike her stepmother and see her through Sarah's eyes as arrogant and dangerous on account of her religion. With regard to her father, Sarah had to tread warily, but Anne was forming a different picture of him. He was immoral; she had always known that; and all men should be like Mr. Morley and Mr. Freeman—moral. Perhaps before their marriages they had had their amours; but all the more credit to them that, being married to good wives, they should forsake their follies.

Anne was changing; she was as placid as ever, but she could be spiteful. The fact was she so enjoyed the scandalous conversations and Sarah was so amusing that sometimes Anne was quite helpless with laughter.

It was so comfortable, to be stretched out on a divan, a dish of sweets beside one, while the talk was all of intrigue and the day when Anne would be Queen. To adventure without stirring from the couch suited Anne.

What would she do without her dear Mrs. Freeman to divert her? She had no notion of the immense and driving purpose behind Mrs. Freeman's discourse.

THE PRINCESS

BEREAVED

It was May and the sun streamed into Windsor Castle.

Anne lay in her bed, her new baby in her arms. The child had just been christened Anne Sophia and it had been such an impressive ceremony with Lady Roscommon and Lady Churchill as godmothers.

It was a healthy baby, but Anne was disturbed because little Mary was not progressing as she wished. The child was pale and listless and she was worried, for so many royal babies did not reach maturity. It was as though there was some blight on them from the day they were born. One could comfort oneself with hopes of a large family, but when a child had been lost and another seemed ailing, fear crept into the heart; and there were memories of Queens and Princesses in the past who had prayed for children—whose whole future depended on the ability to bear children—and who had failed.

Anne's future did not depend on her children; but she had discovered that she was by nature a mother. She yearned for children as she did for nothing else. She wanted to see a whole brood of them, laughing and healthy about her fireside, with good, dear, dependable George loving them in his genial way as she did in hers.

Sarah bustled into the apartment and took the child from its mother's arms; she rocked it with a gentleness rare in her, while Anne looked on smiling benignly.

"The next," prophesied Sarah, "must be a boy."

"I pray so," answered Anne.

Sarah's eyes narrowed. "A boy," she said, "who will one day be our Sovereign Lord the King."

Sarah noticed with pleasure that Anne's eyes were shining with a determination she had never seen there before.

Anne was worried. She had noticed that George had not seemed well during the passing weeks. He had lost his interest in food which could only mean that he was ill.

"My dearest," she cried, taking his hand, "you have a fever."

He did not deny it and she called his attendants to help him to his bed while she sent for the physicians.

George had a restless night and in the morning his condition appeared to have worsened.

The doctors shook their heads. "He is a little heavy, Madam," they told Anne, "and he breathes with difficulty."

Anne had not been so distressed since she had heard that Mary was leaving England; and an additional anxiety was her eldest daughter who was coughing and spitting blood. The sight of that blood terrified her. If her little girl was going to die and her kind George would not be well enough to comfort her, what would she do! She could only turn to her dear Mrs. Freeman, but in the meantime she must do all she could to save them.

She insisted on nursing her husband, and astonished everyone, for never had she exerted herself to such an extent before. He was very weak, but he lay quietly smiling at her and she knew that her presence comforted him.

Sarah was annoyed, but managed not to show it.

"Madam," she said, for others were present, "I like not to see you wearing yourself out in this way. Any of your women could do what you are doing."

"You are wrong, Lady Churchill," was Anne's answer. "He is comforted by my presence and there is no one but myself who could give him that comfort."

Sarah withdrew angrily, but she managed to give Anne the impression that her anger was a sign of fear for her mistress's health.

Anne could be stubborn on occasions, Sarah was discovering. Perhaps it was a warning that she should not take too much for granted. But Sarah was usually in too much of a hurry to heed warnings, too sure of herself to believe she could ever be wrong.

Meanwhile Anne sat by her husband's bed while he held her hand and although he could not speak, his eyes told her how happy he was to have her there.

Anne was melancholy, for she, like everyone else, believed that he was going to die. She thought of the day they had met, of their immediate liking which had made both of them accept the marriage calmly. Rarely could strangers have contemplated marriage with such serenity. But they were serene people—both of them—perhaps that was why theirs was such a happy marriage.

From George's bed, she went to that of her elder daughter. The child lay, panting for her breath, racked now and then by fits of coughing.

Anne wept, then hastily dried her eyes that she might go to her husband's bedside with a smile.

Hourly she was expecting the death of husband and daughter and never in her life had she been so unhappy. She had her baby; she would hold the child in her arms and wonder how long it would be before little Anne Sophia would be the only member of her family left to her.

She was sitting by her husband's bed one day when Sarah came into the room. There was a closer bond between them because Sarah had a boy now whom she had christened John after her husband and as a mother Sarah could understand and sympathize with the anguish Anne was now enduring. Sarah had three healthy children. Lucky Sarah! Her successful motherhood endeared her to Anne. It seemed yet a further proof that Sarah would always be successful.

Now Sarah was subdued which was startling because it was so unlike her.

"Mary . . . ?" whispered Anne.

Sarah drew her outside and put an arm about her.

"It is the little one," she said.

The child was lying in its cradle; her face was scarlet, its limbs distorted.

"No!" cried Anne. "This is too much."

She looked wildly about her, calling for the doctors; but there was nothing they could do.

Anne stood at the window watching the snowflakes falling. She was not weeping; but her limbs felt heavy. She had lost her baby—little Mary was desperately ill and her dear George was sick with a fever.

It was Sarah who came to stand beside her, miraculousy silent for once, but conveying so much by that silence.

"How can I tell him, Sarah?" she asked.

Sarah took her hand and pressed it firmly and it seemed to Anne that Sarah's strength and vitality flowed into her body.

"No matter what happens . . . there will always be you. You'll never change." She added: "Mrs. Freeman."

"Mrs. Freeman will always be at hand to comfort her dear friend Mrs. Morley."

One of the women approached them.

Anne took one look at her and flew to the bedside of her daughter Mary.

It was incredible; fate could not be so cruel. But it was so. Anne had lost both her children.

Strangely enough from that day George began to improve.

They said that he saw he was needed to comfort his heartbroken wife. She would sit by his bed and hold his hand; and they often wept quietly together.

He told her that he had known all the time that she had been in the sickroom, and it was that knowledge and that alone, which had pulled him through.

"I cannot bear to see you unhappy," he said.

"And it grieves me to see you sad."

"Then, my dear wife, we must smile for the sake of each other."

He was growing better every day. This was clear for when Anne brought delicacies to his bedside his eyes lit up at the sight of them.

"Try this, my love," she would say.

And he would take a tidbit and put it into her mouth instead.

They would sample the food, discuss it; and talk of what they would eat tomorrow.

It was a return to the old life.

"Do not fret," he said. "We have lost three but we shall have others."

And as soon as the Prince was about again sure enough Anne became pregnant; and she was sure that if she could only hold a healthy child in her arms she would be ready to forget the anguish of her previous loss.

Anne miscarried, but almost immediately she was again with child.

Sarah was supreme in the Princess's household. She was getting her own way in almost everything, but there were minor irritations. She was shaping Anne's mind and was determined that Mansell and Mansell's wife should go. She was aware that secret intrigues were afoot; that spies were both at Whitehall and The Hague and that William of Orange— and Mary—were waiting for the opportunity to come over to England and take the crown from James. This was what Sarah hoped for. She did not believe that Mary would live long; William, too, was a weakling and there were no children of that marriage. It need only be a few years before the Princess Anne became Queen Anne.

Mrs. Morley, the Queen and her dear friend Mrs. Freeman to guide her in all things! What a happy state of affairs! And she and John were becoming rich. It was so easy, for everyone knew of Sarah's influence and she was approached by many who sought to find favor with the King through his beloved daughter. There were financial considerations but these were willingly paid for a word of the right sort of advice dropped into the Princess's ear by her loving friend.

"Very good, but it could be better," was Sarah's verdict to John. "If only I could rid myself of old woman Clarendon, *I* should be the first Lady of the Bedchamber. Of course I have more influence with Morley than anyone else, but always that old woman bars my way, reminding me of who she is. Clarendon! Who were the Clarendons? The upstart Hydes, that's all—the family which gave itself airs because one of the daughters was made pregnant by the heir to the throne and was clever enough to make him marry her. That's the Clarendons for you!"

John replied it was all true of course, but she must be careful of the Clarendons. The Princess's two uncles held much influence with the King, and his dear Sarah must not forget that.

"I'll give the old hag influence!" muttered Sarah.

She did not have to scheme against Lady Clarendon because at this time Lord Clarendon became Lord Lieutenant of Ireland—there was general gossip about this in the Cockpit.

"What I want to know," said Sarah, "is whether he's taking her with him—or is he going to think of some excuse to leave her behind."

Lady Clarendon herself answered the question a few hours later.

"I shall have to say good-bye to you all for I am accompanying my husband to Ireland."

Sarah gave a great sigh of relief. This was a heaven-sent opportunity.

It was inevitable that the whisperings which went on in the Cockpit did not entirely escape attention. The King had no idea that his daughter was disloyal to him and his wife; no one told him, simply because he would not have believed it if they had and, moreover, he would have been seriously displeased with the informer. All through James's life he had failed to see what was significant and important to his own well-being. He wanted a loving, loyal daughter and he would convince himself he had one no matter what evidence was produced to the contrary.

There was more than the spiteful gossip at the Cockpit. Deep plans were being laid at The Hague. Even those men such as Lord Sunderland, James's Prime Minister, whom James trusted completely, had eyes on The Hague. While James acted with caution, he was safe; but one false step could send him hurtling from his seat; these men knew it, and they wanted to be on the right side when that moment came. Back and forth between Whitehall and The Hague went the Protestant spies and the Catholic spies. Anne was writing frequently to her sister in Holland. Anne was a staunch Protestant and when she rode through the streets the people cheered her with more fervor than the Catholics thought desirable, so they decided that a watch should be kept on the Princess Anne and spies should be placed in her household without her knowledge.

As a result of this, two men met along the riverbank not far from Whitehall.

The elder drew the younger into the shadow of a tree and said: "You know what is expected of you."

"Yes, sir."

"Your task should not be difficult. The Princess and her familiar are not discreet. Memorize what you hear and we will meet frequently . . . though not always in the same place . . . and you can make your reports to me."

"Yes, sir."

"Have you spoken to Gwin?"

"Yes, sir."

"He has been some time in the employ of the Princess so may have to be handled with a little care. But he is a good Catholic and therefore we may rely on him."

"There is one thing, sir. These places are going to be costly. Lady Churchill has the disposing of them and she is a greedy woman."

"We have considered that. You need have no fear. We will pay her prices for you and Gwin to get these pages' places. Then . . . to work."

Sarah was smug. John had been delighted when he had heard; she was his clever wife, but never yet had she made a bargain like this one.

"It is but a beginning," she told him airily. "I sold the two places for one thousand two hundred pounds. It shows what can be obtained for the favors I shall have to dispose of."

"And what manner of men are they to be able to pay such prices?"

"Pages merely, whose tasks will be to stand at the doors of the rooms awaiting orders. They must have rich friends."

"Doubtless, which is our good fortune as well as theirs."

But Sarah's pleasure did not last.

Anne sent for her a few weeks after the two pages had been installed and Anne was clearly shaken.

"News from Holland which is most disturbing," cried Anne. "Those new pages are Roman Catholics. My sister's friends over here have informed her of this and she says they must be dismissed at once."

"Dismissed!" fumed Sarah. "And since when has the Princess of Orange commanded this household?"

"She says that it would be dangerous to keep them, that they would spy on us and could prove to be very harmful."

"They are innocent enough."

"But did you know when you found them for the posts that they were Catholics?"

"They did not tell me so."

"They will have to go," said Anne more firmly than she usually spoke.

"Go!" blustered Sarah, thinking of the twelve hundred pounds which had been paid to her. "But, Mrs. Morley, they have already been accepted."

"My sister is very determined that they shall go."

Sarah's eyes blazed suddenly, but she saw that Anne's mouth was determined. Anne was growing more and more involved in conspiracy every day. She knew that the Prince and Princess of Orange deplored her father's religious leanings; her sister's letters brought a great excitement into her life. Mary and William were coming to England as soon as an opportunity offered itself. Mary would be Queen, for the people would not endure a Catholic on the throne and after Mary . . . Queen Anne! She put her hands on her swollen body. Who knew, she might be carrying the future King of England! She must be careful—for the sake of the child, for her own sake. She must show no favor to Catholics; nor would she have them in positions in her household where they could spy on her.

She guessed what happened. Sarah was always in need of money and had sold the places for a high future. That was legitimate enough, for it was a custom at Court. But she reckoned Sarah had bargained more advantageously than most were able to.

It was a pity to spoil Sarah's bargain, but she could not help it. She would not agree with Sarah over this.

"The Catholic pages must go," she said.

Sarah was furious, but what could she do?

The pages were dismissed and although Sarah refused to pay back the whole of the twelve hundred pounds declaring that they had spent a few weeks in their posts and must perforce pay for that privilege, she was so much the poorer.

Laurence Hyde, Earl of Rochester, called to see his niece the Princess Anne. Rochester was disturbed. He was well aware of the trouble for which his brother-in-law, the King, was heading, and Rochester had tried to be an honest man. He was the Lord Treasurer and he believed that if James would but desert Catholicism his reign could continue in peace and prosperity. James was a King who took his duties more seriously than his brother Charles had done; but he was incapable of understanding human nature and he completely lacked Charles' ability to twist and turn himself out of trouble; James, in Rochester's opinion, was a foolish man, and in this dangerous age a fool had very little hope of survival; and the Queen was an evil influence, because she was Catholic; he had hoped that James's mistress Catherine Sedley would be able to detach the King from the Catholics, but this plan had failed and James had been reluctantly obliged to send Catherine to Ireland after bestowing on her the title of Lady Dorchester. Catherine would not remain there, and when she returned doubtless James would be as infatuated as ever; but meanwhile the situation was worsening.

The Cockpit was the center of scandalous gossip; he knew that letters were going back and forth between Anne and Mary, and what Anne wrote to her sister could only be imagined. Yet James could not see that his daughters were at the very heart of the conspiracy against him.

But Rochester was not calling at the Cockpit to remonstrate with his niece on these matters; it was a much more personal affair. Anne had no conception of how to use money. Her gambling debts were enormous; and Rochester was certain that her favorites were proving a great drain on her.

Anne, like her sister Mary in her youth, was greatly attracted by her own sex. The relationship with Sarah Churchill might have been considered an unhealthy one but for the fact that both the ladies were devoted to their husbands; all the same, one began to ask oneself whether the Princess's devotion to the Churchill woman did not exceed what she gave to Prince George.

He was ushered into her presence by Lady Churchill who hovered near her mistress.

"Good day to you, uncle. It is a pleasure to see you." Anne waved a hand for him to sit.

He thought that she was getting far too fat; of course she was pregnant as usual, but in view of her miscarriages and the children who had not lived Rochester wondered whether she was healthy enough to bear strong children.

The youthful pink of her cheeks was deepening; she was far too fleshy. And who could wonder at it? Even now there was a plate of sweets at her elbow and her beautiful plump ringed hands were reaching for one automatically. The Hydes had always been either drinkers or eaters; there was no doubt from which side of the family she had inherited that tendency. He himself was a drinker. With the Stuarts it was women; with the Hydes food and drink. Rochester had always thought the Hyde indulgence the less dangerous, but he was suddenly not so sure.

He glanced at Sarah Churchill, who met his gaze defiantly and seated herself on a tabouret close to her mistress.

"What I have to say to you is for your ears alone," he told Anne.

"Lady Churchill has my complete confidence."

Sarah was smiling at him smugly. But he was not going to discuss these matters before a third party. He said with dignity: "I see I must call again when Your Highness is free to see me alone."

Anne looked alarmed. "Is it so important then?"

"All the more reason . . ." began Sarah.

Rochester put in: "I will call again," and he rose.

But Anne's curiosity was great.

"Oh, no," she said. "Lady Churchill will not mind in the least."

Lady Churchill flushed slightly, but Anne went on firmly: "Leave me with my uncle, dear Lady Churchill, and come back later."

Incidents like this made Sarah so furious that she could scarcely control her rage; Rochester saw this, and thought: The sooner my niece is free of that virago, the better. If she dared she would insist that they change places and she be the mistress.

However, there was nothing Sarah could do, so she walked to the door, head erect, disapproval in every line of her comely figure.

Rochester wondered at which door she would be listening.

"Now, uncle," Anne prompted placidly.

"A very unpleasant subject, I fear. You are deeply in debt again."

"Oh, that!" said Anne.

"This time to the tune of seven thousand pounds. A fortune, you will see."

"But I cannot understand it."

"You have been losing heavily at cards lately, perhaps. And you are doubtless too generous to . . . your friends." He glanced at the door by which Sarah had just left.

"But seven thousand pounds!"

"Which, I fear, has been outstanding for some time; your debts will have to be settled soon or there will be a scandal."

"But where can I find seven thousand pounds?"

"That is a problem to which you will have to give your thoughts until you find the solution."

Anne's jowls were quivering; she was seriously put out. Debts it seemed there must be. But so much—this was incredible.

"Money," she said plaintively, "is so tiresome. There is never enough of it."

"Yet there is no one in the kingdom who would not agree that Your Highness, due to your father's generosity, is more lavishly supplied with this tiresome article than most of us."

She disliked him; he was not being helpful; he was criticizing her and she hated to be criticized.

"Very well," she said haughtily. "I suppose I must thank you for bringing this matter to my notice. The debts shall be paid."

When he left her, dismay replaced her arrogance.

Where was she going to find seven thousand pounds?

Then she knew, for all her life there had been one who had never failed her.

Anne was sitting idly with Sarah and Barbara Fitzharding when there was commotion outside her apartment. A page looked in.

"The King is here," he said.

"The King!" cried Anne. "Oh, yes. I told him I was in trouble. You had better leave me."

Sarah who was determined to hear what took place between the King and his daughter, signed to Barbara and, pushing her into a cupboard, shut the door on them.

"But why . . ." began Barbara.

"Hush!" commanded Sarah, and at that moment James entered his daughter's apartment.

"My dearest Anne," said the King, taking his daughter into his arms.

"Dear Father, it is good of you to come."

"And you are well, and taking good care of yourself? You must now, you know."

"Oh, yes, but I am so upset."

"You must tell me all about it."

"Uncle Rochester has been telling me I owe seven thousand pounds."

"Seven thousand pounds!" cried James. "It is not possible!"

"That's what I tell him."

"But if he says so, it must be. My dear daughter, it is not the first time you have been heavily in debt. But seven thousand pounds!"

Anne began to weep quietly.

"There now," went on the King, "you must not distress yourself. It is not good in your state. I will pay the seven thousand pounds."

"You are a good father to me!"

"You are my dearest daughter. Now that Mary seems so far away, and how can I know . . ." The tears were in his eyes. "I fear her husband has come between us and we are not good friends as we used to be. But it is different with you. You are my dear daughter and nothing shall come between us. George is a good husband and if you are happy with him that is all I shall ever ask of him. Now you are no longer worried about this money?"

"No, Father."

"But I must speak to you on this matter very seriously, my dear. You must consider your expenditure in the future. Do not bet so recklessly with the cards; and I know that you are far too generous with those about you. Your heart is too soft, my dear. Those who serve you should be content enough to do so. They have well-paid posts and many advantages, which I fancy they are not slow to take. There is no need for you to shower gifts on them. It is no wonder that my dearest daughter cannot pay her debts when she gives so much away."

She embraced him and thanked him.

Now, he told her, she must put all unpleasant matters from her mind; she must forget this wretched seven thousand pounds which he would take care of. But in the future, to please him, and for her own sake, she must promise to be more careful.

"I promise, dear Father," she answered.

He would have liked to linger, to talk of her health and the old days when she and her sister Mary had played together with him and their mother. Anne had heard too much of those days and now that he had promised to take care of the debt, she was anxious to be rid of him; but she was touched by his goodness and she was sincere when she told him he was a good father to her.

As soon as he had gone Sarah and Barbara Fitzharding burst out of the cupboard.

"So," cried Sarah, "Mansell has come to the rescue, and so he should. He has plenty."

"He is a good father," said Anne placidly.

"Over ready to tell you what you should do!" commented Sarah. "There are some who say he should look to his own conduct. The Sedley woman who now calls herself Countess of Dorchester will soon be back to make more scandal, I'll swear. Then Mr. Mansell might more profitably give *himself* some good advice."

Sarah was angry with the King. The gifts Anne bestowed on her were very welcome and she and John were becoming rich. Surely people like herself and John should be rewarded for all they did.

"The real villain," she went on, "is your uncle, that old rascal Rochester."

She would never forgive him for more or less ordering her from the apartment.

Rochester had resigned from the Treasury. He could not serve under James because he could see that gradually the King was introducing Catholics into the most important posts. Robert Spencer, Earl of Sunderland, took his place.

It was characteristic of James that he should have allowed his good friend and brother-in-law to be ousted by a man like Sunderland.

Rochester deplored the King's Catholicism, but at the same time he believed that James was the rightful heir and would have done everything in his power to keep him on the throne. It was true that Rochester had tried to use Catherine Sedley to break the Queen's influence with James, but he had been convinced that by favoring Catholics the King was bringing himself closer to disaster.

Sunderland had let James believe that he had become converted to Catholicism, but he was a schemer by nature and in fact was in close touch with William and Mary by means of his wife, who corresponded with the Princess of Orange frequently, letting her know all that she could discover of what was happening at the English Court.

Sunderland's great plan was to alienate James from the Hydes—Lord Clarendon who had been sent to Ireland and Lord Rochester who had been the Lord Treasurer—and this he did through the Queen. The result was that not only was Rochester impelled to resign his office but Clarendon was recalled from Ireland.

Thus James continued to lose his friends and surround himself with fickle friends, many of whom were waiting for the moment to destroy him.

Now that Sunderland was Lord Treasurer and as such concerned himself with the Princess's expenditure, which still exceeded that of her income, Sarah turned her venom against him.

It was only right, she said, that the Princess of Orange should know what a snake he was, and who could keep her sister informed of what was going on in London as clearly as Anne.

So carefully had Sunderland cloaked his true motives that the Cockpit was unaware that he was really working for the same cause as they were: the deposing of James and the setting up of Mary in his place.

Anne had hoped to visit The Hague during the following spring but James, being unsure of his son-in-law and a little anxious on account of his daughter's health, for he was convinced her miscarriages must have enfeebled her, told her that she must postpone all thoughts of the visit for a while.

Anne pretended to be more angry than she was, for secretly she was not anxious to undergo the discomforts of the journey; but, nevertheless, with Sarah's help she wrote a venomous letter to her sister.

> I am denied the satisfaction of seeing you, my dearest sister, this spring though the King gave me leave when I first asked it. I impute this to Lord Sunderland, for the King trusts him with everything, and, he, going on so fiercely in the interests of the papists, is afraid you should be told a true character of him. . . .

Sarah sat beside her and nodded her approval.

"You should elaborate a little on that, Mrs. Morley, for I am of the opinion that the Princess of Orange should be warned of this man."

Anne took up her pen and continued:

You may remember I have once before ventured to tell you that I thought my Lord Sunderland a very ill man, and I am more confirmed every day in that opinion. Everyone knows how often this man turned backward and forward in the late King's time, and now to complete all his virtues he is working with all his might to bring in popery. He is perpetually with the priests, and stirs up the King to do things faster than I believe he would himself.

"That," said Sarah, with a chuckle, "should warn them. Caliban will be in no mood to tolerate the fellow when he hears of that. But you should tell them of how he hears mass, for instance."

This worthy lord [went on Anne], does not go publicly to Mass but hears it privately in a priest's chamber. His lady is as extraordinary in her kind, for she is a flattering, dissembling, false woman; but she has so fawning and endearing a way that she will deceive anybody at first and it is not possible to find out all her ways in a little time. . . .

The friends smiled at each other.

"That," said Sarah, "will give them a good idea of Rogers and Rogers' wife." Rogers was the name they had given the Sunderlands.

Anne and Sarah had no idea that certain members of their household were sending information about the happenings in the Cockpit to The Hague; and that the Princess of Orange was learning how very much her sister was under the influence of Lady Churchill.

The venomous attacks on various personalities of the Court could not, Mary guessed, have been written by Anne alone. Mary wrote a personal letter to her sister warning her that the reports she received of Lady Churchill did not altogether please her and she begged her sister to be a little more discreet with her woman.

Sarah was with Anne when this letter arrived and as she read it, her face was flooded with angry color.

"There are people who wish you ill, Mrs. Morley," she declared. "That is the reason why they wish to separate us. They know how I carry your welfare in my heart; they know that I would serve you with my life. Oh, it is clear to me that ill-wishers have done this."

"It is folly, Sarah. But I will put this right. I will tell my sister immediately how good you are."

Sarah angrily took the pen from Anne's hand and wrote:

Sorry people have taken such pains to give so ill a character of Lady Churchill. I believe there is nobody in the world has better notions of religion than she has. It is true she is not so strict as some are, nor does she keep such a bustle with religion; which I confess I think is never the worse, for one sees so many saints mere devils, that if one be a good Christian, the less show one makes the better in my opinion. Then, as for moral principles, it is impossible to have better, and without all that, lifting up of the hands and eyes, and often going to church will prove but a lame devotion. One thing more I must say for her which is that she has a true sense of the doctrine of our Church, and abhors all the principles of the church of Rome. As to this particular, I assure you she will never change. The same thing I will venture, now I am on this subject, to say for her lord, for though he is a very faithful servant to King James, and the King is very kind to him, and I believe he will always obey the King in all things that are consistent with religion, yet rather than change *that,* I daresay he will lose all his places and everything he has. . . .

Sarah looked up. She had written some of the fury out of herself.

"This is the sort of letter," she said, "I suggest you write to the Princess of Orange. It is monstrous that one who has done nothing but good should be so slandered. But I know that my dear Mrs. Morley will not allow this injustice to pass. I know she will write this letter to her sister."

"You may trust me, my dear Mrs. Freeman," Anne promised her.

Sarah left Anne to write her letters and went to her own apartments to cool off her temper.

The Princess of Orange had never liked her. A pretty state of affairs if she should return and take the throne. Who knew what influence she would try to exert over Anne—she, and her Caliban of a husband.

Anne could be a sentimental fool. Like her father she was often brooding on the old days of childhood. It was "Dear Mary this" and "Dear Mary that."

Well, thought Sarah, not even the Queen of England shall insult Sarah Churchill.

Sarah came running into her mistress's apartments. She was flushed and breathless and before she spoke Anne saw that something had happened to upset her.

"You have not yet heard the rumors," said Sarah. "I can see that."

"Tell me, Sarah, what is it?"

"The Queen believes that she may be pregnant."

Anne started at Sarah; not until this moment had the Princess realized how deep were her desires, how ambitious she had become.

The Queen pregnant! What if she should be brought to bed of a son. That would be the end of all Anne's dreams. If she had a half brother, neither she nor Mary could come to the throne.

THE WARMING-PAN
SCANDAL

As soon as the news was made public the Court and country was alive with speculation. "This is the end of hope," said some. Others retorted: "On the contrary, this is the beginning. This is the chance."

There were some who said that if James had a son who was Prince of Wales and rightful heir to the throne, the people would have no one but him to be King.

A boy brought up to be a Catholic? And did they think his father and mother would allow him to be brought up otherwise? Then there would be no doubt whatever of the old religion coming back. And were the people going to endure that?

James and his Queen were overjoyed. Neither of them seemed conscious of the trouble all about them. James went on bringing in unpopular measures which favored Catholics; and in the streets the people cried: "No popery."

Anne spent her days in discussion with Sarah. It must not happen, they said; and because it would be the end of all their hopes they believed it never would.

No one was sure who started the rumor that the Queen was not really pregnant but was pretending to be. The theme of these rumors was that the King was so desirous of bringing back the Catholic faith to England that he would foist a spurious baby on the country if necessary. The child would be brought up as a Catholic; he would have only Catholics about him; and how easy it would be when all the important positions were in the hands of papists, and the King was a papist, to turn the whole country back to Rome!

Anne liked this rumor; it appealed to her love of intrigue as well as to her ambition; with Sarah's help she sought to keep it alive.

She wrote to Mary:

Mansell's wife looks better than she ever did which is not usual. I believe that her great belly is a false one. She is positive that the child will be a son, and the principle of that religion being such that they will stick at nothing, be it never so wicked if it will promote their interest, indicates that some foul play is intended.

In Holland Mary read her sister's letters and showed them to her husband, whom she obeyed in all things. It was very comforting to them that the rumors were being spread in England.

James, having heard nothing of the rumors, continued delighted, while he deluded himself that his dear daughters were as pleased at the prospect of a birth in the family as he was.

Mary Beatrice, the Queen, was better informed, although she knew that it was quite impossible to make James face the fact that Anne was not the devoted daughter he believed her to be. She herself was bewildered because she had always been on good terms with both her stepdaughters and at first believed that others were poisoning Anne's mind against her.

But Anne's behavior at the Queen's toilet—at which it was the Princess's duty to attend—began to worry Mary Beatrice. Anne was continually spying on her, attempting to feel her body, to catch glimpses of her naked, and Mary Beatrice, who had a great sense of her own dignity, became very resentful.

The more obvious this became, the more Anne turned against her stepmother; she was now doing everything possible to convince her sister Mary that the Queen was posing as a pregnant woman when she was not so at all.

On one occasion Anne, leaning forward to help her stepmother with her chemise, attempted to touch her body. Mary Beatrice was suddenly so angry that she lifted a glove which lay on a table and struck Anne across the face with it.

Anne drew back in astonishment.

"Your Majesty . . ." she stammered.

But the Queen threw the glove back on to the table and stared straight in front of her.

Anne returned to her own apartments and it was not long before Sarah came hurrying to her, for the story of the slap in the face had been quickly spread.

"The insolence!" cried Sarah.

"She would reply to that, that she is the Queen."

"For the moment," said Sarah darkly. "Oh, it's clear to me that she is a guilty woman. Why, if she were not, should she fly into such a passion? I think you should write to your sister. This is a terrible thing which is about to burst on our country."

So under Sarah's guidance Anne wrote once more to Mary.

> She should, to convince the world, make either me or some of my friends feel her belly. But whenever one talks with her being with child she looks as if she is afraid one should touch her. I believe when she is brought to bed nobody will be convinced it is her child, except it prove a daughter.

This letter brought an unexpected and alarming response. Mary wrote to Anne telling her that in view of all these doubts as to whether or not the Queen was pregnant, she and the Prince had decided that it was desirable that they should come to England to see for themselves whether in fact the Queen was about to bear a child.

Anne was shaking with dismay when she read that letter. She remembered all that she had said of her father to her sister; and she feared that if Mary and James met, too much would be revealed and he would be able to tell Mary that he had been maligned.

If Mary came to England now, if she talked with their father, if she pointed out to him the folly of his ways . . . which she might well do, for Anne did not believe that—although she would support William in everything—Mary wished to see her father deposed . . . there might be a reconciliation between them.

Anne was too stupid to be a subtle intriguer; Sarah was too hasty.

Here was an awkward situation. How were they going to extricate themselves?

Together they found the answer.

"If either of you should come," wrote Anne, "I should be very glad to see you, but really if you or the Prince should come I should be frightened out of my wits for fear any harm should happen to either of you."

Mary's reply to that was that Anne must be present at the birth. She must make sure that the baby was in fact the son of her father and the Queen.

Anne, who had been rather alarmed by the turn of events and desperately disappointed at the possibility of being deprived of her ambition, and at the same time weakened in health by yet another miscarriage, developed a fever and was confined to her bed.

The King came to visit her.

He sat by the bed and held her hand, and when she opened her eyes she recognized him and smiled, for she had forgotten all the trouble of the last months and thought she was a child again.

"Dear Father," she murmured; and James's eyes filled with tears.

"My beloved," he said, "you must get well. You know what you mean to me. I could never be truly happy without you."

She was aware of George on the other side of the bed; and the presence of these two comforted her.

Sarah, who found that her authority was weakened when Anne was not there to help her enforce it, was terrified that Anne was going to die. It was clearly brought home to her that Anne was necessary to her future—hers and John's. If Anne were to die now, what would become of them? They would rise in the world, she was sure of that; but it would take them years to recover what they would lose with the removal of Anne.

Anne was of vital importance to them; Anne *must* live; and when she was recovered they must be closer than ever.

As soon as Sarah could get into the sickroom, she nursed Anne. She amazed everyone with her efficiency, for no one had thought she would make a good nurse; she was gentle with the patient, although fiercely authoritative with everyone else. As for Anne, she drew strength from Sarah and when Sarah said: "You *will* get well!" Anne believed her.

The King and Prince George had to be grateful to Sarah Churchill, although they could not like her, and under Sarah's ministrations Anne recovered more speedily than was hoped.

As the time for the Queen's confinement drew nearer the excitement increased.

Mary Beatrice had said that she would lie in at Windsor.

Anne and Sarah smiled significantly when they heard this.

"Naturally," said Sarah. "Why at Windsor it will not be so easy to summon those people who should be at her bedside. Can you not imagine it, Mrs. Morley? It will be: 'My pains are beginning. Come quickly.' And by the time all those who should witness the birth have arrived, there will be a bonny baby in the bed!"

"Oh, the wickedness!" cried Anne.

It may have been that some of the Queen's friends were aware of this rumor, for shortly afterward she changed her mind and said that she would lie in at St. James's.

"St. James's!" said Anne. "Such a bustle there was about lying in at

Windsor and now it is to be St. James's. St. James's is a better place to cheat in."

It was surprising how she and Sarah made each other believe these spiteful observations. Both knew that St. James's was the palace in which the Queens usually gave birth to their children, Whitehall being unsuitable since it was more or less a public place in which people could enter night and day. It was noisy; matters of state were dealt with there; and the apartments of the Queen looked straight on to the river along which there was constant traffic. St. James's on the other hand was an intimate Palace; it had been the home of Mary Beatrice when she had first come to England and she felt sentimental toward it. Therefore naturally she was determined that this most important child should be born in this Palace.

Certain repairs were in progess on her apartments at St. James's at this time and she gave instructions that they should be hastily finished and her bedroom made ready.

Every small action, every word she spoke, was seized on by her enemies, and made to seem full of significance. Still neither she nor James—least of all James—were aware of the dangers which were overshadowing them, and it never occurred to them that the danger was heightened by the Queen's condition, for those who had been waiting for an opportunity to depose James saw that they could use the birth of a son for doing so. The cry was: "If there is a son, that son will be brought up as a Catholic. A Catholic King; a Catholic Queen; a Catholic Prince of Wales! There can be no doubt then what the fate of England would be. It must never be allowed to happen."

There was a whisper in some circles that if a son was born to the King and Queen, William of Orange would come to England and make a bid to take the crown from him on behalf of his wife.

This was a time of tension and great danger—realized by all except the King.

James, with his penchant for falling into trouble just at the time when it could bring him most harm, sent the Archbishop of Canterbury and six bishops to the Tower for asking to be excused from ordering the reading of the Declaration of Indulgence in the churches. The country was filled with horror, and feeling against the King increased.

Anne was growing alarmed at the speed with which tension was rising. Her sister had said that she must be present at the birth and see for herself that the child was genuinely the Queen's.

This was disturbing because secretly she knew that the Queen was pregnant, and if she were present at the birth how could she continue with this pleasant fantasy? She, who had never had any great desire for action, was becoming too deeply involved. What she liked was to lie on her couch, with Sarah sitting beside her, while she made the most fantastic accusations against anyone they cared to slander. That was quite different from taking an active part.

"I feel very unwell," she told her father. "I think I shall go to Bath at once."

He was immediately concerned. "You should be here for the birth," he said, "but I do not wish you to run any risk of a return of your fever."

"I fear I should if I remained."

"Then, my dear, you must go. The Queen will be sorry, but I am sure she will understand."

The Queen was not in the least sorry. When Anne told her of her decision to leave, Mary Beatrice looked at her coldly. They both remembered the incident of the glove.

"So I shall not be here when Your Majesty lies in," said Anne demurely.

"It may be that you will have returned by then. I think my confinement will be after July."

"Oh, Madam, I think you will be brought to bed before I return," replied Anne.

The Queen did not answer and shortly afterward Anne left.

Repeating the conversation to Sarah, Anne explained: "You will see, the child will be born while I am away."

"One less witness," said Sarah. "You can depend upon it."

This idea pleased them both and they refrained from reminding each other that there was no need for Anne to leave London and it was entirely her own wish that she should go to Bath.

Shortly after, Anne, with a few of her women including Sarah, left London.

The repairs to the apartment in St. James's Palace were not completed by June and the Queen was growing anxious.

"I am determined to lie in at St. James's," she said.

"Your Majesty, there is some work to be completed yet," she was told.

"Please ask them to hurry," she replied.

As the days passed she became more and more concerned, seeming to be very fearful of not being able to get to St. James's in time. Her aversion to Whitehall was unnatural, said her enemies.

All during Saturday, the 9th of June, she was very restless, and she sent to St. James's to ask how the work was progessing.

"It will be finished, Your Majesty, by the end of the day," she was told.

"It must be," she said, "for I believe my time is near and I am determined to lie at St. James's tonight if I have to lie on the boards."

Her remarks were noted and her enemies were ready to see deep meaning behind them. Before the Queen settled down to cards once more she sent to St. James's and the reply came back that the work would be finished before night; her bed was being set up and word would be sent as soon as her apartment was ready.

The play was a little wild that night; the Queen's eyes were on the door and the eyes of almost everyone else were on the Queen.

It was about ten o'clock when the message arrived breathlessly from St. James's, to announce that the Queen's apartments were ready now.

Mary Beatrice half rose in her chair; then she remembered that etiquette demanded the party should not be broken up until the game was completed. She sat impatiently while the play went on as though in fear that the child would be born before she had time to make the short journey from palace to palace.

Her relief was apparent when at eleven the game was completed and she declared her intention of leaving at once. Her sedan chair was brought and because of the solemnity of the occasion, when she was carried from Whitehall through the park to St. James's, her Chamberlain, Sidney Godolphin, walked beside her chair. James joined the party and contentedly Mary Beatrice took possession of her apartments, there to await the birth which, before it was taking place, was causing more speculation throughout the country than any other had before.

On Trinity Sunday, the 10th of June, the Queen awoke and remembered with relief that she was in her apartments in St. James's Palace. She found that she was trembling; the child would be born today she was sure. It was not that she was afraid of the pains of birth; heaven knew she longed for the child to be born; but there were too many enemies about her, and those who should have been her friends were turning against her. Anne, her stepdaughter, had, in the last months, grown sly and secretive. What did Anne say of her when she was not there to defend herself? And there was Mary, she whom she had affectionately called her "dear Lemon" because she was married to William of Orange. Had she really detected a coldness in Mary's letters?

She called to one of her women.

"Send for the King," she said, "and have everyone summoned who should be present when my child is born."

She left her bed then and sat down on a tabouret to wait.

Margaret Dawson, one of her most trusted women, who had been in the service of the first Duchess of York and had attended the births of Anne and Mary, came hurrying in.

"Your Majesty," she cried, "has your time come then?"

"It is close, Margaret," said the Queen.

Margaret saw that the Queen was trembling, and asked if she were cold.

"Strange, is it not?" answered Mary Beatrice. "Cold on a morning in June. Margaret, I am so . . . uneasy."

"Your Majesty, it is often thus at this stage."

"So much depends on this, Margaret. Is the pallet ready?"

"It is not yet aired, Your Majesty."

"Then have it aired immediately and when this is done I will go to it."

The pallet was in the next room and as Margaret went to do the Queen's bidding, the King arrived.

"My dear," he said, taking the Queen's hand and kissing it, "has the time come then? Then all those who are at church must be sent for without delay."

She nodded; for those at church were their enemies, the Protestants, and it was imperative that they should be present at the birth.

"Let me take you to your pallet," said the King.

"They are airing it now."

"Then I will make sure that all those who should be here are summoned."

A warming-pan was being carried into the Queen's lying-in chamber. Margaret Dawson threw back the quilt, the pan was placed in the bed, and the covers drawn over it.

"The bed must be thoroughly aired," said Margaret, "before her Majesty gets into it."

Shortly afterward Lady Sunderland arrived.

"How is it?" she said to Margaret Dawson.

"All well so far. The Queen is in her own bedchamber and will occupy the pallet as soon as it is thoroughly aired. I fancy her time is near."

Lady Sunderland nodded. "I was in the chapel preparing to take the sacrament," she said, "but I was told I must come to the Queen at once."

"It is well that you came," answered Margaret. "She was sitting on her tabouret shivering when I went in so I want the bed thoroughly warmed."

"It is a warm morning."

"But in that state a woman can feel anything. She is so wrought up that I fear the shock will be too much for her—be it boy or girl."

"Much depends on this child," agreed Lady Sunderland. "She has asked that just at first none should say whether it is a boy or girl for she feels that the pleasure or the disappointment would be unbearable. This should be made known."

Margaret nodded.

The King came into the apartment accompanied by Dr. Walgrave and the midwife.

James was clearly anxious. He was talking earnestly to the doctor, making anxious inquiries as to the state of the Queen's health. The doctor thought that all should go well, but he was a little perturbed by the Queen's anxiety.

Seeing Lady Sunderland James came to her and expressed his pleasure to see her there.

"We are all anxious about Her Majesty," said Lady Sunderland. "She is more excited than she has been at previous confinements."

"She longs so much for a boy," replied James.

"I have asked the midwife to pull at my dress, Your Majesty, if the child should be a boy, so that no word shall be spoken to excite Her Majesty."

"You must give me a sign," said James. "I shall be watching you eagerly. Touch your forehead like this . . . if it is a boy. If there is no sign I shall know it is a girl. Then I trust the Queen will be able to rest and recover a little before she hears what is the sex of her child."

It was agreed that that should be the sign and the group broke up as the Queen, accompanied by some of her ladies, came into the apartment.

She got into the bed and it was clear that her pains had started.

Now the room began to fill. The doctors, nurses, midwife, the Queen's ladies and officers of the household with eighteen members of the privy council came into the room.

Mary Beatrice lay back on her pillows groaning.

By half past nine the atmosphere was stifling because of the crowd assembled there. At the foot of the bed the Privy councillors stood watching.

"Margaret," called Mary Beatrice.

Margaret came to her mistress and took her hand.

"I cannot endure this," cried the Queen. "These men staring. Draw the bed curtains."

Margaret firmly did so.

"Pray stand back," she said to the men. "It is unseemly that you should crowd about the bed at such a time."

Shortly afterward the child was born. James was watching Lady Sunderland.

The midwife was bending over the bed. She turned and quickly pulled Lady Sunderland's dress, and when Lady Sunderland touched her forehead the King gave a cry of joy. But he could not restrain himself, and must have the joyous information confirmed.

"What is it?" he demanded in a loud voice.

The nurse had taken the baby from the midwife. She said in a clear voice which could be heard throughout the apartment: "What Your Majesty desires."

James seized the arm of the nurse who held the child and said to the privy councillors: "You have witnessed that my son is born." Then he turned to the nurse and cried: "Make way. Make way for the Prince of Wales."

Mary Beatrice was exhausted but triumphant; the King could not withhold his joy and knighted Dr. Walgrave in the lying-in chamber. The guns of the Tower were firing salutes, and all over London the bells were ringing. There should be a feast for the poor, and wine with which they could drink the health of the Prince of Wales.

But while the people feasted and drank, they asked themselves what this birth would mean. Were they asked to accept a slice of roasted ox, a flagon of wine—for popery?

This would be the end of Protestant England. Was it what the people wanted? Those might who had forgotten the Smithfield fires, the threat of Spain; but there were many who remembered. They said the Court was full of those who were flirting with Rome, not seriously, but only for the sake of commandeering the high posts because the best way of advancement at Court was through the Catholic Faith. But many were false Catholics; and when the time came they would turn.

It was unfortunate that there should be a son at this stage. But was there truly a son?

On a June morning the Queen's bed had been warmed by a warming-pan which had been taken into her bed just before she entered it. A warming-pan! A simple homely implement! But it could be significant, for why should not a child be concealed in a warming-pan and put into the bed before the Queen entered it?

A wild idea? But all knew how wily these Catholics were. They would stop at nothing to do what they wanted.

The rumor grew. The boy whom they called the Prince of Wales was not the Queen's child at all. She had not been pregnant. It had all been a pretence. There were stories which had come from the Cockpit and surely the Princess Anne who lived close to the Queen must know; the Queen would let no one see her without her shift, she would let no one feel her body. Why not? Because she was not pregnant. It was a plot, a wicked plot to bring Catholicism back to England.

And then the confinement. A baby in a warming-pan!

It was a tale that appealed to the people who wanted to believe that the baby who was called the Prince of Wales was not the son of the King and Queen, but a spurious child whom they hoped to foist on the nation for the sake of the Catholic Faith.

When Anne returned to London the air was full of rumors which delighted her.

She was particularly entranced by that of the warming-pan.

She referred to her half brother as the warming-pan baby, and did her best to keep that story alive.

Anne wrote to Mary:

> My dear sister can't imagine the concern and vexation I have been in, that I should be so unfortunate as to be out of town when the Queen was brought to bed, for I shall never more be satisfied whether the child be true or false. It may be that he is our brother, but God knows. . . .

Each day she waited for news from Holland; she knew that something would have to be done now, for she did not believe William would allow the scandals concerning the Prince of Wales to die down. If the people accepted him as Prince of Wales, what hope would there be of Mary's coming to the throne, what hope for Anne?

While she waited for news from Holland, she must keep the rumors alive. The Mansell boy must never be accepted as her brother.

Her father was still unpopular in spite of free feasting and drinking. The bishops were still in the Tower. The foolish man, thought Anne, did he not see that by releasing them he would have won more favor than by roasting a few oxen for the poor?

His enemies made certain that the warming-pan story was the great topic of conversation at all the feasting; and one of the foremost of his enemies was his daughter Anne.

There was a great activity at St. James's as the nursery ceremonies took place. The Prince of Wales must have a governess and the Marchioness of Powis was appointed to this post. His two nurses, Mrs. Royere and Madame Labadie, were already installed; he must have an assistant governess to help the Marchioness and Lady Strickland was chosen for this office. In addition he must have his own laundress and seamstress, four rockers and two pages.

All those who visited him in his cradle declared him to be a bonny child, although in the first hours following his birth there had been a fear that he might succumb to convulsions as other royal children had before him.

There was such anxiety to keep him alive that too many physicians were appointed to look after him and this almost resulted in a fatal accident, for it was decided to give a drug which was believed to be good for babies and this was done; but the physician who had given it did not inform all the other physicians and one of them, not knowing that the child had already had one dose, gave him another.

Mary Beatrice awoke with a start to find no one in her bedchamber. Lady Sunderland, who was lady of the bed for that night, should have been present.

"What has happened?" cried the Queen, while a terrible foreboding came to her.

There was no answer; and as she was about to get out of bed, Lady Sunderland came hurrying in. Mary Beatrice knew at once that something had happened to her son; and when Lady Sunderland told her, she fell fainting back on her pillows.

The news went rapidly round the Court: The Prince is dying.

The King remained on his knees for hours praying for his son; and Mary Beatrice lay without speaking in her bed. Meanwhile the doctors were bleeding the baby and giving him more physic.

For several days the little boy's life was in danger and Anne wrote gleefully to The Hague:

> The Prince of Wales has been ill these three or four days; and
> if he has been so bad as people say, I believe it will not be long
> before he is an angel in Heaven.

It would be the best thing, thought Anne. Then it would be as it was in the days before they had heard Mary Beatrice was pregnant.

In a few days time however the little Prince was well again, and this gave rise to a new rumor. The Prince was now a bonny blooming boy; it was strange, was it not, that a few days ago he had been nigh to death? What if the boy who had been brought in to the Queen's bed by means of a warming-pan was dead—and this healthy boy had been substituted for him?

The twists and turns of the story were becoming farcical, but those who were determined to be rid of James were delighted to accept the rumors as truth.

Now there was a further rumor more important than any that had gone before.

In Holland William of Orange was planning an invasion of England, his object being to depose James and set his wife Mary—James's eldest daughter—on the throne.

The King could not believe it; he shut his eyes to it. It was impossible, he said. He had always detested William of Orange, but he could not believe that his daughter Mary would ever stand against him.

He did not take the threat seriously. He did not—or would not—face the fact that there were many Englishmen, even those close to him who, even though professing an inclination toward Catholicism, were determined never to have a Catholic monarch on the throne.

While James and his Queen had been rejoicing in the birth of the Prince of Wales, these men had seen in the event the sign for action.

Seven of the most influential men had gone so far as to invite William to come to England. These were Danby and Devonshire, Shrewsbury, Russell, Lumley, the Bishop of London, and Henry Sidney.

The bells which James had caused to ring with joy for the birth of his Prince were in truth tolling for his own defeat.

In the Cockpit Sarah and Anne talked in breathless whispers. It was more than a subject for spiteful gossip now. Revolution was in the air. Caliban was coming.

Anne wondered vaguely whether Caliban would be as kind to her as her father had been; but she looked to Sarah who was slyly pleased. Mary, who suffers from the ague, Sarah was thinking. And William, who will be of no account without her, and then . . . Anne.

THE FLIGHT OF
THE PRINCESS

Lord Clarendon called at the Cockpit to see his niece. She kept him waiting a while before receiving him—this was on Sarah's advice—and when he was brought in, Sarah was sure that she was in position to hear everything.

"My lord," said Anne, "to what do I owe the honor of this visit. It is rare that you call on me."

"Your Highness has been out of town lately. I shall be ready to call on you at any time should you have commands for me."

"You have been with my father?" she asked.

"Yes, Your Highness, and it is of him I would speak. Your Highness knows that preparations are being made in Holland."

"Everyone is talking of it."

"The King does not take it seriously enough."

"Is that so? I had thought him much agitated by the reports."

"But he does nothing?"

"What should he do?"

"He should gather about him those friends whom he can trust."

"Ah, uncle, whom can one trust?"

"Those who have never proved themselves false," retorted Clarendon hotly.

"My father is melancholy. He has heard that the Prince of Orange is soon to embark and that Shrewsbury, Wiltshire, and Sidney are with him. It is disturbing news."

"The King your father needs advice and he would listen to you."

"I never speak to the King on state matters," replied Anne.

"If you showed concern for your father now it would give him great pleasure to know that you were anxious on his account."

"But I have told you it is not my place to discuss business."

"Does your Highness realize the danger the King is in?"

"It is not for me to say."

Clarendon flushed. "As the King's daughter does Your Highness not consider it is your place to help him?"

"I have never discussed such things with the King," Anne reiterated coolly. She lifted the watch—which was as large as a clock and which hung at her side. "Why I do declare," she went on, "it is time to prepare for worship and I must not be late for that."

Lord Clarendon saw that he was dismissed. He could see, too, that Anne would not help her father; in fact he was not at all sure that she was not secretly pleased that the King's difficulties were becoming more acute.

Then, thought Clarendon, the rumors I have heard about the treachery in the Cockpit are true.

Clarendon discussed that interview with his brother Laurence.

"The terrible part of it all was that she did not seem to care!" he complained.

"But, brother, have you not heard that many of the evil rumors about the Prince's birth actually started at the Cockpit?"

"I cannot believe it."

"Our niece may not possess a brilliant mind but she has a flaming ambition."

"You think that she wants him . . . deposed. Oh, I can't believe that any daughter would be so ungrateful; and he has been good to her."

"He wears a crown, brother. She covets a crown."

"But it will not come to her."

"After Mary it will."

"I won't believe it. I won't. I shall call on her again. I shall try to make her see that she must help her father, because he seems incapable of helping himself."

"It is what King Charles always feared."

"But who would have believed it would ever have come to this! He should be rallying the country. He should reform his ways."

"He has released the bishops."

"It is not enough. He must let the people know that he will not attempt to foist Catholicism on them. He must gather his faithful friends and prepare for battle. Anne could persuade him I am sure. He would listen to her. You know how he dotes on her since Mary has been under the thumb of Orange. I shall go to her."

He did; and found her with Sarah, Lady Fitzharding, and others of her ladies.

She received him somewhat insolently and would not dismiss her women, who were dressing her. She smiled at him rather maliciously in the mirror and he thought that she took courage from these women about her. "I know what you have come to speak of, my lord," she said. "This baby whose entrance into the world . . . or should I say the Queen's bed . . . is causing such a stir."

"They are saying warming-pans are very commodious these days." That was Sarah Churchill. An odious woman and an evil influence on the Princess, thought Clarendon.

"Yet it does not need a great deal of space to carry hot coals," added Lady Fitzharding.

Spy! thought Clarendon. Sister of the woman whom everyone knew was the mistress of Orange. What a strange pair these sisters were! There was Mary, heiress to the throne of England, meekly adoring a husband who treated her harshly; and, Anne her sister, surrounding herself with women for whom she seemed to have more regard than for her own father!

"I do not think, my lord," retorted Anne, "that you are aware of what the people are saying. It was most unhelpful that those who should have been present at the birth were not there."

"All those who wished to attend were invited to do so, Your Highness."

"I was saying that it was unfortunate it should happen when those who should have been present were prevented from being there . . . and I know that before the birth at Her Majesty's toilet she would go into her private closet and put on her chemise . . . so that those whose duty it was to look on her belly were unable to do so."

The women were tittering; Sarah Churchill laughed out loud.

It was a scene from which Lord Clarendon felt he must escape at once.

He took his leave and went to the King. He could not tell him exactly what had happened for James would not believe him and would be furious, not with Anne, but with him; so he said that he believed that people were endeavoring to poison the Princess Anne's mind and attempting to make her accept this absurd story of the baby in the warming-pan.

James sent the entire Privy Council to his daughter with an account of what happened at the birth of the Prince.

"This is not necessary," said Anne, "for I have so much duty to the King that his word is more to me than these depositions."

Clarendon heard this and was glad of the reply for the King's sake.

But he was very uneasy and he did not trust his niece.

James was truly alarmed now. He sought to modify his policies but it was too late, for the whole of Protestant England was looking to Holland. Then James made another of his mistakes when he attempted to strengthen his army by bringing in Catholics from Ireland.

The English soldiers sullenly discussed those Irish who had been brought in to fight beside them—the Irish who some forty years before in Cromwell's day had cried Lilliburlero while they slaughtered the Protestants.

To Purcell's music words were written and the army began to sing a new song to the old tune and the words inflamed not only the soldiers but the people.

Throughout England that tense autumn it seemed that everyone was singing Lilliburlero, singing it with fervor and indignation.

William set out from Holland, his fleet was scattered by bad weather and he had to return to his own country; but this was only a temporary respite. The next time William made the attempt he reached Torbay in safety; and when the people saw the Orange flags with the motto "Protestant Religion and Liberty," they welcomed William and drank to his success.

It was the 5th of November. A significant day because this was the anniversary of the Catholic plot to blow up the Houses of Parliament.

James now realized the need for action and marched west with his army. John Churchill was one of his leading generals, but Churchill had his own ideas as to what would be the outcome of the battle. As he saw it, there could be victory for either side; but Churchill was a Protestant; he was also an extremely ambitious man; Sarah and he were pledged to Anne and if James were the victor, then the Prince of Wales would follow him.

So here was Churchill, the King's general, secretly hoping the King's enemy would be victorious; and if the King was defeated those who had served him could not expect favors from the new King and Queen. Exile would more likely be their lot.

Churchill was a brilliant soldier; but there was one cause for which he would always fight—the cause of the Churchills.

Churchill left the King at Salisbury and joined William at Axminster. Prince George followed him.

When James heard the news, he knew that he was defeated.

John's great concern was for Sarah who, at the Cockpit, would be in danger. As soon as he reached Axminster he sent a message telling her she must make her escape from London for he was certain orders would be given for her arrest.

When Sarah heard this news she sprang into action.

"We are in danger," she told Anne. "William is going to be victorious, for Mr. Freeman and Mr. Morley are now with him, and we are both in danger of arrest."

"What can we do?" cried Anne.

"There is no need for you to be afraid, dear Mrs. Morley. I will arrange everything. You must tell no one, though. This must be our secret. But we must escape from the Cockpit before our enemies can make us their prisoners."

Anne nodded, but she was a little disturbed. It had been so much more fun to gossip about plots and intrigues than to be caught up in them; but Sarah was at her best on occasions like this.

"Not a word to Danvers, or your old nurse Buss," warned Sarah. "Fitzharding will come with us. We can trust her because she is an Orange woman since her sister is Caliban's mistress."

"Sometimes," said Anne apprehensively, "I do not think we are going to like Caliban as much as my father."

"It will be your sister who is the Sovereign. Caliban is only her consort and we must remember that this is a religious cause and however hateful the Dutch Monster is, he is a Protestant."

"Yes, I understand," agreed Anne.

"You'll see now," went on Sarah, "how wise I was to have our private stairway made. We can use it and very few people know of its existence."

"Oh, Sarah, you are clever! Had you something like this in mind when you had the staircase made?"

"I have always something like this in mind. As you know, my dear Mrs. Morley's safety is always my first concern."

Sarah did not think it necessary to point out that Anne was not in any danger for James would never allow his daughter to be harmed and this elaborate escape was for Sarah's benefit.

But where Sarah was, Anne wanted to be, and she found herself caught up in the excitement.

Sarah's eyes were brilliant with excitement. This was adventure such as she loved; and after it she and Anne were going to be closer than ever. She was certain of William's victory for now he would have John on his side and they could not fail. This was going to be the end of Catholic James and his son; it would be William and Mary and afterward . . . Anne. And Anne meant Sarah. What a future would be hers as uncrowned Queen! The Kings of France were ruled by their mistresses, so shouldn't Anne be ruled by Sarah? There should be no one in Anne's life to compare with Sarah. Sarah had at times been a little anxious about the devotion between Anne and her husband. But George was a bore and Anne's nature was to be more fond of her own sex than the opposite. She had married and as soon as she had borne one child—which unfortunately did not live—she was pregnant with another, and this order of things was becoming an expected pattern; not once during her married life had Anne looked at another man. There had been the abortive affair with Mulgrave, but that, Sarah told herself, had been Anne's desire not so much for a man but to imitate her friend who was happily married. Anne was placid, accepting life as it came. She had married because that was expected of her; she loved her husband because it was impossible to dislike him; she lived a normal married life because it was planned for her. Had she made her own way it would have been to women she turned.

Sarah had no such love for her own sex. Sarah loved herself and her husband and children, and her love was the sort which expressed itself, not in tenderness or unselfish devotion but in getting the best in life for them all.

Sarah saw herself the strong and dominant figure with complete understanding of Anne who could not understand herself.

The plot was laid. Anne was to go to her chamber assisted by Mrs. Danvers and Mrs. Buss and afterward when she was alone Sarah would creep up the private stairway and help her dress; then they would join Lady Fitzharding by the same staircase and escape.

Anne could hear the rain beating against the windows of the Cockpit. It was a wild night, a night of adventure. She was trying to appear normal but she was very anxious; Mr. Freeman had gone over to William; so had Mr. Morley; and of course they had not gone alone but taken their men with them. The country was rising against her father; and she, lying comfortably on her couch, munching her sweetmeats, had helped to bring about this situation.

Of course he was a Catholic. He had imprisoned the Bishops which was a wicked thing to do; he had tried to force Catholicism on a country which did not want it; he had led a scandalous life—as scandalous as his brother Charles's. Charles had loved beautiful and attractive women; James had seemed to choose the most unattractive. Charles had once said that James, in spite of being so devout, loved women even more than he did, but chose such women as his priests might have provided for his penances. Now he had a Queen who was a beautiful creature but he preferred plain Catherine Sedley and others. He was a most immoral man, Anne assured herself. Yet at the same time she did not wish to face him when he came back to London. He would know, of course, that she was with his enemies. There came a time when it was impossible not to show which side one was on; and for that reason she did not want to see him again because she would never be able to look him in the face.

All this she was thinking while she listened to the rain and thought of escape. All would be well because Sarah had planned it. Sarah would see that nothing went wrong.

All the same it was very difficult to hide how excited she was from Danvers and Buss.

Mrs. Buss, who had been her nurse as a child and regarded herself as a specially privileged person came bustling in.

"Oh, my dear Madam! Sitting by the window in the cold . . . and no shawl about your shoulders!"

"I'm not cold, Buss."

"Not cold indeed! Why I saw you shiver."

"Buss, I am not your baby now, you know."

"You will always be my baby."

"Buss, I should like to get to bed quickly. I am rather tired."

"Come then, Madam dear. Let Buss take off your shoes. Danvers, Her Highness is tired. Has the bed been warmed?"

They fussed about her, divesting her of clothes which she would have to put on again. But Sarah would help her dress. It was all set for one o'clock, and it was not yet midnight, so there was plenty of time.

When they had covered her up she said: "Draw the curtains. I am tired."

They obeyed and soon she was alone, lying there, awaiting the summons from Sarah.

At the appointed time the bed curtains parted and there was Sarah with her clothes. Hurriedly she dressed, and taking Sarah's hand went to Sarah's apartment by way of the secret stair so that Danvers and Buss sleeping in the anteroom did not hear them leave.

In a short time they were at the door of the Cockpit.

"Your Highness." It was Lord Dorset whom Sarah had commissioned to conduct them to the hackney coach which Henry Compton, the ex-Bishop of London would have waiting for them. Compton had been the governor of the Princesses Mary and Anne in their childhood and had been chosen by King Charles when his brother was becoming so unpopular that it had been necessary to take his children's education out of his hands. Compton had fallen out of favor with James when he came to the throne and lost his offices, for the Bishop was a sturdy Protestant, but he had kept in touch with his old pupil and heartily approved of her attitude toward her father.

Sarah said: "What a night! Let us make for the coach with all speed, my lord."

"It means crossing the park," Dorset replied.

Sarah made an impatient noise with her lips and Dorset turned away from her to offer his arm to the Princess.

"If Your Highness will honor me . . ."

Anne took his arm, hoping that he had, as she heard, reformed his ways. It was true he was no longer a young man; he had been a great favorite of King Charles, for in his youth he had been one of the wits of the Court; he had taken part in many disgraceful scenes which some members of Charles's Court had seen fit to call frolics, but that was long ago in his wild youth and he must be fifty now. James had always disliked him and Dorset was not one to curb his exuberance to seek favor; he had written satires about Catherine Sedley; and when the Bishops had been imprisoned had openly declared his sympathy with them. This had necessitated his retirement from Court. So both Compton and Dorset were her father's enemies.

More than ever Anne wanted to get away; she was afraid now that their flight would be discovered and they be brought back. "Yes," she said, "and let us hurry."

The rain which had been falling all day had turned the soft soil of the park to mud, and Anne was not equipped for walking—a pastime in which she never indulged if she could help it.

On Dorset's arm with Sarah and Lady Fitzharding beside her they started across the park; but they had not gone far when Anne gave a cry of dismay; her high heeled shoe had slipped off, and she was up to her ankles in mud.

"Where is Her Highness's shoe?" asked Sarah imperiously.

They all peered down into the mud for the delicate slipper, but the night was dark and they could not see it.

"I can only hop," Anne suggested.

But Dorset had taken off his long leather gauntlet and begged leave to slip it on the Princess's foot.

This was done and Anne was half carried by Dorset across the park to where Henry Compton was waiting for them as arranged.

"Now," cried Compton, "to my house by St. Paul's." He turned to his old pupil who laughingly showed him her foot encased in Dorset's gauntlet.

"We will take a little refreshment at my house," said Compton, "and find shoes for Your Highness. But before dawn we must be away."

Before dawn the party set off for Copt Hall, Dorset's house at Waltham, but on his advice and that of the Bishop they did not rest there long. Nottingham was their goal; and there they were received by Compton's brother, the Earl of Northampton.

In Nottingham, Compton dressed himself in a military uniform and riding through the town carried with him a banner.

He cried out: "All people who would preserve the laws and liberties of England, rally to the Princess Anne, the Protestant heiress to the throne."

The people ran out of their houses; they stood in the streets and cheered.

"No popery!" they cried. "A Protestant Sovereign for a Protestant people."

On the morning after Anne had made her way through the rain and mud from the Cockpit to the waiting hackney coach, Mrs. Danvers went to awaken her mistress.

She knocked at the door and, receiving no command to enter, was bewildered.

She went to call Mrs. Buss.

"Her Highness does not answer me," she explained.

"She is fast asleep," said Mrs. Buss. "Open the door and go in. I will come with you."

But when they tried to open the door they found it locked.

"Locked!" cried Mrs. Buss. "I never heard the like of this. Anything might have happened to Her Highness. We must force the door."

"Wait a moment," cautioned Mrs. Danvers and called out: "Your Highness. Are you there?"

There was no answer. "I am going to force the door," said Mrs. Buss. "I take full responsibility."

With that she threw her weight against the door and with Mrs. Danvers to help her they soon had the door open. Dashing in they saw that the Princess's bed was empty.

"She has been abducted," cried Mrs. Danvers.

"Murdered more like." Mrs. Buss began to tremble. "The Queen's priests have done this. We must not delay. Go and tell my Lord Clarendon. He was her friend. Go and tell him at once."

Mrs. Danvers ran to do her bidding; but Mrs. Buss, who looked upon the Princess as her baby, ran out of the Cockpit to Whitehall.

When the guards asked her business she cried: "I want the Princess

Anne." And they, astonished, stood aside and allowed her to force her way into the Queen's apartments.

Mary Beatrice, who was living in hourly fear of what would happen next, could only stare at the distracted woman.

"Give me the Princess Anne," demanded Mrs. Buss. "You have brought her here against her will."

"The woman is mad," said the Queen. "Pray take her away."

Guards seized Mrs. Buss who shouted: "I tell you the Princess has been abducted. You will find her hidden here. Release me, if you value your lives. If you are for the Princess Anne, release me."

"Take here away," ordered the Queen distastefully. "Send her back where she came from."

When she was ejected from the Palace Mrs. Buss began to shout: "You have taken the Princess Anne. What are you doing to her?"

And very soon a crowd had collected.

"The Queen has made a prisoner of the Princess!" was the comment.

"For what reason?"

"Because she is a wicked Catholic and knows the Princess is a good Protestant."

"Shall we stand aside and allow this Italian to harm our English Princess?"

"By God no! We'll pull Whitehall to pieces to find where she is hidden!"

The news spread through the City and soon people were verging on Whitehall from all quarters. The foreigner would have to be shown that she could not harm their Princess.

It was Mrs. Danvers who found the letter on Anne's table. It was addressed to her stepmother and said:

Madam,

I beg your pardon if I am so deeply affected with the surprising news of my husband's being gone, as not to be able to see you, but to leave this paper to express my humble duty to the King and yourself and to let you know that I am gone to absent myself to avoid the King's displeasure, which I am not able to bear, either against the Prince or myself, and I shall stay at so great a distance as not to return until I hear the happy news of a reconcilement; and as I am confident that the Prince did not leave the King with any other design than to use all possible means for his preservation, so I hope you will do me the justice to believe that I am incapable of following him for any other end. Never was anyone in such an unhappy condition, so divided between duty to a father and to a husband, and therefore I know not what I must do but to follow one to preserve the other. I see the general falling off of the nobility and gentry who avow to have no other end than to prevail with the King to secure their religion, which they saw so much in danger from the violent councils of the priests, who, to promote their own religion, did not care to what dangers they exposed the King. I am fully persuaded that the Prince of Orange designs the King's safety and preservation and hope all things may be composed without bloodshed by the calling of a Parliament.

God grant a happy end to these troubles and that the King's reign may be prosperous and that I may shortly meet you in perfect peace and safety till when, let me beg of you to continue the same favorable opinion that you have hitherto had of your most obedient daughter and servant.

Anne.

This letter was immediately published that riots might be averted.

It was a letter, said the people, of a dutiful daughter and a devoted wife. How good was the Princess when compared with her dissolute father!

The mob dispersed. The Queen should not be molested.

But the people were more firmly than ever behind Protestant William, Mary and Anne.

James, a sick and disappointed man, came back to London. It had been necessary to bleed him in Salisbury and he felt not only sick at heart but in body. He was thinking of that dismal supper when the news had come to him that one by one his generals were deserting him. Churchill gone—Churchill whom he had believed was his man, Churchill whom he had favored because he had loved his sister Arabella; then George—not that he had a high opinion of George or that he considered him a great loss—but his own son-in-law! Anne's husband!

Anne! His beloved daughter. She was the only one to whom he could turn for comfort. At least he had his younger daughter. He had been deeply wounded by Mary's coolness; but he told himself it was understandable. She had been away from home for so long and was completely under her husband's influence; her choice had been between husband and father and she had chosen her husband. Yet once she had been his favorite child.

But there was still Anne. He smiled lovingly. She would always remember the closeness of their relationship. To whom had she come when she needed help? Always to her father because she knew that there she would find it.

Her husband had deserted him—but he was a weak fellow and never of much account. It would be different with Anne. When he was with his daughter he would be rejuvenated; together they would stand against his enemies.

As he came near to London he said: "I shall go first to the Queen and then to the Cockpit."

He found Mary Beatrice in a state of great anxiety and terror that the mob would rise against her as they had when they believed she had abducted the Princess.

Unceremoniously she threw herself into her husband's arms and wept while she embraced him and told him how happy she was to see him alive.

"We are surrounded by traitors," she informed him.

"All will be well," he replied. "I am going to see Anne and we will talk of this together."

"Anne!" cried Mary Beatrice. "Did you not know then?"

"Know?" The fear was obvious in his voice and eyes.

"She has gone, like all the others," said Mary Beatrice passionately. "She like all the others is against you." He stared at her and she went on passionately: "You don't believe it. You have blinded yourself. She and Sarah Churchill have long been your enemies. They are for Mary and Orange. She has forgotten her father because she does not want my son to have the crown which she hopes one day will be hers."

"It cannot be true," whispered James.

"Is it not? She has flown from the Cockpit. She has gone to join her husband, she says. She has gone to join *them*. She is against us as Mary is . . . as William is."

James sank on to a stool and looked at his boots; then slowly the tears began to form in his eyes.

"God help me," he said, "my own children have forsaken me."

The conflict was over; it had been a bloodless revolution. A victory for Protestant England against the intrusion of Catholicism.

William of Orange had ridden to St. James's Palace in a closed carriage. It was true it was raining but crowds had gathered expecting a little display; and there was William, with his long twisted nose, his great periwig that seemed too big for his little body, his stooping shoulders, his pale cold face. Not a King to please the English. How different from his merry Uncle Charles who on his Restoration had seemed all that a merry monarch of a merry country should be. But William was a Protestant and religion was more important than merrymaking; and in any case it was his wife Mary who was to be their Queen.

Mary Beatrice had escaped to France with the little boy who was called the Prince of Wales by James's supporters, known as the "Jacks," or Jacobites; but there were many who preferred to believe that the child had been introduced into the Queen's bed by means of a warming-pan.

Anne had joined Prince George in Oxford where the people made much of them and called Anne the heiress to the throne. James had left Whitehall by means of a secret passage and had made his way to Sheerness where he intended to take a boat to France and join his wife and son; but he was captured and brought back to Whitehall.

The position was a delicate one. James had friends in London and even those who had been against him were moved to pity because his daughters had deserted him. He was a prisoner but on the orders of Orange, who was eager to avoid direct conflict, many opportunities were given him to escape.

James took advantage of this.

Only when James was sent out of London did Anne return with Sarah and Prince George.

The people came out into the streets to welcome the Princess who was so much more to their liking than grim William. Having no idea of the intrigues which had gone on at the Cockpit they declared their pity for her—poor lady to be torn between her duty to her father and to her religion. She had chosen rightly though and they were glad of it. This was the end of James; and the fear of Catholicism was over.

James meanwhile had been taken to Rochester, but his guards had had secret instructions to allow him to escape if possible. His wife and son were in France; William of Orange would be pleased if he were to join them there because he foresaw awkward complications if James stayed in England.

James acted as William had believed he would; he left Rochester under cover of darkness and a few days later landed safely in France where Louis XIV, implacable enemy of William of Orange, was delighted to give him sanctuary.

Sarah stood beside her mistress and they gazed at their reflections in the mirror. Sarah looked handsome, her lovely golden hair, her best feature, was decked with orange ribbons.

"Now, Mrs. Morley," she said, "I shall do the same for you."

Anne, whose childish passion for sharing pleasures was one of her most pronounced characteristics, expressed her delight.

"These ribbons are most becoming," went on Sarah.

"They are to my dear Mrs. Freeman, but I fear poor Morley is not as handsome."

"Nonsense," said Sarah, but she smiled complacently at her reflection.

Sarah was delighted. This was not the end of a campaign; it was only the beginning.

The first battle was won. There was no longer a King James II; there would soon be a Mary II; and Mary had no children, so this fat young woman with the mild expression was the heir presumptive to the throne.

"So you like that, Mrs. Morley? *I* think it most becoming."

"Then I am sure my dear Mrs. Freeman is right."

Indeed it was the beginning.

"Let us go to the coach, now," said Sarah.

Anne rose obediently.

So while James II battled against the seas on his perilous escape to France, his daughter Anne, in the company of Sarah Churchill, attended the playhouse—both resplendent in orange ribbons.

THE UNEASY

CORONATION

*W*illiam *of Orange, riding in his closed* carriage through the streets of London, was disturbed. The conquest had been too simple. Perhaps if there had been battles to be faced and won he would not have felt this depression; but here he was, come to England to preserve the land for Protestantism, and he was not even sure that he would be accepted as its King.

William was a Stuart on his mother's side, but he had inherited little of that family's characteristics. The Stuarts were, on the whole, if not handsome, a fascinating family. William had none of those superficial attractions and he was well aware of it. Short, slightly deformed, a sufferer from asthma, tormented by a hacking cough which worried him at awkward moments, he was aware of his disabilities. He never felt happy except on horseback and when owing to the shortness of his legs he looked nearer to the normal size. His expression was sour, his nose long and crooked; and his huge periwig gave him the appearance of being top heavy. Not a figure likely to find favor with the English who remembered gay Charles, tall, dark, and ugly though he might be, possessed of such charm that he made his subjects love his faults more than they would have loved another's virtues. James had been unpopular but he was personable; he had dignity, and his numerous love affairs had proved that he was a man.

How different was William. He would have brought an uneasy reminder of Oliver Cromwell but for the fact that he had a mistress. There had been a certain amount of gossip about Elizabeth Villiers to whom he had been faithful for years. When a man had one mistress for some odd reason that seemed a slight to his wife; it was different when, like Charles and James, he had many.

William was wondering what sort of a reception he would receive. He knew that the people had rejected James and were accepting him. But were they accepting him, or was it Mary?

He had long had his eyes on this crown: England, Scotland, and Ireland. To be ruler of these three kingdoms was a higher position than mere Stadtholder of Holland. But would they accept him as their King? They would have to if he were to remain, for he would be no Consort. But it was Mary who was heiress to the throne.

So he was uncertain about his future. He was uncertain too about his private life. His was a strange complex character and perhaps this was because of his physical disabilities. He longed to be a great hero, a fighter of causes, a worthy ancestor of William the Silent. He was a courageous soldier; he was an astute ruler; this he had proved. But he was lacking in the qualities he most longed to possess.

Beside him now was Bentinck—his dearest Bentinck—his first minister who had saved his life by nursing him through the small pox years ago before his marriage. When the disease had been at its most virulent Bentinck had slept in his bed because he believed—as many did—that by sleeping in the bed of a sufferer at such a time it was certain that one would catch the disease and so reduce the severity of the attack. Bentinck had caught the small pox, had come near to death himself; and by a mercy they had both recovered. That was devotion; that was love.

Love? He loved Bentinck and Bentinck loved him; and for neither of them would there be another love such as that they bore each other.

This was uneasy knowledge. Bentinck had married; his wife had died only a week or so ago, but Bentinck had not been at her bedside, because his first duty was to his master. She had left five children, and Bentinck was sad now, but a wife could not mean to him what his master did—nor could any woman take Bentinck's place with William.

Bentinck had married Anne Villiers and William had taken for his mistress her elder sister Elizabeth. This made an odd kinship between them. For Elizabeth, William had a love he could not give to Mary, and this could be set beside Bentinck's devotion to his wife. Anne had been docile, devoted to her husband and Bentinck would miss her. Elizabeth was shrewd and clever and the cast in her eyes seemed attractive to William because it was in a sense a deformity.

Their relationships were complicated; but at the center of it all was William's love for Bentinck; his interest in members of his own sex which was always greater than what he felt for the opposite one, except in the case of Elizabeth.

His relationship with his wife had always been an uncomfortable one for him. Mary was different in every way from himself; she had been brought up in the merry wicked Court of England where people made no attempt to hide their affections. She had infuriated him at the beginning of their acquaintance by weeping copiously when she had heard he was to be her bridegroom—and not in secret either. She had received congratulations with red eyes and an expression of woe which had made him more sullen and uncouth than ever, so that the English had said what an unsatisfactory lover he was, and he knew that in some quarters he had been called Caliban and the Dutch Monster.

And it was Mary's fault, for had she been gracious he would have been, and the people of England would have had an entirely different notion of him.

And all the years of their uneasy marriage he had wondered what her attitude would be when she were Queen of England. To what position would *he* be assigned? Recently, thanks to the tact of Dr. Burnet who had visited them in Holland, he had discovered that Mary had no intention of not sharing her crown with him. Like the dutiful wife he had forced her to become she had declared that it was always a wife's duty to obey her husband.

Very gratifying, but what of the people of England?

In the Upper and Lower Houses of Parliament fierce debates were in progress.

William was aware of this and was angry. He had come from Holland to save this country from papist rule and because he had come James was deposed; yet they were asking themselves whether or not they would have him.

Some were suggesting that Mary should be proclaimed Regent because they did not care to see the line of succession tampered with. Mary Regent for how long? Until the Prince of Wales was of an age to return?

Others were for making Mary Queen of England and William Consort; and that was something to which William would never agree.

Some had suggested that William should be King, for after all he was the next male in the line of succession; but there was great opposition to this. In spite of his English mother he was a Dutchman, and there were two English princesses who came before him.

Lord Danby, who hoped that if he showed his support for Mary, she would make him her chief adviser when she arrived in England, wrote to her, giving her accounts of all that was happening.

"It is my desire," he told her, "to set you on the throne alone and I do not doubt that I shall do this."

So confident was Danby that the Queen would be delighted with his endeavors and so certain was he that he could persuade the rest of the ministers to follow him, that he summoned a further meeting to which he invited William.

On receiving the invitation William sent for Bentinck.

"What do you think of this?" he asked.

"They are going to put some proposition before you."

"I have no intention of going to hear it. I find it most undignified. I shall remain aloof."

Bentinck nodded. "It is better so. I believe Danby is going to suggest that the Princess of Orange shall be the sole sovereign."

William's lips tightened almost imperceptibly, but Bentinck who knew his beloved friend and master well was aware of the change of expression.

"I shall never be my wife's gentleman usher!" said William furiously.

"You may rely on me to make that plain."

So it was Bentinck who attended the meeting on behalf of his master and he made it clear to the assembly that their terms were unacceptable to William.

Danby was furious.

"The only proposition which would be acceptable to my master," Bentinck explained, "would be a conjunctive sovereignty, and then there would be a condition that he should have sole administration of affairs."

Danby said there was no point in continuing with the meeting.

But when he received Mary's reply he was taken aback.

"I am the Prince's wife," she wrote, "and would never be other than what should be in conjunction with him; I shall take it extremely unkindly, if any, under pretence of their care for me, should set up a divided interest between me and the Prince."

Mary sent a copy of this letter to William and when he read it he smiled in triumph. He had known he could rely on her; he had subdued her completely; he had made that shuddering bride into a docile wife.

He showed the letter to Bentinck. "Now I think," he said, "we can afford to take the strong line and I will see them. Summon them and tell them that I will make my feelings clear to them."

And when they came he looked at them coldly and there was disdain in his expression for that which they treasured so highly and for which they thought he yearned. He was going to show them the contrary.

"I think it proper to let you know," he said, "that I will accept no dignity dependent on the life of another. I will not oppose the Princess's right; I respect her virtues; none knows them better than I do. Crowns to others may have charms, but I will hold no power dependent on the will of a woman. Therefore if your schemes are adopted, I can give you no assistance in the settlement of the nation, but will return to my own country."

They were dumbounded. Was this a monstrous piece of bluff? They could not believe he was ready to throw away so much merely because he was not offered the supreme prize. But what would happen if he returned to Holland? Chaos! James's friends might even ask him to return.

They talked together for a while and they dared not call his bluff because they had seen Mary's reply to Danby's suggestion. What if William returned to Holland, would Mary come to England? Would she leave a husband for whom she had such a regard? William of Orange had proved himself to be an astute ruler. He had strengthened his country and made her of importance in the world. England needed Dutch William unless they preferred to be saddled with Catholic James.

"Nobody knows what to do with him," was the comment, "but nobody knows what to do without him."

Danby said: "This is a sick man. He cannot live long. Let us give him what he wants. Then when he is dead Mary will be our Sovereign. She will not interfere, for if she is docile to him so will she be to us. This is the answer. A King and a Queen . . . until he is dead."

The decision was made. King William III and Mary II should be joint sovereigns of England.

William's reply was that this was a proposition which he could accept.

"There is one point to be settled," pointed out Danby. "This concerns the Princess Anne. By right of succession she should be Queen on the death of her sister. This is unacceptable to William. Therefore we must get her consent. She will have to agree that William shall be King in his own right and that she and her heirs will inherit the throne if Mary and William were without heirs of their bodies."

Thus the matter was settled, but for the consent of the Princess Anne.

Sarah shouted in her rage: "The impudence! It would seem to me that Dutch William is coming very well out of this matter—and at whose expense? Yours, Mrs. Morley. King . . . King in his own right! How can that be when you are next to your sister Mary?"

"I have heard that he refuses to stay here if they do not agree."

"Then let him go. We can do very well without him in Whitehall. Let him go back to his dykes and canals. He looks like a scarecrow. I am not surprised your sister wept day and night when she heard they were marrying her to that Dutch . . . abortion!"

"Dear Mrs. Freeman, you will be heard. What if tales were carried to him?"

"Let them be carried! I care not that he should know what I think of him."

"Do not forget he will be the King."

"Madam, do you think I care for Kings when I see my friend Mrs. Morley robbed of her rights?"

"But what must I do, dear Mrs. Freeman?"

"Refuse! The Princess Mary should be Queen and Caliban her Consort; and when Mary dies then it should be your turn."

"It seems that the Parliaments are prepared to give him what he wants."

"Parliaments! Who cares for Parliaments?"

"Oh, dear," sighed Anne. "How tiresome life has become."

There were many separations in the married life of John and Sarah Churchill and whenever they could be together they took advantage of it.

John was now at Whitehall and able to see his wife frequently, and on this occasion he had something very serious to say to her. They went down to their home near St. Albans, there to spend a few days with their children. There were five of them now: Henrietta, Anne, Elizabeth, John, and Mary. Sarah counted herself lucky when she considered Princess Anne who had lost all hers.

John was thoughtful as they left London and, knowing him well, she sensed there was something on his mind.

"You had better tell me what it is," said Sarah grimly.

He gave her a fond smile. There was little she missed.

"I have much to tell you," he said.

"Good news?"

He nodded.

"Then tell me quickly. I like not to be kept in the dark."

"We took the right road."

"Of course we did."

"Bentinck has talked with me . . . made me promises."

"What, John, what? What a maddening creature you are! Don't you know I am the most impatient woman in the world when there is news of my family?"

"How would you like to be a Countess?"

"John! Stop this teasing. I will not have it, I tell you."

"You may well be ere long."

"An Earldom. Is it true then?"

"Not yet, there is a condition. Bentinck has implied that titles and honors can be ours. Oh, my dear Sarah, what a clever woman you are! Already they realize that you can do what you will with Anne."

"And the condition is?"

"That she agrees to their conditions. Joint Sovereigns. This shall not be the reign of Mary and her Consort but of William and Mary. Not much to ask for an earldom."

"But what if they should have a child?"

"William is impotent."

"And cross-eyed Betty Villiers?"

"It is a blind. He would have the world think him a man when he is only half one."

Sarah narrowed her eyes.

"An earldom," she murmured.

"And that would not be all."

Her smile was triumphant. "Why, John," she said, "Do you think what I think?"

"The Churchills shape the future of England."

She laughed and put her hand in his.

"I shall see that fat Morley agrees to stand aside for Caliban."

She loved her children; the days spent with them in the country were something to look forward to; but all the time she was longing to be back at the Cockpit, for she could scarcely wait to take those steps which would lead her to that earldom.

Playing with the children, riding with John, they talked of nothing else.

"The Earl of . . ." Sarah said again and again, putting her head on one side and looking at him with pride.

"What say you of Marlborough?"

"Marlborough." Sarah tried it on her tongue. "It is a grand sounding name."

"It was a name which was once in my family. The Leys were Earls of Marlborough."

"Marlborough!" cried Sarah. "Oh, I like it." She threw her arms about him. "Oh, my Lord Marlborough, what a happy day this is!"

John cautiously reminded her that the title was not yet theirs. There was work to do first.

So during those days which should have been completely contented, Sarah yearned to be back at the Cockpit.

The Princess Mary of Orange was growing more and more anxious as she drew near to her native land. This was not the best motive for returning; and in any case she had no wish to return. She remembered how, when she had last looked at the receding coast of England she had seen it through a mist of tears and had believed that to throw herself overboard would have given her greater pleasure than anything else. It seemed incredible that now she should be wishing that the boat would turn and take her back to Holland.

But she had changed since the days when she had been a weeping bride. She had come to love William, to think only of William's good and William's desires, and to make them her own.

She had wanted the perfect marriage and she assured herself she had found it. Oh, she would be ready to admit that others might not realize the worth of William. He was a great leader, a great hero; and if he was at times brusque—even uncouth—that was because he hated hypocrisy and pretence of any sort; also he suffered acutely and that everyone knew could make the temper short. William was the most wonderful man in the world; the perfect husband, and Mary would not allow herself to think otherwise.

Obediently she had hated her father when William wished her to although James had always been kind to her; sometimes now she remembered those occasions when he had taken her on his knee and made her talk to the people who came to see him on business, declaring that she understood all that was said. She had believed the evil reports she had heard of him; and when Anne and others had told her of the wicked lengths to which he was ready to go to bring Catholicism back to England—even so far as to introduce a spurious baby in a warming-pan into his wife's bed—she was ready to believe that too. She knew that Elizabeth Villiers was William's mistress and she tried not to believe that. Elizabeth was with her now and she was wondering whether his friendship with her would continue when they were in England.

What pleasure it would give her if she could go back to the quiet life in the Palace in the Wood, at Loo and Honselaarsdijk where William had built and planned gardens. She could visualize such a delightful existence. Planning gardens with William, listening respectfully while he talked of state affairs, playing cards in the evening or dancing. Oh, how she loved to dance, but of course there had been little dancing in Holland. Perhaps in London . . . but William would not want a *gay* court. That would be too reminiscent of her Uncles Charles and William. Never were two men less alike.

Mary would see her old friend Frances Apsley. "Aurelia" as she had called her, and "dear husband." A foolish fantasy, but the love between them had been painfully passionate and Mary had continued to think of herself as wife to Frances even after the marriage to William. There must be no return of that when she reached England. There was no room in Mary's life but to be a dutiful wife to one person—and that person was her own dear husband William.

She frowned thinking of Anne's friendship with Sarah Churchill, Unwise! she thought. And I do not believe Sarah Churchill to be the best friend Anne could have.

Perhaps when they were together again she would break that dominance. Anne was like herself in that she found pleasure in these passionate friendships with her own sex. She, Mary, had grown out of that habit which was not only foolish but dangerous. Perhaps when she reached England she would not see a great deal of Frances. Now that she had such a perfect husband she had no need and no desire to have women friends and had in fact, though she would not admit that this was to protect herself, rigidly refrained from making them.

The land was in sight and she must compose herself. This was going to be one of the most difficult periods of her life. It was no normal homecoming. She was returning to England because her husband had driven her father away. She had not told William, but she had long been praying in Holland that there might be a reconciliation between her father and husband. Mary hated conflict of any sort. She knew so well what she wanted and that was to be on good terms with those about her; to chat incessantly—not of great matters, but of cards and dancing and gardens and fine needlework, although her eyes were too weak nowadays to indulge in the latter. She wanted to hear laughter about her; and although she was devout and her religion, the Protestant religion, was one of the two great passions in her life—the other being her husband—that did not mean that she did not like to be gay.

But William had frowned on levity, although now she had her special instructions not to be melancholy on arrival. He knew that she had felt melancholy when she contemplated the fate of her father; this, he had warned her, must not be shown to the English. They must not have the impression that she came among them as a penitent. She must show no grief for her father's downfall, which he so richly deserved. She must smile and appear happy to be with them. Graciously she must accept the crown; he wanted smiles from her when she landed in England.

How strange! So often in Holland she had been forced to curb her levity; now she must feign gaiety, for the truth was that the nearer she came to England the less gay she felt. She could not get out of her mind the memory of childhood days, of her father's coming into the nursery and picking her up, calling her his dearest daughter. She could not stop thinking of her beautiful Italian stepmother who had shown her nothing but kindness, and had laughingly called her her "Dear Lemon" because she was married to the Prince of Orange.

Instead of this she must remember her father's follies, his promiscuity, his disgraceful rule when he had ousted Protestants from the principal posts and tried to replace them with Catholics, his cruelty after Sedgemoor, for although Jeffreys was blamed James was the King and therefore mainly responsible; she must not forget the wickedness of the warming-pan incident. It was thoughts of Sedgemoor which hardened her heart; it had always been so. After that William had had little difficulty in turning her against her father. When she thought of Jemmy, holding her hand in the dance, his dark eyes aflame with . . . not passionate love, but could she say passionate friendship? . . . when she thought of that charming head being severed from that handsome body, at the command of her father, then she could hate him. James, Duke of Monmouth, the most handsome man in the world (for admirable as William was even she could not call him handsome) had come to The Hague, had danced as only he could dance, had taught her to skate . . . and those had been days which seemed apart from all others. But Jemmy was dead and James had killed him.

My father killed Jemmy. That was what she had to keep saying; and then a fierce anger destroyed her calmness and she knew that she would walk into the palace where her father and stepmother had recently lived and she could laugh and be gay and say to herself: He deserves his misery . . . for what he did to beautiful Jemmy.

"Your Highness, we should be preparing to land."

Elizabeth Villiers stood beside her, smiling her discreet smile, those peculiar eyes, with what some called a squint, downcast.

Mary bowed her head and wondered whether when they stepped ashore William would be more aware of Elizabeth than of her. Oh, no, he would be watching his wife, making sure that her expression was what he had commanded it to be, that she gave no sign of uneasiness because she was coming to take her father's crown. Matters of state would come before any mistress.

But Elizabeth was there and Mary believed in that moment that she always would be. Why? she asked herself passionately. What can she give that I cannot? But who could probe the strange powers of attraction?

A crowd was gathered at the landing stairs, but William was not among them. That was characteristic. He could make no gracious gestures. He would wait and receive her formally at the Palace of Whitehall, to remind her perhaps that although she was the Queen of England, he was the King.

Elizabeth had slipped the cloak from her shoulders and handed it to a page; it seemed to weigh the boy down so voluminous was it with its hanging sleeves and its vivid orange color. The people wanted to see her and she was a handsome sight, for she would have been a very beautiful woman had she not grown so fat. She removed her hood that they might see her face and she stood, tall, stately, and smiling. Her bodice, low cut partly exposing a magnificent bosom, was draped with fine muslin looped with pearls; beneath her purple velvet gown was an orange petticoat which, as she lifted her skirts, showed its flamboyantly symbolic color. Her dark hair was piled high and adorned with agraffes of pearls and ribbons in the same color as the petticoat. She was a magnificent sight: a queen in her glory. Those watching thought: She will be decorative enough to make up for dull William.

Formally she was greeted by the officials of the Court; then she was led to her waiting horse by her Master of Horse, Sir Edward Villiers, as young girls strewed flowers in her path.

A colorful homecoming.

Anne was waiting with Sarah at Greenwich Palace.

Anne was excited at the prospect of meeting her sister. Sarah was alert. Mary had already shown signs of animosity and Sarah felt she would need to be careful. Anne looked enormous, she was pregnant again, but quite attractive in her excitement apart from her bulk, and beside her was her husband, fat and genial.

Sarah was thinking that life would be more complicated now that the two sisters would be together.

As the Queen approached her eyes immediately sought her sister and when she did so, she could not restrain her pleasure.

There could be no ceremony at such a meeting. Mary dismounted and held out her arms and they embraced.

"My dearest Anne!"

"Oh . . . Your Majesty . . . you are that now, are you not, now that our father is gone . . ."

Mary said: "It is wonderful to see you. This meeting is something I have been anticipating for so long."

"To think you will be home again! It is quite wonderful."

"And you have been good, dear sister. William appreciates your goodness."

"Does he?" said Anne vaguely; the mention of William's name had curbed her exuberance temporarily; and Mary was reminded of her duties.

She received her brother-in-law and all those who were waiting to greet her and with Anne beside her they went into the Palace of Greenwich to refresh themselves before going on to Whitehall.

To Whitehall! There would be too many memories for comfort, thought Mary. She could not forget that a very short time ago her father and stepmother had held Court here. It was here that Mary Beatrice had very recently waited for her apartments at St. James's to be made ready that she might give birth to a prince—or pretend to.

As yet Mary had not seen William; she believed that he would be waiting for her at Whitehall and together they would enter the Palace. She hoped so, for she would feel happier if he were at her side.

But when she reached Whitehall William was not there, and she must enter the Palace alone, knowing that everyone was watching her, asking themselves how a daughter would feel who had driven her father from his home.

She must forget she was James's daughter and remember only that she was William's wife. So she smiled gaily.

"Whitehall," she said. "I have thought of it so often. But it does not bear comparison with some of our Dutch Palaces."

"Your Majesty will wish to go to your apartments without delay."

She agreed that she would.

To the royal apartment then. Here was the bedchamber in which Mary Beatrice had lain. It was prepared for her, Mary, now. There were the chairs on which her father had sat; his hands had touched those hangings.

Jemmy's murderer, she murmured; then it was easier.

She laughed gaily.

"It is pleasant to be home in Whitehall," she said.

She could not sleep that night—alone in the royal bed. There were too many memories. She dreamed of her father; she was a child and he had taken her on his knee and was looking at her with mournful reproachful eyes from which tears flowed. And there was Mary Beatrice crying: "I cannot believe it . . . not of our dear Lemon."

"It had to be, it had to be. . . ." She was talking in her sleep. "William said so and William is always right. It was the Papists against the Protestants. It was your own fault, father. And there was Monmouth. . . . How could you. He called himself the King I know, but he was a King's son, and he was your nephew. How could you?"

She awoke and heard herself say: "It had to be. It had to be."

Where was she? In her room in the Palace in the Wood, waiting for William, who would not come because he was spending the night with Elizabeth Villiers? No. She was in Whitehall, in the bed which had been used by her father and stepmother.

This was nonsense. It had to be. He had brought this on himself. William had had no wish for it. It was only because it was his duty to come that he came.

In the morning she chatted gaily as she was dressed.

William would want to hear how she had behaved on her arrival and she must please William. Moreover, it was pleasant to chat. How she loved to gossip; and being back in England reminded her of those carefree gossiping days of childhood.

"I want to go into all the rooms," she announced. "I want to see how much things have changed."

So as soon as she was dressed she went from room to room, opening cupboard doors, turning down the quilts on the bed, laughing and chatting all the time.

Even her friends were a little shocked. They said: "She seems to be quite insensible of her father's tragedy."

Her enemies talked freely to each other. "What unbecoming conduct!" they said. "What an ungrateful daughter, for however misguided he was, he was always a good father to *her*."

As for Mary, she was thinking of him all the time as she went from room to room; she was resisting with all her might the desire to burst into tears, to ask these men to help her plead with her husband to bring her father back. Let them rule together, let William modify James's pol-icy; surely that could have been done.

But William had said: "Smile and be gay. Show no remorse, for that would do ill to our cause."

So she smiled and was gay; and Sarah Churchill watching said to herself: "She is a woman of stone. She shows no remorse for her father. This is most unbecoming. She is behaving like a woman in an inn, peer-ing into cupboards, spying into the beds. . . ."

Sarah disliked keeping her opinions to herself, but on this occasion she would. William and Mary would reward those who helped them and the glorious Marlborough title was not yet won.

Only when Mary was installed in Whitehall Palace did William come to her.

She returned his cool greeting with suppressed exuberance. After the long separation she had forgotten how withdrawn he could be.

"William," she said, "I am so happy to be with you. But you look ill. I fear this has been a great strain on your health."

He shook his head impatiently. Had she not learned yet how he hated references to his infirmities?

"You appear to be in good health," he said shortly. "As for myself, I am well enough. The sooner we are recognized as joint sovereigns the better; and I have arranged for the ceremony to take place in the Banquet-ing room."

"Yes, William. Tell me, are you happy now that all is well?"

"We cannot be sure that all is well. It is early yet."

"But the people want us, William. They have shown that clearly." She laid her hand on his arm. "Your fame is known throughout the world," she went on. "The English know that you will rule them well."

"They were not eager to accept me in the beginning, suggesting that you should rule as Queen and I as Consort."

"I would never have allowed that, William. I would have made them understand that I could not tolerate such a position. You are my husband and I regard it my duty to obey you."

She was looking at him almost piteously, begging for some affection. He felt angry because she was taller than he was and had to look down at him; he was angry because these people wanted her and grudgingly accepted him. There were always these considerations between them. With Elizabeth it was different. With her he could discuss state affairs, make a little play at lovemaking; and he could feel the superior male all the time.

He was eager for the ceremonies to go forward with all speed, for he would not feel safe until he had been publicly proclaimed and crowned King of England.

"I wish the ceremony to be performed with all speed," he said.

"But of course, William."

"I have a great desire to get out of this city. I like not the air and I have seen a palace at Hampton which I think would suit me better."

"Hampton Court Palace! Ah, yes, I remember it so well. . . ."

"It is unsightly and needs alterations; the gardens are a disgrace. . . ."

She began to smile. "Oh, William," she cried, "we must plan alterations. I lack your inspiration in these matters, but I hope you will allow me to help."

She had clasped her hands about his arm; he stood rigid for a while. Then he twisted his lips into something like a smile.

"That might be so," he said.

Then he shook her off and left the apartment.

Dear beloved husband! she thought. I had forgotten how dignified, how remote, how utterly noble he is!

The ceremonial recognition of the new King and Queen took place in the Banqueting room of Whitehall.

Mary, resplendent in state dress, took her place with William on the canopied chairs of state, their attendants ranged about them.

Lord Halifax then asked them if they would accept the crown, and they both declared their willingness to do so.

Were they a little too willing? Those watching thought so; for they did so without expressing the slightest regret at the unfortunate circumstances which had put them into this position.

Those watching had not wanted James but they did not like William's coldness and Mary's apparent indifference. For all his sins James was her father. Was not Mary's blithe acceptance of the crown which could only be hers because of her father's downfall, a little heartless? They would have liked a little reluctance, a little remorse. But there appeared to be none.

The ceremony in the Banqueting room was in February and the Coronation was fixed for April; but William had no intention of remaining at Whitehall until that time.

He said peevishly that he could not endure the London air and he saw no reason why there should be ceremonies and banquets; he considered them an extravagance.

He wanted to explore Hampton Court, and thither he went with the Queen.

The people were not pleased. This was going to be a very dull reign if there was no Court. They remembered Charles sauntering across the park with his dogs and ladies; they remembered him at the playhouse, or playing pell mell. Even James had kept a Court. But within a few days William had retired to Hampton Court; and the Queen had gone with him.

The Queen, however, had shown signs of gaiety, and they were certain that if she were in control there would be a gay Court. It was the Dutchman who was spoiling everything. Perhaps after the Coronation there would be a Court. In any case the Princess Anne would not wish to live in obscurity; she would surely continue with her card parties; and they had heard that the Queen was fond of dancing.

But during those weeks the King and Queen remained at Hampton Court and only came to London for necessary business. Mary felt happier at Hampton, where there were not so many memories; and William, who had already started to plan alterations to the Palace and gardens, was more friendly toward her when he was thus engaged than otherwise; he even allowed her to share his preoccupation.

It was the day of the Coronation and bright April sunshine streamed into the Palace of Whitehall and the Cockpit.

Outside the bells were ringing and the people were crowding into the streets; but this was no ordinary coronation, for it was rarely sovereigns were crowned while their predecessors lived. There were many who shook their heads and said no good would come of it. They had been against James; but when they saw his daughter and her husband calmly taking what was his, their sense of justice revolted. It was so unnatural, they declared.

Many of the Bishops would not take the oath of allegiance, declaring that they had sworn allegiance to a King who still lived. Even some of those Bishops whom James had sent to the Tower were among those who declined to take the oath; and the Archbishop of Canterbury refused to crown them.

The Coronation must not be delayed because of these obstinate men, declared William.

Mary was being dressed in her coronation robes; she looked very regal in purple velvet edged with ermine, a circlet of gold and precious stones gleaming on her dark hair.

Elizabeth Villiers was present, her eyes secretive; she was still William's mistress, Mary knew.

William came into her apartment; he was already dressed and she would leave Whitehall for Westminster Hall an hour after him.

His face was white and set and he came to her and said without ceremony: "I have had bad news."

"Oh, William!"

"Your father has landed in Ireland and taken possession of it. Only a few towns—among them Londonderry—are not in his hands."

"Oh, William!" Her face was ashen and he looked at her with distaste, remembering her childish habit of repeating his name in moments of crisis.

"I have a letter for you. It is from your father."

Mary took the letter in her shaking hands, and as she did so she pictured him sitting down to write to her, the tears streaming down his cheeks while he remembered how once he had loved his dear daughter.

"You should read it," commanded William coldly.

The words danced before her eyes for she could not concentrate. Sentences seemed to leap from the page to wound her.

Hitherto I have made all fatherly excuses for what has been done. I attributed your part in the revolution to obedience to your husband, but the act of being crowned is in your power, and if you are crowned while I and the Prince of Wales are living, the curses of an outraged father will light upon you, as well as those of God who has commanded duty to parents . . .

The letter fluttered to the ground. Mary stood very still staring at it while William with a gesture of disgust picked it up and read it.

"It was well timed," he said; but for once he was unable to hide the fact that he was shaken. James in Ireland—intending to fight for one of the three crowns—meant that his position was very insecure. The Archbishop and Bishops refusing to take the oath of allegiance! James calling down curses on them!

What had he done? He had driven his father-in-law from the throne, that he might take it. Had he not always—ever since the midwife, Mrs. Tanner, had declared she saw three crowns about his head at birth—had his gaze directed on his father-in-law's throne?

He saw that some of those who had come with him into the chamber and those who had already been there were looking significantly at each other.

He said firmly: "This was brought about by the King's ill conduct and what I and my wife have done was forced on us. I would say that I have done nothing which did not have my wife's approval."

This was one of those rare moments when Mary refused to be guided by her husband. It was the second of truth when she saw him not as the supreme being but as a man without charm, without love for her.

She said sharply: "If my father should gain his authority, you have none but yourself to thank for it. It was you who let him go as you did."

For a few moments husband and wife stood staring at each other.

William felt a coldness touch his heart. It was occasions like this—and there had been but a few in the course of their married life which brought home to him that he was unsure of his wife. He could never be certain when her docility might drop from her—like her great orange cloak—and she show clearly that she was a Stuart ruler.

It was for this very reason that he kept coldly aloof from her; it was the very pivot on which their strange relationship revolved.

He said: "It is time I left for Westminster Hall."

And signing to his attendants he left the apartment.

In the Cockpit Anne was being dressed for the Coronation, though she could take no active part in it, being so heavily pregnant.

Sarah was given instructions as to how the Princess's jewels should be worn when one of the women hurried in in some excitement.

"You have heard the news?" she asked.

"What news is this?" demanded Sarah.

"King James has landed in Ireland. They say the whole of that country is welcoming him."

In the mirror Anne sought Sarah's face and she saw it so transformed by fear that she trembled.

"I cannot believe this," blurted out Sarah.

"It's true, Lady Churchill. King James has written a letter to Queen Mary. I heard that she is mighty upset on receiving it and that she has even accused King William of letting her father go."

"This is . . . terrible!" said Sarah, and wished that she could find John at once to discuss the matter with him. What of their fine title now? What would King James have to give the Earl of Marlborough who had deserted to the other side just at that moment when he could have been of greater help to him than ever before?

Anne was thinking: If he comes back, he will forgive me. . . . He always forgave me.

She turned to Mrs. Dawson and asked: "Do you believe the child they call the Prince of Wales is my brother?"

"I do, Madam," said Mrs. Dawson rather sharply, for she had often assured Anne of the falseness of the warming-pan story. "I am as sure that he is your brother as I am that you are the daughter of the late Duchess of York."

There was a deep silence in the apartment; and for once even Sarah had nothing to say.

The ceremony was late in starting. The people were restive. There was whispering in the streets. Was it true that James had landed in Ireland? What would happen next? Would there be a bloody civil war?

Queen Mary was being carried in her chair into the state room of Westminster Hall; she was pale and clearly shaken. What news to receive on the day of one's coronation! How disquieting for a daughter to hear a father's curses in her heart while she took the crown which had been stolen from him!

When they stood together—she and William—and the question was asked: "Will you accept William and Mary for your King and Queen?" It seemed to them both that there was too long a pause before the acclamation.

It was an uneasy coronation. When the offering should have been made William discovered that on account of the upset he had omitted to provide himself with the necessary money and Lord Danby had to count out twenty guineas which he would put into the gold basin on behalf of the King.

An evil omen? asked those who were only too eager to look for evil omens.

Mary and William were fervent in their promises to maintain the scripture and the Protestant religion, holding up their right hands as they did so; between them they carried the sword. It was unlike any other coronation and the absence of the most important figures of the Church— the Archbishop of Canterbury, the Bishops of Durham and of Bath and Wells—was constantly remarked on.

All the principal participators were relieved when it was over. But that was not the end, for later during the banquet in Westminster Hall the champion of the King and Queen failed to arrive to throw down his gauntlet and challenge any to a duel who would not accept the sovereigns. Uneasily they waited; and it was dark when Sir Charles Dymoke made his appearance.

"Why so late?" was the whisper.

"It is because he is the son of James II's champion. He is unwilling to champion those who dethroned James."

But the glove was thrown and a dark figure which looked like an old woman ran to it and picked it up. As she was allowed to disappear among the crowd there was a gasp of horror through the hall.

A challenge!

This threw a gloom on the banquet which the very presence of William in any circumstances would have prevented from being very gay.

The Coronation day was over. What next? asked the people. They would not have been surprised to hear that James had landed in England in order to defend his crown.

On the following day a tall man was seen pacing up and down in Hyde Park at a well known dueling spot. Many people saw him, but Sir Charles Dymoke did not go out to meet him.

There were no cries of "No popery" in the streets now, but were the people satisfied? If Mary had seemed a little contrite, if William had not been so dour, they would have been more ready to accept them.

What had they done? they asked themselves. It was true they wanted no popery; but was it going to be the days of Oliver Cromwell all over again? They did not like sour Dutchmen; they did not like ungrateful daughters. Someone produced a verse which appealed to many, and all over the city it was being quoted. It was written after the Coronation and ran:

> *There through the dusk-red towers—amidst his ring*
> *Of Vans and Mynheers rode the Dutchman King;*
> *And there did England's Goneril thrill to hear,*
> *The shouts that triumphed o'er her crownless Lear.*

A DISH OF
GREEN PEAS

There was little time now for dallying at Hampton Court and making exciting plans for its reconstruction. Ireland was almost entirely in the hands of James; and certain areas of Scotland had declared for him. There was discord in Parliament between Whigs and Tories; William was unpopular with the English who admired a colorful King like Charles II; France had taken the opportunity to increase activity against Holland.

"I wish," said William to his dear friend Bentinck, "that I were a thousand miles away. I am not wanted here. The Queen is regarded as the ruler so I am of a mind to return to Holland and leave her here to govern."

Bentinck regarded him sadly. William had greatly desired this crown and having married Mary for it, it seemed impossible that, now that he had attained it, he should return to Holland.

Bentinck himself would have been delighted to go home; but he did not believe that William would so lightly abandon a lifetime's ambition.

Yet William summoned a Council of Ministers.

"I have made a mistake in accepting this crown," he said. "I can do nothing more for you when you are warring with each other and resent me. The Queen pleases you, so I will leave the government in her hands and go to Holland."

There was an immediate protest from the Council.

"I have been ill-used," William reminded them, "and in such circumstances have no wish to remain. I told you when I took the crown that I did not attach such importance to it as some men did."

So vehement were the protests that William saw how strong his position was.

"If I remained in control of this realm, I should depart at once for Ireland," he said; but there was further protest at his suggestion, for they said they needed his services in England and begged him to remain.

He shrugged his shoulders. "I am a Protestant," he said, "So I must do my duty, for this country could so easily be lost to the papists."

When Mary heard that William had threatened to leave for Holland she was distraught, and went to William with tears in her eyes and begged him not to leave her.

"You have succeeded in making yourself popular with the people," he told her. "They want you, but they are not inclined to accept me."

"They are so foolish, William."

"The Council of Ministers have begged me to stay. So they appear to think I may be of use to them."

"Then I join my pleas with theirs, William."

He looked at her coldly, remembering her outburst on the morning of the Coronation. Deep within her there was great pride, and occasionally it asserted itself. He could not forget the manner in which she had upbraided him for letting James go. What had she wanted? Him to murder her father? Hold him a prisoner? Have him brought to trial?

She had dared to criticize him! It was for this reason that he had threatened to return to Holland, although in his heart he had no intention of going. Marlborough had been sent to Flanders, and Marlborough was one of the most brilliant of his soldiers, although he was a man completely dominated by self-interest and one must, while making use of his services, never forget that fact and be wary of him.

There was no need for William to go to Holland therefore; and he had no intention of going. He wanted his wife to grovel in her desire to keep him at her side, to pay for her insolence on the Coronation morning; he wanted the ministers to acknowledge that he and he alone was the man to deliver their country from the threat of papistry. Once they admitted this he would give his untiring devotion to their Cause—which was his own. But there must be continual appreciation, because there were times when his physical disabilities were almost unbearable. It was bad enough to be smaller than most men, slightly hunchbacked, far from prepossessing, but when in addition he was cursed with asthma, which was improved by riding in the open air, and by hemorrhoids which made riding often an agony, he must remind those about him constantly that in matters of the mind he towered farther above them, in spite of their physical advantages.

He released himself from the Queen's embraces. "Very well," he said. "But I had thought that since you expressed your disapproval of the manner in which I was conducting affairs, you might wish to govern alone."

"Oh, William, you are thinking of that stupid *stupid* remark of mine. I was so distressed. It was the letter from my father coming at such a time. I must implore you to forgive me. I must assure you that I could not endure to live here while you were in Holland. You know that I only live for you.

It was enough.

He said coolly: "Very well, I shall remain. But pray remember in future that I do not care to be treated with disrespect at any time, more especially in the presence of my subjects."

"I will remember, and I crave your forgiveness, William, on my knees. . . ."

"Have done. I shall remain."

He left her and she wept quietly wondering whether he had gone to Elizabeth Villiers or to Bentinck.

The Princess Anne was growing discontented. Looking around her it seemed to her that everyone was benefiting from the new reign except herself.

Sarah and John Churchill had their new title and the revenues that went with it. Mary was Queen of England and William was King, for as long as he should live, which meant that Anne had been set back a place.

This she would have accepted if the new King and Queen had treated her more kindly. All during the years of separation she and Mary had corresponded and deplored their separation; but now that they were together again they found that over the years they had changed. They were not the inseparable companions they had been in childhood. Mary had become the complete slave of that Dutch Monster whom nobody could like because he was so bad tempered and uncouth; Mary was simply not herself. She wanted to talk incessantly and play cards and dance—which was all very well, but at the same time she had to do exactly what Dutch William wanted her to. Mary was, it seemed to Anne, like a shadow of Caliban in spite of her easy manners and love of pleasure. Everything he said was right in her opinion, whereas everything Anne said and did was wrong.

Anne loved cards more than anything; she loved to gossip too, but she found she had little to say to Mary, who did not seem to like Sarah.

Anne was pregnant and she was becoming uneasy because she had had so many disappointments. This time she desired to have a son even more fervently than usual so that she could score over her sister who quite clearly could not get one.

George was pleasant but dull; he provided no excitement. To everything one said, however exciting a piece of gossip, he would murmur: "Est-il possible?" and then nod drowsily. He was getting fatter and slept a great deal of the time, and although Anne was sure he was the best husband she could have, she did not find his company stimulating.

That left Sarah. What would she do without Sarah—dear, violent, amusing Sarah, who could always make her feel alive on her most sluggish days!

Sarah was always fomenting trouble; and now that she had her Marlborough title, she was showing quite clearly her dislike of the Queen.

She came into Anne's apartments to find her mistress drowsing, but as soon as Anne saw her she felt alert. Something had happened to make Sarah indignant.

"My dear Mrs. Morley," she cried. "What now do you think? I have had this straight from Dillon, who heard it from Keppel."

Dillon was a page in the Marlborough household and Keppel one in attendance on the King.

"Pray sit down, dear Mrs. Freeman, and tell me what is agitating you."

"As you can guess it concerns my dear Mrs. Morley, for it is when I see injustice done to her that I lose my temper."

"Oh, dear," sighed Anne. "What injustice?"

"Caliban has summoned Godolphin. He is a mean fellow, this King of ours. He cannot bear that money should be spent on anything but building and gardens and wars to set him more firmly on the throne. He asked Godolphin how it was possible for you to spend thirty thousand pounds a year."

"How possible!" screamed Anne.

"Oh, yes, to mean William that seems a great deal of money."

Anne's face puckered. "But how can I manage on it?"

How could she indeed, Sarah wondered, when she gave such magnificent gifts to her friends and lost so much at cards. Wasting it on cards was folly, but it was well for Anne to have some outlet for spending money or there might be an inquiry as to where it all went. Gifts to the Churchills took care of quite a large portion of it; but the money was not wasted, Sarah assured herself; the Churchills were not people to fritter away their money. John was the most cautious of men—some might call him mean—and Sarah was no spendthrift. They wished to grow richer each year and Heaven knew they had begun poor enough.

No, Anne's income must certainly not be cut for that would mean less gifts for the Churchills.

"One thing I will not endure," said Sarah, "and that is to see my dear Mrs. Morley treated in this way. Where would they be if it were not for you? Who was it who kept them supplied with information? Who was it who made the way easy for them?"

"You, dear Mrs. Freeman."

"Oh, no, no! It was my dear good kind Mrs. Morley. And how do they repay her? Have they forgotten that she stood aside to give him the sovereignty he was greedily demanding? Yes, they have forgotten. Depend upon it, Mrs. Morley, unless you stand firm, William will cut your income and that is something which I shall not allow you to accept."

"Indeed not. My father was so good to me, was he not? Do you remember how when I was in debt he never failed to help me."

"I remember."

Anne looked tearfully at her friend. Life had really been more *comfortable* when her father had been on the throne. Mary and William were not nearly so affectionate. When Anne thought of the letter her father had sent to Mary which she had received on Coronation day and in which he had talked of curses, she wanted to weep, not so much with remorse but with terror, for she felt herself to be included in those curses. A father's curse was a frightening thing to have hanging over one—particularly when one was expecting a child.

She began to wish that she had been a more dutiful daughter, that she had not allowed her fondness for gossip to embroil her in this affair which, from its beginnings as an exciting topic of conversation, had grown into a revolution.

Sarah following Anne's thoughts put a stop to them immediately.

"All will be well as long as you stand up for your rights. They must not browbeat you, which is what they will do if they can."

"Mary has changed so. She talks so much and I have nothing . . . simply nothing . . . to say to her."

"I have thought of something you can say to her. This place is unfit for an heiress to the crown—and whatever they say you are that."

"Unless they should have a child."

Sarah gave a coarse laugh. "My dear Mrs. Morley expects the impossible. William would if he could but he can't. That is why he pretends to spend so much time with his mistress. I tell you this, Bentinck is more to his taste than even Squint-eyed Betty, and between her and Bentinck he has no strength left for the Queen."

Anne laughed. Sarah could always amuse.

"But Mrs. Morley, let us get back to important affairs. Is it right that the heiress to the throne should be housed in . . . squalor!"

Anne looked surprised. The Cockpit was a delightful place and she had always loved it; but for Sarah she would have gone on living contentedly there, never wanting to change.

"No, there are some wonderful apartments in Whitehall; those which your Uncle Charles had rebuilt for the Duchess of Portsmouth. They are the most magnificent in the palace, and if Charles thought only them good enough for Portsmouth, then I say that only they are good enough for the heiress to the Crown."

"I know the apartments you mean, Mrs. Freeman. They are beautiful."

"Then you must ask your sister for them without delay. This will show them that you are aware of your position, of all you have sacrificed for them, and that it is time they began to treat you with due respect. This will make them see that they cannot begin fiddle-faddling with the accounts."

"I believe you are right, Sarah dear."

"I *know* I am."

The Queen looked coldly at her sister. How enormous she was! It must be a large child. Mary hoped it would be a boy for she longed to see a child who would one day carry on the line.

Anne ate too many sweets. Mary admitted that she herself was inclined to corpulence; it was a trait they had both inherited from their mother. Mary dearly loved a cup of chocolate and although she knew she was putting on weight every day, she could not resist that and other delicacies. But Anne was even fatter and even more devoted to her food.

Anne was a disappointment. That absurd infatuation with Sarah Churchill meant that Sarah Churchill was making important decisions which she should never have had the power to do. If they were not careful, these Churchills would be running the country. William had said that it was a matter they must watch and William was naturally right.

Even a foolish creature like Anne could have a great effect on the country's affairs; it was a sobering thought.

We have grown far away from each other, thought Mary; although I always thought her foolish and greedy. She imitated me in everything; I wish she would now devote more of her time to George—though I have to admit he is a fool and not in the least like William—instead of giving way all the time to that Churchill woman.

"I wish to leave the Cockpit," said Anne.

"Leave the Cockpit! But I thought you were so comfortable there."

"Perhaps not leave it entirely but I believe that in view of my position I should have apartments in Whitehall."

"If you wish . . . but being so close . . ."

"I think that the heiress to the throne is entitled to very fine apartments in Whitehall and I have made my choice."

Sometimes, thought Mary, when Anne asserted herself it was as though Sarah Churchill were speaking.

"Oh, and which are these."

"Those which were once the Duchess of Portsmouth's."

"It is strange that you should ask for these," said Mary, "for the Earl of Devonshire had asked me for them and I have promised that he shall have them."

"So then I must stand aside for Devonshire?"

"You know that is not so. But having promised him I must speak to him on this matter."

Anne bowed her head. "I pray Your Majesty to give me leave to retire."

Back to Sarah went Anne.

"So you must wait on Devonshire?"

"She had promised him."

"And when the heiress to the throne asks for apartments she is denied them because Master Devonshire has put in a prior claim? I never heard the like!"

"Doubtless he will give them up when he knows I want them."

"And so the heiress to the throne is to wait on his leavings? You must write at once to your sister and tell her this. It is the only way in which you can uphold your dignity."

Mary was so disturbed by Anne's letter that she went to William. He listened coldly to the problem.

"You see, William," went on Mary, "I had promised them to Devonshire, and I find it difficult to withdraw that promise now."

William narrowed his eyes. "Her income is enormous," he said. "I have been looking into these matters. Why does she need so much money? Why should she keep a separate table? The royal family should eat together. We need money for more serious matters than cards and favorites. Anne will have to reform her way of life; and that very soon. But in the meantime let her have the apartments she covets and retain the Cockpit. Then I shall go into the subject of her income."

"But Devonshire, William. . . ."

William looked surprised. "Naturally you will tell him to stand aside."

Mary bowed her head. She would, as usual, do exactly as William ordered.

"You see," said Sarah, "it is only necessary to stand firm. They have browbeaten you because they believe you will allow it. But let me tell you this, if my dear Mrs. Morley will let others take advantage of her goodness, Mrs. Freeman will not."

"You are right, of course, Sarah."

"And it seems to me that apartments in Whitehall, however fine, and a place like the Cockpit, are not enough for the future Queen of England. I shall never forget Richmond, shall you?"

"Never. We were so happy there and it was in Richmond Palace that I first grew to know my dear Mrs. Freeman."

"It has always been a royal palace and I cannot for the life of me see why it should not be yours."

"Richmond! Oh, how I should love to be there again. The air always agreed with me so well."

"Then you should ask for it, because it is by right yours."

"I believe the Villiers have a lease on it."

"The Villiers! Squint-eyed Betty and her family! It is not enough that Caliban spends the night with Squint-Eye instead of the Queen, but other members of that odious family may snatch your rightful home from you, as their sister does the King from the Queen."

"I think I should have Richmond."

"Then ask for it."

The Villiers were in higher favor than Devonshire, and William was not going to force Elizabeth's family to give up what they wanted to keep. Lady Frances Villiers, the deceased governess of Mary and Anne, had had a lease on the Palace and this was passed to one of her daughters, Madame Puissars, who had no intention of giving it up because Sarah Churchill wanted the Princess Anne to have it.

"You know what this means," Sarah pointed out to Anne. "It is Caliban's decree and of course your sister obeys him slavishly even when it is for the sake of his mistress. I dislike the entire Villiers breed, and I cannot say that I think very highly of the Queen for allowing them to hold such an influence over her husband."

"Mary is quite besotted with the King. And it is not as though he is even kind to her. I thank God I did not have to marry him. Sarah, do you know, I think I was happier when my father was on the throne."

Anne looked plaintive. They must reconcile themselves to being without Richmond, but Anne did not greatly care and it was more Sarah's defeat than hers. Moreover, Anne's confinement was drawing near and her thoughts were occupied with the coming birth.

Sarah was thoughtful. Ever since the Coronation she had been uneasy. The revolution had occurred so easily and she had imagined that once James was deposed that would be an end of him; but it seemed this was not so. James had friends—among them the King of France who was one of the most powerful monarchs in Europe. James was in possession of almost the whole of Ireland and parts of Scotland; he had struck terror into the minds of his daughters by his timely letter; and it was not improbable that he might return.

William was not popular and never would be because he lacked charm, and, although he had his virtues, he was no saint. His manners were bad; he was uncouth; although he was calm and controlled there were occasions when he seemed deliberately to let loose his temper, as he had when he had struck a gentleman with his horsewhip for riding before him on the race ground. This was considered bad manners by the English; it was simply not done, and the story was repeated and enlarged on and those who loved to record such incidents with wise sayings declared that it was the only blow he had struck for supremacy in his kingdoms. It was the age of lampoons and the royal family was spied on and every failing noted to become the inspiration for some gibe.

William was so often ill that only his great spirit enabled him to continue; he could not conceal his terrible cough, and it was the common belief that he would not live long. And after he was gone, pondered Sarah, would Mary be able to hold the country together? In spite of her devotion to William she was gay, and quite clearly if she could escape from his stern eye there would have been dancing every night at one of the Palaces. As it was there was card playing. Card playing, William had said, was a safe occupation for his Queen because it prevented her talking. Mary was affable; she was beautiful, in spite of her growing bulky she was stately; and she had inherited some of her uncle's charm. But her apparent lack of concern for her father's fate had not pleased the people and continual comparisons were drawn to the tragedy of Lear and in some quarters she was known as Goneril.

It did not seem inconceivable to Sarah therefore that one day James might return. If he did Anne must be forgiven by him. Mary he would find it difficult to forgive for she had committed the great sin of allowing herself to be crowned. Not so Anne. It might be possible to convince James that Anne had been led astray by her wicked sister and brother-in-law. Anne was uneasy now; she could not rid herself of the sense of guilt which that Coronation letter had aroused in her. Mary felt the same but dared not admit it.

This was a situation which needed delicate handling and Sarah was not noted for her delicacy. She had always bludgeoned her way to victory and could use no other method. But subtlety was needed here. It was a fact that already certain people were beginning to drink to "The King over the Water"; there was a seemingly innocent trick of what was known as "Squeezing the Orange" but which had its significance.

The people were fickle. They had cried "No popery"; but if James would come back and promise there should be no popery would they welcome him? At least he was the rightful King; at least he was not a semi-hunchback with a Dutch accent, who, when standing, only came up to his wife's shoulder, and had a perpetual sneer on his pale face.

Sarah had decided what must happen. There must be friction between Anne and the King and Queen. They could not disinherit her because there would be a revolution if they did. But at least strained relations between them would show the Jacobites and James, if he should return, that Anne was not in favor of the new King and Queen.

The best way of maddening them, Sarah decided, was to ask for an increase in her annual income.

Sarah was indefatigable; she had determined that the Princess's income should be raised. Sarah had her friends in Parliament and they knew well what an important role the Marlboroughs played in the country's affairs. Anne, pointed out Sarah, was heiress to the crown; yet she was treated like a pauper. Look at her husband. He was snubbed at every turn by the King and whatever the King did, the Queen agreed with. Did they forget that Prince George was the consort of the heiress to the throne? The only way these wrongs could be righted was by voting Anne an annual income of ninety thousand pounds. This was absurd, of course; but as Sarah had said to Anne if they aimed high they would get nearer to the mark than by aiming low.

William who had been contemplating cutting Anne's allowance was not in Parliament when the commons voted Anne an income of forty thousand pounds a year.

William and Mary had not been consulted and when Mary heard what had happened, she was horrified; so was William, but he hid his chagrin and immediately dissolved Parliament before the matter could be settled, and Mary sent for Anne and demanded to know what part she had played in this affair.

Anne, without Sarah to advise, muttered that she believed her friends were of the opinion that she should have an income commensurate with her position.

"Your friends?" cried Mary bitterly. "What friends have you but the King and myself? Others may tell you they are your friends, but their actions belie this."

Anne had nothing to say and, as quickly as she could, took her leave and went to Sarah. It was always such a pleasure to listen to Sarah, raving about her injustices. Anne enjoyed the feeling of self-pity and the pleasure of knowing that her much-loved friend could be so vehement on her behalf.

"Oh," cried Sarah dramatically, "how you have been betrayed! Who gave them help when they needed it. Who invited him over to England? Who kept him informed of what was happening at the Court? Who defied her own father for his sake? For all this you are offered forty thousand pounds and not even that, for Parliament is dissolved before it can grant it to you."

"They have been most unfair to me," cried Anne.

"My poor Mrs. Morley! But there is one who would fight for you with all her might—against King against Queen against all the world for your sake."

"Oh, dear Mrs. Freeman, it is worth being treated thus to know this."

"Do not think I shall allow them to continue treating you like this. We will go on fighting until we win . . . something."

When Mary and Anne met, the Queen was cold to her sister and Anne returned her coldness.

The beginning af Sarah's rupture had started.

William detested Anne whom he thought vapid and ridiculous; he remarked to Elizabeth Villiers that he was delighted he had not had to marry *her*, for if he had he would surely have been the most miserable man on earth. But he realized that there must not be this trouble in the family and much as he deplored her extravagance he must do all in his power to prevent an open rift.

Elizabeth was a delight to him; she was serious when he wanted her to be and she had a grasp on affairs so that he did not have to explain in detail what was worrying him.

"Of course," she said on this occasion, "it is the Marlboroughs who are behind this trouble. Sarah Churchill has persuaded Anne to ask for a bigger grant. And you know why—so that the bulk of it can go into the Marlborough purse. I know through my sister what goes on in that household."

"We shall have to make a settlement—and with as little bother as possible. Although it is disconcerting to see good money thrown away I would agree to a grant of fifty thousand pounds to silence her, for silenced she must be."

"Sarah knows this and I doubt if she will settle for fifty thousand pounds."

"She must, because the country can afford no more."

"I will get my sister Barbara to have a word with Sarah Churchill, telling her that she would be wise to settle for fifty thousand pounds and that if she does not, she will ruin her own chances. For if Anne will not accept fifty thousand pounds, she may well be forced to take much less, and if that is the case, grants to the Churchills will necessarily be clipped."

"What a pass it is," said William angrily, "when a man and his wife hold the country up to ransom in this way."

"How did it ever happen?"

"A clever pair one has to admit. He the brilliant soldier-adventurer, she the controller of the heir presumptive."

"Barbara shall speak to her without delay," said Elizabeth, giving him her slow fascinating smile. "It is ridiculous that with all your responsibilities you should be troubled with such a matter."

"*So you see,*" said Lady Fitzharding, "it would be folly not to take what is offered, for if it is withdrawn that amount might not be offered again."

"A paltry fifty thousand pounds!" cried Sarah disgustedly.

"You call that paltry?"

"Yes, Barbara Fitzharding, I do, when it is offered to the heir of England."

"Don't be foolish, Sarah. Don't you see what trouble *you* may be in if you persist in this quarrel, because we all know it is your quarrel rather than that of the Princess Anne. Do not forget that you are setting yourself against the King and Queen."

"I would rather die than sacrifice the Princess!" declared Sarah.

Barbara smiled and although Sarah had a desire to slap the smile off that silly Villiers' face, she desisted.

"Shrewsbury will come to the Princess to make the formal offer of fifty thousand pounds from the King," went on Barbara.

"And I shall be with the Princess to offer her my support when he comes."

She was true to her word, and when the Earl of Shrewsbury arrived was in her mistress's company.

"It is a private matter, Your Highness."

"All my affairs are known to the Countess of Marlborough," replied Anne.

Shrewsbury had no alternative but to accept Sarah's presence.

"His Majesty says that if Your Highness will refrain from soliciting Parliament he will personally guarantee you fifty thousand pounds a year."

Anne looked at Sarah who burst out: "And what if the King should not keep his word?"

Shrewsbury looked at her in astonishment while Anne's admiration for her friend's boldness was apparent.

Anne knew what she had to say: and said it. "The affair is now before Parliament and events must take their course."

When William heard the result of the interview he was furious with Anne, but did not show it. Instead he summoned his ministers and said he would be happy to accept their will in this matter of the Princess Anne's allowance; at which Anne was voted her fifty thousand pounds.

"Let that be an end to this unfortunate matter," said William.

Mary, who could not let the matter rest, sent for her sister.

When they were alone she burst out: "I cannot understand how you could have behaved so to the King!"

"What cannot you understand?" asked Anne.

"I know what took place at that interview with Shrewsbury. You implied that you would not trust William. I suppose that harpy of yours is behind this."

"I know of no harpy."

"Then it is a pity you cannot see more clearly what is obvious to everyone else. I would like to know when the King has ever shown anything but kindness to you."

Anne was silent.

"Answer me," insisted Mary.

"I do not know what you want me to say. All I know is that I have been less happy since our father went away."

"*You* to talk like that! Have you forgotten what you used to write to me when I was in Holland?"

"I only know that I was not treated thus by our father."

"I am ashamed of you . . . ashamed and surprised."

Anne did not answer.

Her silence maddened Mary, but when Anne had gone the Queen wept a little. She had so looked forward to a return of the old friendship. What had happened to her dear little sister who had so looked up to her and admired her.

She thought angrily: Sarah Churchill has happened to her. How I loathe that woman!

Anne was dining at the royal table. This was one of William's economies; he had ordained that the Princess Anne, the Queen and King must not keep separate tables; it was an extravagance.

It was no great pleasure to dine at the King's table. He said little and never addressed a word even to those who served him. The Queen would have liked a little gaiety—some amusing conversation, a little music and afterward, dancing. But she conformed in every way to the King's desire and was almost as silent as he was.

How different it had been in the days of Uncle Charles! thought Anne. And even in our father's day. . . .

Then her eyes sparkled for a servant had set a dish of green peas on the table. Green peas! the first of the year which always tasted the best.

Anne's mouth was watering. She loved her food and more especially during pregnancies.

She could not stop looking at the peas. Mary could not eat them; they were bad for her; and William was a poor eater. There were not a great many; she would eat the lot and it would be no use asking for more for it was too early yet and these would be all that were ready for serving.

The Queen had shaken her head at the dish. Now it was Anne's turn. Anne leaned forward; but just as she did so William stretched out a hand and drew the dish toward him, and under Anne's agonized eyes ate the lot without even asking her to have a few.

Beast! thought Anne. Uncouth swine! Dutch abortion. Caliban! Was there ever such a King? He belonged more in a swineherd's hut than in a palace.

She was quaking with rage when she returned to her own apartments for although most things did not rouse her from her lethargy, food could.

Sarah came to her and demanded what fresh insult she had been forced to endure.

Anne told the story, her eyes glistening; she could see those peas, smell them, remember the flavor of past peas; she could see them now disappearing into that ugly twisted mouth.

"And he ate them as though he did not care what he was eating."

"Of course he did not care. He only wanted to keep them from you."

"I hate him!" said Anne vehemently.

"Oh, dear Mrs. Morley, he will not always be with us. Let us think of the bright future when he is gone. That will be the greatest day of my life when we crown Queen Anne."

It was pleasant to contemplate but Anne's mind was still clouded with the thought of green peas.

Sarah saw this and had the gardens and forcing houses searched in the hope of finding some that might be found and cooked for the Princess; but none were to be had.

Anne could only ease her disappointed palate by going over and over the list of his sins with Sarah, and from that day she hated him and was ready to follow wholeheartedly in any scheme against him.

AT THE
PLAYHOUSE

Sarah Churchill, thought Elizabeth Villiers, had become one of the most important figures at Court and all because she had so fascinated the Princess Anne that she was allowed to manage her affairs completely. With anyone but Anne, Sarah would have had to use more subtle methods; that domineering know-all attitude would have had to be considerably subdued. But Anne was a stupid woman with an unnatural passion for the friend who was unlike her in every way. Sarah was not exactly beautiful, but was handsome with her magnificent fair hair and her extraordinary vitality. Anne had been pretty enough in an insipid way, but she was growing so fat that she looked much older than her years and of course the perpetual pregnancies had not helped her. She had turned to Sarah as one who was her opposite in every way; and even in their childhood days the sisters had had a great fondness for members of their own sex.

Sarah Churchill would have to be watched carefully.

Elizabeth Villiers's own methods were quite different from Sarah's; and yet there was a similarity, for as Sarah wished to influence Anne, so Elizabeth wished to influence William.

It had been a remarkable achievement to retain his attention all these years; he was a cold man, but between them there was a relationship which was enduring; they needed each other and to be the woman in William's life who could give him exactly what he needed was a tribute to her brilliance.

She had wondered what her position would be in the household when she had accompanied Mary, as a reluctant bride, to Holland, for Mary had little love for her. They had spent much of their childhood together, but she had never been one of Mary's selected friends. And then . . . she had seen the possibilities with William; and miraculously she had succeeded with him.

She must be ever watchful of rivals though; not that Mary was a rival. She would never be afraid of the Queen who was so quick to agree with her husband in every way—even though on one occasion she had, during William's absence, sent her, Elizabeth, out of Holland with a letter addressed to the King, her father, asking him to keep her enemy there. Elizabeth had had some difficulty in returning to Holland, but she had; and after her spurt of independent action Mary had become the docile wife again.

Yet she need not be fearful of Mary when she was looking for a rival in William's affection; she knew full well where the danger lay.

It was with Bentinck, William's devoted friend and Elizabeth's own brother-in-law, for he had married her sister Anne who had died just before they left Holland.

Elizabeth remembered now that deathbed scene with Mary attempting to reconcile the sisters. How characteristic of Mary, who must have everything comfortably rounded off.

Anne had been as docile a wife to Bentinck as Mary was to William—for in a way Bentinck and William were two of a kind, though Bentinck had a charm which William lacked; he was more polished in manners, more diplomatic in his relations with others, but perhaps he could not afford to be as brusque as William was.

Two of a kind! thought Elizabeth; and women were not of great importance to either.

Bentinck had never been a great friend of Elizabeth's; he had even pretended to be sorry for the Queen and had on one occasion dared criticize William for his treatment of Mary; that had meant a rift in that passionate friendship which had not lasted it was true; but it had been an attack on her, Elizabeth Villiers, the King's mistress.

Elizabeth believed she knew why Bentinck had made that attack, why he did not like her. It had little to do with sympathy for the Queen. He was merely jealous of a woman who took up so much of his master's time.

Elizabeth must be watchful of Bentinck. How did she know what he said of her when he and William were alone together. Bentinck was an ambitious man, but he also loved his Prince, even as William loved him; and since William had become King of England he had not forgotten his favorite.

Bentinck was now Baron Cirencester, Viscount Woodstock and Earl of Portland, First Gentleman of the Bedchamber, Groom of the Stole and a Privy Councillor, and William rarely made a decision without him. He was too important. It was not so easy to shower honors on Elizabeth, for William was not a man to flaunt his mistress. He preferred it to be believed that the relationship did not exist and Elizabeth was too clever to insist on recognition. So all that had come her way so far was a large portion of James's Irish estates which was supposed to be worth some twenty-six thousand pounds a year; but because of difficulties in getting the money it was little more than five thousand pounds.

That was not important. Elizabeth would look after herself, but in doing that she must keep her eyes on Bentinck.

She was too clever to attempt to criticize Bentinck. She had held her place by the comfort she had been able to give William; she had never tried to involve him in intrigues for her own advantages. No, the only way of undermining Bentinck's influence with the King was for him to have a rival in the King's affection.

She had been watching that very personable young man Arnold Joost van Keppel who although as yet only a page in William's service had already attracted his master's attention. William could almost smile with pleasure when he looked at that fresh young face and it was already clear that he liked to have the boy near him.

Keppel was bright; it was certain that he was ambitious. Poor Bentinck was growing old and showed signs of strain, for he was as deeply involved in state matters as his master. It was not that Elizabeth hoped to oust Bentinck from William's affections. That would be an impossibility; they would be friends until death parted them; but there was no reason why someone younger, gayer and more handsome, might not take up some of the King's attention.

When she was next with the King she mentioned Keppel.

"A charming boy," she commented, "and one I think who is very eager to serve you."

"I have noticed him," said William, and in spite of his attempt to hide it there was a gentle note in his voice.

"And of good family and breeding," added Elizabeth. "Such a young man should hold a higher post than page of honor."

"The thought had occurred to me," admitted William.

"There will be a vacant place in the bedchamber soon."

"He shall have it," said William, and smiled affectionately at his mistress who had the fortunate knack of anticipating his wishes.

Shortly afterward Arnold Joost van Keppel became Groom of the Bedchamber and Master of the Robes.

During that early summer the city was full of rumors. In Ireland William's army was fighting against that of James. There were constant reports that James had died; that he landed in England; that he was defeated; that he had beaten the King's men.

There was frequent secret drinking to the "King over the Water"; the ominous "Squeezings of the Orange."

William had taken up his headquarters at Hampton Court; he believed that he would soon have to go to Ireland, and he would have been there now but for the fact that his ministers had begged him to remain.

Mary yearned to have a little gaiety, and although this was not possible at Hampton Court when William had to come to London and stayed at St. James's she accompanied him, and on these occasions made some attempt to make a Court there.

William turned his back on such frivolities, but he realized that it was no bad thing that they should take place. He was so unpopular largely because of his uncouth and retiring manners; the people—who would complain of the Court's extravagance, yet wanted an extravagant Court—said he was a dullard and they might as well have no King as King William. But whenever the Queen appeared they cheered, for she obviously liked gaiety. She had been brought up in the right way, to laugh and dance and make merry.

Mary declared that during one of her sojourns at St. James's she would see a play at the playhouse.

Now a play must be very carefully selected because many of them were historical and there must be no references which could apply to the present delicate situation. One which was definitely banned was of course King Lear. That was a play which would never be played during the reign of William and Mary.

Mary discussed the matter excitedly with her ladies of honor: the Countess of Derby, her first lady and Mistress of the Robes, mentioned a play which had been banned under James.

"One of Mr. Dryden's," she said. "I believe it is most enlivening."

"And why was it banned?" asked Mrs. Mordaunt, another of the Queen's women.

"It was thought to contain slighting references to the Catholics, I believe," replied the Countess.

"Then," said Mary, "it might be a good one to have. I have always admired Mr. Dryden's work. What is it's name?"

"*The Spanish Friar*, I think, Your Majesty. Shall I inquire?"

"Pray do," said the Queen. "I can scarce wait to see it. I have always loved the play. I remember in my uncle's time how he was constantly at the playhouse."

They all looked a little wistful for the golden days of the merry Monarch. It was all so different now. So many people were comparing William with Oliver Cromwell, and if he had his way, they were sure there would be a return to puritanism.

But the Queen was different; everyone's hopes were fixed on the Queen.

There were a hundred little irritations in Mary's life. Anne who was aloof and rarely spoke to her; Sarah Churchill was as insolent as she dared be; Elizabeth Villiers, sly and retiring, was nevertheless keeping her hold on William's affections, and as if that were not enough there had to be Catherine Sedley.

Mary had always disliked the woman—no beauty, but like her father, the rake and poet who had been a favorite of Uncle Charles, full of a wild joy in living and a desire to act in such a way as to call attention to herself.

She had been one of the most successful mistresses of James and although he had made several attempts to cast her off, he had never been able to do so. He had made her Countess of Dorchester and given her a fine town house which she now occupied, and she often came to Court which Mary thought was an affront to herself. Such people should have the decency to stay away. It was even said that she was working with the Jacobites to bring James back and that she cared not who knew it.

She was quick-witted and entertained a large company at her fashionable house. There she would talk in an affectionate and slighting way of her lover and drink the health of the King over the Water.

She was almost ugly and she knew it. "One of his penances," she called herself. "He seemed to choose us for our ugliness," she added. "Well, he liked us that way. As for wit, if any of us had any *he* had not enough to discover—so he did not choose us for that."

These remarks were carried back to Mary. It shocked her sense of propriety that her father's ex-mistress should be talking so openly of their relationship.

"The Countess of Dorchester indeed!" said Mary indignantly. "If she comes to Court I shall treat her as no higher than her father's daughter."

When this was reported to Catherine Sedley she laughed and said: "Then I shall treat the Queen as her mother's." An insult, for Mary's mother, Anne Hyde, was of not such a high rank as Catherine's father.

These were minor irritations to which one must submit; William's advice as to how to deal with them could not be asked, for he would not allow himself to be drawn into such trivialities, and Mary must settle them herself.

On this evening she was happily preparing to go to the Theater Royal for Dryden's *Spanish Friar*. To be carried to the theater in her chair, to sit in the royal box and receive the acclaim of the people, would make her feel contented, more as a Queen should feel; and perhaps in time she would persuade William to come to the play, to mingle more with the people. Then perhaps she would be able to make them see what a noble hero he was and him to understand how necessary it was to step down from one's pedestal at times and be a popular hero.

Anne would be present, very far advanced in pregnancy. Surely the child must soon be born! And unfortunately with her would be that odious Churchill woman. Well, it was certainly a royal occasion, for fashionable London had turned out to see the play and it was like the old days. Mary, glittering with jewels, tall, stately, and plumply imposing looking as a Queen should look. The people cheered her, and she smiled her acknowledgment. She had to be doubly charming to make up for William's moroseness. But William was not here tonight, and she must convey to them that he was engaged on the serious matters of kingship, planning how to win the war in Ireland. Oh, no, an unfortunate subject! He was working hard for the good of them all, to bring them peace and prosperity.

A dark thin woman was curtseying before her, and Mary was about to smile when she recognized Catherine Sedley; then she turned her head and looked the other way.

Catherine's malicious face twisted into a smile. "Your Majesty is cool to me," she said very audibly. "It is hard on me. For although I have broken one commandment with your father, you have broken another."

As Catherine had passed on, Mary went white with anger that was touched with uneasiness. How dared the woman! And in a public place! That remark would be repeated all over the Court, all through the city, perhaps throughout the country.

It was true . . . cruelly true. Catherine Sedley had committed adultery—but at her father's request.

"Honor thy father and thy mother: that thy days may be long upon the land which the Lord thy God givest thee."

Was there no escape . . . even at the playhouse?

She turned to the Countess of Derby. "Come," she said peevishly, "what are we waiting for?"

Mary took her place in the royal box and although she smiled graciously at the audience, all the time she was thinking of Catherine Sedley's words; and instead of the stage and the players she saw James coming into the nursery, picking her up, sitting her on his knee; she could hear the whispers: "The Duke dotes on his daughters and his favorite is the Lady Mary." She pictured his bewilderment when he learned that she was with his enemies, at the very core of the rebellion against him which had driven him from his throne and native land.

What were the players saying?

> *"How now! What means this show?"*
> *"'Tis a procession.*
> *The Queen is going to the great Cathedral,*
> *To pray for our success against the Moors."*
> *"Very good; she usurps the throne; keeps the old King*
> *In prison; and at the same time is praying for a blessing:*
> *Oh religion and roguery, how they go together!"*

Everyone was watching the royal box—not the stage. She was horribly aware of Catherine Sedley's malicious eyes and she felt the hot color rushing into her cheeks. The Queen of England in her box unable to hide her embarrassment, her guilt, from the eyes of a playhouse audience! Tomorrow this would be the main topic of conversation all over the town.

Hastily she put up her fan. There was a slight murmur through the audience. Was it a titter of amusement?

What a fool she had been not to read this play before she came to see it. There was nothing to be done now; she must sit through it and pray that there would be no more such references. Mrs. Betterton had come on to the stage. Dear Mrs. Betterton who had taught her and Anne in their youth how to speak lines. She was back in the nurseries at Richmond. Jemmy was there to show them how to dance in the ballet Calista, which had been written for her that she might make her debut. Handsome Jemmy, who had wanted to be a King and had lost his head because of it . . . at her father's command.

Would this play never end? The audience were far more interested in the drama in the royal box than on the stage. Her women were uneasy; they were listening intently for some other reference which could add to the tension in the theater.

It came:

> *"Can I seem pleased to see my master murdered,*
> *His crown usurped, a distaff on the throne?"*

There was a hush in the audience. Recently there had been rumors that James had been killed in Ireland. Mary turned to the Countess of Derby.

"Your Majesty is a little cold?"

"My cloak."

It was placed about her shoulders. The audience watched; Catherine Sedley was smiling: the Queen was uneasy and could not hide it.

"What title has this Queen but lawless force?" came from the stage.

She knew now how the guilty King and Queen in Hamlet had felt as they watched the play staged for their benefit. She was shivering, waiting, tense; and it seemed to her hours before the end.

When it came she rose thankfully. The audience was silent. It had no cheers to offer her. With as little fuss as possible she left the theater.

The next day everyone was talking of the Queen's visit to *The Spanish Friar* and the playhouse looked forward to a run of good business. It would be crowded, and when the telling lines were delivered there would be cheers or boos according to the side the audience were inclined to take. A dull King, a Court that was more often non-existent did not appeal to a people who looked to its royalty to provide some excitement; it would be diverting therefore to have a little battle in the playhouse.

Mary, realizing what was happening, gave orders that *The Spanish Friar* was to be taken off and a new play put on which she would attend.

There was disappointment among those who had hoped to see some sport, but they would all crowd to the theater when the new play was on and when the Queen came it would be amusing to listen and hope for further references which might discomfort her, although it was certain that the script of the play would be well examined beforehand.

It was amazing how difficult it was to find a play in which there was no reference which could be applied to the present situation. But at last something was found and the Queen announced her intention of attending.

She was being dressed for the occasion when William came into her apartment. The very sight of him was enough to scatter her women so he did not have to order them to retire.

"I understand," he said, "that you are going to the playhouse."

"Yes, William."

"I have just heard what happened at *The Spanish Friar.*"

"I did not tell you before William, not wishing to disturb you with a matter so trivial."

"I do not think it trivial."

"It was certainly very uncomfortable."

"And so you propose to go again and possibly submit the crown to indignity?"

"I thought it best, William, not to show that I am afraid to go to the play for fear I hear something that discomforts me."

"I do not think that you acted in a queenly manner. Hiding behind your fan, letting everyone see your discomfiture."

Mary's eyes filled with tears. "I . . . could not help it."

"And now you propose to be a figure of fun once more, should it please them to make you one!"

"I think I should go to the play to show them I am not afraid."

"You will not go to the play."

"But William . . ."

He looked at her in astonishment. Was she going to disobey him? He was afraid; always it was the same. Docility which seemed as though it would be perpetual and then that sudden spark of rebellion for which he must always be on guard because he had to remember that she was the Queen and through her he ruled; and if there was a split between them—which of course there would never be—the people of this country would be with her whom they considered their rightful Queen.

The fear in him made him harden his expression.

"I repeat," he said coldly, "you will not go to the playhouse. I forbid it."

"William, I have said I will go. They are expecting me. I am ready."

"It is the duty of a wife to obey her husband. You know that."

"Yes, William, but . . ."

"Then pray remember it."

The rebellion was there. It was coming. She believed that it was right for her to go to the playhouse. She was English; she had been brought up among these people and she understood them as he could not.

She had been discomfited in the playhouse and she could not refuse to go again because they would think she was afraid.

She was on the point of explaining; but he had turned. She watched him walk from the room—a little figure of a man, slightly hunchbacked, wheezing as he walked—yet a man, she knew, of brilliance, a great leader, the greatest hero alive.

What would she do? thought William. He wanted to be alone to think. A great deal depended on this. He believed that once she disobeyed him, she would continue to do so. The people liked her; they hated him. They did not want him. It was only the ministers who knew him for an astute ruler who had some notion of his genius, who had seen what he had done for Holland who believed he was necessary to them in this difficult time. Later when things were more settled at home, he would go to Ireland and deal with the troubles there. They wanted him for that. They wanted a working King who could lead them in battle, who would plan at the Council table. And they wanted a decorative Queen who could look regal and stately and move among the people as a symbol.

But it was the people who decided in the end—the mob that wanted to laugh and scream, to love or hate. They wanted Mary and not William.

She did not know—or did she—what power she held over him?

This was more than a visit to the playhouse.

What to do? Mary was bewildered. At the playhouse they would be waiting for her. The crowded audience had gone there to watch the royal box rather than the stage. They would try to read hidden meanings in any slightly ambiguous phrases; and she wanted to be there, calm and regal; she had to show them that she was not afraid. Her father had been deposed, true, but they had forgotten that they had helped to depose him. Had they not set their minds and hearts against Popery? She was merely a figurehead; she and William had been sent for. They had not come of their own desire—or she had not.

Her women had come back into the apartment; they would know what had taken place, for there was always someone to listen at doors and report.

He is the master, they would be saying. She must do as he says.

"Your Majesty, it is time we left?" said the Countess of Derby.

Mary hesitated; then she said: "I am in no mood for the theater tonight."

She knew that behind her back they were exchanging glances. They would be saying: She dares not because he has forbidden it.

But she was the Queen and she wanted to bring some gaiety into her life. The spark of rebellion flared.

"I have heard," she said, "that a certain Mrs. Wise has prophesied that my father will return. I have a fancy to go to her and have her tell my fortune."

They were astonished. The Queen to visit a fortune teller! She laughed at them and her eyes sparkled with the thought of the coming adventure. She would not disobey William by going to the playhouse but at the same time she would do something far more daring.

There was excitement in the apartment, for her women, finding Court life dull, were ready enough to enter into the adventure.

She was reminded of the days of childhood when her Uncle Charles indulged in many an adventure incognito, usually concerned with a woman; but how the people had enjoyed those adventures of his! A King and Queen should go among the people; it was what the people wanted. It was not to be expected that every monarch should be a cold aloof hero, who thought of nothing but his country's good . . . except of course when he was enjoying his mistress's company, or that of his beloved Bentinck.

Those were thoughts which Mary tried to avoid, but they were there at the back of her mind; just as was the knowledge that she was the Queen, the first heir; she was the reason why they had been accepted as King and Queen of England. In that case if she wished to have her fortune told, why should she not?

When the royal party arrived at Mrs. Wise's house on the riverside, she somewhat reluctantly invited the party to enter. The Queen, in the rich gown she had intended to wear for the theater, and with her company of almost as splendidly attired ladies, looked incongruous in the small room.

Mrs. Wise, who seemed to think that her wisdom set her on a level with royalty, made a grudging curtsey and said gruffly that she could not understand the object of Her Majesty's visit.

"But Mrs. Wise, I have heard of your prophecies. I want news of my father. I want to know if it is true that he has been killed. I want to know if he will return. I want to know what the future holds for me."

"I will not read Your Majesty's hand," said the woman, "for I'd have naught good to tell you."

"How can you know that until you tell my fortune?"

"The King was driven from his throne. I see nothing good for those who drove him away."

Lady Derby whispered: "She is a well known Jacobite, Your Majesty."

"And cares not who knows it," added Mrs. Wise.

"Then read Her Majesty's future. That is all she asks of you," suggested one of the women.

But Mrs. Wise refused.

Mary, who admired the woman's obvious loyalty to her father laughed lightly and said: "I see our visit is in vain. Come, let us look in at one of the curiosity shops. I hear they are worth a visit."

So they left Mrs. Wise and went along to a notorious shop where extraordinary curiosities were sold; this was one of many which had sprung up since the Restoration. On the lower floor were the objects to be sold and upstairs were rooms where gallants could entertain ladies or vice versa. The laxity of morals which had become an accepted part of life after the years of Puritan rule had made these shops a commonplace; and the most notorious of them all was Mrs. Graden's.

Here Mary was led and Mrs. Graden came out with great glee to welcome Her Majesty. It was rather pleasant to be so treated after the rudeness of Mrs. Wise; and when Mrs. Graden ordered her servants to prepare a supper and on her knees implored the Queen to partake of it, Mary agreed.

It was a merry little supper party with good food and music.

Mary felt soothed by the evening's entertainment, particularly as, while not disobeying William, she had done something of which he would not approve.

That was the beginning of a new kind of entertainment.

The Queen's visits to the bazaars pleased the people. They liked her to move among them, to show that although married to Dutch William, she was not like him.

Having visited Mrs. Graden's, she must go to Mrs. Ferguson's and to Mrs. De Vett's; she would buy ribbons and headdresses and knickknacks which they had to sell. It was so good for business.

But it was not possible to please everyone, Mrs. Potter who had a house in Exeter Change wanted to know why the Queen did not come to her house. Being a garrulous woman she did not keep her observations to herself.

"Why am I not chosen?" she demanded one day as she stood at the door of her shop. "Is Mrs. Graden any better than I? Does she sell finer ribands? Do higher nobility entertain in her back rooms than in mine? I tell you this much. The Queen has more reason to come to me than to Mrs. Graden's, because the plot to bring William and Mary to the throne and to send James off was hatched in *my* house."

Lady Fitzharding who was buying silks for the Princess Anne at the time heard this tirade and went at once to her sister Elizabeth Villiers to report what was being said; and Elizabeth realized that it was a matter which should be passed at once to her lover.

When William heard he was furious. She had done this to defy him, of course. He had been pleased when she had refrained from visiting the playhouse, but he had not known then that she had committed the folly of visiting these low shops which were little more than bawdy houses. She might think little of that having been brought up in one of the most dissolute courts in Europe, with a reigning King who was not content with one—or even two—mistresses, but kept a dozen at a time. His Dutch soul was nauseated at the thought of those immoral houses; if he had his way, he would have them abolished. And to think that the Queen had been foolish enough to visit them was infuriating.

It was not enough to go to her and express his displeasure. He wanted the country to know that he deplored the existence of these places, so he waited until they were dining in public.

"I have heard," he said, "that you make a custom of dining at houses of ill repute."

Mary answered: "I have visited the houses of several women in The Hall."

He knew that the name The Hall was applied to both Westminster Hall or Exeter Change where most of the bazaars of this kind were situated.

"It seems a strange choice of yours."

"Do you think so? We found the visits amusing."

He looked at her sardonically. "It is only proper," he said, "that when you visit such places, I should accompany you."

She hated to anger him and she knew that he was very angry, more so because he had chosen to reprove her in public. She knew why, of course. He would insist that she never went to such places again and he wanted everyone to know that it was his command and that she would obey it.

She said rather sullenly: "The last Queen visited these places."

"I beg of you do not use her as an example," retorted William sharply.

It was rare that he was so conversational at meals; usually he ate in silence, although Keppel had reported that when he was with his Dutch friends, drinking Holland gin, he talked often with abandon; and there was frequent laughter at the table.

This conversation was listened to eagerly. He talked of these places which in his opinion should not exist and expressed the view that it was strange indeed that the Queen should find pleasure in them.

Mary was ready to burst into tears, which always had come so readily to her.

She knew that William was very displeased and that this would be an end of her efforts to amuse herself in the gay old way.

She was right. Very soon she and William returned to Hampton Court; and there she was expected to live quietly, walking six or seven miles a day, planning the new building and gardens, praying a great deal, and sometimes listening to a little music while she played cards or knotted her fringe, a pastime which she had to take up since her eyes had become too weak for the fine needlework she had once so much enjoyed.

But for the pleasure of living closer to her husband, Hampton Court would have been dull after Whitehall. The news was neither good nor bad but remained undecisive; but at least at Hampton Mary was secure from criticism; there was less danger of hearing one of the scurrilous lampoons being sung; and since the night at the playhouse she had begun to listen for them.

Hampton was delightful in the summer and William was more healthy there; he could breathe more easily; and there was no doubt that he was delighted with the prospect of improving the place. This brought them closer together.

Mary had grown plumper since coming to England and her doctors had told her to take more exercise, so while she ate heartily of fattening foods, she attempted to lose weight by walking.

Often she would be seen stepping out with her women and since some of them came from Holland they liked to wear their native styles which caused some amusement among English spectators. To see Mary and her Dutch maids walking in the grounds at Hampton was one of the sights of the times. Mary would walk at some speed and the ladies would flutter after her and her favorite spot was the long walk close to the walls of the Palace. This became known as the Frow walk.

There were occasions when William would walk with her, discussing his plans for building and laying out the gardens; sometimes he even talked of state matters. She cherished these walks and was delighted to have his company, although he slowed her down by hanging on her arm and they made an incongruous pair—she so tall, fat, yet stately, he, small, pulling on her arm so that it seemed she almost had to drag him along while he wheezed uncomfortably, and she was always afraid that an attack of asthma was coming on.

One day he said to her: "Your sister will certainly soon be brought to bed."

"I am expecting it in a week or so," Mary answered.

"Then," went on William, "as the child, if it lives, could be heir to the throne, it should be born under the roof we are occupying at the time. We should be present at the birth."

"It is usual for the heirs to be born at St. James's," began Mary. "Perhaps we should go there."

She thought of the feasting they would have if the child should live and prove healthy. A royal birth should be such a joyous occasion.

But William was frowning. "I do not wish to leave Hampton. The air suits me better than that of London—which I find most obnoxious."

Mary looked contrite as though the contamination of the London air were due to some fault of hers.

"You should invite them to Hampton without delay," commanded William. "The child must be born here."

𝒯*oward the end* of June Anne and George arrived at Hampton Court. Anne was so large that some anxiety was felt for her safety. But she herself was unperturbed. She had already given birth so many times that it seemed to be becoming less of an ordeal, and each time a natural optimism made her certain that the child would be a boy and that this one would live.

Sarah was with her, which did not please the Queen, but Mary was too kind to show her displeasure at such a time. Anne settled comfortably into her apartments and each day would sit and play cards with

Sarah and Lady Fitzharding and others of her ladies, or gossip with them, and look out of the windows at the river or at Mary with her ladies in their Dutch costumes or at Mary herself, like a galleon in full sail with William hanging on to her like a fisherman's barque, as Sarah said.

Anne indulged her fancies, usually for food; and whatever she asked for, Sarah managed to get for her. Mary came to see her and talked tenderly of her health, as though all enmity between them was forgotten.

The first weeks of July passed thus pleasantly and on the twenty-fourth of that month Anne's pains started. Mary came into the apartment and said she would remain until the child was born. William and officials came too, but they retired after an hour or so, when the pains became more frequent.

After a three hour labor Anne's child was born.

There was triumph in the lying-in chamber, for it was a boy.

Mary was almost as delighted as she would have been if the child were her own. She carried him about the apartment, marveling at him, while Anne lay back in bed smiling placidly.

Prince George could not suppress his delight. A son at last—and a son who looked as though he would live! He kept examining the baby's hands and feet and murmuring "Est-il possible? Est-il possible?"

Even William expressed his approval.

Mary said to her husband: "I think he should be called William."

Did Anne approve of the choice of name? Sarah was not in attendance at that moment and she smilingly agreed that she was happy in the choice.

He was to be baptized in the chapel and the King and Queen would proclaim him Duke of Gloucester without delay.

"I feel," said Mary, "that he is *my* own little son."

The sisters smiled at each other; it was as though all misunderstandings had been swept away by this child whom they both adored.

THE ARRIVAL OF
MRS. PACK AND
DEPARTURE OF WILLIAM

There was desperation at Hampton Court, for it appeared that little Gloucester, like his predecessors, was doomed to an early grave.

Mary and Anne would sit together by his cradle watching anxiously.

"Why is it?" cried Anne. "How can life be so cruel? Oh, Mary, I cannot bear it if he should die."

Mary could not answer; she would burst into tears if she attempted to speak and she had to find some way of comforting poor Anne.

"I fancy he is a little better than he was yesterday."

"Do you in truth, sister?"

"I feel it is so."

But she did not; and they both knew she was saying it only to comfort.

Sarah was in the apartment, silently resenting the presence of the Queen. Anne had changed; she had forgotten the quarrels with her sister; and merely because the Queen could gurgle over the baby and prattle besottedly, she was ready to call her "dear sister" again. This state of affairs was *not* going to last, Sarah decided.

Meanwhile the baby did not thrive. He was pitiably thin, would take no nourishment, and lay silent in his cradle.

In the streets they said that it was due to a curse on ungrateful daughters. One was barren and the other, while constantly enduring the pain of childbirth, could only bear children who lived for a week or so.

They were waiting for the announcement of the death of the child.

One morning while Anne and Mary sat with the little boy, who looked more frail than ever, there were sounds of voices outside the apartment.

"I tell you, I will see the Princess."

"You must ask first for an audience."

"It is an urgent matter . . . a matter of life and death . . . for the baby."

The Queen had risen; so had Anne.

Mary threw open the door. "What is this . . . ?" she began, and even as she spoke a big and buxom woman almost pushed her aside and came into the room.

"I wish to see the Princess Anne."

"About my child . . ." began Anne.

The woman looked at her shrewdly and said: "You are she?" Then she strode to the cradle and looked at the child. "And this is the young Prince?"

Mary was beside her. "Who are you and what do you want here?"

"I am a mother," answered the woman, "and I have never lost a child. I have enough milk in my breasts to feed two, and I have only one. I can save that child."

The Queen and the Princess exchanged glances.

"How can you be sure?" asked Mary.

"I will answer to the child's mother and no other."

"You are speaking to the Queen," Anne told her.

"Well, Madam," said the woman, "I am Mrs. Pack—a Quaker woman—and I come to tell you that this child is dying through lack of good milk, of which I have plenty."

The disturbance had brought Prince George into the room. He was pale through lack of sleep for he, with Anne, had been awake for almost the whole of the night watching the baby from time to time and discussing what they might do to save its life.

He looked at the woman, at her pink healthy face and full breasts.

He murmured: "Est-il possible?"

His eyes had begun to shine with tears as he put his arm about his wife. "We cannot afford to miss an opportunity, my dear," he murmured.

"Pick up the child," said Anne, "and see if he will take nourishment from you."

So Mrs. Pack took the Prince in firm yet gentle hands and he did not whimper as he had when other nurses had handled him. She sat on a stool which George had placed for her and undoing her blouse placed the child's lips to her breast.

For a second he whimpered; then he was sucking.

Anne had turned to George who put his arms about her. Mary was weeping silently. Perhaps it was not too late.

At last there was hope.

Mrs. Pack, the Quakeress, had saved the baby's life. He was now taking nourishment regularly and screaming if he did not get it on time.

Anne was delighted; George would gloat over the baby and remind people of how he had looked a little while ago. "Est-il possible?" they would ask him smiling and he would smile with them for he did not know that he was nicknamed "Old Est-il possible."

Mary was so happy, for she told Anne that she looked upon the baby as her adopted son; and Anne at this time was ready to share him. It was so pleasant to be on easy terms with Mary. She even found William tolerable.

As for Mrs. Pack, she was to be treated like a Queen. Nothing anyone could do would be too much for her. The Queen and the Princess could not express their gratitude sufficiently and declared they would never forget what they owed the young Quakeress.

Mrs. Pack cared nothing for rank and she deemed the baby the only person of importance in the nursery; therefore his nurse came before any lady-in-waiting.

It seemed as though there would be trouble when she ordered Sarah away from the baby's cradle.

"If I wish to take up the baby, I shall," said Sarah, her eyes glinting.

"You'll do no such thing," declared Mrs. Pack.

"I think, nurse, you forget yourself."

"It's you who are forgetting that that child is in my charge and in my charge he shall remain."

"My good woman, because you have fed the Duke of Gloucester you imagine yourself of some importance at Court."

"Since what they wanted was this child's life and I gave it to them, *my* good woman, I *am* of some importance at Court."

"Insolence!" cried Sarah.

"You can use your tongue the way you fancy, but keep your hands off my baby."

"I shall report your conduct to the Princess."

"Do what you like; it means nothing to me."

Sarah looked down at the baby and for a moment it seemed as though the two women were going to have a tussle over him. Sarah thought better of that and instead went to find Anne.

"Mrs. Morley," she cried, "that nurse is an intolerable creature."

"You mean our good Mrs. Pack?"

"Good Mrs. Pack! I verily believe she imagines herself worthy to be *crowned* because she happens to feed the Duke of Gloucester."

"I can never be grateful enough to her; nor can Mr. Morley. He was recalling only the other night how sickly our little darling was and saying . . ."

"Est-il possible? I know. But really she is nothing but a wet nurse. We could have found one of those at any time."

"But we couldn't. We tried nurses and none was any good until Mrs. Pack came."

"The Prince will soon be old enough to do without her."

"Mr. Morley and I should be afraid to let her go. We feel she is a sort of talisman."

"She has been very insolent to *me*."

"To my dear Mrs. Freeman? Oh, I am sorry. But remember, she is not exactly a well-bred lady. She is brusque with the Queen who forgives her all because of what she has done for our little darling. And to me also . . . and to Mr. Morley."

"I find it not easy to forgive slights to my dear Mrs. Morley."

Anne smiled. "Have one of these sweetmeats, dear Mrs. Freeman. They are especially sweet. I must send for some more. Now sit down and forget about Mrs. Pack. Tell me something *interesting*."

So she was weary of accusations against that woman. In fact she was on that woman's side . . . against Sarah.

And what could Sarah do about it? It was clear that however much she schemed against Mrs. Pack she would never get her removed because the Queen and Anne believed that the child still needed her.

Sarah Churchill, Countess of Marlborough, insulted by a wet nurse!

And that was not all. The sisters were together again. "Dear Anne, how is my little darling today? I could not rest until I had seen him." "Dear Mary, I am sure he knows you. See how he is smiling?"

Bah!

"Now that you have given them the heir to the throne your allowance should be increased," said Sarah firmly.

"Oh?" murmured Anne.

"It is disgraceful. Here you are at Hampton—dependent on the King and Queen. Should you not have your own establishment? Yet you are asked to live on a *pitiable* sum."

Anne was not listening; she was dreamily reaching for one of the sweetmeats and thinking of going into the nursery and wondering if Mrs. Pack would allow her to hold the Duke of Gloucester for half an hour.

Sarah ground her teeth in anger.

One must be patient, she supposed, but it should not go on.

Because her child was thriving Anne was happy; all she wanted was to talk of him. She and Sarah would chat together of Sarah's children and they decided that when the little Duke of Gloucester was older,

Sarah's son John should be his companion. But Sarah continued to talk of Anne's wrongs and persuaded her that something should be done to right them; consequently with Anne's permission Sarah sounded certain ministers as to methods of increasing Anne's allowance.

When William discovered this he discussed it angrily with the Queen, and Mary went to see her sister to reproach her with her duplicity.

"And I thought that we had become good friends again," complained Mary.

"So did I," replied Anne.

"And all the time you were going behind our backs . . . trying to get more money. Don't you realize how generously you have been treated?"

"There is my son now . . ." pointed out Anne.

"Anne, there is a war in Ireland which is draining our resources."

Anne wiped a tear from her eyes. "A war against our own father," she said.

"This is not the time to go into all that. You must be sensible. We are all together on one side. . . ."

Anne knew vaguely that that was just what Sarah did not want. Anne was not on their side; neither was she on her father's; she was somewhere in between—ready to jump either way, depending on what happened.

"I think I should have the money," she said.

"You are . . . stupid!" cried Mary.

And she left her.

Sarah who had been listening came into the room.

"Congratulations, Mrs. Morley. You dealt admirably with Mrs. Dutch Abortion."

"Oh, Sarah, you'll be the death of me. What a name for her."

"I do not think we should stay here at Hampton Court," went on Sarah. "The Duke of Gloucester, as heir to the throne, should have his own establishment. I was speaking to Lord Craven and he would be delighted to lend his house at Kensington Gravel Pits. It would make an excellent nursery for the Prince because it is a very fine house."

"I must see Lord Craven at once."

"I fancy Mrs. D-A will not be very pleased to have her little darling taken from her, but people who will not oblige us cannot expect to be obliged."

Very shortly afterward the little Duke of Gloucester was set up in his nursery at Kensington Gravel Pits.

While Mary had been worrying about the health of her little nephew and rejoicing at Mrs. Pack's success with him it had been becoming obvious that the conflict between the reigning sovereign and the Jacobites was not going to be easily settled.

The Battle of Bantry Bay had been fought against the French who were supporting the Jacobites and the result had been defeat for the British fleet.

Clarendon had come to William and Mary and begged to be allowed to go to Ireland where he believed he could be of service to them, but Anne had so poisoned her sister's mind against their uncle in her letters that both William and Mary failed to see that the very fact that he had supported James pointed to his loyalty, and regarded him with suspicion.

Clarendon's great desire was to save the Protestant community in Ireland who were in danger of elimination, and much as he disliked William, much as he abhorred the manner in which he—and he blamed him rather than his niece Mary—had treated James, he believed that this was not the time for partisanship. Peace in Ireland was necessary and he was sure that he, as a former Lord Lieutenant, could persuade the present Lord Lieutenant, Lord Tyrconnel, to declare for William.

But William and Mary turned their backs on him and looked about for some other ambassador whom they could trust. They favored Count Hamilton and when John Temple—son of Sir William—who had been made Secretary of War, recommended that Hamilton should be sent to Ireland, he was given the commission instead of Clarendon.

Hamilton was the brother of Frances Jennings's first husband, and Tyrconnel was now that lady's husband; so that the relationship should, it seemed, prove helpful.

The result however turned out to be disastrous, for Hamilton persuaded Tyrconnel to stand firm for James. They had sent the wrong man, but it was too late to alter that now.

The situation in Ireland was worsening; John Temple, having made such an error of judgment in advising the sending of Hamilton, filled his pockets with stones and jumped into the Thames near London Bridge. There was great public interest when his body was found and the reason known.

"We have nothing but ill luck," said the people. "This is the curse of a father on his ungrateful daughter."

"There is only one thing to be done," said William. "I myself must go to Ireland."

The little Duke of Gloucester, although frail, continued to survive. Crowds collected to see him taken out each day in his tiny carriage which had been made especially for him. Four of the smallest horses ever seen had been chosen to draw it; and Prince George's coachman held the reins and drew it along. There were cheers as the baby with his little retinue passed by; and no matter how cold the weather he always went out. Mrs. Pack had brought her children up to face all weathers, so little Gloucester must do the same.

No matter what criticism was thrown at the King and Queen, and even the Princess Anne, royal babies were always assured of public acclaim; and this little one who had survived when so many of his brothers and sisters had failed to get a grasp on life was regarded as something of a phenomenon.

He was a good baby, rather solemn but very interested in everything and at an early age his eyes would light up at the sight of soldiers.

The Queen sent eager inquiries as to his health and there were presents too. Even William was interested in his progress. As for George and Anne they could think of nothing else; and Anne deserted even Sarah that she might be with the baby and marvel at his intelligence.

It was all most irritating to Sarah, and as Marlborough was away she could confide her rage to no one.

This, she thought, is the biggest trial of patience I was ever called upon to endure.

But it would not last. Soon the arrogant Pack would be told to do what her name implied and get out of Court. When she was no use she would soon be forgotten, and Sarah would come into her kingdom once more, ruler supreme of the Princess Anne's household.

Mary was desolate. The thought of William's going away terrified her. She was obsessed by the fear that her father and husband would meet and that one would kill the other.

He talked to her of his plans as they walked about the gardens of Hampton Court. He had bought the Earl of Nottingham's house in Kensington and planned to build a palace there. It seemed astonishing to some that while he was so anxiously thinking of the war he must carry on in Ireland he could at the same time be planning Kensington Palace, but Mary understood that building was his hobby and relaxation and while in his mind he planned the apartments of Kensington Palace and the gardens he would have, he was giving his mind that rest which it needed if he were to succeed in the difficult tasks which lay ahead.

While he was away, the government of the country would be in her hands, he reminded her grimly.

"Oh, William, how can I govern without you?"

"It is something you will have to learn. If you have doubts of yourself the people have none. They have shown clearly that they prefer you to me."

"Only because of their ignorance, dear William. Oh, this is a great tragedy. To be left here alone . . . unable to ask your help!"

"You are a Queen and must perforce shoulder your burdens."

"If you could but stay at home . . ."

"I have stayed too long. Think of Bantry Bay. Of Hamilton and Tyrconnel. Who knows what next."

She thought sadly of the days ahead when she would not have him beside her. Those who saw them smiled at the picture they made. She so large; he so small; and they quoted the lines which had caused so much amusement throughout the country.

Man and wife are all in one, in flesh and in bone,
From hence you may guess what they mean.
The Queen drinks chocolate to make the King fat
And the King hunts to make the Queen lean.

Neither of them knew what was written of them; and if they had they would not greatly have cared.

William saw himself as a great hero, and Mary saw through his eyes.

And all she could think of at this time was that soon she would have to be without him; and he could only turn over in his mind whether it was wiser for him to stay in England than to go to Ireland and settle the Jacobites once and for all. It must be done, he was sure of that; but to do so he must leave the reins of government in the plump white hands of his wife.

How would she fare without him? And even if he settled affairs in Ireland, what would happen in England during his absence?

Gilbert Burnet, Bishop of Salisbury, that staunch supporter of William and Mary who had enjoyed their hospitality in Holland before they had come to England and had so often given them the benefit of his wisdom, now called on the King and Queen.

The interview was for the three of them alone and as Mary greeted him there were tears in her eyes for the occasion recalled those happy ones in Holland when she and Burnet had chatted together, while she knotted her fringe close to the candles the better to see, and William sat a little apart listening to their conversation. Such happy days! thought Mary. Never perhaps to be equaled, for in those days her father had been King of England and although they had talked of deposing him, until the deed was accomplished the guilt did not have to be so acutely suffered.

"What I have to say is for our ears alone," said Burnet, speaking lower than was his custom. "It must not go beyond these walls."

"Speak on," commanded William.

"There will never be peace while Ireland stands against us," went on Burnet. "And when I think of the Protestants there I feel very melancholy. That is why I am bringing this to the attention of Your Majesties. A certain captain has approached me and I promised I would tell you what he suggests. He is a true and loyal subject. That I can vouch for."

William nodded and Mary found that her heart was beating so fast that she feared it would be heard.

"What is his suggestion?" asked William coolly.

"That he takes a ship to Ireland. Aboard her will be men whom we can trust. They would have to be very carefully selected. No more Hamiltons. They will sail to Ireland and when they reach Dublin will declare for James. The captain will invite him aboard. He would go, not suspecting a trap . . ."

Mary gave an exclamation of dismay which made Burnet halt and William frown at her.

"Pray go on," said William testily.

"When he is aboard, the ship sets sail and James is taken away from Ireland."

"Where to?" demanded Mary sharply.

"To Spain perhaps."

"And then?" said Mary.

"Then, Your Majesty, he would be put ashore with say twenty thousand pounds."

William shook his head.

"Oh, William!" murmured Mary, and there was a sob in her voice.

"Your Majesty does not like the plan?" said Burnet.

"James was a misguided man, but he was a King and is my father-in-law. I could not agree to this."

Burnet nodded slowly. "I understand, Your Majesty. I merely thought that to end this miserable war . . . to save lives and money and to restore the peace . . ."

"There is much in what you say," said William. "I think the plan might well succeed. But I want no hand in treachery."

"There was no harm to the King intended," said Burnet.

"Picture it," interrupted William. "James stepping aboard—perhaps with a few attendants. When he realized that he was to be a prisoner he would attempt to escape. What if he were killed in the struggle? No, no. I like that not."

"I see that the scheme would not fit in with Your Majesty's honor."

"That is what I feel."

"Then I will tell this captain of Your Majesty's decision."

"Yes," said William. "But send him to me for I would compliment him. Although it is a plan I do not wish to follow yet this captain is a man who should be thanked for his services. Clearly he wishes to serve us well."

"I will send him to Your Majesty."

"Pray do so quickly, for soon I shall have little time to spare as the day of my departure grows nearer."

When Burnet had left them Mary threw herself on to her knees and taking William's hand kissed it.

William, who disliked dramatics, looked at her with distaste, but she did not notice, for her eyes were blinded with tears.

"William," she cried, "it is small wonder that I adore you. You are the noblest man alive. Oh, how fortunate is my father that it is you who stand against him. Who else would have been so good and honorable as to reject such a proposition. We were right to come here. England needed you, William. Oh, how happy this has made me."

"Get up," said William. "You are too large to grope on the floor."

She rose abashed and he looked at her sardonically.

"Spain!" he muttered. "Twenty thousand pounds! What nonsense! He should be delivered to the Dutch sailors. They will remember how often he has fought against them." William almost smiled as he said softly, "Yes, to the Dutch sailors, to be disposed of as they think proper."

Mary stared at him in horror, but he scarcely seemed to see her; he had seated himself at the table and begun to write.

William was on the point of departure. He was disappointed for the scheme to abduct James had come to nothing. James was too wary to be caught like that. He was evidently full of hope, for the campaign was going in his favor so far. The French were behind him as the battle of Bantry Bay had shown; but for the fact that he was sick in body for he was no longer young, and sick at heart because of the defection of the daughters he had loved, he would have been a very much more formidable adversary.

The Duke of Schomberg, William's friend and favorite, had been sent to Ireland with a small army, inadequately armed, and inadequately fed; whereas James had one hundred thousand Irish Catholics behind him.

It had been decided that Prince George should accompany William to Ireland, and this pleased Anne, although she was constantly declaring how much she would miss her husband. Sarah and she discussed the campaign. Marlborough had returned to London yet he was not to go to Ireland, but would remain in England as a member of Mary's Advisory Council and to be in command of the remnants of the army which would remain behind.

Sarah was pleased to have him at hand; and at the same time saw a further means of fermenting more trouble between Anne and Mary.

"Mr. Morley should have a high command in the Army," she said. "Why, he should take precedence over everyone—under the King; and he should accompany William wherever he goes. It is his due."

"It is, but I do not believe these privileges will be granted him."

"Oh, no! Caliban will be surrounded by Dutchmen. You mark my words. Unless of course the King's duty is pointed out to him."

"Who would do that?"

"The Queen of course."

"Do you think she would?"

"Dear Mrs. Morley, it is her duty, and if this were pointed out to her, she might well realize it."

So there was a further estrangement between the sisters.

George to have a position of trust! cried William. Were they mad. Of what use was George to any campaign but to provide light relief with his perpetual bleating: "Est-il possible?"

Anne was sulky and refused to speak to the Queen except in public. Sarah looked on, amused.

The day of William's departure came.

Mary wept openly.

"You must take the greatest care of yourself," she cried. "I fear the climate. They say it is very damp. It will be bad for your chest. I shall pray for you . . ."

"Pray rather for yourself," suggested William. "You will need prayers, for you have a mighty task before you."

"Oh, William, is it too late to beg you to stay behind?"

"Too late and quite foolish," said William, but not unkindly for it pleased him to see her distress. "Going into a campaign is no unpleasant thing compared with governing this country, I do assure you. I pity you. Indeed I pity you."

"William!" she threw herself into his arms and he kissed her almost gently.

He had an affection for her which increased as he grew older.

"Those who have some regard for you must help you all they can. I must speak to them . . . impress on them . . . the difficulties of your task."

"William, I trust I shall act as you would have acted. That is what I shall try to do."

"I am sure you will govern wisely."

She was overcome with joy at such praise and almost immediately plunged into despair because of his departure.

"You will guard your dear person well, William. You will not expose yourself to danger. I trust that you . . . and my father . . . will never come face to face."

"Pray for it," he said.

BEACHY HEAD

AND THE BOYNE

On the morning after William's departure Mary awoke with a swollen face.

She called for a mirror and looked at herself with dismay. Her expression was dismal; she had a feeling of foreboding. William gone and herself swollen-faced and inadequate without him! She lay back on her pillows carefully touching her face. She hoped it did not mean a return of the ague. She must not, however, brood on her affliction, but call a meeting of the Council at once; and she would have to impress them with her knowledge of affairs; William had been so kind lately and had talked to her so carefully that she had a good grasp of what was going on. Dear William, he had been really concerned on her behalf. People did not understand that beneath that rather harsh exterior was great kindliness.

He is a great good man, the best in the world, she assured herself. And I must be worthy of him. That was what alarmed her—consciousness of her own unworthiness.

She thought of her nine councillors and wished that Shrewsbury was among them. Charming Shrewsbury, with the gentle voice and the noble

air, reminded her of Monmouth; not that they were alike, but Shrewsbury was attractive, as Jemmy had been, and there was not one of the nine
councillors whom she could really like. Four of them were Whigs and
five Tories. How clever of William to assure a good division!

She would speak to them earnestly and sincerely and she would pray
that no situation arose which would be too difficult for her to handle.

When the Countess of Derby came to her she exclaimed with horror
at the sight of the Queen's face.

"But Your Majesty is ill."

"It will pass," replied Mary.

"I must call the doctors while you rest in bed."

"My dear friend," insisted Mary firmly, "I cannot lie abed now. The
King is on his way to Ireland and I have the sole responsibility of ruling
in his absence. Why do you not know that almost always *he* is in pain. Do
you not know that he is fighting a battle for his breath most of the time,
but does he stay in bed? Does he complain?"

The Countess did not reply.

"There is one thing I know I have to do," went on Mary, "and that
is follow his example. Then I cannot fail."

"I am sure no one ever performed royal duties more graciously than
Your Majesty."

Mary smiled a little sadly. She understood the implication. It was
most perverse of those about her continually to defend her against
William.

"Graciousness is not a necessary part of greatness," she reproved
gently.

And the Countess of Derby in sudden affection kissed her hand. She
wanted to say that it was an asset when a sovereign knew how to win the
love of the people. Mary had that asset—William never could.

"The first thing I shall do is to pray for the King's safety and success," said Mary. "And then that I may have the help I shall surely need."

The Council meeting was held in Nottingham's apartments in
Whitehall. Mary sat at the head of the table with the nine members of

the Council about her; the five Tories were Marlborough, Danby, Nottingham, Pembroke, and Lowther; and the four Whigs Dorset and Devonshire, Mordaunt and Russell.

They expressed their concern at the Queen's appearance and she replied that she believed the swelling to have little significance.

"The King worked with greater disadvantages," she told them smiling.

The Earl of Devonshire said that the strain of the last days had been great, and if Her Majesty wished to retire to bed they would work without her and have sent to her bedchamber any important documents which she would wish to see.

His voice was caressing. Devonshire was a courtier for ladies, she mentally commented; she considered him weak and unfit for the post he now held.

"I shall remain," she told him pleasantly, "and I pray you cease to think about this ailment, which I know to be trivial."

There was a touch of command in her voice which they were quick to note; Mary without William was a different woman from Mary with him. She had become a Queen overnight—not merely William's shadow.

"We must be doubly alert now," she said. "I trust that we are on the watch for a move which might come from France. Now that the King is away we should be very vulnerable."

"The King in his wisdom has not taken all his best men, Your Majesty. We are few who remain but some of us do not lack experience."

That was Mordaunt. She had never liked him, but thought him a little mad. He had visited William in Holland before the revolution and had declared himself willing to help rescue England from popery. He had put forward several plans for William to study. William had laughed at most of them and had said to Mary and Burnet: "This fellow wants to be at the heart of all the adventures which are planned not for the establishment of the Protestant religion in England but for the glorification of Mordaunt. Such a man would be setting himself up as King before long, I'll swear."

Marlborough was nodding approval of this speech. Marlborough, Sarah's husband. The one she trusted least of all. How much was he in league with his wife to turn Anne against her and William? What was their idea? To rid themselves of William and Mary and set up Anne—as

William and Mary had made away with James—that they might be the powers behind the throne?

He was a handsome man, this Marlborough—his features clearly cut; his eyes alert, his voice soft and gentle—very different from the somewhat strident tones of his wife—but of all these men who had been chosen for her councillors, Marlborough was the one of whom she must be most watchful.

"What we should look for," said Marlborough, "is an attack from the French. They might well seize this opportunity while the King's army is in Ireland."

"Torrington will look after *them*," said Nottingham complacently.

Mary glanced sharply at him. She was uncertain of Nottingham and had heard that he was a secret Jacobite. He certainly had a sinister look; was it because he was as dark as a Spaniard? He was aloof and his expression was melancholy; it was no wonder that he was nicknamed Don Dismallo.

"I believe the Earl of Torrington to be a good admiral and an experienced one, but I believe too that he is over-fond of soft living," growled Danby.

Danby! thought Mary. He was growing old now; he looked almost like a corpse already; but he was experienced and he was one of the few around that table on whom she felt she could rely. Russell, Pembroke, and Lowther were decent men, she believed; but they were insignificant compared with eccentrics like Mordaunt and self-seekers like Marlborough.

"We will hope for a quick success in Ireland," said Mary, "and a speedy return of the King. Now let us get to work."

They were deep in discussion when a messenger arrived and because of the nature of the news he brought was taken immediately to the council chamber.

The French fleet had been sighted off Plymouth.

William on his way to Ireland! The French Fleet on its way to attack! And all about her men whom she was not sure she could trust. Within a few hours of taking her place as ruler—which William had never allowed her to do before—Mary was confronted with this dangerous situation.

Whom could she trust among all these people around her? Yet she must succeed for William's sake. She would never be able to face him if she failed now. She must be suspicious of everyone.

She heard that her uncle Charles's widow, Catherine, had refused to allow prayers for William's safety to be said in her chapel. Therefore Catherine, a Catholic from birth, was suspect. What plots went on in her apartments? Her Chamberlain Feversham was a Frenchman, and the French were enemies.

Feversham was reprimanded. Oh, how easy it was to strike terror into the hearts of these people! In tears he assured her that he planned no harm to her or to William.

"Yet you said no prayers for the King's safety," retorted Mary. "I might forgive you for your insults to me, but I cannot forgive those to the King, who has sacrificed his health for this country."

Catherine herself came and made tender inquiries as to the swelling of Mary's face; it was difficult to believe that this gentle lady was an intrigant. She was getting old now and she had never been a fighter.

Mary accepted her condolences; but gave orders that she should be closely watched.

Her uncle, the Earl of Clarendon, was sent to the Tower. He was less self-seeking than many, she knew, but he had never approved of the revolution. He was a stern Protestant; but he had made his vows to James and he was not a man to easily break vows. She knew that he was the man of honor; but men of honor were as ready as others to make trouble if they believed they were in the right.

She had no wish to send her uncle to the Tower; but she must act as William would act if he were here; always she must think of William and do that which would win his approval.

She wote to William, assuring him of her devotion telling him of the danger. She trusted that she was acting as he would wish, which it was her intention to do at all times.

The news grew more alarming. The French fleet, consisting of over two hundred ships, was lying off the south coast.

Arthur Herbert, Lord Torrington, was dismayed. He was a man who, while a good sailor, loved his pleasure so much that in this age of parodying he had quickly earned the name of Lord Tarry-in-Town.

Some months before he had foreseen an attack by the French and believing himself inadequately prepared to meet it, had written to Nottingham begging for reinforcements, but Nottingham had merely replied that he need have no fear for he would be strong enough for the French.

He had replied then: "I am afraid now in winter while the danger may be remedied, and you will be afraid in summer when it is past remedy."

Well now it was summer; and if Nottingham cared for the good of his country he must be taking Torrington's words to heart.

The Battle of Bantry Bay had been a defeat; Torrington wanted at all costs to avoid another—and here were the French . . . waiting for the moment to open the battle.

"And here are we," cried Torrington, "unprepared. I will not go into battle against them."

But even as he made this declaration he received a note from the Queen, reminding him that he had a Dutch squadron at his disposal under Admiral Evertzen, and commanding him to go into action without delay.

Torrington disobeyed the order, because he believed to act on it would mean crushing defeat.

Around the Council table Mary presided. She felt ill yet stimulated at the thought of danger; she was facing a great crisis and William was not near to advise. She must succeed.

Nottingham was saying that Torrington had deliberately ignored orders, and that the French were still off the south coast though the battle had not yet begun. Torrington had done nothing, in spite of orders.

"This is mutinous," cried Mordaunt.

"He should be court-martialed," growled Danby.

"At this stage," Mary intervened, "we should only be adding to our danger by a court-martial in such a high quarter. How do we know what effect this might have!"

Marlborough supported her in this.

"I will go to Portsmouth," suggested Mordaunt. "There I will board the flagship, arrest Torrington and myself lead the fleet."

Mary looked at him with a hint of scorn. How like Mordaunt to plan an action with himself as the hero set for glory!

"Impossible," she said coldly.

Nottingham put in: "Before he left, the King commanded me to take command if Torrington should prove unfit."

Mordaunt glared at Nottingham.

"My lord, would that be wise?"

"And why should you believe that you could lead the fleet to victory and I fail?"

Heaven help me, thought Mary, they are vying with each other for power. What good will this do us? We must all stand together.

"The King gave me no instructions that you should leave for the fleet, my lord," she told Nottingham. "And I could not allow it. You are needed too badly here."

Nottingham was mollified and graciously thanked Her Majesty for her compliments.

"Who then should go?" asked Danby sharply; and she saw the gleam in his eyes. Is he too looking for naval glory, wondered Mary, at his time of life?

"I need you all here," she said after a moment's hesitation. "I shall send a dispatch to Lord Torrington immediately telling him that I *order* him to attack."

She was exhausted. If only William were here! It was not that she feared herself inadequate to deal with the situation, only that William might disapprove of what she had done. How could she know what he would do in similar circumstances?

Her women were helping her to bed and she was silent, which was unusual for her. Usually she liked to chat for, to her, talking was one of the pleasures of life and since she was never able to indulge in it to any great extent with William she did so whenever possible with everyone else.

"Your Majesty's face is slightly less swollen," said the Countess of Derby.

"Do you think so? I fancy it is less painful."

Then silence. They were thinking of the change in her, for they had been hoping that once William was away there would be a little gaiety at Court. Dances perhaps, visits to the play; perhaps little jaunts to some of the houses in the bazaars.

But this was quite different. William's absence had made of Mary a Queen with solemn duties.

Even at such an hour there was no respite. A messenger was at the door now with an urgent letter for the Queen.

Mary seized it and began to tremble as she read that the French were occupying the coast of the Isle of Wight.

The Council meeting was stormy.

What had Torrington done? Nothing! He ignored the Council in London, replying that his council upon the spot did not advise action as yet.

Devonshire was demanding action. "Does Torrington realize that the fate of three kingdoms is in his hands? Torrington must be replaced."

"Make him a prisoner," cried Russell.

"No, no," interjected Marlborough. "That would please the enemy too much and put heart into them."

Mordaunt said: "Let me go to him. I will engage the Frenchmen and drive them off . . . or die in the attempt."

That someone should go was finally agreed by the Council and Mordaunt and Russell left.

In the privacy of her own apartment Mary awaited news with trepidation, feeling that disaster was very close indeed. She was unsure, and could only pray that the actions she took were the right ones.

She did not trust Mordaunt and wondered what he would do when he reached Torrington. Russell was the most outspoken of the ministers; he was coarse and crude but she believed trustworthy; and trustworthiness was a very desirable quality at such a time.

She could only find comfort in writing to William to tell him that she faced dire trouble at home as doubtless he did in Ireland. But she was far more anxious, she would have him know, for his dear person than for her own poor carcass.

"I can say nothing, but pray to God for you, and my impatience for a letter from you is as great as my love, which will not end but with my life."

Before Mordaunt and Russell set out Mary had sent an order to Torrington to engage the enemy; and this he did, in his own way, before it was possible for the two ministers to reach him.

He attacked; or at least commanded the Dutch to do so, and this they did valiantly, but were so outnumbered that they could not hope for success. Many ships were disabled and Torrington's contribution was to leave the Dutch to the enemy while he towed the damaged ships to the Thames mouth in order to blockade it.

There was utter defeat. The navy—Britain's pride—had let her down shamefully; and England lay at the mercy of the invader. The French were at her coast. Torrington was locked up with the fleet in the estuary of the Thames; and while the King was in Ireland the Jacobites, who may well have been waiting for this opportunity, could now rise—and who knew who would support them?—and bring back James.

Marlborough, thank God, was at hand. He could, better than any man, protect his country should an invasion be attempted—if he would. But what of Marlborough, who could, Mary was sure, jump this way and that with agility? It would depend of course on which attitude would best serve Marlborough.

She felt that she had reached the very depth of despair, but two events, following closely on one another, brought fresh hope; and she believed them to be an answer to her prayer.

She was in her apartments writing a letter to William—for her only solace was in writing to him—when the Countess of Derby came to tell her that the Earl of Shrewsbury was asking to see her.

As Charles Talbot, Earl of Shrewsbury came into the room, Mary's spirits lifted. He would have been extremely handsome—perhaps the handsomest man at Court, now Monmouth was gone—but for a blemish in one eye. Even so, he had been called "The King of Hearts"; it was said that women loved him on sight, but he had never taken advantage of that, being gentle and retiring. He would be faithful, Mary was sure, to a woman . . . or a cause.

His character had begun to show in his face for he was almost thirty now; gentleness blended well with the features which could almost be called beautiful; delicacy was there; his enemies might call it nervousness.

He did not enjoy good health, and this was the reason he had not been a member of the Council. Strange that an old man like Danby clung to office; and a young one like Shrewsbury pleaded ill health in order to stay out of it.

They had been children together for he was only a few years older than Mary, but there was a stronger bond than age and similar environment between them. When Mary had been a child she had constantly heard scandals about her father's affairs with women and there was one— the case of Margaret Denham whose husband had murdered her because of her association with James—which had shocked her deeply. Shrewsbury had suffered a similar shock when his mother's lover, the Duke of Buckingham had killed his father in a duel because of his mother; and then created a scandal by living openly with her.

Both Shrewsbury and Mary had been deeply affected by the adulterous intrigues of their parents. Mary had sought companions of her own sex until marriage with William had made her build up an ideal so that she convinced herself that she adored her husband. Shrewsbury wanted to shrink from the world of intrigue and responsibility, which was difficult for a man in his position. He had become abnormally interested in his health and whenever a situation from which he flinched arose he would invariably become ill and make this the excuse of his retirement from it.

This was what had happened when William announced his intention of leaving England for Ireland. Shrewsbury, contemplating those who would have been his fellow councillors, had no wish to be in office; and to the chagrin of William and the disappointment of Mary he had pleaded "the comfortless prospect of very ill health."

And now here he was, looking serious but determined; and the most attractive man Mary had seen—since she last saw him.

"Charles!" she cried affectionately.

He knelt. "Your Majesty."

"Rise and welcome. I am pleased to see you. You are in better health?"

"Your Majesty, I could not lie abed while you are in such straits. I have come to offer you my services in whatever capacity you wish to use them."

She began to smile; she was beautiful when animated and as the strain of the last days dropped from her she was young again.

"That makes me very happy," she said. "I have great need of friends whom I can trust."

Meanwhile William had arrived in Ireland. He was more melancholy than usual, for the climate did not suit his health, being even more damp than that of England. He said grimly to the Earl of Portland, who had been Bentinck, that he would give much to be back in London, even Whitehall; and having tested this climate he wondered why he had ever cursed the other.

Portland replied that he must guard his health; it was all important that he should not be sick at this juncture.

William nodded grimly; his hemorrhoids were very painful after so many hours in the saddle, but riding was good for his asthma—or would have been in a better climate.

"You should rest more frequently," chided Portland.

"There is no time for resting. You know that well, Bentinck. We must go with all speed to Belfast to take over from Schomberg. How long do you think the army can hold out with inadequate food, and with all the disease there is among them? What do you think they are saying of a King who stays in London while they fight his battles for him. They may not like me—these English; but to see me here, fighting with them, one of them, will put heart into them, I promise you."

Portland smiled at him affectionately. Many would be astonished that William could be almost garrulous in his company when he merely snapped out a word or two with almost everyone else.

"You will do it," he said. "More than that you'll conquer Ireland."

"I have to. If not, James will be back in England. There are many who won't have him and many who will. That will mean bloodshed, Bentinck. We don't want it. That is why I have come to Ireland to stop his chances of ever making a bridgehead from here to England. I may die in the attempt, but at least I am going to put everything I have into driving him right off this island."

He began to cough and hastily put a kerchief to his mouth. He tried to hide it, but not before Portland had seen the blood. Portland snatched it from him and anger blazed from his eyes.

"Again?" he demanded.

"Come," said William lightly, "you forget your manners, Portland."

Portland looked at him, and the anger was there to hide the tears. All the love which was between them was visible in that moment and neither attempted to hide it, for it would have been useless. This was Bentinck, the friend of boyhood who would be the friend until death; who had nursed his Prince through small pox and caught the disease himself by sleeping in his bed in the hope that he would divert something from the Prince to himself, as he might have stood between him and an attacking lion.

Portland wished he had not shown petulant jealousy of young Keppel whom William had favored more and more since Elizabeth Villiers had asked for a place for the boy; William wished he had not often neglected Portland for the young page.

"I shall insist that you rest before going on. You must at least do that."

"Dear Bentinck," said William softly, "I shall insist that there be no delay. Do not grieve for my ailments. God, man, they have been with me all my life. When I was in my cradle they despaired of my life; but I kept it. Those who loved me have been despairing since while those who hate me have been hoping; but I'm not going yet. I have decided to stay alive."

He leaned forward and touched Bentinck's hand.

Again they looked at each other, defenses down. For as long as they lived there would be love between them. Bentinck knew it; William knew it.

It must be for a long time, prayed Bentinck.

Ulster was shouting its joy and relief.

He was a little man with a long hooked nose dominating a pale face; he was without personal attractiveness; he suffered from undignified illnesses; he was ungracious in manner; but when he was conducting a campaign he was a great leader; and these men who were so in need of inspiration saw in William that nobility which Mary had discovered and which had made her accept her marriage as an ideal one.

At Loughbrickland, William concentrated his troops; and from there they marched south with him at their head.

And they sang as they went; and their feet kept time with the music; and their eyes were on that small but inspiring figure on horseback whom they were certain could lead them to victory.

"Lilliburlero bullen a la!" they sang.

In battle he was intrepid; because his body had always served him ill he treated it to a certain amount of contempt. Death had no terror for him. Bentinck scolded that he took unnecessary risks; but he only shrugged his shoulders and continued to take them. He was not a man to enjoy life so wholeheartedly that he held it dear, he said; and he had not come to Ireland to let the grass grow under his feet; he was going to settle this matter once and for all.

He was growing more and more certain of success.

"They have some good Frenchmen on the other side," he told Portland, "but they are few and the majority of James's army are Irish who are untrained and too emotional. We'll have them running never fear."

By evening they had come to the River Boyne on the opposite bank of which Lauzun, the French commander, had taken up his stand. His position was strong; he had made entrenchments and he had the river between him and the enemy.

Schomberg was worried, believing that they should wait before attacking, but William wanted to go quickly ahead into battle.

They rested for the night and the next morning as William breakfasted on the bank some Irish sentries saw him, and guessing him to be an important personage fired at him and his party.

One man and two horses were killed. In dismay William's friends closed about him but not before a shot had grazed his right shoulder blade.

Portland was beside him, white faced and trembling.

"My time has not yet come," William assured him. "This must be dressed quickly, for I am in a hurry."

The wound was dressed and when Portland anxiously inquired if it were painful William retorted: "I have suffered much pain in my life, I can endure a little more."

"Postpone the battle. Rest awhile. Schomberg feels we should not go into action yet."

"Battles are rarely won by postponement, Bentinck. We have the superior force. Let us use it now before the enemy have time to strengthen themselves."

As soon as his wound was dressed he mounted his horse and for the rest of the day went about his affairs as though nothing had happened. He was determined that everything should be ready for battle the next day.

That evening at nine o'clock he called together his generals and there was a council of war. His plan was to cross the river the next day and attack. There was opposition but he overruled it, and as soon as day broke on that 1st of July Schomberg with Portland beside him made a crossing of the river and at Slane Bridge they found a regiment of Irish guards whom they quickly beat. Lauzun had placed his own countrymen at the Pass of Duleek to prevent the right wing of the English army making a crossing; so the left and center of the force had only to face Irish Catholics.

As William made the crossing he called to his men to remember they were fighting for the Protestant religion: and they plunged into fierce battle.

The Irish went down before them. Schomberg fell, fired at in mistake by one of his own men; but William fought on; and James, who was watching from the Hill of Donore began to understand that this son-in-law whom he disliked was one of the greatest generals of his day; and that though courtiers might turn shuddering from him, soldiers rallied to him and fought as they would only for a great leader.

"Your Majesty." It was a voice at his elbow and he knew what would be said before the words were spoken.

"It is time?" asked James.

"There is not a moment to be lost," was the answer.

James turned away; he had lost the battle; now it remained to save his life.

His horse was waiting.

"To Dublin, Your Majesty."

"To Dublin," he repeated.

He took one last look at the battlefield. The bitter truth was becoming clearer with every moment.

The Battle of the Boyne would soon be over, with victory for the Orangemen.

It was more than a bloody battle; it could be the end of hope. William of Orange was in Ireland to drive out James II and he would not rest until he had done it.

The only hope now was help from France.

But first he must think of preserving his life.

$\mathcal{S}$*hrewsbury at her* side; William victorious in the decisive battle of the Boyne; James fled to Dublin and to France!

"Thank God," prayed Mary, "he is safe. Thank God they are both safe." If her father would stay in France and live there peacefully; if William would come and take over the task of troublesome government. But that would come, for the tide had changed.

William was no longer in danger from battle; but what of his health? Portland was there to look after him and she trusted Portland to do that well, although often she had been hurt because he had seemed to think it was a duty better performed by him than a wife.

Torrington had been recalled to face eventual court-martial and there was the task of appointing a new Admiral which no one was going to agree about. Perhaps the greatest piece of good luck of all was the stupidity of the French who, after the Battle of Beachy Head, having England at their mercy, could have landed and did not. Marlborough would have done his best to deal with them when they did, but the pick of the army was in Ireland and even the brilliant generalship of Marlborough could not achieve success without soldiers.

Invasion of England had always terrified the foreigner; it was believed to be well-nigh impossible, because the English had special protection from Providence; they had never been invaded. Somewhere deep down in the heart of every invading force was the fear that it never would be.

The French Admiral Tourville procrastinated. Anchored off Torbay he sent a small experimental force to Teignmouth. The little village was sacked and from his flagship, Tourville contemplated the flames with satisfaction. There were many Catholics in England, and he imagined that now he was at hand they would be ready to rise against the new rulers and stand for James, and make his landing easy.

But his soldiers had burned the church, and the men of Devon, shocked that their navy had failed to protect them, were incensed because an enemy had dared set foot on their land.

All other grievances were forgotten. If foreigners were attempting to land in England there was only one enemy. Whether James or William and Mary should rule was a matter to be settled internally. But foreigners must always be shown that England belonged to the English and no hostile foot should ever be allowed to set itself there unbidden.

Never mind the "Squeezing of the Orange" or drinking to the King over the Water now. It was: Curse the invader. We'll show him what he can expect if he sets foot on Devon shores!

The whole of the West Country was rising against the Frenchmen. Bonfires were seen along the coast; the men of the West were ready and waiting.

It was true, Tourville realized; they were unbeatable. A small success at sea did not mean that the land could be conquered.

He had had that success; was it going to be forgotten in the ignoble failure of attempting the impossible?

Tourville was certain there was only one action to take; he took it and sailed back to France.

It was imperative that Torrington should be dismissed his command, and two names were put forward as his successors. These were Sir John Ashby and Sir Richard Haddock, both excellent men of wide experience and well capable of taking command of the Navy.

Mary had believed that the affair could be quickly settled, but she had forgotten the jealousy of those about her. The Admiralty was incensed because it had not been consulted. Why should the Cabinet decide who should command the Navy? Was it not the prerogative of the Admiralty?

The Cabinet said that they, with the Admiralty, should discuss the matter, but the Admiralty wanted no easy solution. The Queen had discussed the matter originally with the Cabinet; so why, when the Admiralty was represented, should she be absent?

Mary, angered by the pettiness of all this, refused to see them and Lord Lincoln, one of the Privy councillors, came bursting into her apartment, acting, as she said, like a madman, shouting at her, demanding this and that. She ordered him out; but weary of the ridiculous conflict agreed to make an appearance at the meeting.

It was a stormy meeting. The Admiralty rejected Haddock and Ashby, not on their merits, for they could find no fault with their records, but simply because they had been chosen by the Cabinet.

It was Russell who suggested that the two men should share the responsibility with a third man of quality whom they could all trust. The Earl of Shrewsbury was now recovered in health and he was a man of whom they all had a high opinion.

This pleased Mary, for if Shrewsbury held a high command she would feel that she had someone in an important place on whom she could rely.

Her suggestion was that Haddock and Ashby be given command and that William should name a man of his choice to stand with them. She was certain that William would choose Shrewsbury for he had been as sorry as she was when the Earl had retired from public life.

Sir Thomas Lee answered her curtly that he and his Commission would make the choice. "We refuse," he added, "to accept Haddock."

"It would seem," said Mary, who was always stung to action by any criticism of William, "that the King has given away his power and cannot make an Admiral whom the Admiralty do not like."

"No," snapped Lee. "He cannot."

The entire company was shocked by this outburst and Danby immediately closed the meeting.

Danby now showed his strength and advised that if the Queen insisted on the nomination of Haddock who was the best man for the job, her ministers would see that her commands were obeyed.

"Your Majesty," pointed out Danby, "not one criticism have they been able to raise against Haddock. Their only reason for refusing him is that they did not choose him."

Mary replied: "I am very angry with Lee—at the manner in which he spoke of the King. I have rarely been so angry. Yes, Haddock shall be appointed and Ashby with him."

The Admiralty, themselves shocked by Lee's outburst, now saw that they would have to accept Haddock and Ashby; and the names which were put forward as the man of quality who should assist them were four in all: Shrewsbury, Russell, the Duke of Grafton, and Henry Killigrew.

Russell would not leave the Cabinet, so it was a choice between the other three. Grafton had a reputation as a sadist and seamen would not wish to serve under him. Henry Killigrew was suspected of being a Jacobite, and Shrewsbury was the Queen's man.

The Admiralty preferred to choose Killigrew; and with Ashby and Haddock he was given command.

Shrewsbury, who had hoped to receive the command immediately became ill when he had heard that it had been given to Killigrew.

He came to the Queen—his face set into lines of resignation.

"I came out of my retirement too quickly," he told her. "I fear I must go at once to Tunbridge Wells."

Mary was desolate; but clearly the charming Earl must consider his health.

This was a time of waiting for Sarah—always so irksome. John was in England and for that she was thankful. How she enjoyed those occasions when they could be alone together, planning, always planning for the grand future which lay ahead. He did not always agree with her and there were frequent quarrels, but he was as ambitous as she was, and they were working toward the same goal, although they did not always want to take the same road. He told her that she was too domineering, that she made too many enemies; she retorted that he wasted time on attempted diplomacy. But they always made up their quarrels; they knew they were bound together for the glory of the Marlboroughs. If he could get command of the Army and she could get command of the Queen—which Anne would be one day—they would be for all important purposes King and Queen of England. It was a wonderfully exhilarating prospect and worth a lifetime's plotting, planning, and occasional disagreements.

Marlborough was almost hoping for an invasion of England that would give him an opportunity to show his skill. He had hoped that it might happen because there had been rebellions in Deal and Rye, and as far north as Berwick. Scotland was always suspected of being firmly behind the Stuarts and therefore for James against William. But French folly in making the hit and run attack on Teignmouth had quelled all thoughts of rebellion against William and Mary because of a need to stand against England's enemy: France.

They must wait in patience, said Marlborough; but patience was not one of Sarah's virtues.

She looked about for some light diversion and found one.

She was playing cards with Anne and a few of the Princess's women when they began to discuss the effects of the victory in Ireland.

Sarah commented that this would probably mean that there were estates in Ireland which would come to the King's faithful supporters. Then she noticed that Lady Fitzharding was looking a little smug.

Sarah could guess what this meant.

It was an astonishing thing that Elizabeth Villiers should have received so little from the King. She supposed it was because he hoped to keep his relationship with her secret. What a fool Elizabeth was not to feather her nest while she had the chance. Little Hook-Nose was not going to last forever, and if she could believe her spies, which she could for they would not dare deceive *her*, he was spitting blood. And what would Elizabeth Villiers have when he was gone? Would Queen Mary offer a pension to the lady who had served her husband so well?

Sarah snorted with amusement.

Impatiently she played her cards, bringing the game to an early end; then she sought an opportunity of cornering Barbara Fitzharding.

"It would not surprise me," she said, "if your sister did well out of this Irish business."

Barbara's lips closed quite perceptibly tighter.

Does she think I'm blind! thought Sarah.

"Well," said Sarah, "have you lost your tongue?"

"His Majesty has not taken me into his confidence," replied Barbara.

"I didn't think His Majesty had. But it's no use pretending your sister isn't his mistress when we all know it. I think she'd be a fool not to get what she can out of Ireland and I don't think she's all that much of a fool."

"I agree with you on that. I do not think my sister is a fool either."

"She will be rich in a short time. It wouldn't surprise me if the Earl of Portland has his picking."

"It may well be," answered Barbara.

May well be! thought Sarah. It is.

She told Anne about this. "It is quite funny. That Dutch Abortion. Such a clever general, my dear! Why wasn't Marlborough sent to Ireland? He would have settled them long ere this. No, Caliban must go! He must be the great hero."

"They say he is a great soldier."

"Great soldier indeed. Ha! Great soldier and great lover! Do you know he has the Irish estates to dispose of now? He is going to shower them on . . . whom do you think? Two guesses, Mrs. Morley. I should have thought he was neuter. But he teeters half one way half the other. There is Betty Squint-Eye on one side and his dear Bentinck on the other, with Keppel waiting for his turn. It will be pickings for Betty and Bentinck."

"My sister will not be pleased," said Anne.

"They hope to keep it secret from her. *I* think she should be told. After all, think to what good use she could put the Irish estates."

Mary sat alone in her apartment weeping.

Life was too difficult. There had been the dreadful affair of Torrington and the disaster of Beachy Head; then all the trouble over Haddock and Ashby and she knew Killigrew was a most unwise choice; dear Shrewsbury had become so ill over the matter that he had retired to Tunbridge Wells; she had been frantic with worry as to what was happening to William in Ireland; and when she had visited her dear little nephew for solace, her sister Anne had been there and had hinted that William was going to bestow Irish estates on Elizabeth Villiers.

Often she was able to dismiss that woman from her mind. It is not so, she had told herself. It used to be, but it is no longer. But for all that, she knew that Elizabeth continued as his mistress.

Why? she demanded. Why?

William was not a sensual man like her uncle Charles and her father. Women were essential to them—not so to William. Why then could he not be contented with his wife?

She understood his affection for Portland. She herself had once loved Frances Apsley better than anyone else in the world; it was for this reason that she no longer saw her; she did not want to be tempted again into passionate friendship with a woman.

She accepted Portland's influence with William. She could tell herself that it was good for a man to have ministers whose fidelity he could rely on.

But Elizabeth Villiers was his mistress and while he was in Ireland he was thinking of her.

She would not allow it. She was after all the Queen and should have some say in matters.

She thought of gentle Shrewsbury and she wondered whether he would have been a faithful husband.

What an extraordinary idea! Her thoughts then skipped to the visit of Monmouth to The Hague. How they had danced and skated together, and if Monmouth had not been so devotedly attached to Henrietta Wentworth at that time and she married to William, there might have been gossip about them. Perhaps there had been, for who knew where gossip was? Did William know how there were always men and women to discuss his relationship with . . . that woman.

She took up her pen and wrote:

> You will have Irish estates of which to dispose. I believe it would be an excellent idea to set up schools on these estates and instruct the Irish. If you will give me leave I must tell you I think that your wonderful success and deliverance should oblige you to think of doing what you can for the advancement of the true religion and the promoting of the Gospel . . .

She reread what she had written. Would he be angry that she sought to dictate to him. She wanted to cry out: "This you must do and not shower such gifts on your mistress while all London, all the Court, all the country titters behind your back.

"I will not endure it," she said aloud.

But she knew that when she was face to face with him she would do exactly as he wished.

He would be home soon. Her great plan now was to have Kensington Palace ready for him. In her frequent letters she had told him how progress was going on and she knew that he would consider her very incompetent if it were not ready for him to take up residence when he arrived.

But there was so much to be done; she looked with dismay at the apartments not yet painted. Every day she was at Kensington urging the workmen to work faster, while at the same time they made sure that all the skill of their craft was put into practice.

"The King's homecoming will be spoilt if Kensington Palace is not ready for him," she complained.

She herself was planning the gardens with feverish activity. She longed for William's return and yet at the same time she was terrified that he would come too soon.

She was at Kensington when the news of fresh trouble reached her. The Jacobites were rising in Scotland.

The pleasant trips to Kensington were over; now it was no longer a matter of, Will it be finished in time? It was And who are these Scottish traitors?

There were Scotsmen in London and the Scottish songs were sung in the streets.

Ken ye the rhyme to porringer?
Ken ye the rhyme to porringer?
King James the Seventh had a daughter
And he gave her to an Oranger.
Ken ye how he requited him?
Ken ye how he requited him?
The dog has into England come
And taken the crown in spite of him.
The rogue he shall nae keep it lang
To budge we'll make him fain again
We'll hang him high upon a tree
King James shall hae his ain again!

Was there to be no end to it? Would there always be the "Jacks" lurking behind every corner? And how could she sleep peacefully at night when she heard threats against William?

There was a scare when a man and woman were overheard in Birdcage Walk plotting her assassination. The woman was thought to be Catherine Sedley, although there was no real evidence of this. The Queen was guarded but no attempt was made on her life; and the rebellion in Scotland was ended by the capture of the ringleaders. Catherine Sedley was involved with them, but Mary could not allow her to be punished very severely for, after all, had she not been James's mistress and she must have had some affection for him. How difficult it was to punish those men whose crime was that they were loyal to her own father?

Several of them were in the Tower. She did not want to think of them. How she longed to be back in Holland, tending her gardens, living quietly, peacefully. How she wished that she had never been drawn into this conflict between her father and husband.

Each day she rose wondering what new crisis would be brought to light. She had always been one to form habits and her days ran to a pattern; she awoke at six, had tea brought to her and worked at her papers until eight when she went to prayers; then she worked again through the day until evening when if there were no public engagements she relaxed at her favorite cards; she rarely went to bed before two of the morning. Each day she wrote to William; she had always been a great letter writer and she found it so much easier to write to him than to talk to him.

She had had no reply to her letter about the Irish estates, but William was no letter writer. He was a soldier with serious business to occupy his time; and she, good ruler though she had proved herself to be, was first of all an emotional woman.

Her success as a ruler would have meant nothing to her if William's campaign had been a failure. She was constantly turning attention from her own achievements to point to his. If the people cheered William, which they never did, that would have given her greater pleasure than their cheers for herself. She longed for the people to appreciate him, to understand why he had taken the crown. It was not for his own glory, she would have them understand; it was to save England for Protestantism.

He would soon be home now. She had heard that he was on the way.

She drove home from Kensington where she had been to see how the building was progressing and there was an anxious frown between her eyes. It would not be ready—she was certain of it now—and he would be very disappointed.

I should have made sure, she scolded herself.

As her coach had turned into the courtyard, the horses shied suddenly; they reared and plunged . . . onto the statue of James II.

Her hand on her throat, she alighted. She stood for a moment staring at the remnants of her father's image, which her coach had destroyed.

She was shivering, seeing in everything that happened a symbol.

William was home, and as Kensington Palace was not ready the meeting took place at Hampton Court.

She smiled at him, her face illumined with great joy.

The bells were ringing and the people were giving him a welcome. He was uncouth and Dutch with a hooked nose and crooked back, but he was a conqueror for all that. He took Mary's hand and managed to smile at her. She had done well and her letters with their adulation and deep sincerity had been a comfort to him. He had molded her until she had almost become the wife he wanted; and he was well pleased.

"You see me in a very happy condition," she told him. "You are home and well. The people know you for the leader you are and that makes me rejoice."

He answered: "You have done well in my absence."

His mouth twitched a little at the corners. She had shown herself capable of ruling. She would have increased her popularity. Were the people going to wish that she was the sole Sovereign? Would they say now that they could well dispense with him?

She said: "I shall now be rid of all the troublesome business I was so little fit for."

"You showed yourself fit," he told her.

"Perhaps I wished to please you and I always said to myself, 'What would he do?'"

Again that half smile. He was well pleased.

She could not show him a completed Kensington Palace, but she could assure him that she was his devoted docile wife.

It was a happy homecoming.

MARLBOROUGH'S

DEFEAT

*I*t was impossible for *Marlborough* to advance his fortunes in England; and he had no intention of wasting time. Life was too short, he explained to Sarah.

They took a few days from Court to be together with their family. Henrietta the eldest was now nine years old, and John, four, was the pride of them both. There was also another boy—little Charles. Sarah had great plans for her four daughters; but for her boys she wanted the whole world.

Exciting days. She wished that they could have been longer. Each one was filled to the last minute with the mingling joys of family life and dreaming dreams—practical dreams. Sarah was always practical.

"A successful campaign in Ireland," Marlborough whispered to her, "and I'll have the command of the Army."

"Dutch William wants all the glory, don't forget."

"He has his kingdoms to rule."

"He prefers to lead his armies. Why if he had had the sense to send you to the Boyne the Irish troubles would be all over now."

Marlborough smiled at her affectionately.

She went on: "He's spitting blood and I can't believe he's much longer for this world. As for Mary, she grows fatter every day and looks well. I would to God she would go back to Holland with him and leave the place free for Anne."

"You always want to move too fast."

"And you, my lord, are too slow."

"They do say that the more haste often means less speed."

"Nonsense. I continually move fast. I have Anne exactly as I want her. She cannot bear me out of her sight. As soon as Gloucester's a little older I'm going to get John to Court. He shall be Gloucester's companion as I was Anne's. You can't start too young."

He laid his hand over hers. "As I said before, be careful."

She threw him off impatiently. "John Churchill, I know what I am doing. I trust you do."

They understood each other. They were close; she was dynamic, so it was natural that sometimes she bubbled over with the emotion of the moment; he believed in diplomacy; he had been born with a natural charm which it would have been a sin not to use. Sarah had no such charm; she was impatient of subterfuge. She believed in saying what she meant—although she would not tolerate others being so frank to her.

They were convinced that they would succeed.

But events did not work out quite as they had hoped.

The Cabinet did not wish Marlborough to go to Ireland, but William did; therefore the King persuaded the Cabinet of the wisdom of the move. But, thought William, who was Marlborough? He was a good soldier, but so far he had done little. But for the fact that he had a forceful wife—an obnoxious woman whom he, William, personally disliked intensely and would have preferred to banish from Court—who had bullied the Princess Anne into giving her rich gifts, where would he be? There was a great deal of noise around the Marlboroughs, but what had they done?

Still, William had an instinct where soldiers were concerned and he believed Marlborough to have talent. Moreover, he had come over to his side at the beginning of the revolution and such an action was worthy of a reward.

So Marlborough was allowed to go to Ireland—not with English soldiers trained by himself but with a company made up of Danes, Huguenots, and Dutchmen. This was the first disappointment for Marlborough. The second was that he was placed under the Duke of Württemberg instead of in supreme command. This was a terrible blow which made Sarah almost dance with fury. But Marlborough exercised his diplomacy, was ingratiating to Württemberg, who very shortly was ready enough to hand over the command to this able general.

The result was great victory, all due to Marlborough. He was fighting his brother-in-law the Duke of Tyrconnel, who was the second husband of Sarah's sister Frances; and so successful was he that Tyrconnel was forced to escape to France. His place was taken by the Duke of Berwick who was the son of his sister Arabella. He won the towns of Cork and Kinsale; and then returned to England.

He was certain now—and so was Sarah—that having served so brilliantly William must reward him—perhaps make him a Duke, perhaps give him some high office at Court.

William received him graciously. He even congratulated him on his success.

"I never knew one who has seen such little service so fit for great commands," he said.

A good compliment coming from William. But surely he did not think Marlborough could be rewarded by *words*.

As the weeks passed it seemed that he did.

"We shall not endure such treatment...indefinitely," said Sarah ominously.

Since the Battle of the Boyne and Marlborough's southern campaign, Ireland was no longer a major menace; but the French who were sheltering his enemies were a continual threat to peace and William decided that he must go to Holland and take his place as commander of the forces engaged there; and Marlborough, having proved his worth in Ireland, should go with him.

"This is another chance," Marlborough told his wife.

"If this does not bear fruit," she said, "we must then consider new plans."

Marlborough was inclined to agree with her.

She told him that Prince George had almost been in tears over the King's treatment of *him.* Anne had told her how upset he was and how unfair he thought his brother-in-law.

"He treats him like a lackey," said Sarah. "Of course we all know he *is* no better than a lackey, but Caliban might show a little civility. After all, George does happen to be the husband of the Princess Anne. She says he is treated as though he were no better than a page of the backstairs."

"William should be more careful," agreed Marlborough. "He hasn't too many friends. He should be more diplomatic."

"As you are, my love?"

"It worked with Württemberg."

"It would never work with William, my dear. He has not your handsome countenance, your soft voice, and your charm of manner. William could never be anything but what he is—however much he tried. Hooky Nose is a Dutch abortion and I cannot see how Elizabeth Villiers endures him for the silly creature gets little for her pains."

"And George?" asked Marlborough, for she had raised her voice and he was always afraid that her vituperations against William would be overheard.

"He does not want to go to Flanders with William, to be treated like a page of the backstairs. He wants to go to sea and he is going to ask William's leave to do so."

"He won't grant it."

"So much the better," snapped Sarah. "Then there will be a big fat quarrel between our sisters. Now, my lord, do not look alarmed. What if anyone *did* overhear me."

"They might tell Anne how you speak of them all."

"Pah!" cried Sarah. "They are a fine family, the lot of them." She laughed aloud and began to quote one of the Jacobite couplets.

There's Mary the daughter, there's Willy the cheater,
There's Geordie the drinker, and Annie the eater.

"Now don't fret my lord. Why if anyone carried tales of me to Annie the Eater I'd have it all explained away in a minute and have her falling on her knees to ask my pardon for having suspected me."

"It's never wise," he warned her, "to be too sure."

But she only laughed at him, and told him that he kept his boldness for battles. He should be more like his loving wife. Bold and adventurous every minute of her life.

William, on the point of leaving for Holland, came to the Queen's apartment for a private word with her.

"George has a notion that he wants to go to sea," he said. He gave a snort which was meant to be an expression of derision. "George!" he said. "We should soon be having another court-martial like that of Torrington."

"Oh, William, what are you going to tell him?"

"I refuse to discuss the matter with him. You must prevent his going."

"You mean, William, that I must forbid George to go to sea?"

"I should try to arrange it more diplomatically, if I were you."

"But if he wishes to go?"

"I have said he is not to go."

"Then I . . ."

"You will use methods of persuasion. If they fail, of course you will have to forbid him."

"It is going to be very difficult."

"You are the Queen," said William. "In my absence you take sole command."

"William, if you could explain to him."

William did not answer. It was an indelicate task, he agreed; and therefore one more suited to a woman's skill.

There was one thing he must insist on: George was not to go to sea.

The expedition had left for Holland and Mary was once more sole ruler.

An idea had come to her that if Anne would persuade George that she wanted him to be with her, for she was as usual pregnant, he would abandon the idea of going to sea. As it was he was going ahead with preparations, for when he had said good-bye to William he had mentioned the matter. William had not answered but had merely said good-bye and George had taken that for consent. Unfortunately she was not on good terms with Anne so she could not approach her; then she thought of Sarah and summoned her.

Sarah was astonished for she knew that the Queen disliked her and had even tried to break up her friendship with Anne. She was therefore very excited when the message came.

The Queen was affable.

"Pray be seated, Lady Marlborough. I want you to help me."

"If it is in my power, I will," said Sarah with a trace of arrogance.

"I want you to ask the Princess to prevent the Prince from going to sea."

Sarah opened her eyes very wide. "Am I to tell her that Your Majesty does not wish him to go?"

"I do not want you to mention me, but to persuade the Princess to keep her husband at home."

"Not mention to the Princess *why* I make the suggestion?"

"That is what I ask."

This was power! thought Sarah. The Queen was actually asking her to persuade Anne to do this. Indeed she was recognized even by her greatest enemies as an influence at Court.

"Your Majesty," she said haughtily, "I will ask the Princess to persuade her husband to stay at home."

"Thank you," said Mary, hardly able to hide her dislike.

"*But,*" went on Sarah, her voice rising triumphantly, "I could not hide from her the fact that *you* had asked this of me."

"You mean you refuse to do what I ask?"

"Your Majesty, I am in the service of the Princess Anne. I could not reconcile my honor to doing this—unless I could tell her that I did so on Your Majesty's orders."

The Queen rose to indicate the audience was over.

"You may leave, Lady Marlborough."

Sarah swept a curtsey. "Thank you, Your Majesty. You understand that . . ."

But the Queen had turned away.

To be in the company of that woman was an alarming experience! There was venom in her flashing eyes. Would to God there was some means of dismissing Sarah Churchill from the court! thought Mary. What a fool I was to betray myself to her. What is she plotting? What does she say to Anne when they sit together? Anne is her slave, her creature. Cannot Anne see how the woman uses her? She is capable of anything. What does she want? To see Anne on the throne? That is it, so that she can be the Queen in truth. She will say "Do this" and "Do that" and my silly sister will do it.

What a state of affairs! There is a serpent at our Court who is watching and waiting to destroy us. What will she do now? Of course she is planning to take the crown from William and from me . . . as we took it from my father.

Was it true that when such a wrongful act was committed, others planned to imitate it?

There was nothing to be done now but to summon Nottingham. He was to carry the news to George. He must tell him that there would be no sea campaign for him because it was against the orders of the King and Queen.

Sarah went straight to Anne.

"The impudence! Oh, my dear Mrs. Morley and poor, poor, Mr. Morley!"

"Dear Mrs. Freeman tell me what has happened."

Sarah told.

"Oh, the wickedness, the slyness of it! 'Lady Marlborough, I wish you to persuade the Princess to persuade her husband . . . and not a word that you do so because I have asked you.' What do you think of it!"

"They exclude us from everything. Poor George, he did so want to go to sea."

"So he will not be allowed to. Caliban wants all the credit."

"And to think that the Queen should try to make *you* work against me."

"That would always be in vain."

"I know it. I know it."

George came into the apartment, his face bewildered like a child's who has been ordered to stop a favorite game.

"Est-il possible?" he murmured. "Est-il possible?"

Marlborough had no opportunity of distinguishing himself in Holland and on the return to England expressed his dissatisfaction to Sarah.

"We are not moving forward," he said.

"I am glad you realize it," she retorted. "Great names are not made by marking time."

"Well, my love, we will look out for our opportunities, and when they come I am sure we can trust ourselves to seize them."

But Sarah was going to make opportunities, not wait for them.

"Is it not a strange thing," she said to Anne as they sat together one day, "that those who serve this King and Queen are not rewarded if they happen to be English."

Anne agreed as she always did with Sarah.

"Poor Mr. Morley longed to serve his country," went on Sarah, "but no! He is not allowed to." Sarah slid over the fact that he was not an Englishman and went on quickly: "And Mr. Freeman. I am sure Mrs. Morley will agree with me that there is not a man in this country who has done as much for it as Mr. Freeman."

"He is a great soldier and I know you are proud of him and he of you, which pleases me, for I like well to see those I love appreciated."

"Dear Mrs. Morley, what should I do without your sympathy? I had thought that after his services Mr. Freeman would have received some decoration. He is worthy of the Garter. But my poor Freeman is too modest to think of these things. I declare he is like Morley in that. So we, my dear Mrs. Morley, must think for them."

"What would they do without us to think for them!" sighed Anne, smiling.

"If I could see Freeman wearing the Garter I think I should be the happiest woman alive."

Sarah glanced sideways at Anne. It had worked. A conspiratorial expression had flitted across the plump highly colored face. Anne was going to see what she could do about procuring a Garter for Mr. Freeman.

"*The Garter for* Marlborough!" said William. "They'll be asking for the crown next."

Mary shivered. That was what she feared. There were so many Jacobite plots. One never knew where they were going to spring up next; and prisoners when questioned told strange stories. She was certain that the Marlboroughs were not to be trusted. They had betrayed James and people who betray once will do so again. Mary's nightmare was that they rose and deposed William. It would break his heart if that happened. He always seemed so indifferent to the three crowns of England, Scotland, and Ireland but this was not so. He believed that in possessing them he fulfilled a destiny which he had known was his ever since the midwife at his birth had seen three circles about his head which were believed to signify a prophecy that he would one day inherit three crowns.

"Anne is very eager to get a Garter for Marlborough," said Mary.

William frowned. "They do what they will with her. They have bewitched her."

"It is that woman."

"The sooner Anne rids herself of Sarah Churchill the better."

"She never will."

"No, I've aways said that the most stupid woman in England is your sister."

"Poor Anne!"

"Not poor in worldly goods, only in mental equipment," growled William. "And I'd as lief decorate one of your dogs with a Garter as Marlborough. So that's an end of it."

But it was not the end, for now Marlborough was agreeing with Sarah that little would be achieved under William.

His services were unrewarded. William did not believe it was necessary to consider him. Very well, he would show William.

In the first place he had great influence in the army. He had good looks and great charm of manner. He was also a first-class soldier and a born leader of men. Therefore what he said carried weight.

He began to point out how extraordinary it was that so many high posts in the Army were held by foreigners. One would have thought it was a foreign army. Of course the King was a Dutchman. That was the reason why favors were always given to the Dutch, and the English passed over.

Sidney Godolphin, Earl of Godolphin, who was a friend of the Marlboroughs, became aware of what was happening. Godolphin, a brilliant statesman and a Tory, had voted for a Regency at the time of the Revolution and was by no means satisfied when William and Mary were made King and Queen.

He sought out Marlborough and when he invited him to walk in the park, Marlborough guessed that something was going to be said that was too dangerous to be mentioned inside four walls.

Godolphin said: "You're dissatisfied with the manner in which affairs are being conducted and I understand why."

"I am a soldier," said Marlborough, "I do not care to see the Army in the hands of foreigners."

"It is inevitable when we have a Dutchman for a king."

"What is, must perforce be borne, I dare swear."

"Unless it were changed."

Marlborough was alert; this was what he had expected.

"I never believed that they should have taken the crown," went on Godolphin. "Had there been a Regency we might have made some compromise. James might have been made to accept certain conditions and return. In fact I am sure he would."

"It would have been preferable to this."

"I believe so."

"Alas, it is too late." There was almost a question in the remark.

"Some of the old King's friends are still in touch with him."

Marlborough's cool brain was rapidly weighing up the possibilities. Men like Godolphin were in this. Then it had a good chance of success.

"I have often felt contrite," he said, "because of the way I acted."

"James would be ready to forgive, if forgiveness were asked."

They were silent for a while. Godolphin was waiting for Marlborough to speak and when he did he said what he expected him to.

The Marlboroughs' policy had always been that where they went, the Princess Anne must follow, for their fortunes were inextricably bound up with hers.

Marlborough was writing to James, asking forgiveness for the part he had played, hinting that he would be ready to bring down the regime he had helped put up, assuring James that he would persuade his daughter Anne that she had been an undutiful daughter.

The task of persuading was, of course, Sarah's, and Sarah accomplished it with speed. When she had a definite project Sarah was happy and this was not a plan to bring back James, but merely to depose William and Mary. They wanted no Catholic monarch; therefore with the Dutchman out of the way, and his wife with him, for she would not reign without him, it would be Anne's turn.

When Sarah came to her mistress's apartments the cards were laid out. Sarah sat impatiently drumming her fingers on the table.

She had already spoken to Anne and she was sure the Princess was now ready. She hated William; she disliked Mary; and she was ready to wish she had been a better daughter. Once she had put her intentions in writing, the matter would be sealed.

Cards! thought Sarah impatiently. What a preoccupation when there was life to be lived! Not that Sarah did not enjoy a game of cards. They were her favorite recreation, for she had never had much patience with books. "Prithee do not talk to me of books," was a favorite remark of hers. "I know only men and cards." It had not occurred to her that had she looked into books she might have learned some invaluable lessons; she might have been able to see herself in relationship to others; but Sarah could not do this—it was her great fault. She could only see herself as a giant in a world of pygmies, and, as John often feared, this could be her downfall.

She played the game with a careless abandon which was not lost on Lady Fitzharding, who had come to know Sarah very well. When she played like that, her mind was on other things and it was clear that she wanted to be alone with the Princess Anne.

Sarah lost heavily and made no accusations against the others, which was unusual; and very soon she had contrived to be alone with Anne.

It was on such occasions that Barbara made sure that she was aware of what went on between Anne and Sarah. She owed that to Elizabeth.

"Oh, those tiresome women!" cried Sarah in her resonant voice. "I thought the game would never end."

"It was a good game, and you, my dear Mrs. Freeman, played very badly."

"I know. My mind was on more important matters."

"Oh?" said Anne, her eyes shining. "Do explain."

"There is news from your father. He is delighted that you are with those who are ready to show him friendship."

"My poor father. Do you know, Mrs. Freeman, I have been haunted ever since the morning of the Coronation. That letter! To be cursed by one's father. And all the babies I have lost. And my little Gloucester . . . sometimes my heart almost fails me when I look at him. He is such a clever little boy, so alert, so brilliant . . . oh, but dear Mrs. Freeman, so frail."

"I know, I know. If you had your father's forgiveness everything would be better, for it is not a good thing that there should be enmity between a father and daughter."

"What can I do, Mrs. Freeman?"

"Well, I believe that if you were to write a letter to him and tell him how sorry you are, he would be ready and willing to forget the past and be friends again."

"How I wish that could be."

"We will write that letter and see what happens. It can do no harm. Now . . . pen and paper and to work."

Sarah bustled about the apartment, laid out writing materials, and helped Anne to the table.

"Now . . . what do you think? Something like this. 'I have been very desirous of some safe opportunity to make you a sincere and humble offer of my duty and submission to you; and to beg you will be assured that I am both truly concerned for the misfortune of your condition and sensible, as I ought to be, of my own unhappiness . . .'"

"That is wonderful."

"Well write that down."

Anne obeyed.

Sarah went on: "'As to what you may think I have contributed to it, if wishes could recall what is past, I had long since redeemed my fault . . .'"

Sarah went on dictating; Anne went on writing; and in the anteroom Barbara Fitzharding's ear was pressed against the keyhole that she might not miss a word.

Elizabeth Villiers made William lie on her bed and rest, for she said that when he came to her he must, for a short time, forget his troubles.

She smiled down at him and he regarded her with affection—the face which so many failed to appreciate, that fascinating cast in the eyes which had endeared her to him in the first place, and the clear alert mind which she devoted to his interests. He was blessed in his mistress as he was with his male friends. He was a man who was loved by few, but those few gave him wholehearted devotion.

Wife, mistress, and friend. He could rely on them all—though perhaps not his wife because, for all that she was the meekest of the three, her exalted position and the power she could wield if she wished meant that he could never be completely sure of her.

"My sister reports disturbing news from the Cockpit," she said. "Anne is writing to her father."

William raised himself on his elbow and stared at her.

"It is so. No suggestions . . . yet. A little contrition; the dutiful daughter is haunted by the wrong she has done her father and asks his forgiveness."

William was silent; then he said. "The Marlborough woman."

Elizabeth nodded. "She dictates all."

"Marlborough will be aware of it."

"I am sure of it," said Elizabeth. "That woman continually abuses you, but I do not think she would take this step without Marlborough's being aware of it."

"He's a good soldier but his ambitions run ahead of his achievement," said William. "I wonder how far this has gone."

"I think that James is too tired for action and the French have refused him the army which he needs to invade. The Marlboroughs are intent on mischief. They don't want James back."

"No," said William, "they want Anne on the throne so that the Churchills can rule the country. Anne, being the most foolish of women, does not see this."

"Barbara declares that it is quite sickening to listen to them. Dear Mrs. Freeman and poor silly Mrs. Morley! Anne looks upon it all as a girlish game, but Sarah is no girl. She's the most ambitious woman at Court—and since she is married to the most ambitious man, they are a pair to be watched."

"He could be taken up for treason."

"He could be," admitted Elizabeth, "but I am sure you would consider that unwise at this stage."

"At this stage," agreed William. "I think, though, that we could well dispense with their services. I can bring a charge against Marlborough. He has been talking seditiously in the Army, complaining that foreigners are favored. He is very fond of money and having little is always seeking ways of finding it. On account of his position in the Army he has posts to dispose of. He could be dismissed for bribery and extortion."

Elizabeth nodded slowly and leaning toward William kissed him.

He took her wrist and said: "It is a pleasure to me to talk of these matters with you. There are times when a woman's wit is . . . agreeable."

Elizabeth was well pleased. The rivalry between herself and Bentinck was never forgotten. Bentinck was devoted; but his mind worked along similar lines to William's; the viewpoint of a woman was invaluable, particularly when that woman was his devoted mistress.

He went from Elizabeth to the Queen's apartments. Her women disappeared as he entered. Mary came to him, arms outstretched, delighted, as always, when he sought her out.

"I wish to speak to you," he told her. "The matter is urgent and concerns your sister."

"Oh, dear William, I trust Anne has not been causing you anxiety again."

"It is what we must expect. She is a constant anxiety."

"What now, William?"

"She is writing to your father."

"No!"

He looked at her with mild contempt. How different from Elizabeth! Elizabeth made it her business to have a spy established in the Cockpit who could report to him, yet Mary, who had so much more power and opportunity, had failed to do this.

"At the moment it is merely, 'Please forgive me.' But that is of course a preliminary. You will know of course who is at the bottom of this."

"Not that odious woman!"

"Who else?"

"I loathe her. The airs! Really, my sister is a fool. How can she so far forget her royalty as to grovel at the feet of that woman."

Mary felt a twinge of conscience. She had remembered suddenly the humble letters she used to write to Frances Apsley. Anne was no more humble to Sarah Churchill. She could well understand Anne's devotion to Sarah as she had once entertained a similar feeling toward Frances. Perhaps Frances wondered now why she was never invited to see the

Queen. Mary was determined not to become enslaved to a woman as Anne was to Sarah Churchill.

"These Churchills seem to have some unnatural power over her. We have to be rid of them. You must start. Try to persuade your sister to get rid of the woman."

"But William, she never will."

"You must talk to her. I want them out of Court."

"You have only to order them to go."

He looked at her in exasperation. How obtuse she could be! One of the more dangerous occupations of the Marlboroughs in recent weeks had been to increase the popularity of Anne. She had been appearing in public, smiling at the people, distributing alms, visiting the playhouse, laughing when the people laughed, being one of them.

In any case, of all the royal family she was the favorite; she was the mother of the heir to the throne and when she appeared with him in public, playing the fond mother to perfection—not that she had to act in that role; for she always had been devoted to her children—the people applauded her. They knew of her quarrels with her sister and brother-in-law and they were ready to believe the worst of Dutch William.

"Anne will refuse. Don't you see that this time we cannot afford to upset Anne. She is too popular. We have to be wary. You must speak to Anne and try to make her see what harm this woman is doing. I will deal with Marlborough if you will deal with his wife."

"I will do my best of course, William, but . . ."

"Do it then . . . and without delay."

The two sisters faced each other. It was rarely that the Queen came to the Cockpit. She would visit her nephew frequently, take him toys and if she was prevented from visiting him, send to inquire for his health; but she was not on such good terms with his mother.

Mary looked with distaste at her sister who was growing so fat. Mary herself was a big woman and getting fatter every week, but Anne had had a start of her, and she was becoming enormous.

Mary's eyes went to the dishes of sweetmeats in the apartments. Her own mouth watered for she dearly loved them; but what a temptation to have them always before one! She supposed Sarah Churchill encouraged the habit; the fatter Anne became, the more lazy she was—and therefore the more ready to do as she was told.

"Anne," she said, "I want to talk seriously to you."

Anne looked mildly interested.

"There is one woman in your suite who, I am sure, is a bad influence. I'm going to advise you to consider ridding yourself of her."

"I know of no such woman."

"You must be aware that Sarah Churchill attempts to govern your life."

"Govern my life. How?"

"Does she not tell you what you must do and are you not inclined always to do it?"

"Sarah Churchill is my friend . . . my greatest friend . . . the friend I trust more than anyone in the world."

"Then I am sorry for you."

"I know of course that you hate her. You haven't a great friend now, have you? I am sorry. You must have forgotten how once Frances Apsley was your great friend. She is still mine, but not such a great friend as Sarah, of course. I see no harm in having friends. Nor did you once. I suppose William has asked you to do this."

"I am asking you because I believe you would be better without Sarah Churchill."

"I think I should be allowed to choose my own household."

"I am advising you."

"I could advise you."

"Do not be so foolish, Anne. If you are not careful I shall take away half of your income."

"You couldn't do it," retorted Anne. "The Parliament has voted me my income . . . although I know you and William tried to deprive me of it."

"And how much do you allow the Marlboroughs?"

"That is my own affair."

"Anne! You forget . . ."

"That you are the Queen? I do not. You won't allow me. You come to talk to me like a sister, you say, and then you are reminding me that you are the Queen. Well, I am the Princess Anne—our father's daughter no less than you, and the heiress to the throne, for you and William have no children—nor ever will have. So I and my little Gloucester are entitled to some consideration."

Mary interrupted her. "You give the Marlboroughs a thousand a year. That is ridiculous and extravagant. Why should they have this money. Are they not paid for their services . . . he in the Army and for his Court duties . . . she for her duties here at the Cockpit? Why these extravagant gifts? Shall I remind you that your income has to come out of the royal purse and if it is so large that you can afford to give rich gifts of one thousand a year—to those who don't deserve them—then I think it high time your income was reconsidered."

"This is monstrous," cried Anne, wiping her eyes. "To think that you come here . . . and me in my present state . . ."

"I do not mean to upset you, merely to make you see a little good sense."

"Which in your opinion is to rid myself of my best friends."

"Your friends are the King and myself."

"I have yet to see any signs of your friendship."

"Oh, you are the most ungrateful wretch!"

"Should you talk of ingratitude?"

Anne's lips were pursed together, for she was remembering the letter she had written to her father. How much happier she had felt since writing that! Mary had asked no forgiveness. How could she, tied as she was to Dutch William? The only way she could repent was to go back to Holland and take her Dutchman with her.

How much more pleasant for Anne; all she had to do was write her penitent letter and continue to live at the Cockpit with Gloucester nearby and perhaps another little one soon, and dear Sarah her constant companion.

Her constant companion—that was the point at issue.

"Sarah shall remain with me," she said stubbornly. "No one shall take her away from me."

The Earl of Marlborough, one of the lords of the bedchamber, arrived at the King's apartment to perform his duties as usual.

William, wigless, in bed, was not a handsome sight; but all his attendants were accustomed to that by now.

The ceremony was never a very pleasant one. Charles II had made of it a very merry occasion, with his quips and jokes and the King's wit was something worth listening to. James's rising ceremony had not been amusing, but it had been dignified and there had been conversation, although it was almost always confined to horses and women. William's was silent and was merely the grim purpose of dressing the King.

It was Marlborough's duty to put on William's shirt. He did this as usual, and if the King looked at him as though he did not exist, that was not unusual.

The duty over, Marlborough was leaving the apartment when Lord Nottingham approached him.

"My Lord Marlborough, a word with you."

Marlborough and several of the bedchamber people halted to listen, for there was something grave—even ominous—in Nottingham's tone.

"The King has asked me to inform you that he has no further use for your services."

"What!"

Nottingham nodded. "All your employments should be sold or disposed of, for neither the King nor the Queen wish to see you at Court."

Marlborough was stunned. This could mean discovery. Then why not imprisonment? Dismissal. Banishment. How could he possibly go forward with his schemes if he were forbidden the Court?

Curious glances were directed toward him. He must pull himself together. He lifted his shoulders, smiled and went quickly on his way.

There was gossip all through the Court. What is Marlborough's sin? What a disgrace! To tell him in that way with so many looking on! And after his campaign in Ireland! Why, if Marlborough had not deserted James when he did, William would not have had it so easy.

It was circulated that he was accused of taking bribes. Well, that was true enough. But if everyone who took bribes was going to be driven from Court there wouldn't be many left.

Ah, here was the real reason. He had spread infection in the Army by complaining of the privileges given to the Dutch and denied the English.

Dutch William did not like that.

So . . . that was the end of Marlborough.

Sarah was stricken between sorrow and rage. That this should happen to her John, to the most brilliant commander in the Army, was unthinkable! If ever she had disliked William and Mary she hated them now. Loathed them! Detested them! And she was determined that they should pay to the full for this.

She went at once to her husband.

He took her into his arms and tried to soothe her for he had never seen her in such a state of rage and excitement.

"My dear, be calm," he begged.

"Calm! When you have been insulted . . . by that monstrosity, that gorilla, that abortion! How dare he!"

"He has discovered that I am writing to James."

"No!"

"I think so."

"He has not said . . ."

"No, he is too clever. He knows that if it were said half the country would rise up behind me. They do not want him here."

"And a good thing if they did."

"No, Sarah. Bring back James . . . and the Prince of Wales? What are you thinking of?"

"It would not do, of course."

"No. Remember it, my dearest, and be calm."

"They want to drive me away too."

He nodded. "They will not feel safe while you are at the Cockpit."

"But I am staying at the Cockpit."

"I fancy they won't allow it."

"We shall see. We shall see."

There was nothing for him to do but retire to St. Albans.

"Not for long," said Sarah fiercely.

She went to Anne for comfort and it was one of the rare occasions when Anne saw Sarah weep.

"My dearest, *dearest* Mrs. Freeman," cried Anne, the tears flowing down her plump red cheeks. "I beg of you, do not weep so. You distress me. I cannot bear to see my proud Mrs. Freeman thus."

"I think of what he has done. But for him they would not be here. He could have prevented them. He has helped to subdue Ireland; he has fought for them bravely and this is how they reward him. Dismissed the Court! Banished . . . and all on trumped-up charges!"

"They must not be allowed to do this," said Anne ineffectually.

"They have done it; and what is more they have only just begun. You know what they will do next. They will separate *us*."

Anne was fierce suddenly. "Never!" she cried.

She threw her arms about Sarah and clung to her.

Sarah remained quietly at the Cockpit; Marlborough was at St. Albans; and three weeks had passed.

On February 6th, which was Anne's birthday, Anne was invited to Kensington Palace to celebrate the occasion.

"I shall accompany you," announced Sarah.

"Of course, dear Mrs. Freeman."

"They will not be expecting me. They will think I want to hide myself because of my husband's so-called disgrace. I will show them that nothing he has ever done makes me ashamed. I am proud of him. I wonder they do not forbid *me* to go to Court; but they have not done that yet."

"They know that I should never go without you," said Anne.

"Dear Mrs. Morley. My one comfort in my trouble."

"Dearest Mrs. Freeman, what are friends if not to comfort each other in adversity?"

They left the Cockpit together; and as the Princess's carriage passed along, the people cheered her; but the surprise of the people was obvious when they saw that Sarah Churchill was accompanying her; the entire city knew of Marlborough's disgrace and believed that would be an end of his ambitions. Therefore it was odd to see Marlborough's wife in the Princess's carriage.

When they arrived at the Palace even greater surprise greeted them.

"Was Marlborough's wife mad?" courtiers whispered to each other. "How could she be received at Court when her husband was in disgrace?"

Sarah was well aware of the stir she created; she walked a pace or so behind Princess Anne, her head high, her eyes flashing scorn, through the royal apartments, which even now retained a whiff or two of fresh paint, into the state apartments so lovingly designed by William and watched over by Mary, to where the King and Queen were waiting.

Anne curtseyed; so did Sarah; and when Mary saw the latter she was almost unable to suppress a gasp of dismay and astonishment.

Mary drew her sister aside and spoke coolly to her. Sarah she ignored.

Many would have tried to hide themselves in the throng; not so, Sarah; it was as though she flaunted her presence in the royal apartments, as though she were saying: "You may not want me, but here I am and here I remain."

The next day a letter was delivered to the Princess Anne from the Queen.

> I hope you do me the justice to believe it is as much against my will that I now tell you that, after this, it is very unfit that Lady Marlborough should stay with you, since that gives her husband so just a pretence of being where he should not. I think I might have expected you should have spoken to me of it; and the King and I, both believing it, made us stay thus long. But, seeing you

so far from it, that you brought Lady Marlborough hither last night, makes us resolve to put it off no longer, but tell you she must not stay, and I have all the reason imaginable to look upon your bringing her here as the strangest thing that ever was done. Nor could all my kindness for you (which is always ready to turn all you do to the best way) at any other time have hindered me from showing you so that moment, but I considered your condition, and that made me master myself so far as not to take notice of it then. . . . I tell you plainly that Lady Marlborough must not continue with you in the circumstance her lord is.

Sarah, who was with Anne when she read this letter, snatched it from the Princess and gave vent to her rage.

"You see how they treat you! Who would believe that you are the heiress to this crown when you are treated like a serving wench!"

"Sarah, we are *not* going to be parted."

"Until you dismiss me, I would never go," was Sarah's rejoinder.

"Then what can I do?"

"You can write to her and tell her that you resent her unkindness and have no intention of parting with Lady Marlborough."

"What will they do then?"

"What can they do? It is for you to choose those you wish to have about you."

So once more under Sarah's dictation Anne wrote to her sister, and when the letter reached her Mary sent orders that Lady Marlborough was to leave the Cockpit.

"There is only one thing to do," said Sarah; "I must leave the Cockpit, so if you do not want us to be parted you must come with me."

"Where can we go?"

"My dear Mrs. Morley forgets she is the heiress to the throne. There will be some who are ready to lend her a lodging, I'll swear. What of Sion House? That would be comfortable. I am sure the Duchess of Somerset would not deny you shelter there if you asked it. Shall I arrange for a letter to be taken to her while we prepare to leave."

"Oh, dear Mrs. Freeman, you think of everything!"

"Then write immediately. Someone must take care of Mrs. Morley.

Remember her condition, and she is never well during these times. A miscarriage could be brought on. I am sure the people will realize how harsh your sister and her Dutchman are to turn you out of doors at such a time."

So Anne wrote the letter while Barbara Fitzharding immediately went to her sister to tell her that Anne was proposing to move to Sion House with Sarah.

When William heard this he sent to the Duke of Somerset asking him to refuse the request of the Princess Anne.

As one of the foremost noblemen of England, Somerset was furious to be dictated to. What did this Dutchman think he was doing? He must realize that England was not Holland. They wanted no uncouth foreigners here. A request had been made to his wife by a kinswoman who happened to be heiress to the throne, and Somerset implied that he had received the Kings *request* too late, and his wife had already offered Sion House to the Princess Anne.

Anne, with Sarah and George, left for Sion House, and William's retort was to rob them of all the honors which they had enjoyed; these included their guards, so when they left, they rode in their carriage unaccompanied.

The people watched them: the Princess Anne, large with child; her faithful woman beside her and her husband, holding her hand, assuring her of his affection during all their troubles.

What was the Dutch monster doing to their Princess? asked the people. She was no favorite of his because she was English and the King had no favor to bestow on the English. Was not Marlborough in disgrace for pointing this out?

Anne smiled wanly and waved her hand in acknowledgment of the cheers.

"Poor long-suffering lady!" said the watchers.

A few days later when she rode out in her carriage, with Sarah beside her, her coach was held up near Brentford by two masked men.

Anne was terrified. Such a thing had never happened to her before. Sarah demanded: "What does this mean?"

"It means, lady, you hand over your valuables and keeps your life . . . or if you don't, you loses both. The choice is yours."

"Do you realize this lady is the Princess Anne and I am Lady Marlborough."

"Thanks for the information, lady. You should have some very nice valuables."

Anne was lying back against the upholstery, her plump cheeks quivering. The coachman dared do nothing. Trembling she removed her jewelry and put it into the grimy outstretched hand; she dared not look at the eyes glinting behind the mask.

To her chagrin, Sarah was forced to do the same.

Then satisfied, the highwaymen allowed them to go on their way.

The Princess Anne held up in her coach and robbed of her jewels—some said to be priceless!

What next? Had she not been robbed of her guards, of course, she would not have been robbed of her jewels. This was no way to treat a royal Princess. It was Dutch William's doing. He had taken away her protectors and she, poor lady, not far off her accouchement, was in peril of being robbed—perhaps murdered—on the highways.

The lampoons began again. The popularity of the Princess had never been so high, that of the King never so low.

Rebellion all about him, thought William. How ready the people were to take sides against him! They were cheering Anne, that fat, stupid creature who hadn't a mind of her own, and obeyed the odious Churchill woman in everything.

He was continually wondering what news was coming from Ireland and Scotland. Three crowns! he thought. How much better had there been but one. Ireland and Scotland—they were not worth the trouble.

In the last weeks he had heard that MacIan of Glencoe had refused for some time to take the oath to live peacefully under the Government. William had believed that if he promised pardon to all who had been in rebellion, provided they took the oath before the end of the last year, he would succeed in quelling rebellion. The majority, tired of conflict, had taken the oath.

William did not know that MacIan, head of the McDonald clan, had waited until the last day of December and then had gone to Fort William to take the oath, only to find there was no magistrate there. This had meant that he must travel to Inverary, through the Highlands in difficult weather, and thus he had not taken the oath until the sixth day of January.

The Campbells decided that this would be a good way of destroying the rival clan, and keeping from William the fact that MacIan had belatedly taken the oath, assured him that if he ordered that justice should be done, they would see that it was.

William, weary of troublemakers, believing that he had to show a strong hand, decided to make an example and gave the required order.

As for the McDonalds of Glencoe, if they can well be distinguished from the rest of the Highlanders, it will be proper for, the vindication of public justice to extirpate that set of thieves. W.R.

Captain Campbell rejoiced to receive orders which were to fall upon the rebels, the McDonalds of Glencoe, and put all under seventy years of age to the sword.

Taking his band of soldiers to the glen, he was welcomed by the McDonalds, given hospitality, as was the custom of the district, and invited to stay as long as he wished.

There was revelry for a day or two; then the order was given; the passes were closed so that none might escape, and men, women, and children were slaughtered in what came to be known as the Massacre of Glencoe.

The news of what had happened was hurried south.

Innocent men and women murdered by the orders of the Dutch Monster! MacIan *had* sworn the oath——but because he was a few days late doing it his entire clan was destroyed.

"This is a deed which will be remembered long after Dutch William lies in his tomb," growled the people.

There was no peace to be had. Ireland was still not completely sub-dued; the news of the Massacre of Glencoe was shocking the British Isles, and in Scotland many were ready to rise against the Dutchman whom they blamed for that tragedy.

On the Continent James was raising an army and Louis was helping him. His wife was pregnant and James had sent invitations to all those who should be present at the birth of one who was in the line of succes-sion to the throne. Mary and Anne were sent invitations——and all were promised a safe conduct into France and liberty to return to England when they wished.

The discovery of Marlborough's duplicity, while it had made Wil-liam and Mary so apprehensive, had put heart into James. He believed that if he could gain one big victory many important men who now served William——somewhat discontentedly——would come over to him. Marlborough was one; Godolphin was another; he believed that Not-tingham was a Jacobite at heart; and who was most important, Admiral Russell who could bring over a part of the fleet.

William's health had taken a turn for the worse and he was spitting blood so frequently that he found it difficult to keep this a secret. Mary was beside herself with anxiety. But when he came to her and told her that he must go to Holland, for matters seemed to be coming to a head on the Continent, she knew that she could do nothing to dissuade him.

"I know that I can safely leave the government in your hands," he said with more kindness than usual.

"I trust I shall not disappoint you," she answered.

He pressed her hand, which was as near a caress as he could get.

"One thing that pleases me is that the greatest of all troublemakers is banished from Court. But what of the woman? I fancy she is more deadly than the man."

So once more he sailed away and Mary was left to govern her turbulent realm alone.

Soon after he had left she developed a cold which because of the pressure of business she ignored. In a few days she was delirious and those about her feared she was dying.

In Sion House Sarah was so delighted she could not hide her pleasure.

"Think what this is going to mean, Mrs. Morley. *He* was spitting blood before he went to Holland. *She* is laid low. After all Providence cannot go on forgetting us. Evil is always punished; good rewarded. You will see."

But Sarah had her anxieties; when she looked at Anne whose pregnancy should end in a month or so, she wondered if she were not in as bad a state as her sister and brother-in-law. She was enormous. Surely something must be wrong for a woman to be so large. If Anne should die that would be the biggest misfortune which could befall the Marlboroughs. Sarah bustled around Anne, never allowing her for one moment to be in a draught, cosseting, fussing to such an extent that Anne was often in tears merely to contemplate the devotion of her beloved Mrs. Freeman.

Meanwhile Mary was growing so ill that those about her were certain she was near her end.

Mary herself believed this. She was young to die—thirty; and she felt that she was leaving her affairs in the utmost disorder. William needed her, she was sure, far more than he realized. She thought of him, driving himself to work in Flanders when he was suffering acutely from all the disorders which had been with him so long that he considered them a part of his life.

There were times when she was so ill that she was not sure where she was. Sometimes she thought she was a little girl again playing in Richmond Palace with the Villiers girls. Sarah had intruded there, and was a shady figure in her dreams to disturb her. The pleasantest dreams were those in which Monmouth figured—gay and dashing, dancing with her at The Hague; and sometimes the face of Monmouth changed to that of Shrewsbury. She was depressed to be dragged from such dreams to the reality: her sickbed, with troubles crowded about her; rebellion abroad and at home; surrounded by spies so that she did not know whom she could trust; her own sister, under the influence of that venomous woman—her enemy.

To her surprise and that of everyone else Mary recovered.

She believed this to be a sign. She had been spared because she had more work to do on earth. She surprised everyone by the speed of her recovery.

There were letters from William. She must realize that James was amassing an army in Normandy at this time, and she must be prepared for invasion. She must be watchful for it was possible that those whom she felt she ought to be able to trust were at this moment working against her. If there should be an invasion he would immediately send Bentinck to her. He himself would not be able to come until he had raised the siege of Namur.

"He shall not be disappointed in me," she murmured.

Sir Benjamin Bathurst was asking for an audience with the Queen.

In the midst of all the preparations, when a knock at the door would make Mary start and wonder what fresh disaster was about to be announced, Mary's heart began to beat fast, for Benjamin Bathurst was the husband of Frances Apsley, the woman whom Mary had once loved best in all the world.

"Frances's husband . . . to see me," she murmured; and her thoughts ran on. Is Frances dying? Is she asking for me?

She was trembling a little when Sir Benjamin entered.

"Welcome, Sir Benjamin," she said. "Pray give me news of Frances."

"She is well, Your Majesty."

"Ah!" Her relief was apparent.

He said: "I bring you this letter."

She seized it and her eyes sought the once familiar handwriting which had meant so much to her, but this was another handwriting which she knew well.

"The Princess Anne has asked me to deliver this letter into your hands."

So he came from Anne. Of course Anne had kept up her friendship with Frances. Anne had always had to imitate her in those days and because she had loved Frances passionately, Anne had had to do so too. And now Anne had turned to Sarah Churchill—a friendship Mary certainly did not share.

"Thank you," she said. "I will read it at once. Pray wait a while. There is much I wish to ask you . . . about dear Frances."

The letter was in Anne's childish scrawl. Her pains had started and as she feared she was much worse than usual, she thought the Queen should come at once to Sion House.

Mary folded the letter, and put it into her pocket.

"Pray tell me of your wife," she said. "It is long since I have seen her. She comes so little to Court. But of course now she has her family. I know how happy she must be with her children."

Benjamin said that the children were well and that their mother was devoted to them.

"Dear Frances!" sighed Mary.

Sir Benjamin was surprised that the Queen should make him talk of Frances for he knew the contents of the letter he had brought.

Sarah said: "So she does not come. Her sister may be dying for all she cares."

Barbara Fitzharding shrugged her shoulders. "It is because *you* are here."

"And a mercy it is that there is someone to look after the Princess!"

"There are many of us," Barbara pointed out.

"She needs someone whose sole care is for her. She needs affection and there are few who can give that."

Barbara lowered her eyes. She would like to have told Sarah Churchill that she was not subtle enough; her loud voice and her loose tongue didn't deceive anybody. Those who believed her motives were altruistic would have to be very simple indeed. But Barbara had no wish to quarrel with her, for Sarah's behavior was just what was needed to give everything away. It would not be nearly so easy to gauge what was going on in this household but for her audible vituperations.

The midwife was with the Princess. This had been a longer labor than usual and Sarah was anxious.

She was at the bedside when the child was born.

A boy. A poor frail little boy, who breathed for a few minutes and then like so many of his predecessors, died.

Mary came to Sion House expecting, from the reports she had had, to find her sister on the point of death.

Anne was propped up in her bed and when Mary saw that she was no worse than after other accouchements she was angry. A campaign, doubtless, started by Sarah Churchill, to call attention to the poor neglected Princess who had been brought to bed in Sion House instead of Whitehall or St. James's.

All this, when the country was in danger of invasion, and sisters could not stand together!

Mary sat beside the bed and said: "I had expected to see you in worse state."

"I have had a very bad time," sighed Anne.

"You look a little tired, that is all."

Anne put her kerchief to her eyes. "And I have lost my baby."

"You have little Gloucester, so you should be thankful. You have been more fortunate than I."

"But think how many times I have been brought to bed . . . only to suffer loss."

"We must accept our fate. I have come to talk seriously to you. There should not be quarrels in families. The times are too dangerous. We should stand together. So I have made the first step toward ending our quarrel by coming to see you. You must make the next."

"But how so?" asked Anne.

"You know what I mean. Get rid of the Marlborough woman."

"I have never disobeyed you but in this one respect," said Anne. "I believe that some time you will see how unreasonable it is of you to ask me to give up my greatest friend. I will not do it."

Mary stood up. "Then I have nothing more to say to you now."

When she had gone, Sarah, who had naturally been listening, came into the apartment.

"Well done, Mrs. Morley. I am proud of you."

"She came just to ask me to get rid of you."

"Insolence! She is worried you know."

"I gathered that. It is the thoughts of invasion."

"James has an army assembled in Normandy. If he comes, you should be prepared. He will hate them . . . but he will be ready to forgive you. You should write to him without delay." Sarah brought her mouth close to the Princess's ear. "Tell him that when he comes to England you will go at once to him."

"Oh, Sarah, you think he will soon be here?"

"No. But it is as well to be prepared. One can never be sure."

"How right you are on all things, Sarah."

"It is because my undivided attention is given to the affairs of my dearest Morley."

THE FLOWERPOT

PLOT

There were many people in England at this time who were wondering how to turn the situation to their advantage—some low born as well as high—and one of these was a man named Robert Young.

He was lying in Newgate Prison when he conceived the idea of fabricating a plot which would be a sham, of course, but which could be used by people in high places to rid themselves of their enemies. He had tried to get this taken up and even succeeded in having it brought before William himself, but William had treated the suggestion with disdain and had thought it too trivial to inquire from what source it came.

Robert Young had been cheating all his life—he lived by it, he delighted in it, and if it had not brought him great wealth it had brought adventure. His greatest skill was forgery; he could copy a signature after a little practice so that it was impossible to tell it from the original. Such a gift was invaluable to his schemes and he longed to make use of it. He had spent most of his youth in Ireland although he had been born in Lancashire. He claimed that he had been educated at Trinity College, Dublin, and although he had diplomas to authenticate this his name was not on the list of graduates. By producing his forged certificates he procured admission to deacons orders and became a curate in Waterford. He married, tired of his wife, and went through a form of marriage with Mary Hutt, the daughter of an innkeeper who, liking the adventurous life, was more to his taste. He did well as a curate, performing all sorts of illegal acts for a good price, but he had to run away when one of his flock became pregnant.

He was arrested for bigamy and sent to prison but was released when he promised to divulge a Popish plot. This he did by forging the signature of various people to whom he had written at some time or other merely for the purpose of supplying himself with signatures he could copy: On the point of being discovered he came to England.

It did not take Young long to forge more documents which he pretended had been written by the Archbishop of Canterbury. With these he managed to delude several clerics, live on their bounty, and extract money from them, until he was found out; at Bury he and Mary Hutt were imprisoned.

While he was in jail he wrote to the Archbishop of Canterbury telling him that he had been ill-used, giving him a long account of a fictitious Irish background, asking for his help and promising in return to uncover plots against the state. The Archbishop ignored this and on being released from Bury jail Young forged the Archbishop's signature and worked the same trick in England as he had in Ireland, visiting wealthy clergymen, telling them he came from the Archbishop, and extracting large sums of money from them.

Eventually the Archbishop heard of the fraud, and Young and Mary Hutt went back to jail—this time to Newgate.

Failing to gain interest in the plot he was trying to fabricate, Young decided that he would work by himself. If he could disclose a plot involving famous people he believed he would not only be released from prison but would be substantially rewarded and given an opportunity of being in the company of men who could be of use to him—if only giving him opportunities of forging their signatures.

The great scandal at this time, even in the prisons, was the dismissal of the Earl of Marlborough. Marlborough had distinguished himself in Ireland and Holland; he had been a soldier of importance even before the coming of William; yet he was deprived of all his commands and employments and living in disgrace. It was said that he had spread disaffection in the Army by complaining of favor shown to foreigners and had taken bribes. Was this the real reason? It was whispered everywhere that Marlborough was a "Jack" planning to bring back James.

A plot, thought Young, which would involve Marlborough, would make them notice him.

He drew up a document which was meant to be a declaration for the restoration of James II. He had had opportunities of examining the signatures of the people he wished to involve, for he had seen Marlborough's signature on military papers and those of others on public declarations; and his knowledge of church affairs decided him to involve the Bishop of Rochester, who was known to be easygoing and something of an opportunist.

It was amusing to while away the weary hours of captivity formulating a plan which should be foolproof. All the men he intended to involve were already suspect; but of course Marlborough was the one who was going to cause the greatest stir.

This document had to be put in the house of one of the suspects, and then attention called to it so that it could be discovered there. But how operate all this from prison?

Young's agile brain enjoyed nothing more than working out an involved and seemingly impossible scheme; and as he was searching for the solution he thought of a disgruntled prisoner named Stephen Blackhead.

Blackhead had suffered badly in the pillory and as a result part of one of his ears was missing, the other being badly mauled. He hated society on account of this injury.

Young began by talking to him about his wrongs—a subject Blackhead was always ready to discuss.

"You have been cruelly treated, my friend. Society is against people like us."

Blackhead was mollified by the attention of the apparently well educated Robert Young, particularly when he was allowed to talk of his early days, of his poverty and of all he had suffered in an unsympathetic world.

Blackhead was only in prison for a short while, and Young had no idea when he himself would be released; so Blackhead was the man for the job.

"There is a way of getting your revenge on them," said Young. "They are worse criminals than you, my dear fellow. You are trying to get enough to eat; *they* are trying to make wars and bring rebellion into the country."

"Who?" asked Blackhead.

Young appeared to consider. Then he said: "I know I can trust you with an important secret. This is a matter which concerns the state. Will you swear to secrecy?"

Blackhead swore.

"I happen to have a document in my hands which could bring important people to the scaffold."

Blackhead looked incredulous.

"You think I'm mad. What if I showed it to you?"

"You would?"

"I trust you my friend."

Young brought the document from inside his jacket and showed Blackhead. Blackhead could not read, but he was impressed by the writing.

"You see that name," Young pointed. "That is Marlborough. And you see that—that is Thomas Sprat, Bishop of Rochester. That is the Archbishop of Canterbury and those are Lord Salisbury and Lord Cornbury."

"All those famous people! But how did you get it?"

"Never you mind. I make it my business to discover these plots and help the government. In this it says they'll kill the King and Queen and bring back James."

"The King and Queen ought to know about it."

"That's exactly what I think."

"But you could send it to them."

"Do you think they would believe me? I've tried to help them before, but I'm a poor man, wrongly accused. What chance have I against them?"

"There's one law for them, another for us. Why, I wasn't given a chance . . ."

Young interrupted; he wanted no further meandering through the wrongs suffered by Stephen Blackhead.

"The only way to get this brought to light is to put it in one of their houses and then let it be known that it will be found there."

"How'd you get into one of their houses?"

"I would if I were free."

"But you're here and so you can't."

"No, but you'll be free next week."

"Me?"

"You want a slice of the reward, don't you? I can tell you it will be a big one."

Blackhead licked his lips and although he had turned pale he said: "What would I have to do?"

"It's easy. You go to the Bishop of Rochester's house to take a letter."

"What letter?"

"Don't worry about that. I'll give you the letter. It will have been sent by your master."

"What master?"

"Some Doctor of Divinity. You're his manservant and he has sent you to deliver the letter. When you get there you'll be in need of refreshment and it will be given to you. You'll be taken to the kitchens by the servants. You will talk to them, tell them how honored you are to be in a Bishop's house; you can ask to see where the Bishop works. You'll touch his table with reverence. 'Is this where His Honor does his writing? Is this where His Honor sits?' you'll ask. You'll flatter them. Lucky people to work for a great bishop. You're just the servant of a humble priest. Then, when none of them is looking you slip the document somewhere . . . behind a picture . . . in a drawer, pushed well back so that it won't be easily discovered. You'll have to find the place when you get there. All you have to do is to make sure it is somewhere where the Bishop is not going to find it for a little while. Once you've done it, we shall inform the government that the document is in the Bishop's house and where it is. They will find it and we shall be rewarded."

Blackhead was staring at Young

"Suppose they won't show me into his rooms?"

"Then you'll put it somewhere else. I can see you're a man of resource. Think what your reward will be. The state owes you something in my opinion."

"In mine too," grumbled Blackhead; but he was bemused.

Young was slightly anxious. Would Blackhead have the sense to work this thing? He wasn't the accomplice he would have chosen. But how else was the plan going to work? Young was accustomed to taking chances. Well, he had to take a big one now.

Stephen Blackhead arrived at the Bishop of Rochester's house in Bromley, hot and dusty.

Could he be taken to the Bishop for he had a letter to deliver from his master and he had been told he must himself put it into the Bishop's hands.

He was taken into the study of the Bishop who received him cordially.

"A letter for me from your master?"

Stephen Blackhead handed over the letter which Robert Young had given him.

It was a beautifully written letter complimenting the Bishop and asking his advice on a matter which, the writer pointed out, would seem trivial enough to him but was of some importance to a humble deacon.

The Bishop glanced at the signature. He did not know the name but the letter had come from some little distance. He was pleased with the terms in which it was couched, and the subtle flattery put him into a good humor.

"I will answer your master and in the meantime you will be refreshed. I see you have traveled far." He sent for his butler and told him to take the messenger to the kitchen and give him food.

This was working out exactly as Robert Young had said it would and Stephen's spirits began to rise. He had never been inside such a magnificent house; he had never tasted such food as the butler was putting before him.

"This is a grand house," he said, for Young had told him he must admire the house and he could do it with sincerity.

Yes, it was a fine house, agreed the butler and the Bishop was a good master. It was a comfortable living serving such a man.

Stephen looked wistful. "I have never been in such a fine house."

The butler was clearly proud of it.

"I'd like to see a little more of it," said Stephen. "I'd like to see the Bishop's study."

"The Bishop's study! But he's working there."

This was where the plan was going wrong. How was he going to plant the document in the Bishop's study if the Bishop was working there; and how was he going to put it somewhere without the butler's seeing?

"The Bishop," said the butler, "is very fond of his gardens. He plants things himself. You see those flowerpots all along the windowsill; he's got his special plants and things in there. Would you like to see the gardens? I could show you them."

"Well, yes," said Stephen blankly. How was he going to put the paper in the gardens?

"Flowerpots," said the butler. "They're everywhere." He showed Stephen a little parlor leading off from the kitchens. "A lot of them go in here. We've got to put them somewhere. Now would you like a piece more pie while you're waiting?"

Stephen said that he would and while he was eating it the butler was summoned to his master's study for the reply which Stephen was to take back to his master.

"I'll be with you in a minute," said the butler.

And Stephen was alone, but he could hear the voices of other servants in some of the outhouses. This was the moment, he knew; he might not be alone again; and how was he going to rid himself of the document unless there was no one to see him.

He looked wildly about the kitchen; then he thought of the parlor with the flowerpots. He went into it quickly, picked up a large flowerpot, and knocking out some of the earth it contained, put in the document; he managed to conceal it by covering it with earth. Then he slipped back to the kitchen.

When the butler returned he was sitting at the table eating his pie.

He felt triumphant. He had done the job assigned to him; now all he had to do was wait for his reward.

The butler took him around the gardens as promised and as he feigned an interest he did not feel, he believed himself to be a grand conspirator.

As soon as he could get away he hurried to London and went to Newgate to visit the prisoner, Young.

"Well?" said Young.

Blackhead told him of everything that had taken place and how the incriminating document was in a flowerpot in a parlor which was clearly rarely used.

Young was delighted. "It couldn't be better," he said.

Mary sat with her Council to discuss the latest scare.

A prisoner in Newgate had written to the Privy Council warning them that he had evidence of a plot in which the ringleaders were the Bishop of Rochester and the Earl of Marlborough. These men had been in correspondence with James II and a letter containing the signatures of the conspirators and an offer of their services to James, had fallen into his hands. The letter was now in the house of the Bishop of Rochester at Bromley and if they would allow him to explain in detail, he would give them all the information they needed.

"Young?" said the Queen. "I fancy I have heard his name before."

"I have ascertained, Your Majesty, that he is a criminal, in prison for forgery," Danby told her.

"These are dangerous times," replied the Queen.

The Council agreed with her; also that no sources of information, wherever they were, should be overlooked.

As a result Young was able to tell them that if they searched the flowerpots in the Bishop's house they would find the document.

As a result the Bishop was arrested and a search party was sent to the Bishop's house and his flowerpots investigated.

Fortunately for the men whose names had been forged, for they would have been sent to the scaffold had the document been discovered, since Young's signatures were very good indeed, the disused parlor was overlooked; and the party came away without discovering the document.

Sarah was with Anne at Berkeley House in Piccadilly, whither they had come from Sion House as soon as Anne had recovered from her latest confinement, when news was brought to her from St. Albans that her youngest child, Charles, was ill.

"You must go at once to him, dear Mrs. Freeman," said Anne, "and write to me every day that I may know what is happening to you."

Sarah promised and when, arriving at St. Albans, she found the child with a high fever, she immediately put all her energies to nursing him.

It was pleasant to be home with her family, but not, as she told her husband, for such a reason.

"This ridiculous state of affairs must be over soon," she said. "Time is being wasted."

"Anything can happen in the next few weeks," replied Marlborough. "There are going to be mighty battles either at sea or on land and they may well decide great issues."

"And Marlborough skulking at home . . . in disgrace!"

"Which may be as well," he said grimly. "It is difficult at this stage to know which side one should be on."

Sarah was ready to launch into discussion of great plans, but the sickness of the child worried her and as the days passed he grew worse.

She was in the sickroom one day when she heard the sounds of horses galloping and looking from her window she saw a company of guards coming toward the house.

She called to her husband, but he was already on his way down. Rushing after him she was in time to hear what the leader was saying.

Marlborough was arrested on a charge of high treason, and orders were to conduct him without delay to the Tower of London.

Sarah was in despair. She thought of the letters Marlborough had written to James and trembled. Had one of these fallen into the Queen's hands? If so, he was doomed. But Sarah was not one to believe the worst until it had happened.

Marlborough must be freed from the Tower. He must be proved innocent.

How?

She must go to him. She could be with him in his lodging, make sure that he was well cared for, plan his escape if necessary.

She was preparing to leave when one of the nurses came to her and begged her to come at once to the child's sickroom.

Little Charles had taken a turn for the worse.

Sarah, numb with misery, sat reading a letter from the Princess Anne.

"I am very sensibly touched with the misfortune that my dear Mrs. Freeman has in losing her son, knowing very well what it is to lose a child, but she, knowing my heart so well, and how great a share I bear in all her concerns, I will not say more on this subject for fear of renewing her passion too much."

Anne was right. There must be no renewal of passion. The grief was overwhelming. Her beloved son for whom she had planned such a grand future—a corpse in a coffin. But that was past. There were the other children—her dear son John still left to her; her girls, Henrietta, Anne, Elizabeth, and Mary. She still had them.

And her own dear husband, that other John, who was at this moment a prisoner in the Tower.

She must go to him at once. She would take up her lodging there that they might be together.

No. Wait a while. She would go to see him, but she would not stay. She would return to the Princess Anne, because there she could work more hopefully for his release.

Meanwhile there was heartening news for the Queen. The fleet, under Admiral Russell, had beaten the French at La Hogue after a mighty sea battle lasting five days and nights. It was a complete victory. How delighted Mary was! All the anxieties of the last days seemed to be lifted if only temporarily.

Her first thought was for those men who had been wounded in the battle and she sent fifty doctors and hospital supplies to Portsmouth; she gave thirty-seven thousand pounds to be distributed among those who had taken part in the victory; she ordered all the bells to be rung throughout London.

"This has decided the issue," was the comment. "James will never come back now."

Young, who feared that, since the paper Blackhead had deposited in the Bishop's house would never be discovered and therefore the plot founder, sent Blackhead back to the house in Bromley to recover the paper.

Blackhead this time went as an emissary of the government and forced the astonished servants to allow him to search the house. He went straight to the disused parlor and there found the paper where he had put it. He carried it back to Young, who immediately sent Blackhead with it to the Secretary of State.

Meanwhile the Bishop of Rochester had been questioned; so had his servants; and he certainly had the air of an innocent man.

Blackhead had brought the document to them so it was decided to bring both the Bishop and Blackhead before the Council and question them together.

This was more than Blackhead had bargained for, and he was terrified when he was brought into the great chamber and saw the lords seated around the table. He was even more alarmed when the Bishop was brought in.

"This fellow came to me with a letter from his Deacon," cried the Bishop.

"So you are a servant of a Deacon. His name please?"

Blackhead could not remember. "Er...sir...he was a very good master..."

"His name?"

Blackhead bit his lips. For the life of him he could not think of a name. Young had not prepared him for this.

"The fellow's scared out of his wits," said one of the men at the table. "Give him time to think."

Blackhead thought hard and he mentioned a name and a town he knew. This was written down. He breathed more easily.

The Bishop said: "There is no such Deacon. There is no such living."

"Well, you had better tell the truth." Blackhead's knees were shaking.

"It were no fault of mine," he said.

"Then whose fault was it?"

"Well 'twere Robert Young. He said as how it would be easy like. These men had plotted against the King and Queen and 'twere the only way to bring 'em to justice."

"Why did you take this false letter to the Bishop?"

"So as I could put the paper there."

"So you put the paper in the flowerpot did you?"

It was no good. He couldn't think of any story to tell them, so had to tell them the truth.

Young was brought before the Council.

"Do you know this man Stephen Blackhead?" he was asked. "Yes, my lord. He was in prison with me. I was wrongly accused . . ."

"And you used him in this plot, to incriminate the Bishop, my Lord Marlborough, and others?"

"My lord, I have never spoken of the matter to this fellow."

"Yet he seems to have a good knowledge of the plot which you promised to disclose."

"It is all simply explained, my lord. The Bishop has bribed Blackhead to tell this preposterous story."

"Yet you informed us that this letter was in a flowerpot in the Bishop's house?"

"That is not so, my lord. It is part of the plot against me."

Young defended himself fluently and with an aplomb which suggested innocence; but his story lacked authenticity. He had in fact warned the Council to search the flowerpots; moreover, he had a criminal record.

When the results of the examination were brought before the Queen she said that Young was a rogue and that the plot against the Bishop had clearly been fabricated by him.

She still believed the men implicated to have Jacobite leanings, but they could not be found guilty in this case.

"Send Young and Blackhead back to Newgate," she commanded, "there to await their trial. As for Marlborough . . ."

She looked at the members of her Council. She would have liked to keep Marlborough a prisoner; but that would be unjust. He had been sent to the Tower for being implicated in this plot and the plot was proved to be a sham, fabricated by a villain with a criminal record.

Marlborough must be released.

"On bail," was the verdict. Marlborough was not entirely free from guilt, they were sure.

Thus Marlborough was released from the Tower, but suspicion of guilt clung to him and he could not call himself a free man.

Even as the bells were ringing for the victory of La Hogue came the news of the defeat of William's army at Namur.

Mary was astounded.

"Such a sudden change," she cried to Lady Derby, "is more than I can bear."

She had been planning great celebrations, for it had not occurred to her that William could be defeated; it seemed ironical that he should have failed, and the fleet which was operating under her jurisdiction should have been victorious. She would, in her heart, have preferred it to be the other way about, just for William's satisfaction; but of course that was folly. The victory of La Hogue was of far greater consequence than the defeat at Namur. That sea victory might well have made a future invasion impossible.

"But," she insisted, "I am quite stupefied."

There was more bad news to follow. Turning from Namur where he had failed to break the siege William was defeated at Steinkirk, but fortunately inflicted such losses on the enemy that it was impossible for them to take full advantage of the victory.

Moreover, there was news of a plot to assassinate William which had been miraculously discovered in time. A French officer named Grandval was caught by the English and executed; but before he died disclosed that James II and his wife had been involved in the scheme.

When Mary heard this, although horrified at the danger through which William had passed, she could not help feeling a kind of exultation. Her father was guilty of such a thing! It seemed as though there was a balance of their sins—hers against her father, his against her.

A little of the guilt which had oppressed her so often was lifted. She talked often of the Grandval affair with those about her, stressing the part her father had played in it.

"When I heard that he whom I dare no more name father was consenting to the barbarous murder of my husband, I was ashamed to look anyone in the face," she declared.

William came home from Holland, not this time a conqueror, planning to return again after a time.

Robert Young faced a trial for perjury and Blackhead promised to turn King's evidence. Having been granted freedom because of this, he promptly disappeared which meant a delay of the trial.

Eventually Young was found guilty of conspiracy and perjury; the plot was proved to be one fabricated entirely by himself, and the people whose signatures he had forged were clearly innocent.

Young was sentenced to imprisonment and to be set in the pillory where he suffered greatly from the attentions of the mob before he was returned to Newgate.

Marlborough still remained on bail and neither the King nor Queen were eager to grant him his freedom. But Marlborough had no intention of submitting to such treatment and had his case brought before the Lords, declaring that it was an infringement of privilege to retain bail after the charges against him had been dropped.

William presiding, was very loth to allow Marlborough to escape. He wanted to keep a close watch on the man, for he was well aware that he was corresponding with James and that although he was guiltless of implication in the flowerpot intrigue, he was nevertheless as much a traitor to the present regime as Young had implied.

There was a noisy session and William, knowing the Marlboroughs, could well imagine their using this to represent themselves as martyrs in the public eye. Martyrs were the biggest enemies a King could have, and the Marlboroughs were not going to be allowed to join that band.

Marlborough should be watched; he should be excluded from favor; but he should be free.

William therefore exercised the royal prerogative and brought the case to an end.

So Marlborough returned to his wife, but there was little to make them rejoice.

They had lost all they had carefully built up; their son was dead; they had little money. All they could rely on was the bounty of Anne; and her fortunes were not very high at this time.

She was living at Berkeley House and thither she invited the Marlboroughs.

In Kensington Mary found the outlook disturbing. The Marlboroughs influencing Anne; the quarrel with her sister growing; the people cheering her and disliking William.

The people were cruel and they did not hesitate to express their thoughts in the fashion of the day.

Lampoons and verses were circulated in the streets and the latest one, calling attention to William's failures and the success of La Hogue which they called Mary's triumph ran:

> *Alas, we erred in choice of our commanders.*
> *He should have knotted and she gone to Flanders.*

She hoped William would never hear that cruel couplet. How she wished that she could make everyone see him as she did! But that was impossible. He would make no concessions. He was only friendly with his intimate friends . . . like Bentinck, and now Keppel, and Elizabeth Villiers.

Bitterly Mary thought of that intimate circle in which even she was locked out.

But she would not dwell on it. She must continue to see William as the hero she had made him in her thoughts.

HIS HIGHNESS'S
SOLDIERS AND STAYS

*D*uring the months which followed Mary's health was not good; there were frequent attacks of the ague, that disease which had first attacked her in Holland. To add to her troubles there were constant rumors of Jacobite plots; William was obliged to return to the Continent which meant that she must give up the role of Queen Consort which she happily took on when he was in England and become the reigning Queen.

She had a natural aptitude for ruling; perhaps it was something she had inherited; her flashes of wisdom still astonished her Parliament for she was apt, when William was present, to offer no suggestions and thus appear to be merely a figurehead.

She was popular, for she had a natural dignity and because she liked to go among the people they were reminded of her uncle's affable manners. She was a Stuart, they told themselves; she looked like a Queen; she acted like a Queen; she was what they expected in a ruler.

With her ladies she often made excursions from the Palace; and would visit the fairs and, to the delight of the stallholders, made her purchases. She was a fine figure—large enough for three Queens, was the comment; but they preferred this to meagre William. Had she not been so big she would have been extremely beautiful in her coronet headdress consisting of three tiers of guipure point; beneath it her hair, drawn back from her forehead, showed dark and glossy. Her brocade dress was magnificent with the bows of ribbon at the shoulders; diamonds and pearls were about her neck and her garments. A Queen, said the people, of whom they could be proud.

But there were many, of course, who favored the Princess Anne. Why should she not have the friends she wanted? Did it not show how faithful she was to insist on keeping the Marlboroughs with her? There was the Princess Anne, heiress to the throne, not received at Court, deprived of her privileges.

It was interesting, though, to have such a quarrel in the royal family. What material it provided for the lampoon writers! And all the time, of course, there was the excitement of having a King over the Water.

The rumor was circulating that Mary and Anne had passed when driving in Hyde Park and Mary had pretended not to see her sister.

What next!

As for William, nobody wanted him. The English had never liked the Dutch and the idea of having a Dutchman for a King was intolerable, in some respects. He was so small, and to see him pulling on the arm of the Queen when they took their walks in the gardens about Kensington Palace was a comic sight, and therefore provided some amusement; but they would never like him.

Oh, for the days of good King Charles who gave them peace and pleasure! Wars, wars, it was all wars now—and there had to be taxes to pay for them. But what could be expected with a King over the Water and his daughter on the throne, and her not on speaking terms with her sister!

It was something to laugh at and as long as the English could laugh they were ready to be lenient.

But Mary was the one they cheered; nobody was going to raise one little shout for Dutch William.

Fortunately he was often abroad. "Let him stay there," said the people.

Anne was now living at Berkeley House, although she had apartments in Campden House where her son, at this time about four years old, had his household. Anne was a devoted mother and could not bear to be long away from her son; consequently she was often at Campden House.

The little boy's health caused constant anxiety; although he was extremely intelligent his body did not keep pace with his mind and the members of his household who loved him were terrified that, like his brothers and sisters, he would not survive. But that one of Anne's children should have lived four years was a triumph; Anne herself was continually fretting about his health and talked of it until, as Sarah complained to John, she nearly drove her mad.

The young Duke of Gloucester suffered from hydrocephalus and his head was out of proportion to the rest of his body so that it gave the impression that it was a great burden he had to carry around. He found difficulty in walking and had to be carried almost everywhere so that he was never without a retinue of nurses and attendants. Wherever he happened to be, his high young voice could be heard asking questions. Although only four, he wanted to hear about his uncle's campaigns in Flanders and what the war was all about. His manner was that of an adult, and although those whose duty it was to look after him were anxious about his physical state they were extremely proud of his mental capabilities.

When he was taken into the parks, in his carriage, he would demand to stop when he saw a soldier and discuss his uniform, medals, and campaigns with him like a veteran.

The Duke of Gloucester was by no means the least picturesque member of the family.

Anne adored him; so did Mary. Even William had to turn away to hide a smile at some of the boy's drolleries; and when he visited Campden House it was noticed that he would linger by the boy's side and answer his questions with a patience, and amusement, that no one had ever seen him display before.

It was expected that this common interest in the young heir to the throne might bring the sisters together, but this did not happen. Mary had given Anne her ultimatum which was that she did not wish to see her until she rid herself of Lady Marlborough. Anne's reply was to keep Lady Marlborough with her.

So the rift continued.

Each day the Duke of Gloucester was taken to Kensington Palace to see the Queen, for although his mother was forbidden the Court, this naturally did not apply to him.

He was interested in Kensington Palace where work was still going on, for he was always delighted to watch men at work, and if he could persuade them to let him have a tool so that he could join them, he was very happy.

Mary looked forward to his visits and was never with him without wishing that he were her son.

Mrs. Pack, the Quakeress, who had saved his life when he was a baby by feeding him at her breast, had remained with him in spite of Sarah Churchill's endeavors to get rid of her. Anne had shown herself very stubborn on this point; she was clearly terrified that something would happen to Gloucester if the outspoken, somewhat domineering Quakeress departed. It was disturbing for Sarah to have someone with a temperament like her own near the Princess Anne, but she realized that it was something she had to accept. Moreover Mrs. Pack was attached to the little boy's household in Campden Hill and therefore was not, as Sarah said, constantly under her nose to worry her.

Mrs. Pack rather naturally took as firm a dislike to Sarah as Sarah had to her; and with her plain good sense deplored the state of affairs in Anne's household. She thought Anne a fool; her only redeeming characteristic being her love for her son. In the quarrel between the sisters Mrs. Pack sided with the Queen; and as a result carried to her any little piece of information which she thought might be important to Mary, who, recognizing the shrewdness of the woman, was very glad to have her spy in Gloucester's household.

Mrs. Pack could tell the Queen when the Princess Anne was likely to be at Campden House which meant that Mary would not go at that time, thus avoiding an awkward meeting. But of course Mrs. Pack had other information to offer.

Anne often occupied her suite of rooms in Campden House, for she could not bear to be parted too long from her son, much to the disgust of Mrs. Pack who preferred to have the household to herself.

Gloucester was watched over with the utmost care. His food was sent from Berkeley House and knowing her own fancy for sweet things, Anne had banned confectionery, lest he develop too strong a taste for it.

Gloucester at the age of four was as intelligent as a seven-year-old; his quaint remarks were a delight to Mary, and when he called on her at Kensington Palace she enjoyed taking him around and showing him the men at work, for there were constant alterations and extensions being made at the Palace.

It was such a pleasure, in the midst of her anxieties, to spend an hour with the child. He always greeted her gravely, giving her the required homage and then having done his duty he would chat in a carefree way without a hint of shyness.

"How is my nephew today?" asked Mary.

"My dear Queen," he answered, "I am taken too much care of. Did they take too much care of *you* when you were a child?"

"I don't think they did," replied Mary.

"You were lucky. 'He mustn't walk too much.' As if I could? 'He is getting over excited. He must be bled.' Do you know there is a blister on the back of my neck?"

"No. Show me."

He did.

"It is the doctors. They are always doing something to me." He began to laugh. "They tried to fit me with a periwig. The blister was in the way."

"So no periwig," laughed Mary. "I think I like you better without."

"Still, as heir to the throne I should have a periwig. I should like to be Prince of Wales. Why cannot I be?"

A difficult question. He knew nothing of his grandfather who had been driven from his throne, for all those about him had been forbidden to mention the matter. Why couldn't he be Prince of Wales? How could one explain that in France there was a boy who was called the Prince of Wales. Not that he was accepted as such over here. But to give this boy the title would immediately give the Jacobites a fresh cause for complaint.

"You are young yet. All in good time."

"Some people have been Prince of Wales when they are babies."

"I think Duke of Gloucester a better title."

"I don't," said the boy.

"Well, come and look at the men working on the masonry. You will be interested and I want to see how they are getting on."

"It is good."

"What?"

"To be a mason. I would like to be a mason."

Mary smiled. Prince of Wales one moment, a mason the next.

"I think," she said, "you enjoy these little jaunts to the Palace."

"It is good to escape from them all. There is Lewis, my governess and her husband, and Mama as well as Pack. They are always there to see I do not tire myself, or if I need the leeches. Of course I wish I could walk better."

"You will when you're older."

"There is so much to wait for. I wish I were older."

"Most of us grow up too quickly."

That was a point which made him pause to consider. Later he would inform someone that most of us grew up too quickly—that was as if he had convinced himself that it was so.

But when he watched the masons he was a child again, crying out with pleasure when one of the masons gave him a tool and showed him how to work with it. His big head on one side, an expression of deepest concentration on his face, he did as instructed and then turned to Mary, his eyes alight with triumph.

"I wish I were a mason," he said.

"You are all wishes."

"And you are not?"

She was silent and he went on: "But then you are the Queen. You can have everything you want so you don't have to wish long."

She looked at him wistfully and thought: If you were my son I should be very happy.

When she left him she told him that a surprise would be coming to him.

In a few days he received a set of exquisite ivory tools. They had cost twenty pounds, which was a large sum, but worth it, Mary thought, to give him pleasure.

He played with them for a few days; then he saw the soldiers when he was out on one of his trips in the carriage with Lewis Jenkins, his Welsh attendant. He insisted on stopping to watch them drill, and spoke to them.

Then he knew that more than anything on earth, more than a mason, more than Prince of Wales, he wanted to be a soldier.

There was consternation at Campden House. The Duke of Gloucester had whooping cough—not a serious complaint in itself, but when one considered the delicate state of health of the little boy every ailment struck terror into his family.

Anne, whose greatest quality was her devotion to her family, went to Campden House and stayed there. Sarah was with her. Mrs. Pack resented the intrusion into the nursery but could do nothing about it and silent enmity reigned between her and Sarah.

Mary was worried, but knowing Anne was in the nursery could not face the embarrassment of calling and coming face to face with her sister, who had so disobeyed her by keeping Sarah Marlborough and, moreover, had the woman with her at this time.

She therefore sent Lady Derby to inquire after the child's health and to bring her back an account of how he was getting on.

"Go straight to Mrs. Pack," said Mary. "She will give me a truthful account; and try not to have any conversation with either my sister or Lady Marlborough."

Lady Derby, informing the servants that she came from the Queen, went straight to the nursery where Anne was seated in a room next to that in which Gloucester was sleeping. With her was Sarah.

Lady Derby walked past the Princess and Sarah into the nursery where she found Mrs. Pack, while Sarah and Anne exchanged glances before Sarah's fury burst forth.

"You might have been a rocker, the way she behaved. You know whose doing this is!"

Anne nodded. "I know," she said, "and I pray you, Sarah, say nothing

to Lady Derby who but does what she is told. I care nothing for my sister's attitude at this time. There is only one thing I pray for; and that is
my boy's recovery."

Anne the mother had a dignity which she lacked in other roles. Sarah
recognized it and, although it was a great strain, forced herself to be
silent.

In the nursery, Lady Derby was questioning Mrs. Pack.

"He'll get better," Mrs. Pack assured her. "He's over the worst. He
wants to be a soldier, he told me today. He wants his own company and
he does not want to wait till he is grown up. That's a good sign."

"I will tell Her Majesty and she will be pleased."

"Tell her too that I am keeping that Churchill crow out of *my*
nursery."

"I will tell her," Lady Derby promised.

When she walked out Anne and Sarah were sitting together, and
they ignored each other.

Mrs. Pack was right; the Duke of Gloucester began to recover quickly.

To mark the occasion and because she had heard of his desire to be a
soldier, Mary sent him a toy sword which was set with real jewels.

"*If you will* eat this," Gloucester was told, "you shall be a soldier."

Gloucester would do anything to become a soldier—even eat the
hideous potages that were put before him to build up his strength.

"If you will wear this, you shall be a soldier."

He wore what they wanted him to.

He went out for rides in his carriage when he would have preferred
to stay in, because a soldier must go out every day.

He was not one to allow these promises to go unfulfilled.

"Mama," he said, "I was promised that I should be a soldier and it is
not good to break promises."

"My boy shall be a soldier when he is old enough."

"Mama, he is five years old."

"It is a little young to be a soldier."

"Not when promises have been made."

Anne consulted with George. "He will have his way," she said fondly. "And we promised him to make him get well quickly."

"We must get him a toy musket, cannon, and a uniform. That will please him."

Anne smiled at George; no one could have had a kinder husband. He never interfered with what she wanted to do; they supped and drank together; he had taught her to like the same wines that he did; and the pleasures of the table delighted them both. There was no excitement to be had with George; for that one had to go to Sarah; but the fact remained that he was the kindest husband in the world and as devoted to their boy as she was.

The cannon, the musket, and uniform pleased the little boy, but he said: "I am the Duke of Gloucester and cannot be a soldier on my own. I need a company. I have to drill them and lead them into battle. I shall start recruiting immediately."

The parents exchanged glances. This was an extraordinary child they had begotten. He was full of energy in spite of his physical weakness. What a King he would make when he grew strong!

Even they were surprised when they saw him drilling five or six boys in the gardens.

When they spoke to him about it he shook his head. "It is not enough," he said. "I need many more for a company of soldiers. And I must have more uniforms and muskets and swords for them all, for they can't be soldiers without."

Naturally they wanted to please him; and it was so pleasant to see him well again. The Queen heard of the new project and muskets and cannons began to arrive. It seemed that to serve in the Duke of Gloucester's army might be a good opening for many little boys. So it did not take the little Duke long to form his army and soon he had ninety boys to be drilled each day. He had his drummers and his pipers—all of the ages of six and seven, a little older than himself but he was old for his years.

This occupied his thoughts to such an extent that he could talk of little else. The people could come and watch him drilling his army and they laughed and cheered.

The most popular member of the royal family was the Duke of Gloucester.

Mary was forced to reign alone while William was on the Continent and both she and William greatly regretted that Shrewsbury was not in office.

William had taken the seals of the Secretary of State from Nottingham and offered them to Shrewsbury before he left, but Shrewsbury would not accept them. Shrewsbury was piqued because he supported the Bill for three-yearly parliaments which William was against for he sensed that this would curtail the royal prerogative. The Tories opposing the Bill in the Commons enabled the King to refuse his assent; thus it was thrown out. William, however, believed he and Mary needed Shrewsbury and while he offered him the office of Secretary of State he hinted at a Dukedom. Shrewsbury, ever ready to plead ill health, retired to the country, expressing indifference to the King's offers.

William was harassed. His defeats on the Continent had depressed him; he had heard the rhymes about himself and Mary and the continual fear that he would be regarded merely as her consort—and which had been with him ever since their marriage, souring it and filling it with misunderstandings—returned.

He believed he needed Shrewsbury, and he was afraid that if he did not bind him with high office, Shrewsbury would go to the Jacobites. This affair of the Bill for triennial Parliaments was unfortunate, and he consulted one who never failed to comfort him and give him sound advice.

Elizabeth nodded shrewdly. He wanted Shrewsbury and there might be a way of persuading the Earl that he should become a member of the Government.

"He was completely without interest, but when I mentioned a dukedom there was the faintest flicker and then that died and he seemed adamant."

"Would you like me to try to see what could be done?"

"My dear, do you think you could?"

"He has a mistress—Mrs. Lundy. She is a foolish woman, but he is devoted to her. It might be possible to persuade her. Have I your permission to try?"

He took her hand.

"I know you to be completely discreet."

"You can trust me always to work . . . as you would yourself . . . and what higher compliment can there be than that?"

He wondered what he would do without her. Fortunately the Queen never mentioned her now. She knew of his relationship with her and accepted it. That was well.

And it was largely due to the cleverness of Elizabeth who never irritated the Queen, never intruded. She should be rewarded; yet how could he reward her without calling attention to their relationship.

She never asked for rewards. Incomparable woman!

He had forgotten that she had her small rewards. Bentinck was falling out of favor, although William would always have an affection for him; Keppel was rising in power; and Keppel had been the protégé of Elizabeth. They stood together while Bentinck had been the enemy who had dared criticize her.

Elizabeth had her power. It was enough.

It was absurd, said the Princess Anne, for her boy to be dressed as a child. One only had to look at him drilling his soldiers to realize how advanced he was.

Sarah yawned. She was a little weary of Anne's obsession. She would tell her so, but for the fact that John had warned her; and it was true their fortunes were not very bright at the moment. As soon as that child was a little older she would have her own son brought to be a companion to him; but not yet; she did not want her young John to be drilling with that band of boys. When Gloucester had a worthy post to offer her son he should have it.

The Princess Anne went on: "Mr. Morley and I were talking of him last evening . . ."

I'll swear you were! thought Sarah. What else do you talk of but food and drink.

She was getting very restive and finding Anne more boring than ever; and she was often angry at the way things were going. William was spitting blood and looked as if he would soon be in his tomb; but Mary recovered from her illnesses and in fact seemed a great deal more healthy than Anne. Life was madly frustrating at this time. But she was subdued—for her; Marlborough's sojourn in the Tower had had a very sobering effect.

"So we have summoned Mr. Hughes to make him a suit in white camlet and the loops and buttons are to be of silver thread."

"I am sure the little Duke will look charming thus attired." Poor little monster, thought Sarah, complacently, thinking of her own handsome son. Then her expression clouded when she remembered little Charles lying in his coffin. There was no safety anywhere now, it seemed. Tragedy could hit the Churchills just as any other family. They were meant for distinction, she was sure; but they had their troubles.

"When Mr. Hughes comes I want to take him to my boy for I wish to discuss with him how the clothes shall be made."

Sarah hid a yawn; and was rather pleased when Mr. Hughes came so that she could be rid of Anne.

"Mrs. Pack," said the boy, "I do not like Mr. Hughes."

"Why not. He's a good tailor."

"My stays are so tight, they hurt me."

He looked incongruous with his enormous head and his bright darting eyes which seemed as though they should be on the body of a boy in his teens instead of that fragile little creature.

He pulled at the stays under his waistcoat. "Do stays always hurt like this, Mrs. Pack?"

"They are meant to make you straight so they are bound to restrict a little."

"They do not make me feel very friendly toward Mr. Hughes," said the Prince.

Mr. Hughes the tailor called at Campden House on the orders of the Duke of Gloucester. As he entered the hall he was almost knocked over by a noisy crowd of small boys—ninety of them. One stood apart shouting orders.

"This way. Bring him here. Hurry, men."

"What the . . ." gasped Mr. Hughes as his legs and arms were seized by small hands and he was dragged to the floor; for small as his attackers were, they were numerous and they swarmed over him.

"Over here," was the order. "This way. We'll teach him to make stiff stays."

"Help me!" cried Mr. Hughes, so bewildered that he could not imagine what was happening to him.

A voice said: "Your Highness, what is this?"

"My men are in control," was the answer.

"It's Mr. Hughes, the tailor. Why Mr. Hughes, what has happened to you then?"

Mr. Hughes gasped his thankfulness to hear the voice of his friend and fellow Welshman, Lewis Jenkins.

"I do not know. These . . . imps fell on me as I came into the hall."

"We are taking him to the wooden horse," said a high pitched voice. "He is to be punished for making stiff stays that hurt."

"Mr. Hughes," said Lewis Jenkins, "get you up then, man. Now stand away, you boys."

"They take orders from none but me."

"The wooden horse, Mr. Hughes, man, is the punishment they use for soldiers who disobey. Take no notice. Mr. Hughes is not one of Your Highness's men."

"He makes stays that hurt. They're hurting me now."

"Why don't you ask him to remake them for Your Highness. That would be more sensible than this game you're playing."

Mr. Hughes was on his feet, but hands still pulled at his clothes. He said: "I'm sorry the stays are too tight, Your Highness. You must allow me to alter them."

"You can alter them?" asked the Duke.

"Certainly, Your Highness. I can make them so that you won't feel you're wearing stays at all, and would have done so, had you asked me."

"Men . . . dismiss!" cried Gloucester. "Mr. Hughes, to my apartments quick . . . march."

So Gloucester went off with the tailor and in a short time the stays had been altered to fit comfortably.

Lewis Jenkins laughed at the affair with his fellow attendants. "He'll get what he wants, that little one," he commented, and it struck him that they were fortunate to be in the service of the Duke of Gloucester. It was time he was acknowledged the Prince of Wales, for the more honors that befell him, the more they would all benefit.

THE END OF
A LIFE

Mrs. Lundy, daughter of Robert Lundy, who had been Governor of Londonderry, where he had served with little distinction, and had betrayed William and deserted the town during the siege—smiled at Elizabeth Villiers and wondered why the woman was being so gracious to her.

"You have great influence with my lord Shrewsbury," said Elizabeth, "and I can well understand that."

Mrs. Lundy, a vain and pretty woman, laughed. "He's an obstinate devil," she said, "once he has made up his mind."

"What man is not?" asked Elizabeth. "But sometimes—nay, often—it is possible to use a little gentle persuasion."

"You think Shrewsbury would listen to me?"

"If he would not listen to you he would listen to no one."

That pleased the woman; she tossed her head. No doubt she was proud of her conquest, for Shrewsbury was reckoned to be a fascinating man. He had a damaged eye which some people found repulsive; yet that seemed but to add to his attractions where others were concerned.

Elizabeth herself knew the value of some slight imperfection and how it could be turned to an asset.

She must get Shrewsbury to take office. William would be so delighted if she did; and she was eager to bind him closer and closer to herself.

"A Dukedom. That is worth having," went on Elizabeth. Surely, she implied, you would rather be the mistress of a Duke than an Earl? As the mistress of a King, Elizabeth could show that the rank of one's lover was of the utmost importance.

"He doesn't seem to care for titles."

"He is well equipped in that direction," added Elizabeth. "But I have yet to know the man who was not ready to take a little more. I'll warrant you will make him do as you wish."

Mrs. Lundy was not at all sure that it was her wish; but Elizabeth was subtly convincing her that it was.

Well, Mrs. Lundy was thinking, Secretary of State, a Duke . . . that was rather pleasant. And the King—and the Queen—would know that it was Mrs. Lundy who had persuaded that obstinate man to change his mind. They ought then to be very respectful toward Mrs. Lundy.

"I will talk to him," she said.

"I know you will succeed," Elizabeth assured her.

Gloucester was suffering from the ague and his mother was frantic with anxiety until she remembered that a Mr. Sentiman used to make up a prescription of brandy and saffron which he claimed would cure any sort of ague. Anne's uncle, Charles II, had dabbled in the making of medicines and she had heard him recommend this prescription. So Anne immediately sent for Mr. Sentiman.

The mixture was brought to Gloucester who, protesting, took it. It cured his ague but made him so ill that his parents feared he was on the point of death.

Anne sat on one side of his bed, George on the other.

"He must not die," whispered Anne brokenheartedly, and George came to stand at her side and place one of his fat hands on her shoulder. Dear comforting George, who loved the boy even as she did. Gloucester looked weakly from one to the other and smiled faintly.

"You must not fret so, Papa and Mama," he said. "I shall get better soon. I have to drill the men I intend to offer the King to go to Flanders with him."

Then he closed his eyes and slept.

He was right; he did improve.

It was a glorious day when Anne and George knew that he was out of danger.

"He should be proclaimed Prince of Wales," said Anne.

George shook his head, meaning that it would not be wise.

"Mary is fond of him; she gives him almost everything he asks for. I think sometimes she would give everything she has for a son like our boy. George, I have just thought of something. The Duke of Hamilton has died. Does that convey anything to you?"

"No, my dear, only that the Duke of Hamilton is dead."

"He had the Garter."

"It's true," said George.

"A blue ribbon vacant. Why not for our boy?"

"It should be his. Why not?"

"My lord Shrewsbury to see Your Majesty."

"Pray tell him to come to me at once."

Mary was pleasurably excited as always by this man.

He came to her and bowed low. What was it about him that reminded her of her youth in Holland when she had danced with Monmouth? He was not in the least like Monmouth—he had far more to commend him. He was more serious. Poor Monmouth had tried to snatch at office and had lost his head in doing so, and Shrewsbury had been remarkably shy in taking it.

"I hope, my lord," said Mary, flushing slightly, "that you have come to give me the news I shall best like to hear."

"Your Majesties have been most gracious to me, most complimentary."

"I know the King desires you to take office. There are few men here whom he can trust."

"I once heard it said to him that there was no one in England who could be trusted and he replied, 'Yes, there are men of honor in England, but alas, they are not my friends.'"

Mary nodded. "In his great wisdom he knew that to be true. You, my lord, are one whom he would trust; and if I could write to him and tell him that you have accepted office that would be the best news he could have."

"It is my desire to serve Your Majesties."

Mary gave a little cry of pleasure and laid her hand on his arm, then flushing still deeper, removed it.

"I am so delighted that you have made this decision."

They looked at each other intently. He was suspected of being a Jacobite; but he was also a man of honor. Perhaps he had refused office because he had no wish to serve against the King to whom he had once sworn allegiance. This taking of office, in the case of a man like Shrewsbury, must mean that he had accepted the revolution, that he had decided that it was impossible to attempt to bring back James and would work therefore for William and Mary.

William was right. There were few men of honor who had been his friends. If they had been men of honor they would not readily have deserted the old King in favor of the new. That was why William had had to look for his friends among Dutchmen.

But Shrewsbury was a man they knew they could trust, and the Queen felt a mingling of relief, delight—and excitement.

Gloucester was preparing to visit the Queen; he had recovered from the ague and was as full of vitality as ever. He looked like an odd little man in his white camlet suit with the silver thread decorations and he was pleased now because Mr. Hughes had taken most of the stiffness out of his stays.

His mother put a blue ribbon over his shoulders and stood back to admire the effect.

"But what is that?" he asked.

"Do you not like it?"

"Soldiers don't wear them."

"Ah, yes they do, if they are honored enough."

"I have never seen a soldier in a blue ribbon."

"It is the ribbon of the Garter."

"A garter, worn there . . ."

"They have a garter too."

"Where is it?"

"You haven't got that yet. It has to be given by the Queen. Perhaps when she sees how that blue ribbon becomes you she will give you one."

Gloucester was not greatly impressed, but was always pleased to visit his aunt; and when he was with her he forgot about the blue ribbon for she did not mention it either.

Mary had noticed it though and understood the implication. Anne wanted her to bestow the Garter on her nephew.

She would have liked to do so, for nothing pleased her better than bestowing honors on the little boy; but she had already made up her mind who was to have the vacant Garter.

A Dukedom was not enough for one whom she admired, as she did Shrewsbury; and the Garter should be his.

"*So it is* the Garter for Shrewsbury!" cried Sarah. "A Dukedom and the Garter!"

"She knew that I wanted the Garter for my boy."

"You can want all you like. She can't do enough for that man. You can guess why, Mrs. Morley."

"You don't mean . . ."

"What else? I have heard that she starts and blushes every time he comes into the room. Well, you can't wonder at it when you consider Caliban. And what of the Villiers woman too! Naturally the Queen wants a little fun."

"As you say considering Caliban . . ."

They laughed together, Anne a little bitterly because she was furious that Gloucester had been denied the Garter.

"You know what Jack Howe says . . ." went on Sarah.

"Pray tell me."

"You know, Mrs. Morley, that Jack Howe was dismissed from the Queen's service, but he knew much of what went on there and he said that if William died she would go so far as to marry Shrewsbury."

"He is supposed to be handsome, Mrs. Freeman, but that eye of his is so repulsive."

"William has Squint-eyed Betty and you know the Queen thinks William has such good taste."

It was like Sarah to be able to make her laugh when she was feeling so miserable about the loss of Gloucester's Garter.

"Oh, Mrs. Freeman, do you believe this?"

"I do," said Sarah.

More than that she was determined that others were going to believe it too.

Mary wondered whether the child had expected to have the Garter; she guessed that there would be a good deal of light chatter when his mother was about; and his ears were alert for everything that was said. She feared he might be disappointed and therefore decided that she would give him a present instead.

She had a beautiful bird in a cage brought to her; it was of a rare species and the same blue colors as the Garter.

Surely a bird would be more exciting to a child who could not understand the honor implied.

When Gloucester next came to see her she received him with great affection, complimented him on his glowing looks and asked how the army was progressing. He delighted to tell her that his men were shaping well and when they were ready he intended to offer them to the King.

Mary assured him that the King would be delighted.

"And now I have a present for you," she said.

He looked pleased; he was certain that she was going to offer him a blue ribbon. He had heard so much talk about the Garter between his parents that he had begun to regard it with awe and look forward to the day he would wear it over his uniform. All his soldiers must be told in advance that it was a great honor and they must have a special field day to mark the occasion.

So when the Queen's woman brought in a bird in a cage he was taken aback.

"There!" said Mary. "Is that not a beautiful creature."

Gloucester regarded the bird intently. "Yes, it is a beautiful creature," he said.

"I knew you would like it. How much more beautiful than a Garter."

He looked stonily at the cage.

"I will give it to you," said Mary.

He bowed courteously but distantly.

"Madam," he said very distinctly, "I would not rob Your Majesty of the creature."

Then to the astonishment of the Queen he began to talk of other matters.

Sarah had been talking to Princess Anne when suddenly she rose and throwing open a door found Mrs. Pack standing very close to it.

"Ah, Mrs. Pack, I expected to find you there!"

"Did you?" said Mrs. Pack, for the moment abashed.

"Oh, yes. A favorite spot of yours." Sarah smiled and then let her expression become grim. She shut the door with a bang and went back to the Princess.

"There we have our spy," she said. "I have told you before, Mrs. Morley, that you should suspect her."

"I wish she would go."

"You wish she would go? But in this household your wishes are law."

"My boy has an affection for her."

"He cares for nothing but his soldiers. Give him a few more to drill and order about and he'll gladly exchange Mrs. Pack for them."

To order about? thought Anne. Sarah liked to order people about.

She dismissed the thought at once; it was so unfair to Sarah who thought only of her comfort. But what to do about this Mrs. Pack? The woman was a spy for the Queen. There would always be spies. If you were rid of one, others took their places. That was why Barbara Fitzharding had remained. She was a good governess to Anne's boy even though she did report everything to her sister. There must always be spies.

"Pack must pack," said Sarah facetiously.

But Anne shook her head. "My boy wouldn't like that. Remember she fed him. I shall never forget the day she came to the nursery. Dear Mr. Morley and I were breaking our hearts because we thought we were going to lose our boy."

"My dear Mrs. Morley, because Pack was a good wet nurse that does not mean that she should be allowed to spy on your household."

"The boy is fond of her."

"Then you will not let her go?"

"I do not care to make a hasty decision on such a matter."

Sarah was quite obviously angry, but Anne was firm.

It was Mrs. Pack who made the decision. She had been found out and she guessed her usefulness was at an end. She told the Queen what had happened and Mary gave Mr. Pack a place in the Custom House which Mrs. Pack gratefully accepted on his behalf.

Then Mrs. Pack addressed herself to Anne.

"Madam," she said, "I am begging leave to retire as the Duke is now growing too old for a nurse and I find my health failing me."

Anne was pleased. This gave her an opportunity of pleasing Sarah without upsetting a woman to whom she must always be grateful, so she settled an annuity of forty pounds a year on Mrs. Pack who went to join her husband and family at Deptford.

It was true that Mrs. Pack's health was not as good as it had once been; and the Deptford air did not suit her as Kensington had.

Only a few weeks after she had left she caught the small pox.

The Duke of Gloucester who had been distressed when she left was even more so when he heard that she was ill. He wanted to visit her, but when this was forbidden, he sent messengers each day to inquire for her health.

He was noticeably less exuberant than he had been; and the attendants said that there was a closeness between a wet nurse and a child she had suckled which nothing could break.

The Duke of Gloucester stood staring disconsolately out of the window. Several of his attendants noticed that he had been quiet that day.

Mrs. Wanley, one of the women of the household, asked him if he were feeling ill.

"No," he told her; and continued to stare out of the window.

There was something odd about the child, yet at the same time lovable. He was so grown up in his mind and yet so physically delicate. Everyone in the household was constantly on the watch for a cold or an ague or fever.

"I know what," said Mrs. Wanley; "you miss Mrs. Pack. You haven't been the same since she went."

He did not answer and she went on: "Poor Mrs. Pack. I always said the Deptford air wasn't to be compared with this at Kensington. Why, she hadn't been there a week when she took this small pox. Mind you, I haven't heard that she's got it badly . . ."

Gloucester said slowly: "Mrs. Pack will die tomorrow."

Then he walked slowly out of the room.

Mrs. Wanley staring after him, murmured: "Lord have mercy on us!" and then shrugged her shoulders.

She remembered the remark the next day, though, for Gloucester did not send to Deptford as he had every day since he had heard of Mrs. Pack's illness.

Lewis Jenkins, thinking that he had forgotten, reminded him.

"It is no use sending," said Gloucester gravely, "for Mrs. Pack is dead."

"Dead!" cried Lewis. "How do you know."

"That is no matter," answered Gloucester, "but I am sure she is dead."

The entire household was discussing this strange incident and Jenkins, out of curiosity, sent a messenger to Deptford to find out the state of Mrs. Pack's health.

When the messenger returned several of the servants were eagerly waiting for him.

"Mrs. Pack died today," he said.

They looked at each other. The little Duke of Gloucester was strange in more ways than one.

Oddly enough now that Mrs. Pack was dead he ceased to grieve for her, and it was almost as though she had never existed.

Mary, hearing the story, was struck by the strangeness of her nephew and wanted to know more about the incident and asked him if he were very upset because his old nurse was dead.

His expression was stony suddenly. He looked into his aunt's face and said coldly: "No, Madam."

Then in that disconcertingly adult manner, he began to talk of other subjects.

The news from the Continent was not good; Mary was beset by troubles. The Whigs were in revolt against William's policies both at home and abroad, for they had supported him in the first place—expecting him to take orders from them, and the Tories were naturally dissatisfied. Why, Mary wondered, did men covet crowns? When she thought of the pleasant life she and William might have had, living quietly in Holland she could cry with frustration. But then William was a born leader; he would never have been content with the simple life.

She herself was discovering a talent for government which surprised no one as much as herself. She was gracious to all; she wished to be just; she was rarely arrogant and the people liked her, in spite of the spate of lampoons which were written about her and William. She had inherited some quality from her Uncle Charles which meant that when she came face to face with trouble she would be inspired to act in a manner which could best avert it.

This she was able to prove when she was with her Cabinet; as it was a ceremonial occasion she was wearing her velvet robes lined with ermine and there were jewels on her gown.

The defeats the Army had suffered on the Continent meant that the Exchequer was low and there were rumors that the country was on the edge of bankruptcy. Servants of the state had not been paid for some time and this was a condition which could not continue.

She was discussing this matter with her ministers when there were sounds of angry voices in the courtyard, and she sent one of her pages down to discover what was happening. Shortly afterward—while the shouts became nearer and more menacing—he returned to say that it was a party of sailors' wives from Wapping who had come to demand their husbands' pay.

Mary was aware of the consternation on the faces of her ministers. This was the first riot, they were thinking. Where was it going to end?

It was then that Mary showed her special talent.

"Go down to these women," she said, "and tell them to select four of their group as spokeswomen; these four shall be brought to me here and I personally will talk to them and they shall tell me of what they complain."

Her ministers were astonished.

"Did she realize that there was a mob of angry women below threatening to tear the palace apart? And did she know what a mob could be like when it was aroused?"

She answered: "They have a grievance and have come to Whitehall, I believe, to see me. It would be discourteous of me to refuse to talk with them."

She insisted that four women were brought to her presence chamber.

When she, in her ermine and jewels, faced them in their patched serge, her ministers trembled, but she was unafraid.

So royal did she look; so large, so glittering, so very much like their picture of a Queen that even the leader of the four was temporarily overawed. And when Mary spoke to them in a beautiful soft voice which betrayed at once her sympathy they were still further taken aback, that someone who looked so sumptuous could at the same time be kind and sympathetic.

"You are anxious because your husbands have not been paid, and I understand that full well. So you came to see me about it which was a wise thing to do, and I am glad you did it. Now tell me everything that is in your minds."

They told her. They spoke of their poverty, of the arrears which had not been paid and how the sailors' wives of Wapping had decided that they would not accept this state of affairs.

She did not attempt to interrupt, but listened gravely, nodding her head.

When they had finished she said: "I will tell you this: Everything that is owing to you shall be paid in time. The first payment shall begin at once. I give you my word."

There was a brief silence. Promises had been made before. But this was a woman like themselves who seemed to understand. She was magnificent yet kind; she was a Queen and they did not believe such a woman could deceive them.

"We believe Your Majesty," said the leader of the group, turning to her companions for confirmation. They nodded.

"Then," said the Queen, "take your friends back to Wapping, and take them in peace, for riots would serve no good to any of us."

The four retired, reported what had happened to their friends and assured them that the Queen was a lady whom they could trust; the mob went quietly away, and, summoning the Cabinet, Mary ordered that whoever else suffered the sailors must be paid.

She made them see the wisdom of this move and that having given her promise it must be honored.

The sailors were paid and what might have been the beginning of disaster was avoided.

William was in England, rather weary, rather dispirited and poor in health.

Mary noticed that he was turning more and more to Keppel and that there was an unhealthy rivalry between him and Bentinck for William's affections. She was sorry for this because Bentinck had been a good and faithful friend; and she was afraid that William's obvious preference for the younger man would turn Bentinck from him.

It was Elizabeth Villiers' doing, she knew; for Elizabeth had promoted Keppel when Bentinck had shown himself to be against her, and so subtly had she done this that she had undermined the friendship of a lifetime. Mary felt very sad to see William's neglect of his old friend in favor of the gay young man; and more so because it was an indication of the hold Elizabeth Villiers still had on William.

It was pleasant, however, to discover that he could be amused by young Gloucester. Perhaps the boy with the grown-up manner and the big head reminded him of what he himself had been at that age; and Gloucester's preoccupation with the Army was something they had in common.

When the boy announced that there was to be a grand field day in Kensington Gardens and invited the King and Queen to attend, William's mouth turned up at the corners and he said to Mary: "It is an invitation we must accept."

Mary was delighted. "Such a droll creature he is, William. He is most unusual. I never knew such a boy. If only his health would improve we should all be so much happier."

"He certainly does not resemble his father or mother."

"He is not in the least like them."

"If he were, I for one would not wish to see him."

"I think you must have been rather like him when you were a boy, William. He is so bright and so interested in his soldiers. To see him drilling them is better than a play."

William grunted and they set out together for the gardens where Gloucester had his troops lined up in readiness.

Gloucester saluted the King and Queen and conducted them to the grand stand with their attendants.

"Such guards you have!" he commented. "Once my Mamma had Guards. Why does she not have them now?"

There was a brief silence. The boy certainly had a habit of firing awkward questions. Then the Queen said quickly. "I am always rather pleased to escape from guards and formality. Tell me are you going to fire the cannon?"

Gloucester was thoughtful for a second or so which Mary knew meant he was making a mental note of her answer. He would probably want to know later why she did not wish to discuss his mother's lack of guards.

He turned to William. "Have I the King's permission to fire the cannon?"

"It is readily granted," answered William, and Mary was happy again.

"I hope the King will inspect my troops," said Gloucester. "I have assured them that this would be a great honor."

To Mary's delight William expressed his willingness to inspect the troops and he carried out the performance as gravely as though it were a real military display.

Gloucester walked with the King through the ranks of boys who stood at attention, toy muskets on their shoulders, wooden swords at their sides. An incongruous sight, some might think—the boy with his enormous head and little legs which hardly seemed strong enough to carry him so that he gave the impression of tottering, and William stooping forward, his great periwig overbalancing his body. They might have been father and son, thought Mary; and how wonderful it would have been if they were.

The cannons were then fired; there were four of them but the fourth had gone wrong and only three of them worked. Gloucester was very downcast about this. "That this should happen on the field day when the King is inspecting my troops!" he moaned. "Oh, be doleful!"

William replied that he would send a cannon to replace that which had failed to work and Gloucester was mollified.

"My dear King," he said, "you shall have both my companies with myself to serve you in Flanders."

William gravely thanked him and watching them Mary almost wept with joy, for never would she have believed William capable of such make-believe.

She said to herself then: This is one of the happiest moments of my life.

In May William prepared to leave for Flanders and Mary decided to accompany him as far as Canterbury.

As the weather was impossible for William to cross the Channel they decided to stay for a while in Canterbury and Mary was glad of these few days' respite.

She felt there was little to look forward to but these separations which meant long periods of anxiety for her when she must shoulder the burden of sovereignty alone. That she was admired and respected by her ministers was some comfort; and she had Shrewsbury to lean on. But her relationship with him was a little uneasy for she could not be unmoved in his presence and somewhere at the back of her mind was a thought which she refused to consider. There was a man whom she could have loved. It had been thus with Monmouth; and if she had loved one of them how different her life would have been from that which she shared with William.

She was thirty-three, which was not after all very old; yet she was weighed down with responsibilities; and it was disconcerting to remind herself that she had never had a lover.

These thoughts were suppressed before they had time to become complete. Fragments of disappointment and frustration were stifled by the ideals which demanded that she accept her union with William as the perfect marriage.

She fancied that he was turning to her more than he ever had before. Was he admiring the manner in which she ruled in his absence, and of which her ministers approved? In fact she believed they were glad to see William go, for they preferred to serve her. William was aware of this and it did not really please him. It was natural, she hastened to assure herself, for he was the man, he was the master; and he had always been afraid that he would be regarded merely as her consort.

But he was turning from Bentinck to Keppel; could it be that he was turning from Elizabeth Villiers to his wife?

He had been less irritable; he had treated her with more respect; he was forced to discuss state affairs with her; and he did like to walk, leaning on her arm, through the gardens of Kensington, talking of the plans for rebuilding which never seemed to be completed.

He seemed to have made up his mind that he could not win the affection of these alien people, and he made no attempt to do so.

When he had ridden through Canterbury only that day he had had an opportunity of pleasing the people. Knowing that he would be riding that way they had gathered the flowers from their gardens to dress up the High Street and some of the boys of the neighborhood had called "Long Live King William!" as his coach drove along; they had run beside it shouting loyal greetings.

And William, instead of bowing, smiling, and showing his pleasure, had scowled at them. "It is enough," he said dryly.

They had fallen away from the coach, crestfallen then, but they would be sullen and resentful later.

What a King! Those boys could remember tales of royal progress. Good King Charles had always known how to please the people. What William did not seem to understand was that whenever his name was mentioned those boys would remember a sour face against a coach window grumbling: "It is enough!"

Soon afterward they went on to Margate and there she took yet another farewell of her husband.

A few weeks after William had left came news of the disastrous expedition against Brest when many lives were lost.

Sarah heard the news in silence. Another failure for William! She believed that she had had a hand in this for she had heard from John that the expedition was to take place and she had written of it to her sister Frances, Lady Tyrconnel, who was in France with James and his exiled Court. If the element of surprise had been removed, then it was hardly likely that the expedition should succeed.

Well, thought Sarah, I have no reason to be grateful to this King or Queen.

She felt an immense sense of power—which had deserted her lately—when she could convince herself that she had had a hand in this disaster.

Anne was becoming more and more boring; she was completely wrapped up in her son and this brought her and George closer together. As for Old Est-il possible? he was even more of a bore than his wife.

I shall go mad if something does not happen soon, thought Sarah.

William returned in November. The English received him sullenly. What sort of a King was this whose heart was clearly on the Continent. He had suffered many defeats, but he had inflicted great losses on the French and it was believed that they might be pleased to make peace.

William did not want peace. He was a soldier and his military skill had won him adulation abroad—if not in England. He had a greater interest in Holland than in England and chose Dutchmen for his friends.

He was more morose than ever on his return, having no time to be with Mary, nor to visit young Gloucester. He was brusque and showed no respect for his wife's wishes. When her devoted friend John Tillotson, the Archbishop of Canterbury, died she had wanted to give the office to Dr. Stillingfleet who was most suited for it, but William had given it to Thomas Tenison, although previously it had been understood that she was to bestow such offices where she thought fit.

It was impossible to discuss anything with William. He became aloof and cold, or even sarcastic, when she tried to. So Mary shrugged the matter aside and accepted his rule.

But with the coming of the winter she was feeling depressed. Often she heard news of her sister's household and she knew that slanderous stories about herself and William had their beginnings there; and although Sarah Churchill was her enemy, Anne was to blame for keeping her.

Information had reached William that the failure at Brest was partly due to betrayal on the part of the Marlboroughs, and he was furious, yet afraid; for the people chose to see in Anne a martyr and while she supported the Marlboroughs it was dangerous to attack them.

He summoned Marlborough and told him that he was deeply disturbed by what he believed had happened.

"Upon my honor," cried Marlborough, "I never mentioned it but in confidence to my wife."

"I never mention anything in confidence to mine," murmured William.

"My wife must have mentioned it to her sister."

William looked at him through narrowed eyes and thought of how he would have this man's head . . . if he dared.

What a country! What was this crown worth? The men whom he would have chosen to have on his side, and Marlborough was one of them, were all against him. He was feeling weary and wished that he had allowed this ungrateful land to turn papist, to keep its King.

There were continual pinpricks, such as when the new coins were issued. The heads of William and Mary were to be engraved on these coins, and there had, in fact, been difficulty in getting them made because Philip Rotier, the artist who had worked for the crown, refused to do so for William and Mary, boldly stating that he did not consider them the true King and Queen. His son, Norbert, however, was less scrupulous and undertook the work.

When these were completed the head of William looked as though it belonged to a satyr. It was deliberate, and of the same pattern as the lampoons which were circulated daily. The people did not like Dutch William. They had not wanted papist James but they did not want William either. It was only Mary, he knew, who kept them on the throne. What he had always feared was, in a way, happening. It had been one of his nightmares that Mary would become Queen of England and he merely her consort. That had not happened; but again and again he was reminded that he was only accepted on her account.

The political situation was dangerous, and William was constantly at Whitehall. Mary who was suffering from a cold which she could not throw off, remained at Kensington to take advantage of the purer air. Occasionally William would come there; but when he did he would be working all the time and rarely stayed long before he was called back to business in Whitehall.

Mary was melancholy; she worried about William's health for the spitting of blood had started again and his asthma was worse. She heard through the gossip of his pages that he drank a great deal—always Holland's gin—when he was with his Dutch friends, and although he never showed signs of intoxication he became irritable. He was working too hard, planning new campaigns, and was never at rest.

One day when she was at her toilet the ruby fell out of the ring which he had put on her finger when he married her. Of all the splendid jewelry she possessed this ruby ring was the most precious to her. Often she would remember the occasion when he had placed it on her finger, the horror in her heart, the ready tears; and all because she was marrying William whom, she assured herself, she had come to love more than she had believed it was possible to love anyone.

"The ruby!" she cried as it dropped to the floor.

Her women were on their hands and knees searching for it, and one of them, finding it, held it up.

"Your Majesty will have it reset."

She was trembling. "I do not like that," she said.

"Your Majesty has had it for many years. Stones do drop out now and then."

"I am afraid," she said, "that it is an omen."

"Your Majesty is tired," soothed Lady Derby. "Will you allow me to take the ring and have the stone put in?"

Mary handed it to her, but she could not shake off her melancholy, and when the ring was returned to her she did not wear it. She wrote an account of how William had slipped it on her finger, how she had always treasured it beyond all other jewelry, and then how frightened she had been when the stone had fallen out.

She put it on her finger while she wrote. Then she thought: I shall never feel it is safe. I shall always be afraid of losing it now.

So she put it into a box with what she had written about it and locked the box.

That gave her a feeling of security; as though she had taken precaution against fate.

Mary had felt ill throughout the day; she had slept badly and in the morning was filled with such a sense of foreboding that she did not wait for her women to come to her. Instead she got up and examined her arms and shoulders. It was almost as though she had been expecting what she saw there. They were covered in a rash.

She went back to bed and lay there waiting.

There was one disease which all feared, for although some took it and survived, mostly it was fatal. If she were suffering from small pox she would have very little chance of recovery. She was only thirty-three, but she loved rich foods; her habit of drinking chocolate every night had made her put on a great deal of weight and she had heard that those whose blood was rich with a surfeit of food fared badly in the sickness.

When her women came to her she said: "Do not come too near me, but call Dr. Radcliffe."

When Dr. Radcliffe came, he said she was suffering from the measles.

The news was quickly circulated that the Queen was sick.

At Berkeley House Sarah felt as though new life was being pumped into her. The Queen sick. Measles, they said. But was it? Doctors who wanted to cheer the patient and not spread alarm sometimes said "Measles" when they meant "Small pox."

If it were small pox, she couldn't survive. She was not strong enough. She was too fat; and moreover she had suffered recently from the ague. She hadn't a chance.

The great moment might be at hand, for if she died, would the people keep William? And if they would not, it was Anne's turn.

Sarah went to her mistress who was lying on her couch. She frowned at her. Anne herself was in a poor state; She had suffered in the last year so badly from gout and dropsy that she could scarcely walk and had to be carried everywhere. She was enormous, and the fact that she was once more pregnant made her look larger than ever and feel more indisposed.

"Mrs. Morley has heard the news?"

Anne looked surprised, and as obviously she hadn't, Sarah lost no time in telling her.

"Radcliffe says measles, but the man's a fool. From what I hear it's the pox."

"The pox!"

Sarah clicked her tongue impatiently. "You know what this can mean, Mrs. Morley?"

Anne looked startled. Then she said: "Of course. Oh, dear, we must act quickly."

"There is nothing much we can do at the moment, Mrs. Morley, except be patient for a while."

But Anne was not listening. "My boy must leave Campden House at once. If there is small pox in Kensington he may be in danger."

If Dr. Radcliffe diagnosed measles, Dr. Millington could not agree with him.

The Queen was suffering from small pox, said Dr. Millington, and Mary believed him.

She assured them that she felt a little better and that night dismissed her women. "If I need you," she said, "I shall call. If I do not call, I wish to be left in peace."

When she was alone, she rose, and taking the boxes in which she kept her writings and correspondence she sat at her table. Many candles had been lighted at her command and piece by piece she destroyed what she had written in her journals, the letters she had received from William during his campaigns, those which she had received from her father and Frances Apsley; she wanted no one to pry into her life, for she had expressed herself too frankly in her journals about her relationships with others. She had always intended to destroy these things at the last moment; and she believed that moment had come.

All through the night she sat there, reading those letters which recalled so much of her life; they brought back memories of a passionate young girl—a girl who had dearly loved another woman before she had been thrust into a marriage for state reasons; of the reluctant marriage which she had done her best to make into the perfect union; of the love she might have had for two men, Monmouth and Shrewsbury, but had never been given, only dreamed of.

"My life has been like a succession of dreams," she said aloud, "and it has never been easy to know where the world of dreaming ended and that of reality began. And now it is too late to discover."

She thought of William who from the time she was fifteen had dominated her life. That meant for eighteen years. Eighteen years with William and they had never known each other. She pictured those eighteen years. She saw herself dancing with Monmouth, pleading with Shrewsbury to take office, offering him his Dukedom and the Garter. And she saw William going stealthily up the back staircase to the apartments of the maids of honor to be with Elizabeth Villiers, of his devotion to Bentinck and Keppel.

Perhaps, she thought, it would have been better to have looked for truth rather than to have made dreams.

She smiled at the ashes. The past was dead now and no one should read the truth through her.

But there was one thing she had forgotten. William and Elizabeth Villiers! She believed that she was close to death; yet William had been the one whom everybody had thought would go first. He spat blood; he was in constant pain and his asthma was dangerous. He could die suddenly.

She thought of his dying with the guilt of adultery on him.

She would write to him, implore him to repent of his sin, and warn him that there was only one way he could hope for forgiveness and that was to sin no more.

Writing had always come easily to her; that was why there had been so much to burn during this night. Now her pen flowed smoothly. She knew, of course, of his adulterous intrigue with Elizabeth Villiers and she implored him not to go to his death with that stain on his soul or she feared he would not be received into heaven. He must repent. She begged him to. He must give up that woman. She herself had known of his adultery all through their married life and it had given her great pain. He must repent now. She was going to put this letter into a casket which she would entrust to the Archbishop of Canterbury. And with it she would write to the Archbishop himself telling him the contents of the letter. Then William must take notice of it. It was the only way in which she could save his soul.

She wrote long and passionately; and enclosed the letter in the casket which she addressed to Thomas Tenison, Archbishop of Canterbury, and on the letters she wrote "Not to be delivered excepting in case of my death."

Then she retired to her bed, exhausted. In the morning her condition had worsened.

Sarah had regained all her old vitality. Gloucester was now with his mother at Berkeley House and Anne watched over him constantly, terrified that he might have contracted the disease.

He went about the house asking questions. How was the Queen? Why did she not want to see him?

His mother explained that she was sick.

"More sick than you?" he asked.

"Much more," she answered.

He looked at her sadly, his great head on one side.

"Poor Mama," he said. "Poor Queen!"

There was excitement everywhere. Servants at Berkeley House who knew servants at Kensington Palace discussed the latest news.

Sarah could not restrain herself; she sat by Anne's chair and insisted on discussing the importance of all this and the possibilities which must ensue if Mary died.

"You should write to her now," advised Sarah. "You should if necessary see her. It would not be good if she were to die and you two not friends. Who knows what would happen. What you do now is of the utmost importance."

"I should feel unhappy if I did not have a chance of being friends with her again. I remember when we were little. I used to think she was so wonderful. I copied everything she did."

"Yes, yes," said Sarah, "but it is now that is important, not the past."

Sarah *was* a little overbearing, thought Anne. She herself felt depressed. It was terrible to think that Mary—once her dear Mary—might be dying. They had not spoken to each other for so long and that made her very sad. She wished that they had never banded together against her father. The last year or so when she had been confined so much to her couch had made her more thoughtful.

She would write to Mary and ask if her sister would see her. There was no danger to herself for she had had the small pox. In any case, she would have risked danger to see Mary and be friends again.

Sarah was pleased. As Anne's chief lady she would write to the Countess of Derby telling her the Princess Anne's wishes.

A reply came, written in the hand of the Countess of Derby.

Madam, I am commanded by the King and Queen to tell you they desire you would let the Princess know they both thank her for sending and desiring to come, but it being thought so necessary to keep the Queen as quiet as possible, hope she will defer it. I am, Madam, your ladyship's most humble servant.

E. Derby.

There was a postscript to this letter which Sarah found significant. It read: "Pray, Madam, present my humble duty to the Princess."

"It is the most polite note we have had for some time," said Sarah gleefully. "And what do you think Madame Derby means with her postcript?"

"She presents her duty to me."

"Her duty! She is suddenly very dutiful. Why? I ask you, Mrs. Morley. It is because when Mary is gone, Mrs. Morley will hold a very important position in this land."

Sarah looked at Anne who had begun to weep silently.

But Sarah was right. During the next few days there were many callers at Berkeley House. Those who of recent months had not thought it necessary to be aware of the Princess Anne's existence, now wished to pay their humble respects to her.

No wonder Sarah was gleeful.

In Gloucester's apartments the servants were talking of the topic which was on everyone's lips.

"Well, Mr. Jenkins, I have just had it from the Queen's usher. It is not the small pox. It's only measles."

"Oh, be joyful!" cried Jenkins. "Dear lady, she will recover soon."

"Oh, be joyful," murmured Gloucester.

"What did you say, sir?" asked Jenkins.

"What you did, Lewis. You said 'Oh, be joyful' but soon you will be saying 'Oh, be doleful'."

He walked away from them with his strange gait, for he had never yet been able to walk straight on account of his affliction.

They looked after him and then looked fearfully at each other. He was such a strange boy.

The Queen was dying. There was no doubt of it now.

In her bedchamber it was stifling, for so many people came to see her die.

The scent of herbs and unguents filled the room; there were the sounds of whispering voices, of prayers and of weeping.

Mary was not aware of this; she did not see her doctors or her ministers and those who called themselves her friends gathered together to see her die.

The Princess Anne had sent a message by Lady Fitzharding who, determined to deliver it, forced her way to the Queen's bed. She said in ringing tones that Her Highness the Princess Anne was deeply concerned for her sister.

Mary understood for she smiled faintly and whispered: "Thank her." Then she closed her eyes.

William who had been told that her end was very near lost his indifference. She would have been astonished if she could have seen his grief. Never while she lived had he shown such feeling for her; but now that he was losing her he remembered all her goodness, all her affection; and he was struck with a sense of great desolation.

Bentinck was at his side—Bentinck who had grown away from him; but at such times it was to old friends whom one turned.

"I must go to her," he said, "I must ask forgiveness . . ."

"Your Majesty yourself is ill," said Bentinck.

As William rose he swayed and would have fallen had not Bentinck caught him.

The King had fainted.

Half an hour passed before, leaning on Bentinck for support, he was able to go to her sickroom. All calm deserted him, and as he stood by the bed he cried aloud: "Mary!"

But she did not answer him. She who had always longed for his affection could not respond now when it was given as never before.

The irony of the situation came home to him. He wanted to show her that he loved her, for now that he had lost her he understood her goodness to him, all that she had offered and he had rejected.

But she had gone. She would never speak to him again, never give him that fearful tremulous smile.

He covered his face with his hands; his body had begun to shake.

Those in the death chamber of Queen Mary saw the astonishing sight of William of Orange giving way to his grief.

TO BE DELIVERED

AFTER DEATH

Slowly recovering from the grief which surprised him no less than it did those about him, William began to consider his own position, and he was alarmed. He had threatened often to return to Holland, but the prospect of being forced to do this was not pleasing. At his christening the midwife had prophesied three crowns for him; he had won them and he intended to keep them.

He was a wise man; he was a brave man, and his somewhat sour outlook prepared him more for disadvantages than for advantages. He had never tried to gloss over the fact that he was unpopular and that he lacked those qualities to inspire affection. Even his enemies respected him as a great leader; but for the nature of his coming to England and its inevitable conflicts, his rule would have been beneficial. No one who lived close to him and realized what physical torments he suffered uncomplainingly could but admire him. But the fact remained that though he had virtues which bordered on greatness he was completely unlovable.

He turned now to Bentinck, who, like the true friend he was, forgot the estrangement of the past and was by his side in this crisis.

Bentinck, so like himself in many ways, lacked his powers of endurance, his calmness in adversity, his great leadership, but, in place of this lack, possessed a charm and an ability to inspire affection.

He knew that he could trust Bentinck as he could no one else now that Mary had gone.

"Well Bentinck, what news?"

"Some mourn the Queen, some rejoice."

William nodded.

He wanted the worst so Bentinck would not hesitate to give it.

"In some of the taverns, they are singing Jacobite songs. They are shouting: 'No foreigners. No taxes!'"

"Do they want James back?" said William wearily. "They will say 'No popery' then. What's it to be, foreigners and taxes to keep him out or popery to bring him in? They can make their choice."

"They have made their choice. If he came back they would be shouting 'No popery' through the streets again."

"And the lampoons?"

Bentinck nodded.

William held out his hand.

"Do you want to look. They are so silly."

William took the paper and read:

> *Is Willy's wife now dead and gone?*
> *I'm sorry he is left alone;*
> *Oh, Blundering Death, I do thee ban,*
> *That took the wife and left the man!*
> *Come, Atropos, come with thy knife,*
> *And take the man to his good wife;*
> *And when thou'st rid us of the knave,*
> *A thousand thanks then thou shalt have.*

William screwed it up in his hands with a wry smile.

"So foolish," murmured Bentinck.

"Yet in these outpourings we have an indication of public feeling. We should never shut our eyes to that, my friend."

"And you have thought how best to act?"

William nodded. "I have been considering the Princess Anne. You know how I loathe the woman." Bentinck nodded and William gave a sharp laugh. "As much as she loathes me. But this estrangement should end, of course. They will all be looking to her, for now there can be no doubt that she is the heir to the throne."

Bentinck knew his master well enough to understand what was passing in his mind. What was his position now that Mary was dead? Would the people allow him to keep the crown? Would they remember that in the direct line of succession, Anne came before him.

If this were so, a continuance of the estrangement between them could make great trouble. There was enough conflict abroad; William must have peace with Anne. Therefore a reconciliation was essential.

Thomas Tenison, Archbishop of Canterbury, was asking for an audience with the King on a matter of vital importance, and William ordered that he should be admitted without delay.

The Archbishop was surprised by the signs of grief in William's face, for never before had he seen him betray any emotion. Never during his married life had he shown how much affection he had for his wife; and in view of the Archbishop's mission the latter was doubly surprised.

"Your Majesty," he said, "I come on an unpleasant duty and an indelicate mission. I pray you will forgive my frankness."

William said coldly: "Pray proceed."

"The Queen left me a casket which contains a letter addressed to you."

"Left you a casket! With a letter for me! Why was it not left to me?"

"Because her late Majesty wished me to give this to you; there was also a letter for me in which she explains the contents of her letter to you. She wished me to remonstrate with you and to point out the evil of your conduct."

William was startled out of his calm. "This seems to me both incredible and monstrous."

The Archbishop's eyes were as cold as those of the King. "Her

Majesty suffered greatly from your infidelity and she fears that if you continue in your adultery you will not be received into heaven."

"I do not understand how . . ."

The Archbishop held up a hand. William might be angry but Tenison was in command. The Queen had entrusted him with the saving of the King's soul and he was going to perform his duty no matter how he offended him.

"The Queen was, of course, right to be anxious. You endanger your soul by continuing with this liaison."

"I will be responsible for my soul," retorted William.

"To God or to the Devil," murmured the Archbishop. "I will leave the casket with you so that you may open your letter."

"Pray do."

"Then, Your Majesty, if there is anything you wish to discuss with me, if you wish my help in any way . . ."

"That is unlikely."

The Archbishop bowed his head. "Then have I Your Majesty's permission to broach a matter of a different nature, something which concerns the temporal position rather than the spiritual."

William bowed his head.

"This concerns the Princess Anne. Your Majesty will be aware that many of those who have ignored her in the past are now flocking to pay their respects to her."

"I know this."

"And it is well that the people should know that she is recognized by Your Majesty as the heiress to the throne?"

"This is so."

"The people would accept no other heir. Had you and her late Majesty been blessed with a child, that would have been different. But you were not." The Archbishop looked reproachful as though suggesting that the barrenness of the late Queen was a punishment for her husband's sins. It was an indication of how the people were feeling that the Archbishop should dare censure him in this way. He was now implying that if William married again and had issue, the child would not be accepted as heir to the throne.

He understood this, and of course Tenison was right.

"I propose," went on the Archbishop, "that I speak to the Princess Anne and remind her of her duty. I believe that a reconciliation between Your Majesty and Her Highness should not be delayed."

William answered: "Pray do this." And in spite of the shock he had just received his spirits lifted a little. Tenison was an honest man. He disapproved of William's relations with Elizabeth Villiers and said so; but at the same time he was anxious that there should be an end to the quarrel with Anne which was necessary if William's reign was to continue in peace.

A good friend, this Archbishop, though an uncomfortable one. But William was wise enough to know that the best friends a King could have were often those who spoke their minds and made as little concession to royalty as possible.

He shut himself into his cabinet and opened the letter. He read it and as he did so he could scarcely stop the tears falling from his eyes. He understood her now as he never had when she had lived. She had been so constantly aware of his infidelity; and yet she had rarely given a sign of it, outwardly accepting it, behaving as though it did not exist, when all the time it was souring her existence. Poor, foolish Mary! Courageous, clever Mary! He had thought her more simple than she was. He remembered how she had sat knotting her fringe, close to the candlelight, because her eyes troubled her so; he could see her looking up at him smiling tenderly, radiantly, giving him the homage and humility he had demanded. And all the time she was thinking of him with Elizabeth.

Again he read her letter. He must give up Elizabeth. His immortal soul was in danger. She implored him to do so. Marry again if he must, but marry someone worthy to be a consort of a great King.

She was gone; he had lost her, never to see her again, to see her start at his entrance and flutter her hands in that helpless way which had so often exasperated him; and yet he had been annoyed when she had seemed more composed. Never to be able to talk to her, to have her give him all her attention, to let him see in a hundred ways how she adored him.

He had lost the best wife he could have had; she was all that he had needed in a wife; and he had never appreciated that when she was here with him. He had never thought of what he would do without her; in fact he had never believed he would have to be without her. He had been the delicate one, he had been the invalid.

But now she had gone. Mary, whom he had never quite understood.

Oh, there was the subtlety of his emotion. She had wanted to save his soul and that was the reason why she had left this last letter. But why had she thought fit to write to the Archbishop of Canterbury on this very private matter? Would it not have been enough to write to him? Now he was wondering about her motives as he constantly had during her lifetime, and he realized that he could never be sure of Mary—no more in death than in life. Perhaps she had believed that if she had not sent him the letter through the Archbishop he would not have taken it seriously. Now the Archbishop would remonstrate with him, for that was what Mary had asked him to do.

It was surprising that now he must be unsure of her, even as he had in life.

He touched his cheek and it was wet. He, cold stern William, was weeping. He wanted her back with him; there were so many questions he wanted to ask her. He wanted to *know* what was going on in her mind. Suddenly a sense of desolation swept over him. He understood that he had loved Mary; and he had lost her: he would never be able to tell her that he had loved her—in his way. Why had he not, when she was alive? Perhaps he had not known it.

He shut himself in his closet and gave orders that he was not to be disturbed. He opened a drawer and took out a lock of her hair. She had given it to him before one of his departures in what he had considered to be an excess of unnecessary sentimentality, and he had thrust it into this drawer, exasperated by her action.

Now he took it out and looked at it. It was beautiful hair, and he wished that he had appreciated it during her lifetime.

How odd that he felt no resentment toward her for writing that letter to him and worse still writing to the Archbishop. He would never feel resentment toward her again, and wished with all his heart that she were with him now.

He made a bracelet of the hair and tied it about his arm with a piece of black ribbon.

No one would see it; only he would know it was there; but he would wear it, in memory of her, until he died.

There was someone at the door of his cabinet. He cried out angrily: "Did I not say I did not wish to be disturbed?"

"The King will see me."

He recognized the voice of the Archbishop and for the second time was too taken aback in the presence of this man to assert himself.

The Archbishop shut the door and faced him.

"I see," he said, "that Your Majesty suffers remorse. I come now to ask you for the promise as Her Majesty wished me to."

"Promise?" demanded William.

"The promise that you will not see Elizabeth Villiers again."

William was silent. The Archbishop had found him in the midst of his remorse; there were even traces of tears on his cheeks. Perhaps Tenison knew that what he felt today he would not feel next week: and that this was the time to complete the commission left to him by the dead Queen.

"It was her dying wish," went on the Archbishop. "All her thoughts were for you. She died in fear that as an adulterer you would never enter the Kingdom of Heaven. Perhaps she is watching us now, waiting, praying for you to give the answer she wants."

William was choked by emotions. It seemed to him that he could never miss anyone as he missed Mary. He longed for her meekness, her tender docility—all that he had lost.

"She is watching us," said Tenison. "Do you not sense her near?"

William murmured: "I promise. Please leave me now."

The Archbishop, smiling serenely, left him.

William sat down and covered his face with his hands.

Elizabeth Villiers was alarmed. It was long since she had seen her lover. There was so much to discuss; she had news for him of how the Queen's death was affecting the Princess Anne's household.

But he did not come.

He would though, she was sure of it. He could not do without her. It might be that, knowing they were spied on he did not want to give his enemies the scandal they were hoping for.

It was only a matter of waiting, Elizabeth assured herself.

There was excitement in Berkeley House. Sarah had dismissed everyone so that she could have a private talk with Anne before she left.

This was a change in their fortunes, she assured her friend.

"His Majesty will graciously see you. He has changed his tune a little. And that does not surprise me, for I can tell you this, Mrs. Morley, the people are not so fond of William on his own as they were when your sister was Queen. They ask themselves what right he has to assume the crown. And what right has he? It is you, Mrs. Morley, who should be wearing it. You should be thinking of riding to your coronation instead of being carried in your chair to wait on Caliban!"

"It is true enough, Mrs. Freeman; but my sister would not have wished it so."

"Oh, she was bemused and bewildered by that Dutch Abortion."

"How I wish that we had been good friends! I was sitting here remembering, dear Mrs. Freeman, when we were little girls. I could not bear her out of my sight. I always wanted to do what she did, wear what she wore . . . I loved her, I think, more than anyone in my life at that time."

"Children at play!" said Sarah sharply. "Well, now she is dead and gone."

"Alas! I would I could have her with me for a while so that I could mend our quarrel."

"You have another to consider, Mrs. Morley, and therefore little time to waste on regrets for the past. What of the young Duke of Gloucester. You must make sure of his future."

"My precious boy! How right you are, Mrs. Freeman, as usual."

"And," went on Sarah, "when you talk to Caliban, you must make sure that he does not forget that he cannot thrust your son from his position."

"He wouldn't dare."

"Caliban would dare anything, I do assure you. What if he married again? What if he had a son? Ah, Mrs. Morley, I can see that he would be very anxious then to make sure your boy did not have the throne."

Anne's lethargy dropped from her. "There would be a revolution if he ever attempted to take my boy's rights from him."

"Remember that and make sure *he* understands it. You need friends, Mrs. Morley, as you never did. And those who would be the best friends to you are languishing in exile. Banished from Court. It is something you can remedy now, I'll warrant."

"You are thinking of Mr. Freeman."

"He is the best friend Mrs. Morley ever had, and if he were brought back to Court would be ready to defend your rights and those of the young Duke with all his skill, which I assure you, Mrs. Morley, is formidable; and it is for this reason that Dutch William has kept him from you. Ask him now to bring him back. Now is the time for you to ask favors. He wishes to show the people he is on good terms with you. Bring Mr. Freeman back and then Mrs. Morley will have two Freemans to protect her from whatever ill wind is likely to harm her and the precious little Duke."

"My dear good friends!" murmured Anne.

"And here is Mrs. Morley's chair."

"I need it. I do not think I could walk a step."

"You must save all your energies for facing that monster!" said Sarah.

Anne was lifted into her chair and carried from Berkeley House first to Campden House and from there to Kensington Palace, where William was waiting to receive her.

Anne was suffering so much from gout and obesity that her chair had to be carried right to the door of the King's presence chamber, where William, making an unusually gracious concession, came out to receive her and himself opened the door of her chair.

Taking his hand, Anne hobbled out.

Anne said tremulously: "I am sorry for Your Majesty's loss."

William answered: "I am sorry for yours."

For the first time in her life Anne saw that he was moved by his emotions and this let loose her own; she began to weep silently.

William said gently: "Pray come in and be seated."

He closed the door and they were alone. He brought forward a chair that Anne might sit and then he brought another for himself and placed it close to hers. For a few seconds they remained silent as though to control their grief.

Anne said simply: "If we could have been friends before she died . . ."

William nodded. At one time he might have given her a sardonic look, but he too had his remorse to disturb him.

"It is too late," he said. "We must forget the past for the future could be troublesome. I want to make that safe for our heir." Anne was alert at once. William's voice was dry as he went on: "In this we must stand together. Do not forget that your father calls himself the King of England, Scotland, and Ireland; and that his son in France is known as the Prince of Wales. We must not deceive ourselves. There are some here who drink secretly to the King over the Water and who insist that that young boy *is* the Prince of Wales."

Anne nodded slowly. They disliked each other intensely, but they must be allies.

"We have to make sure that you are accepted as heir to the throne to be followed by your son. I think this is a matter in which we are in complete agreement. Therefore we must forget all other differences. Are you of my opinion?"

"Your Majesty is most kind and gracious."

"Then . . . we must show the people that we have settled our differences and are . . . friends."

"Your Majesty will remember that the cause of my quarrel with my sister was that she wished me to dismiss my best friends."

William was alert. "The Marlboroughs?" he muttered.

"Marlborough has been long in exile. He desires above all things to serve Your Majesty."

"You mean to serve himself?"

"He is an ambitious man, but then so are most men. He would serve himself through serving his King."

"Which King?" asked William drily.

"For me and for my Lord Marlborough, there is only one King of England."

"It did not always seem so."

"I can assure Your Majesty that if you would allow him to return he would serve you faithfully. He is too brilliant a man to be left in banishment."

Too brilliant a man, thought William. There was something in that. Too dangerous a man. What was Marlborough plotting in his retirement? There was no doubt of his great ability.

Moreover Anne was making a condition. Peace between us providing you bring Marlborough back into favor.

He must have peace with Anne. Without that his crown was unsafe.

It might well be that Marlborough at Court was safer than Marlborough in banishment.

William knew that in this he must grant the Princess's request.

Marlborough should come back to Court.

Through England the bells were tolling for the state funeral of the Queen. Although she had died at the end of December, this ceremony did not take place until the following 5th of March.

A wax effigy of the Queen was placed over her coffin, and in the royal robes of state it looked lifelike. Following as mourners were all the members of the House of Commons; but Anne was not present and the Duchess of Somerset took her place as chief mourner.

Anne in her apartments was too dropsical to be able to leave her bed; in addition she was pregnant once more.

Sarah sat beside her, bubbling with vitality, her head full of plans that she would not disclose to the Princess.

Anne was melancholy listening to the tolling of bells, overcome by memories of the past. Not so Sarah. This was the great opportunity. The Dutch monster spitting blood, growing more sick every day. How long could he last? Six months? Surely not more. And then . . . then . . . it would be Anne's turn and that meant the turn of the Marlboroughs.

Elizabeth Villiers listening to the tolling bells was as apprehensive of the future as Sarah was hopeful.

So long and he had not sought her out! What did it mean? Surely he needed her now, as always?

He would come to her. Perhaps he was waiting until after the funeral. They would have to be more careful even than before, but he would come.

THE TWICKENHAM
INTERLUDE

*A*nne was completely absorbed in her son. *She* was looking forward to having a child and as usual she was praying this one would survive; the little Duke of Gloucester was the living proof that she could bear a child that could live and although his health gave cause for great alarm no one could deny that he was not extremely intelligent. Dr. Radcliffe, that blunt man who had little respect for rank yet was reckoned to be one of the best doctors at Court, had said the little Duke's affliction—he had water on the brain—could mean that his brain was consequently more agile than was normal. In any case the young Duke was the delight and terror of Anne's life. This was a cause of irritation to Sarah who again and again found herself and her affairs relegated to second place on account of the boy.

Mary's death and her interview with William had made Anne feel the need to rouse herself from her customary lethargy. There was her boy's future to protect and as a poor invalid unable to move she felt she could not do all that might be required of her.

Therefore she decided that she must recover the use of her limbs; one of the reasons why she found walking so exhausting was because of her size so she decided to take cold baths to help reduce her weight, to eat a little less—although this was torture to her—and to hunt more frequently. She had always hunted from childhood so this was no hardship.

In her condition she was, of course, unable to ride on horseback and she had had a chair made which was just big enough to hold herself and this was set on high wheels and drawn by one horse. In this she followed the chase indefatigably.

These efforts combined with her determination to improve her health for the sake of her son, had their effects. She was able to walk when her gout and dropsy were not too painful.

She and George would sit together for hours discussing their boy. The child was often with them and was fond of them. They watched him anxiously and were very concerned because of his difficulty in walking straight; it was a perpetual topic between them.

One day Anne said to George: "Something must be done. He is still walking as though he were first learning. He is like a child of two in this respect."

"I know, I know," murmured George.

"It grieves me. Do you think there is anything we can do about it."

"That we can do?" repeated George.

"Do you think that he is not making enough effort to walk?"

George was thoughtful, his head on one side. "It might be possible."

"Then, George, we must make him walk straight. We must make him walk without the aid of his attendants."

"How so?"

"By . . ." Anne winced . . . "punishing him if he does not."

"Punishing our boy?"

"It is going to be more painful for us than for him, but if it is the only way . . ."

"If it is the only way . . ." murmured George.

"George, you are his father. You must do it. You must take your cane and beat him if he will not walk alone."

"I . . . beat our boy!"

"I shall feel every stroke, but if it is the only way . . ."

George looked as though he were about to burst into tears but he murmured: "If it is the only way . . ."

Anne was determined. She sent for the boy. He came to them, kissed their hands in his grown-up way, but with him were two attendants who walked beside him to steady him and to keep him from swaying from one side to another.

"My dear boy," said Anne. "Papa and I want you to walk without help. You are old now, you know."

"Mama, I cannot." A fear came into the boy's face. He wanted to explain to them that when he tried to walk alone he was so giddy that he feared he would fall; and when an attendant walked on either side of him, that kept him straight and prevented the giddiness.

"You must, my son."

"But I cannot, Mama."

"Papa and I think you could if you tried."

The boy was for once unable to explain what was in his mind. How could he tell these people who had normal heads what it felt like to carry one which was top heavy and would not allow him to walk as they did.

His face was set in obstinate lines, but all he said was: "No."

Anne ordered the attendants to stand back. "Now walk," she said.

"No," said the boy.

"Papa," said Anne signing to George.

The boy saw the cane in his father's hands and looked at it in some astonishment. He could not believe it was intended for him, for never before had he experienced anything but kindness and indulgence from his parents.

"Walk," said Anne.

He stood there looking at her.

Then he felt the cane across his shoulders. He started with horror that *they* should do this to him. He could not understand it.

"Walk," said his father. "Walk alone."

The cane descended again and again across his shoulders; and suddenly he was aware of the pain it inflicted.

He cried out and began to run . . . straight out of the room . . . alone.

George and Anne looked at each other.

"My poor, poor darling!" cried Anne. "But you see, George, it was effective."

They were both trembling and on the verge of tears. Only they could know what pain it had caused them to inflict suffering on their beloved boy; they could only bring themselves to do it because they earnestly believed it was for his own good.

A gentle scratching on the door of Elizabeth Villiers' chamber made her start up in delight. It was the well-remembered signal of happier days.

She ran to the door and flung it open.

"William!" she whispered.

He stepped into the room and shut the door behind him before throwing off the cloak which had completely concealed him.

"I knew you would come," she cried, almost hysterically. "I knew it."

"It must not be known that I am here," he said.

Her spirits sank; he was different—changed toward her. He had surely come to tell her that this was an end of their relationship. How incongruous! The end . . . now that his wife was dead! All those years they had met clandestinely and he, the stern Calanist, had imperiled his soul by committing adultery for her sake; and now that there would no longer be the need for such sin, he had come to tell her that the relationship was over.

"It has been so long," she murmured. "I have been so unhappy."

"I found it long," he repeated. "I too have been unhappy."

"And now?"

"I have given a promise to Tenison."

"But . . . why?"

"There was a letter she wrote—two letters, one to me, one to the Archbishop. It concerned us. She asked me to end our relationship; and she asked Tenison to extract the promise from me."

"She would rule you from the grave as she never could in life," said Elizabeth bitterly.

"I will not be ruled."

Her smile had become radiant, but he would not look at her.

"Do not imagine," he went on, "that I have not thought of you over this long time."

"This long, long time," she murmured.

"I have thought of ways . . . and means . . . and this is what I plan. We must not meet . . ."

He saw the despair in her face and he was as delighted with her as he had been when he had first discovered the nature of her feeling for him.

". . . in England," he went on. "I will keep my promise. But there is Holland."

She looked puzzled and he took a step toward her as though to lay his hands on her, but he stopped himself.

"I have decided that you shall have a husband, a husband will give you a position worthy of you."

"And you?" she asked.

"I shall be often in Holland; you and your husband shall accompany me there; and there it shall be as it was in the past."

"I see."

"This pleases you?"

"I accept as always Your Majesty's commands," she answered.

How like her! So clever, and yet so amenable. It had always been so; she had always given him what he needed. He was not a sensual man and the sexual act would never be of the utmost importance to him. He could contemplate this separation without despair; but he would not have her believe that he had deserted her.

He said swiftly: "I am bestowing on you the private estates of James II in Ireland."

She caught her breath; she would be a rich woman in her own right.

"And," went on William, "when we have decided on your husband, rest assured I shall give him an earldom."

She lowered her eyes so that he might not see her exultation.

All her efforts had not been in vain.

Lewis Jenkins stood by the bed of his little master and he was smiling broadly.

"This is the best day of the year," he announced.

Gloucester sat up in bed and demanded to know why.

"St. David's day, the day of the Welsh, and I hope Your Highness will wear the leek in his hat today."

"Well, Jenkins, as I should be the Prince of Wales if I had my rights I will certainly wear the leek."

Jenkins put into the boy's hands one of the ornaments which were made of silk and silver in the shape of a leek and which were worn at Court on St. David's day by the Welsh.

"So this," said Gloucester, "is the leek. But of course it is not a real leek."

"Certainly not, but it is a fair imitation."

"I like not imitations."

"Then we will go down to the gardens and I will show you the real leek growing there."

"I will then compare it with this bauble. Help me dress, Lewis."

When he was dressed he said: "Do not call any of the others to walk beside me. I must walk alone. Papa beat me for not walking straight. It hurt a great deal. But he did not wish to do it. It was only for my good. And although, Lewis, it is not easy for me to walk straight, I do walk straighter since Papa caned me."

"I trust it was not too painful, Your Highness."

"I could see that it was for Papa and Mama," answered the boy gravely.

In the gardens he examined the leeks. "But these are far more interesting than the silk ones, Lewis. There are layers and layers, and smell them."

"I am pleased that the leek finds favor with Your Highness."

The gardener gathered several of the finest leeks and with a bow presented them to the boy.

"I am pleased to accept them, and as I cannot wear them all in my hat, I shall decorate my cannon with them, or perhaps my ship. Lewis, summon my men. It is only fitting that there should be a parade on St. David's day."

The boys were summoned and the parade begun, and, the leek in his hat, Gloucester shouted orders and reviewed his men.

When the parade was over he was very tired and Mrs. Buss, who had been his mother's nurse and was still attached to the royal nursery, said that he should rest for a while.

Gloucester did not care to take orders from his mother's old nurse but he was exhausted and allowed himself to be led to his bed where he very soon fell into a deep sleep; and when he awoke began to shout orders to his men. His attendants rushing in saw at once that he had a fever.

The alarm spread through Campden House. The little Prince had been poisoned by handling leeks.

Sarah was sitting by Anne's bed and her voice went on and on.

"It is a marvelous thing indeed that Marlborough should be allowed to return to Court, should be allowed to kiss those Dutch fingers, should be allowed to declare his loyalty . . . Oh, a marvelous thing indeed, but Marlborough has a better mission in life than to slobber over that Abortion's fingers. What of Marlborough, I say? What position is he going to have at Court? None it seems. Is this the way Caliban keeps his promise?"

Anne answered: "It is a scandal, dear Mrs. Freeman. But I don't trust Caliban, you know. So much and no more, is his way. He has offered me St. James's Palace and for that I am grateful, but there is no suggestion that I should move in."

"He offers it because he must. He is giving nothing away."

"I am sure you are right, but it would be pleasant to be in St. James's once more."

"But to return to my Lord Marlborough. He should be given a chance to use his great talents."

There was a knock at the door, and Sarah swept to it in indignation. "Do you not know that the Princess and I wish to be alone together. What disturbance is this? Go away."

"My lady, there is news from Campden House."

"I have told you . . ."

Anne's voice broke in imperiously. "News from Campden House! Pray bring the messenger in. I trust my boy is well."

"Your Highness, the Duke is in a fever. We fear he has been poisoned by the smell of leeks."

"Poisoned!" cried Anne. "Call my chair, Lady Marlborough. Send for Dr. Radcliffe. Quickly . . . without delay. I must go to Campden House."

"Radcliffe is in Oxford," began Sarah coldly.

"Send to Oxford. I know Radcliffe to be the best man. My chair. Send for it at once and tell my bearers that I must be carried without delay to Campden House.

Sarah obeyed, fuming. How maddening these delays were. When, oh when, would she be able to get her John where he deserved to be!

$\mathcal{D}$r. $\mathcal{R}$adcliffe arrived in due course, and pronounced that the little Duke was suffering from a fever. The boy was bled and in a few days began to recover.

Dr. Radcliffe, however, recommended rest for a week or more, for the little patient after the first recovery developed a slight fever again.

"Keep him in bed," said Radcliffe, "and keep him amused there."

When Anne, at the bedside of her son, asked what her darling wanted most, the answer was prompt: "My soldiers. Let them guard the bedchamber. Let Harry Scull come to me. I wish him to do a tattoo on his drum and I will select those who shall build the fortifications about my bed."

"My dearest boy, should you not rest?"

"How can I, Mama, when I have to be protected by my men."

"There is nothing to protect you from."

The boy's face crumpled then brightened. "Those who will one day wear the crown are always in need of protection."

Dr. Radcliffe said in his brusque way: "These amusements will do no harm, if he stays in bed."

"Send my men," said the Prince, "and I promise to stay in bed."

So at the Prince's door were posted his guards, who marched back and forth and challenged all those who would enter. Enough, said Mrs. Buss, to drive you mad, when you came along with a posset to find a wooden sword flourishing under your nose and the basin all but knocked out of your hands.

"Halt! Who goes there? Friend or foe?"

"Friend, you silly boy. I've a posset for His Highness."

"Pass, but you will have to make your way through the fortifications."

"Drat the fortifications!" said Mrs. Buss.

She and others would have complained, but they knew it was no use. Dr. Radcliffe had wanted the patient to be amused and so they had rowdy boys, playing soldiers all over the place.

Not content with his soldiers, Gloucester called in his attendants and coachmen to take messages as he said through the lines. Lewis Jenkins was always ready to throw himself into the game; Mr. Pratt, Gloucester's tutor, was pressed into service; and the two that amused Gloucester most were coachmen Dick Drury and Robin Church.

The language of these two was full-blooded and Gloucester liking it, learned it quickly.

"Confound you!" Gloucester would cry. "God damn you, man, can't you see that gap in the fortifications? By God, I damn you to hell."

All the young soldiers took up such cries to the concern of Lady Fitzharding, Mrs. Buss, and others.

Mrs. Buss remembered that a short time ago the Duke had delighted to receive wooden figures of great soldiers in battle-dress; and she believed that if he were presented with a very fine specimen, he might play with this and be lured from his rougher games.

She bought a magnificent figure of a soldier and summoned one of the Duke's coachmen, a man named Wetherby, to take it to the sickroom with her compliments.

When Wetherby arrived, the Duke was sitting up in bed surrounded by a dozen or so of his "men."

The Duke heard his guards outside his door halting the arrival, demanding to know whether he was friend or foe and what his mission was.

Wetherby said in a voice which was audible in the sickroom: "I've brought His Highness a toy from Mrs. Buss."

All the young soldiers clambered off the bed and stood at attention. "Bring him in," ordered the Duke.

Wetherby came in and laid the doll on the bed. "Mrs. Buss thought Your Highness would like this to play with."

Gloucester lay back on his pillows and closed his eyes. "Escort the messenger from my apartments," he said coldly.

Wetherby, agreeing with Mrs. Buss that these boys' games were enough to drive you mad, left as soon as he could.

As soon as he had gone, Gloucester said: "This is an insult from the enemy. Call a Council of War without delay. Confound it, this is an insult which shall not pass unheeded. A toy to play with! I gave up toys last year!"

The Council was held about the bed, and the order for execution given; the doll was immediately torn to pieces with shouts which echoed through the Palace.

"The bearer was insolent," said the Duke, thinking regretfully that he dared not punish Mrs. Buss. "He should not go unpunished. Let us decide on his sentence."

It was decreed that Wetherby should undergo the water torture; and the next day when he appeared at the Palace he was seized by some fifty small boys. They dragged him to the floor, clambered all over him, and bound his feet and hands together. Then they brought water with which they doused him until, breathless and panting, he begged them to desist.

They then tied him on the great wooden horse which they wheeled into the Duke's bedroom, headed by Harry Scull's drumbeats.

"Your Highness's orders have been carried out," announced the herald. "Here is the prisoner for your inspection."

Gloucester sat up in bed, shaking with laughter—a supreme commander.

Dr. Radcliffe was anxiously questioned by the Princess.

"He is recovering," said the doctor, "but I think what he needs most is a change of air. Get him away from Kensington and his noisy friends for a while. Keep him interested and occupied, but these soldier games are too rough for him."

The Princess was thoughtful. She knew how he hated to be separated from his "army"; but she did see that horseplay in the sickroom, although much to her son's taste, was not what was needed for his convalescence.

She thought longingly of Richmond—the home of her childhood. It would be pleasant to return there; but she remembered how she had once asked for Richmond and been refused. Perhaps Epsom or Hampstead? And she had always been very fond of Twickenham.

The news that the Princess was seeking a house in Twickenham where her son might recuperate in the salubrious air, was circulated and several people, remembering the change in the Princess Anne's position, begged her to make use of their houses.

Anne hesitated; and one day Lord Fitzharding, who with his wife shared the governorship of young Gloucester, came to her and told her that his great-aunt, Mrs. Davies, who had long retired from Court life, had heard of the Princess's need and would welcome her, the little Duke, and a few of their attendants to stay with her.

It would be a quiet life in the country and his aunt, who was then eighty years old, lived on fruit and vegetables which she grew herself, and was certain that these would be of great benefit to the little Prince.

It was comforting to receive this offer, for Anne remembered the old lady, who was related to the Berkeleys, was gentle, devoted, strong-minded, and she was certain that this was the place to which she should go, so she accepted the invitation without telling Sarah; and for once Sarah made no protest, deciding that she would spend the time with her own family.

So while Sarah went to St. Albans to plan earnestly with her husband, Anne, her son, and very few of their servants and attendants set out for Twickenham.

"What shall I do?" asked the Duke, "without my soldiers to command?"

"You will eat fruit and herbs and vegetables."

"But, Mama, one does not eat all day."

"*You* have to get strong and well."

"But to be right away in the country!"

"You cannot command your soldiers forever from your sickbed.

Whoever heard of a general doing that? No, if generals are ill they take care to grow well quickly . . . and then they are welcomed back with a guard of honor and . . ."

"A guard of honor," said Gloucester and he was silent, planning the great occasion of his return.

In the meantime for four weeks—or perhaps more—he must eat fruit, vegetables, and herbs; he must live quietly and grow strong because it seemed that was what a general must do to get well quickly.

She was an old, old woman. Gloucester had never seen anyone so old; her face was rosy and wrinkled and her eyes bright blue; she was quiet, but she would answer questions if one caught her alone. She would sit in her garden on her rocking chair and the sun shining on her white hair made it seem like the halo on the heads of saints if you half closed your eyes and imagined it was there.

Her estate was large and it was given over almost entirely to the cultivation of fruit trees, vegetables, and herbs. When Gloucester arrived with his mother and her retinue some of the trees were laden with red cherries. He had never seen so many before.

The old lady stood in the hall when they arrived to receive them; he had stared up at her curiously, wondering what it was like to be so old. Perhaps he would ask her one day.

She smiled at him and told him that he would soon be well and strong enough to return to his army. Meanwhile he could eat as much fruit as he liked from her trees but he must always remember that trees were living things and must not be harmed.

It was an interesting thought. He liked the old woman.

He was put to bed in a room smelling of lavender and herbs which seemed small after his apartments at Campden House. Lewis was with him and asked how he liked the place.

"It is early to say yet, Lewis," he answered. "But I feel like an ordinary boy, not a Prince."

"Then Your Highness won't like that."

"But I do like it, Lewis. I like it for now."

He fell asleep quickly, wondering about the old lady.

There was little ceremony at Twickenham. The Princess Anne's servants joined those belonging to the house; Anne, herself, spent much of her time in the rooms which had been allotted to her; and the little Duke liked to explore the house and grounds.

When he saw the old lady gathering fruit or herbs or sitting in her rocking chair he would go and stand by her, watching. She would smile at him, but not always speak. He found this refreshing; she seemed to understand that he did not always want to ask or be asked questions. Sometimes she would show him the herbs she was gathering and tell him what uses they could be put to, how they cured this and that. He listened intently and sometimes he himself would pick a leaf and hold it out to her. She always had something interesting to say about it.

He looked for her every day; and when he found her on her rocking chair he would sit at her feet.

Sometimes they would talk and sometimes be silent. He enjoyed both moods.

He asked her one day what it felt like to be so old, and she answered that it felt very much the same as being very young; the young thought highly of some things, the old of others.

"Like battles," he said, "and gathering herbs."

She nodded and went on rocking.

Then he told her about his soldiers and the wonderful battles they fought; and she told him how when she had been at Court his great-grandfather had been King.

"Tell me about him."

"He quarreled with the Parliament and had to go away."

"Where?"

"Far away where he could not come back."

"My grandfather has gone far away where he can't come back. At least not while William has the crown. But they are not supposed to tell me that."

"Then how do you know?"

"I listen. I am always listening. You see, I always want to know . . . everything. Is that wrong?"

"I think it is good to want to know."

"Well I want to know everything . . . except Scripture. I don't want Scripture. I won't listen when Mr. Pratt tries to teach me."

"Why don't you like it."

"Because I don't like going to church."

"Oh," said Mrs. Davies and was silent for a long time.

Soon it seemed to Gloucester that he had always lived at Twicken-ham; it seemed that the sun shone every day and strangely enough he could always find something to do. His chief pleasure was the company of the old lady. The affection between them was noticed and it was re-marked how strange it was that the very old woman should attract the young boy.

When she talked she told him of the Court of his great-grandfather who had been gentle and of his French great-grandmother who had been fiery; she told him of the wars between the King and Parliament; and he listened avidly.

She talked to him of the Bible and told him stories from it; he had never heard the stories told in such a way before. She could quote from the New Testament and she told him that she loved the Bible which had been a great comfort to her.

"It has never been a comfort to me," he said. "I will tell you some-thing: I do not like going to church and I have sworn never to say the psalms which I do not like."

"But they are so beautiful."

"Beautiful?"

"Yes," she said. "Listen. 'I will lift up mine eyes unto the hills, from whence cometh my help. My help cometh from the Lord which made Heaven and Earth.'"

"Go on," said Gloucester.

He watched her mouth as she spoke the words; and although he had heard them before they had never seemed beautiful until then.

"It is you," he said, "who make them beautiful."

"I only repeat what is in the book."

"You love them; you believe them and you make them good."

"They comfort me. There is much in the book that comforts me."

"It does not comfort me."

"But it could."

"You mean if I loved it . . . and believed it as you do?"

"You can. Say it with me."

He did, and he found that the words were beautiful. He wanted to know them so well that he would be able to say them when he was alone without her to prompt him.

He learned quickly. Then he learned other psalms and to say the Lord's Prayer.

And each day he was more and more with the old lady.

The Princess Anne liked him to be present while she was at her toilette. She was delighted to see the fair skin, which he had inherited from his Danish father, tanned with the sun and air. There was a sprinkling of freckles across his nose; and his eyes seemed several shades more blue than before: but for the fact that his head was so large he would have been extremely handsome, for he had the Stuart features which matched up charmingly with his fairness of skin.

"So my boy is happy at Twickenham?" asked Anne.

He smiled. "Very, very happy, Mama."

"Come here," she said. He came and she kissed him and held him tightly for a moment. He endured the embrace with fortitude. He knew that out of many, he was the only child who had survived, and that made him very precious.

"Confound it, Mama!" he said. "You are not old like Mrs. Davies. You will have many children yet; then you will not have to watch over me with such care."

Anne wanted to say that however many children she had he would always be infinitely precious to her, but to hide her emotion she said: "And pray where do you learn such language?"

"What language, Mama?"

"'Confound it', you said."

"Oh, that is nothing. It is not like 'God damn you to hell, sir.'"

Anne was truly shocked.

"I demand to know where you heard such talk," she said.

"It was Lewis, I think . . ."

"Lewis! Then he shall be dismissed."

"Oh, Mama, no . . . it was not Lewis. I am remembering now."

"I want to know where you learned such talk."

He hesitated then, "Why, Mama, I remember now. I invented it myself."

He smiled at her disarmingly and once more she had to fight to resist the temptation to embrace him and cover him with kisses.

Anne sent for her treasurer, Sir Benjamin Bathurst, the husband of her great friend, Frances Apsley, whom her sister Mary had loved so dearly. Frances had remained Anne's dear friend and naturally Anne had wanted to honor her husband and this she did by bestowing on him the post of treasurer of her household.

"Sir Benjamin," said Anne, "we have been here some four or five weeks and all this time we have enjoyed the hospitality of Mrs. Davies. I want you to pay her a hundred guineas, for although she is a wealthy woman, I and my son and our servants must have been a great drain on her."

Sir Benjamin said that he would see to the matter without delay and the next day he returned to the house with a hundred gold guineas.

Gloucester was with the old lady when Bathurst came in and when he saw that the treasurer wished to speak to her he retired to a corner, and both seemed to forget that he was present.

"Her Highness wishes to recompense you for your hospitality during the last weeks," began Sir Benjamin.

"To recompense me? I need no recompense."

"Her Highness believes that to feed so many people must have been costly."

"I am not in need. I have plenty here for my use and for that of my friends."

"Still it is Her Highness's wish that you should take a hundred guineas."

"I pray you return to Her Highness and tell her that I have no intention of accepting payment."

A hundred guineas, thought Gloucester. A great deal of money. How many muskets could one buy with it? Was the old lady wondering? But she would not want muskets, of course.

Sir Benjamin, believing that Mrs. Davies merely wished to be persuaded, emptied the bag of guineas into her lap.

"There," he said, "with Her Highness's thanks."

Mrs. Davies stood up and the guineas rolled in all directions. Then she rose and walked from the room without even looking where they went.

Gloucester watched Sir Benjamin on his hands and knees gathering them up. Some had come close to him so he took them to Sir Benjamin.

"So Your Highness saw what happened?"

"She told you that she did not want it."

"People say of money 'Take it away. I won't have it.' But they are only waiting to be pressed."

Gloucester considered this.

"But she is not people," he said gravely. "She is Mrs. Davies."

"Mama," *said* *Gloucester,* "may I come to church with you?"

Anne opened her eyes very wide. "I thought my boy did not care to go to church."

"I wish to go now," he said.

"I am pleased."

"She is pleased too."

Anne knew that he meant Mrs. Davies.

"I can say 'Our Father' now. And I know the Commandments. She says them and I say them after her. The psalms too."

"You once said that you would never say the psalms."

His face puckered for a while. It was true. Then he smiled. "I shall have to sing them."

Anne thought then how happy they had been at Twickenham. It was a strange little interlude in her life—perhaps it would be in his, too. To live quietly in the country, like an ordinary family, walking across the fields to church; and she felt so much better that she was able to walk that little distance. The fruit and vegetables had seemed to do them all good—and to be away from Court in this quiet house of an old lady who could not live much longer, away from bickering and strife, ambitious men and women, the ranting of Sarah. . . .

What was she thinking? She was longing to be back with her dear Mrs. Freeman. Heirs to thrones could not endure the quiet life forever.

"You must be eager to be back with your men," she said to her son.

His expression was intent. He thought of his soldiers marching up and down in the Park, while he took the salute, and the excitement made him tremble.

Then he thought of sitting with the old lady and enjoying her talk or her silence.

He was unsure.

He was very sad when the time came to say good-bye to his friend, and, understanding how he would feel, his mother had ordered that his soldiers should be posted as sentinels at Campden House to give him a welcome back.

As he rode up they presented arms and he felt a great joy to be back.

The old lady and her quiet house at Twickenham seemed like part of a dream, something to think about when he was in bed at night, when he could close his eyes and repeat the Lord's Prayer and the psalms and recall every inflection of her beautiful but sometimes quavering voice.

This was real. This was living.

There was a new pistol waiting for him which delighted him. It was made of wood, but there was a trigger which could be pulled so that it looked like the real thing.

Yes, he was glad to be back.

GARTER AND GOVERNOR
FOR GLOUCESTER

While Gloucester was drilling his soldiers in the gardens before Kensington Palace William was in Flanders fighting the French, and at the end of the summer he won his most significant victory of the entire campaign when he captured Namur. There was rejoicing throughout the country as the people believed that this must mean the end of the war was in sight. No more taxes; a settling down to peace; that was what was needed and they believed that William could bring about this state of affairs.

Gloucester listened to the war news and immediately planned a capture of Namur between his own men. During the fight he fell and grazed his forehead with his own pistol and although it was bleeding insisted on carrying on with the mock battle.

Every little ailment or accident must be reported to his mother and she came immediately to his apartments to see the damage for herself.

"A bullet grazed my forehead," he told her. "If I had been a boy I should have cried, but as a soldier, of course, I cannot."

Anne commanded that the wound be dressed; and wished that she could put an end to these rough games.

She did order that no one was to fence with the Duke of Gloucester. "For," she declared to Lady Fitzharding, "I have heard of many accidents coming about through fencing."

But almost immediately she saw Gloucester practicing with the sword, though alone, and she demanded to know why he did this.

"Have you forgotten that I have forbidden anyone to fence with you?"

"I hope, Mama," replied the Duke gravely, "that you will give them leave to defend themselves when I attack them."

She marveled at his wit and intelligence. Was there ever such a boy. He was the delight and terror of her life.

At the beginning of autumn, William returned from Flanders.

William, returning as a conqueror, had begun to think that he was firm enough on the throne not to have to bother to placate the Princess Anne. He had promised her St. James's Palace but had not yet given it to her. Why should he give the foolish woman anything, particularly as Sarah Churchill was at her elbow, pressing her to demand this and that.

But when he went to visit Campden House he could not help being charmed by young Gloucester, who had his army drawn up to form a guard of honor for him. The boy was bright and amusing, a born soldier, for he would not have had this little army otherwise.

He walked beside William inspecting the "troops" and asking his advice about them. William gave it seriously, enjoying the occasion, feeling more at ease with the boy than he did with his mother, or any of his English ministers.

"It will not be long," Gloucester assured William, "before my men are serving you in Flanders. I shall be with them to command them, of course, and willingly I offer you my services."

"I am sure you and your men will serve me and their country well."

Gloucester saluted with the utmost seriousness and the King gravely acknowledged this.

"What horses have you?" asked William.

"I have one live and two dead," answered Gloucester.

"Dead horses? Soldiers do not keep dead horses."

"What do they do with them then?"

"They bury the dead horses."

"Mine shall be buried at once."

William watched with amusement while the boy gave orders that his two wooden horses be buried.

"I shall need replacements," he said.

"What of the one live one?"

"I ride on him in the park. He is not very big, but later I shall have hundreds of big ones."

"I see," said the King.

And all those who watched them marveled at the boy's power to charm even William. Anne was delighted. This was a clear indication that William happily accepted the boy as his heir.

That was a brief interlude in the King's day. He was feeling wretchedly ill and was forced to face the fact that he was growing more and more feeble.

He had never been a happy man, but since the death of Mary he had become even more morose than before. He had lost her adulation, and the comfort of Elizabeth's companionship, for having given his promise to Tenison not to continue his liaison with her, he could not do so... in England. There was little left to him but his Dutch friends. Keppel was his first favorite, a handsome charming gay young man, who had not the worth of Bentinck, but somehow he craved for his company. He did not want Bentinck's frank advice; he was impatient with his friendship and Bentinck knew this and kept away. He had even left Court—a matter which often gave William deep misgivings. Mary, Elizabeth, and Bentinck—all lost to him—and in their place young Keppel.

There were times when he wanted Bentinck back—yet such was his pride that he would not command or request. Bentinck must come back on his own desire—and Bentinck stayed away.

William had improved the Banqueting House which stood close to the Palace of Hampton Court on the banks of the river and there, with his Dutch friends, he spent most of his evenings. He was drinking heavily—mostly Holland's gin—and although he never showed signs of intoxication, after a night's drinking he would awake next morning in such a mood of irritability that he was approached only by those servants who found it impossible to keep away. Then at the slightest misdemeanor William would lift the cane, which he kept for the purpose, and slash it across the offender's shoulders.

The English who preferred to see a man merry in his drink, disliked Dutch William more than ever and jocularly referred to those poor servants who suffered through their master's irrascibility as "the Knights of the Cane."

Moods of melancholy beset the King; he shut himself into his cabinet and brooded on the wretched turn his life had taken. He mourned for Mary; he had not believed it would be possible to miss anyone as he missed her; he wanted Elizabeth; and he wanted Bentinck.

To Bentinck he had given the vested rights of the Prince of Wales—a move which he soon began to see was a stupid one. He had meant to imply by it that he cared nothing for Anne and believed he could hold the throne without any help from her; also that he would do what he wished with affairs under his control. The people disapproved of this act; and it did not bring Bentinck back to him. Only his morbid and melancholy mood could have made him do such a foolish thing.

He sent for Lord George Hamilton, a soldier who had done good service at the Battle of the Boyne and who had been wounded at Namur.

"I wish to reward you for your services," said William. "I trust you are recovering from your wounds."

"Your Majesty, I trust soon to be back in your army."

"Let me see," said William. "You were made Brigadier General after Namur were you not?"

"Yes, Your Majesty."

"And you are unmarried. You should have a wife."

"Sir I . . ."

William said: "I am going to honor you. I will give you an earldom. What do you say to that of Orkney?"

Hamilton was stammering his thanks, wondering whether Holland's gin was having a new effect on the King; but William silenced him.

"Your cousin, the daughter of Sir Edward Villiers, is a very marriageable young woman. I wish to see a union between you two."

Hamilton was astounded. So he was being offered the King's mistress! This could mean one of two things: Either he and an earldom were being offered to Elizabeth as a reward for past services or he was being given the role of complacent husband.

Time only would show which, for William was not a man to make himself clear on such a delicate matter.

An earldom! Promotion in the army, doubtless! And it was not as though he had marriage plans elsewhere. His cousin Elizabeth? She intrigued him. Not a beauty, but she must be fascinating to have held a strange cold man like the King all these years. She was a clever woman; and they would be partners. It was a good bargain he was being offered.

"A union with the lady would be very agreeable to me," he murmured.

William nodded dismissal. That was one matter settled. That would quieten gossip; and when he was in Holland Elizabeth should come to him and it would be almost as it had been in the old days.

It became clear to William that it was a mistake to think that he could afford to flout Anne. No matter how many victories he might win abroad, to the English he was still a foreigner, and they resented a foreign King. Yet when Anne was carried out in her chair they cheered her; they looked upon her as the heiress to the throne and on Gloucester as her successor. He could not hope for a peaceful existence while he was outwardly not on good terms with her.

He renewed his promise of St. James's Palace and this time Anne was able to move in. Then he made a gesture which gave Anne more pleasure than anything else could have done.

Lord Strafford, Knight of the Garter, died; and William wrote to Anne to say that it would give him the greatest pleasure to bestow the vacant ribbon on his nephew.

Anne went at once to her son's apartment where he was having breakfast. In spite of her excitement she was shocked to see that Lewis was sitting beside him spooning the food into his mouth.

"That," she said, "is no way for a Prince to eat. Lewis, stop it at once."

"Your Highness it is the only way in which we can induce him to eat."

Anne looked at her son with the familiar mingling of pride and terror. She had lost the last child as she had all the others, and Gloucester was her great hope. And he did not like food when his father and mother had such a delight in it! Was it a sign of delicate health?

"My boy," she said, "do you not like the food which is prepared for you?"

He considered this and said: "I like crumbs on the table but I do not care much for food on plates." He then wet his finger and picked up some of the crumbs about the table.

"You eat like a chicken," she said.

"Oh, Mama, I am a chick of the game."

His bright eyes, his quick smile were enchanting. Oh God, she prayed, preserve my darling. Keep him well. Take anything from me but leave me my precious boy.

"I have good news for you. You are to have the Garter."

His eyes shone with pleasure. "The Garter. But I have long wanted it and do you know, Mama, Harry Scull dreamed he saw me wearing it. Pray, Lewis, bring Harry to me without delay. I must tell Harry."

Back to Campden House came Gloucester, eyes brilliant with triumph, wearing the blue ribbon. He paraded before his parents telling them about the ceremony. "There were eleven knights with the King," he said. "William knighted me with the sword of state and then put the ribbon on me with his own hands, and that, Papa—are you listening Mama?"

"To every word, my dearest."

"Well that is most unusual, for one of the knights usually does it, but William wanted to do it for me. It was a special occasion. I am a favorite of his."

"Well, you are an heir to the throne."

"Yes, but it is a most unusual thing to be a favorite of the King's, Mama."

Anne exchanged glances with her husband. How could anyone help but make him a favorite? she was asking.

"Now may I go to my men. They are all anxious to see me in the Garter. I shall always wear it . . . until the day I die."

"We will not speak of that," said Anne sharply; and George laid a hand on her shoulder reassuringly.

They were silent, listening to Gloucester's voice shouting orders to his soldiers.

It had been wonderful to see the boy wearing the ribbon, but the mention of his death could plunge them both into deepest melancholy.

There was a visitor for the Princess Anne. This was John Sheffield, Earl of Mulgrave. Anne could never see him without remembering that love affair of her youth when she and John Sheffield had planned to marry. She still remembered the poems he had written to her. He had been sent away on her account and she had been given her dear George who was the best of husbands; but that did not mean she had not still a tender spot for Sheffield.

He was handsome; he was an excellent poet; and she believed he was at heart a Jacobite, for he had remained loyal to James longer than most men.

"My lord," she said, "it does me good to see you."

He kissed her hand with a lingering tenderness. He was married and so was she, but memories lingered.

"I came to congratulate you on the Duke's honor."

"It was good of you."

"I thought you would like to hear an account from an eye witness. I never saw the like. One would have thought he was a mature man. Such dignity! Such grace!"

"He is a most unusual boy."

"Which is only to be expected."

Their eyes met. He was thinking: He might have been ours. And if he had, she wondered, would he have been stronger? She compared John with George. Poor George, who was so fat and ineffectual; and John, tall, handsome, a man who would leave his mark on the world with his literary achievements and his parliamentary career.

"My lord," she said, "I would that you would watch over the Duke. Sometimes I feel that his education is not in the best hands. His mind is so alert; he picks up such *odd* pieces of information. And we find it so difficult to make him eat nourishing food. His servants feed him . . . to entice him. It causes me anxiety."

"If Your Highness would wish me to keep an eye on the boy . . ."

"It is what I do wish. I can trust you as I can few people. Will you do this?"

"With all my heart."

She sat smiling to herself after he had gone. It was pleasant to sit dreamily contemplating what might have been. She could do this without heartbreak. She had her dear husband, her beloved boy, her hopes of inheriting the throne; but romance was sweet.

Sarah came in and found her thus.

"Mulgrave was here, so I learn."

"Why yes."

"And what did he want?"

"He came to tell me how my boy conducted himself at the ceremony. Why, Mrs. Freeman, he said that the child behaved like a mature man. I do not think there is another boy in the world to compare with him and that is the truth."

"My young John must come to be his companion. I am sure they would be good for each other."

"It shall be so. John Sheffield is a charming man, I think."

Sarah grunted. "Not much guts I'd say. Remember how he fled at the first sign of trouble?"

"He did not fly. He was sent away to Tangier by my uncle."

"Some men would have refused to go."

"Refused to go? Refused the King's command?"

"Some would have found a way."

Sarah did not notice the slightly sullen expression about Anne's mouth, nor the hint of firmness in her voice as she said: "He is going to superintend the Duke's education."

"What?" cried Sarah.

Anne had turned away, murmuring: "Oh, not in an official capacity, of course, but I confess I shall be glad to have such an excellent man at hand."

What of Marlborough? thought Sarah, with difficulty suppressing her anger. If the Duke was to have a Governor naturally it should be Lord Marlborough. But at least Sheffield had not been offered the post officially.

Marlborough should have it, decided Sarah. And I shall see that he gets it.

The Princess Anne was preparing to leave for Windsor Castle. William had been unusually gracious. Not being content with seeing her installed in St. James's Palace, he offered her Windsor Castle in which to spend the summer with her husband and their son.

Having seen Anne's interest in John Sheffield, Sarah had decided that if she could do nothing for her husband it was time she brought her son forward, and before they left for Windsor she suggested to Anne that the little Duke should have some boys, near his own age and rank, to play with.

"My John is a little older than he is, but I am sure your boy would find him a good companion."

Anne who was sorry that Sarah had been put out over the favor she had shown to Sheffield, readily agreed; and it was decided that John Churchill together with three other boys, who were all studying at Eton, should be the companion of the Duke at Windsor.

It was inevitable that Anne should remember her dear Frances Bathurst's boys; there were two of them of suitable age and they with another named Peter Boscawen were invited to Windsor.

Gloucester was delighted at the prospect of going to Windsor, a castle he had never before visited, and expressed the hope that there would be many towers and bastions to be defended. And what were the fortifications like? he wanted to know.

As they drew nearer to the castle he was clearly pleased with the impressive towers and immediately began planning a battle which should be fought between the new companions he was to have, since his army had not accompanied him to Windsor.

He explored the castle looking for suitable spots to defend, and was delighted when his four companions arrived. John Churchill was a charming boy who had been well prepared by his mother to make himself agreeable to the young Duke; Peter Boscawen was a little older than the others and more serious, but the Bathursts were mischievous and ready for some good sport.

Gloucester immediately called a meeting and explained the plans for the campaign. He had, he said, chosen St. George's Hall for the action; then the music gallery and the stairs which led to it would represent a castle which had to be defended on one side and taken on the other.

This would be a new kind of game for he would not have all his soldiers to command; but he sent at once back to Campden Hill for his weapons which consisted of swords, muskets, and pikes.

He was eagerly explaining the plans of battle to his parents as he walked with them in Windsor Park. Anne and George exchanged glances; they were both wondering whether the boys understood that they must not be too rough with the young Duke.

Gloucester went on ahead of them as Anne said, "I must speak to Lewis. He must explain to them when our boy is not present. I wish that he did not so love these rough games."

"You would not have him girlish, my dear," George soothed.

"No, I would not. But how I wish that he were as strong and healthy looking as those others. I almost wish I had not asked them here. John Churchill is so big and strong."

"He is several years older than our boy."

Anne took her husband's hand and pressed it. "You are a comfort to me," she said; and she was suddenly angry because of the cruel lampoons which were written about this good man. The latest one which came to her mind explained that he was not quite dead but had to breathe hard to prevent being buried because no one saw any other sign of life in him. He was not stupid, as they implied, thought Anne angrily. He was just good and kind, a lover of peace.

She caught her breath in dismay, for she saw her precious son rolling over and over on the grass; he had come from the top of a steepish slope and there was earth on his face and the stains of grass on his clothes.

"My dearest . . ." she cried.

George had gone to the child as quickly as his overplump body would allow him; but before he could reach him Gloucester was on his feet.

He stood, legs apart smiling benignly on his parents.

"I must be able to descend hills quickly if I am to defend castles," he told them with dignity.

Lewis took Peter Boscawen aside and said to him: "Now look here, my boy, you must be the enemy, and you must see that no harm comes to His Highness."

Peter Boscawen nodded.

"Lose the game, rather. His mother's orders are that he is not to be hurt on any account. Who will you have on your side?"

"I'll take young Peter Bathurst."

Lewis nodded. "I shall be near to give a hand, but be careful. He's full of fire, but he's not strong."

"His head is too big, I think," commented Peter Boscawen.

"He's a game one. Won't say when he has any sort of pain. Think generals have to forget all that. But as I say, have a care."

Peter Boscawen was a cautious defender of the gallery and stairs, all the time giving way when in combat with Gloucester. But Peter Bathurst could not restrain himself; he became over excited and determined to hold the gallery at all costs. He had slipped the sheath from his sword and as Gloucester began to mount the steps dealt him a blow on his neck which started the blood to flow.

Lewis, horrified, saw what had happened and called: "Truce! Truce for the wounded!"

Gloucester looked at him in astonishment. "What wounded?"

"You, General, are wounded in the neck."

"I shall not give up for a scratch, man," cried Gloucester and charged up the stairs sending young Bathurst sprawling.

By the time the fortress was taken, Lewis was at hand with a doctor. The wound was slightly more than Gloucester would admit until the battle was over.

When his mother saw the bandage about his neck she was worried.

There was no way of protecting him, she told George, for he was the bravest boy in the world.

"My dear," said George, "there must be other children. If you had another son . . . two other sons . . . you would not fret so much over him."

"Perhaps next time we shall be more fortunate."

Next time! Since her marriage she had been pregnant for most of the time—to what avail? Continual disappointment—and one boy who, while he was the most precious thing in her life, was a continual anxiety.

With the passing of summer Anne and her family returned to St. James's. Two events occurred which caused consternation, not only in Anne's household but throughout the country.

The first was the affair of Sir John Fenwick, the well known Jacobite who had insulted Queen Mary when she was riding in the Park by refusing to take off his hat. Fenwick was suspected of being involved in the Assassination Plot with Sir George Barclay and Robert Charnock. The plot was that with forty men they were to ride out to a lane between Brentford and Turnham Green and when William came past in his coach-and-six on his way from Richmond to London, set upon him and kill him. The plot was divulged before it could be carried out; Barclay escaped to France and Charnock was captured, found guilty of treason and hanged, drawn and quartered at Tyburn. Fenwick's name was mentioned in papers which were captured on Charnock and he was named as a general in the army which was to be raised after William's assassination in order to put James II back on the throne. Fenwick getting wind of his danger at once went into hiding and made efforts to leave the country. These failed and he was captured and made a prisoner in the Tower while investigations went on. Realizing that he must eventually be found guilty he accused some of the leading Whigs of being implicated. Among these was Marlborough.

Sarah was in a panic. Just as she had brought her son to Court and was hoping to have her husband proclaimed Governor of the Duke of Gloucester, there was this fresh scare.

So far William had given no honors to Marlborough and although he was allowed to come to Court he was almost as much in the shadows as ever. This could be a further check to her hopes—and as she knew that her husband had been corresponding with the King over the Water, she was terrified of further revelations.

William, however, was well aware of Marlborough's Jacobite tendencies. But he knew that Marlborough would work for the winning side, and at the moment William was on that. He was turning over in his mind whether Marlborough should be given a post, for he was certain that hope of advancement was the best way of making sure of his loyalty.

William ignored Fenwick's accusations; the man was found guilty and beheaded on Tower Hill. His goods were confiscated and William took possession of them. One of these, it was remembered later, was a particularly spirited horse named Sorrel, which became one of William's favorite mounts.

The King returned to Flanders and because of his successes there the Treaty of Ryswick was signed and this, to a war-weary people, caused great rejoicing.

But the event which was somewhat startling to so many was a rumor that William was considering bringing home a bride.

William returned to England, minus a bride. It was only necessary to take a glance at him to realize that there could scarcely be truth in a rumor of that sort. He looked old and wizened; his asthma was noticeably worse; his cough was troublesome and his intimate servants knew that he frequently spat blood; he suffered torments from hemorrhoids and during the last months had begun to feel pains in his legs which had begun to swell alarmingly. He was more irascible than ever, and more liberal with his use of the cane; many of those close to him whispered hopefully together that he could not last much longer.

There was a revival of the old Jacobite songs and often William heard them whistled, although none of them dared sing the words in his hearing. The favorite at the moment was one which had come from Scotland, where most of them originated and called Willie the Whig.

He whiggit us out of our rights
And he whiggit us out of laws
And he whiggit us out of our King
Oh, that grieves us worst of all.

Popular favor was turning more and more to Anne, and this was largely due to young Gloucester. Crowds gathered to see him drilling his soldiers in the parks; they applauded and called "God bless the Prince." They were looking forward to the day when he would be their King; they were weary of Dutch William; he would like to have told them that he was weary of them.

Elizabeth Villiers was now the Countess of Orkney and seemed satisfied with her marriage. He met her at Loo, but it was not the old relationship which he had enjoyed for so many years. He was tired and very sick; yet still some belief in his own destiny drove him on and he knew he would never give up his three kingdoms until death overtook him.

It was written that they should be his; and his they had become and should remain until death took him.

He called on Anne. It was necessary to show the people that they were on excellent terms. He had given her St. James's for a residence; he had allowed her to spend her summers at Windsor. He himself was content with Kensington Palace and most of all Hampton Court. He could not breathe the damp air of Whitehall for long.

He inspected Gloucester's troops and never did the people cheer him so loyally as when he was in the company of his nephew.

The boy seemed well; perhaps he would grow out of his delicateness, and the water in his head disperse; if this could be, he would make a fine King, one to whom William could happily leave his inheritance.

He talked pleasantly with Anne, curbing the irritability which she always aroused in him.

"My boy is no longer a child," she was saying. "He should have a governor and I know of none who would fill the post as skillfully as my Lord Marlborough."

"Marlborough," repeated William thoughtfully; and he thought of the Fenwick affair and how mischief could always be found for idle hands. Better to have Marlborough occupied at Court, well satisfied than in half-banishment plotting. Marlborough was too clever a fellow to fail every time. "I think it a good choice," he said.

Anne's plump cheeks quivered with pleasure.

"I am glad to have Your Majesty's gracious consent to the appointment," she replied.

She could scarcely wait for him to leave; she was longing to call her dear Mrs. Freeman to tell her that at last their desire was achieved.

To annoy her, William stayed longer than he had intended, and when he rose he could scarcely walk. He would have to do something about this new complaint in his legs.

Keppel was beside him. Dear Keppel! Beautiful, fresh faced, attentive—for what he could get most likely, but when one was old and weary one was grateful even for bought attentions.

Oh, for the good days, the days when he had felt like a god among men; when the affection of Bentinck and the adoration of Mary had supported him in the role he had chosen for himself.

On horseback he was more comfortable—apart from the accursed hemorrhoids. He had always felt better mounted; he touched his horse's flanks lightly and they were off. The creature responded to a touch. All his horses knew their master and because he showed more affection for them than he did for many people within their limits they gave him what he wanted—respect and devotion.

In the Palace he said he would rest for a while and told Keppel to send for Dr. Radcliffe who was known to be one of the best doctors in the country. A blunt man, an unashamed Jacobite who had declared openly that he had little time for the Whig Sovereigns. He had been physician to the King of England and if that King was across the water that didn't mean that others who called themselves Kings were worthy of the name.

A man, thought William, who in some reigns would have been in the Tower. All the same he was the cleverest of doctors and when one was ill one did not think so much of politics.

In any case, thought William, I am surrounded by Jacobites; and such was the spirit of the age, fostered by the spate of writing so often in the form of lampoons and songs, that they must be endured.

Radcliffe came; he examined the King.

What a wreck of a man! he thought. He's breaking up all over. Spitting blood for years; cough that racks his body; this alone would have killed most men years ago. And his legs? Just a further sign of decay.

There was a touch of contempt in the manner in which he prodded William's body. A Whig Sovereign who had usurped the throne from the true King and a wreck of a man into the bargain! But a King—with a belief in his own destiny that was an inner vitality which kept him afloat.

"The climate's no good to you," said Radcliffe with a touch of mischief. He meant Get back to Holland and leave England for those to whom it belonged. William sensed the insolence. That word "climate" was often used ambiguously in his hearing. How often had he been told that the climate was not good for him.

"Perforce I must endure it," replied William coldly.

"At Your Majesty's peril," continued the doctor.

The man was getting offensive; he need not think that his reputation as a doctor gave him the right to insult the throne.

"And my legs?" asked William tersely.

"I wouldn't have Your Majesty's two legs for your three kingdoms," retorted the doctor.

William was now incensed; if his cane had been handy he might have been tempted to slash it across that insolent face.

"You may retire," he said coldly.

Radcliffe bowed.

"I do not mean from my presence merely. You are dismissed from the Court."

Radcliffe bowed again, smiling as though the King had bestowed some honor.

He left the apartment; some minutes later William heard the sound of whistling beneath his window as someone passed by. He looked out.

It was Radcliffe on his way, whistling as he went, "Willie the Whig."

THE GREAT
TRAGEDY

*S*arah *was jubilant.*

"This is our chance at last," she told her husband. "Anne is delighted. And I can tell you this: Caliban won't last long. He dismissed Radcliffe for telling him the truth so it must have been mighty unpleasant. Now, John, we can begin to plan."

Marlborough shared his wife's enthusiasm. He was in at last; a pleasant state of affairs after years of neglect.

Their son John was a companion of Gloucester's and it had not taken Sarah long to persuade Anne to appoint him Master of the Horse to the young Duke.

She was in a whirl of excitement, plans flooding into her brain. She asked Anne if she might retire to St. Albans to have a few days with her family, to which Anne replied fondly that she could deny her dear Mrs. Freeman nothing—even leave to absent herself from her.

Those were thrilling days.

"Just think, my dear," cried Sarah, "Anne will soon be Queen and she will obey me in all things. You are the Governor of Gloucester who will immediately become Prince of Wales. We shall rule the land."

"A moment, my love. There will be the Parliament to be considered. You have overlooked that. Do you imagine that they are going to stand aside?"

She laughed in his face. "There is something you have overlooked, John Churchill. We have two daughters who will soon be marriageable."

He stared at her and she went on: "Henrietta is seventeen. Anne is sixteen. Henrietta is ready now for marriage. I intend to see that my girls marry in the right quarter."

Marlborough marveled at the power of his wife to astonish him; he raised his eyebrows and murmured: "Doubtless you have already decided on matches for our daughters?"

"I am casting my thoughts," she answered. "Sunderland has a son— so has Godolphin."

"You are . . . amazing!"

"Someone has to work for this family. You are the best soldier in the world, John, but sometimes I think you are a little dilatory in other matters."

"I thought you hated Sunderland."

"I do not hate his son; and I might find my hatred turning to affection if he belonged to my family."

"You think Sunderland would . . ."

"My dear John, in a very short time any family in England is going to think itself fortunate to mate with the Marlboroughs. Mind you, Godolphin will be easier. I shall invite young Francis to visit us and that will give him an opportunity to become better acquainted with the girls."

She was invincible, he was sure of it. What she wanted she would have by the sheer force of her character.

When they returned to Court a minor irritation awaited them. William had appointed Dr. Burnet, Bishop of Salisbury, to be in charge of Gloucester's education.

Burnet had been with William and Mary in Holland and had done a great deal toward bringing them to England and deposing James. He would possibly not look with favor on a suspected Jacobite like Marlborough and there might be trouble there.

Sarah was angry. Burnet, to whom William owed some loyalty, could easily poison his mind against a man who had come near to losing his life through Jacobite activities. She was for going into battle with Burnet.

Here it was that Marlborough showed himself her superior in tactics.

He listened courteously to Burnet's plans for the Duke's education and immediately assured the Bishop that he was ready to accept the rule of a man whom he knew was far more learned than himself. In a very short time Marlborough's tact and diplomacy had averted a situation which Sarah's blunt vitality might have made a disaster.

All was going well. Marlborough and Burnet in accord; Henrietta falling in love with Francis Godolphin; his father clearly delighted with the possibility of a union between the Marlboroughs and Godolphins. Charles, Lord Spencer, Sunderland's son might have to be angled for more insistently, and Marlborough himself was not as eager for the match as Sarah was, which meant that she would have to persuade him of the importance of alliance with the Spencers. Sunderland was an opportunist, she knew, and she had loathed him at one time, but he was one of the richest men in England and his son Charles would be rich one day. Not that money was everything. Power was the goal. And with the Spencers and the Godolphins allied to the Marlboroughs by family ties they would be supreme.

Sarah would bring her husband around to her way of thinking eventually, she had no doubt. And in the meantime she could rejoice in the way the Godolphins were being drawn into her net. And for her son John there should be the greatest triumphs of all . . . but he was young yet.

All was well then—William's health was declining rapidly, and although Anne was not well, anyone who would miscarry so frequently and continue to live must be strong. She had had three miscarriages in the last three years.

Never had Mrs. Morley and Mrs. Freeman been so close. Anne liked to sit, her beautiful hands lying in her lap, while she talked of her boy, and Mrs. Freeman betrayed her hopes for her dear daughters.

Such a comfort to talk together of these family affairs! sighed Anne.

When Henrietta Churchill was engaged to Francis Godolphin, Anne said Mrs. Freeman must allow her to give them a useful little wedding gift. This turned out to be five thousand pounds—a useful sum indeed.

"Like her mother she will always be grateful to dear Mrs. Morley," murmured Mrs. Freeman.

Those were glorious days. To Sarah it seemed that she only had to plan, exert her powerful energy, and what she desired was hers.

Anne, with what Sarah called to Marlborough her constant slobbering over her boy, often drove her to distraction. "I find the need to get away some times."

"Be careful," warned Marlborough. "You can be too frank at times."

"John Churchill, it is my frankness which has endeared me to the fool."

"Perhaps, but never forget that there are others just waiting for the opportunity to leap into your place."

"And you think it is as easy as that! They just jump and are there?"

"No, but be careful."

"Well, I don't intend to waste all my time playing cards and listening to her gossip! I am going to put someone in to do some of my duties so that I can get away now and then more easily than I have done."

"Who, in God's name?"

"I'm thinking of my uncle Hill's girl. That family will have to be helped in some way, I may as well make use of them."

"She is doing good work looking after the children at St. Albans."

"The children are growing up. She shall come into Anne's bedchamber. She will be so grateful and she is such a mouse no one will notice her. Then I shall be at liberty to get away when I want to, knowing that there will be no smart madam to try too much friendship with old Morley."

"You think of everything," said Marlborough fondly.

Shortly afterward Abigail Hill joined Anne's household; and it was as Sarah had prophesied; so quiet was she, so humble, so retiring, it was hardly noticed that she was there.

A new century, thought Sarah. The century of the Churchills. She commanded the household of the Princess Anne. She was looked upon as the future power behind the throne for with every passing week William looked more and more frail.

Yet he clung to life with the obstinacy of a shriveled leaf in spite of autumn gales.

In the spring Anne was brought to bed once more and again miscarried. She was sad for a while to think of another child lost. But there was her boy to comfort her and she believed that as he grew older he was growing stronger.

She herself was feeling the strain of the last miscarriage; Dr. Radcliffe had told her that she must show more restraint at the table and she did try; but it was difficult; and when she had to pass by her favorite dishes she grew melancholy.

She often felt sick and faint and one evening on rising from the table she felt so ill that she sent for Dr. Radcliffe. Since William had banished him, Dr. Radcliffe had not lived at Court and had often been summoned to the Princess's bedside and obliged to make a journey through the night from his house. Being certain that Anne was merely suffering from indigestion caused through overeating he declined to go.

He sent a message back: "Her Highness is not ill. I know her case well. Put her to bed at once and she will be better in the morning."

He proved to be right; she was better the next day; but a week later she felt ill again at that same hour which Dr. Radcliffe found inconvenient.

This time Dr. Radcliffe was more blunt. "Go back to the Princess and tell her that there is nothing wrong with her but the vapors. Let her go to bed and rest and she'll be better in the morning."

Anne was angry and the next time she saw him she told him that on account of his unforgivable conduct his name was no longer on her list of physicians.

"Was I not right?" he demanded. "Did you not feel better in the morning? There was nothing wrong with you but the vapors."

"Nothing would induce me to put you back on my list," said Anne.

"Nothing would induce me to come," retorted the doctor. "I have never hidden my feelings and like as not, on account of them, I'd be accused of poisoning you Whig Sovereigns. So 'tis better as it is."

He left in his insolent way, as though having the reputation of being the best doctor in England meant that he could flout royalty without fear of retaliation.

He was now no longer a Court physician and glad of it.

Anne forgot her anger over Radcliffe, because her boy's birthday was approaching. He was eleven years old; he still drilled his soldiers, and under Burnet was becoming very wise. It was fortunate for him that he had a natural aptitude for learning which grew out of his lively curiosity, for Burnet was determined to make him a scholar.

How delightful he looked on his birthday. He was wearing a special suit which had been made for the occasion. The coat was blue velvet—a color which suited him and made his eyes more vivid than ever; the buttons were diamonds and the Garter ribbon matched the coat; he wore a white periwig which made his head look bigger than ever; but he was a charming figure.

Anne could not take her eyes from him; she thought: He is the whole meaning of life to me.

There was flatttery among courtiers, of course, for the heir to the throne, but surely all who saw must admire him as much as they implied.

He had asked permission to fire his cannon in honor of his parents and when this was given and done he approached them and bowing to them he said in his high clear voice: "Papa and Mama, I wish you both unity, peace, and concord, not for a time but forever."

They were both overcome with emotion; George pressed Anne's hand to show he shared his wife's pride and emotion in their son.

"It is a fine compliment," George told the boy.

"No, Papa, it is not a compliment; it is sincere."

There never was such a boy. Anne had been so often disappointed through the children she had hoped for; there were so many failures that she had to think hard to remember the number and then she was not sure; but, while she had this son, she was the proudest, happiest mother in the world.

Young Gloucester sat at the head of the banqueting table and welcomed his guests. All his soldiers were present and taking advantage of the good things to eat, for they needed refreshment after their exertions.

Dancing followed. Gloucester danced tolerably well although he told his mother he could not abide Old Dog—his name for Mr. Gorey who had been dancing master to Anne and her sister Mary when they were Gloucester's age—and he felt that dancing was not for soldiers.

He was very tired when the banquet was over and not sorry to retire to his apartments where he told John Churchill that birthdays were better to be planned for, than to have, and he would rather one big battle any day.

In their apartments Anne and George sat together reminding each other of how he had danced, how he had reviewed his soldiers, what he had said.

"I can never thank you enough for giving me such a son," said Anne.

"Nay my dear, it is I who should thank you."

And they went on to talk of him. They laughed and rejoiced in him.

"We cannot say we have been unfortunate while we have our boy," said Anne.

The next morning when Gloucester's attendants went to awaken him they found him feeling sick. He said he had a sore throat and did not want to get up.

This news brought his mother to his bedside immediately, and when she saw his flushed face she was terrified.

"Send for the physicians!" she cried. They came; but they did not know what ailed the boy. They bled him, but his condition did not improve. Before the day was out he was in a high fever and delirious.

"Dr. Radcliffe must come," said Anne. "Go and bring him."

"Your Highness, you have dismissed him."

"Go and bring him. Tell him I order him to come."

Dr. Radcliffe arrived at Windsor in due course but he clearly came reluctantly.

"Your Highness," he said, "I am no longer one of your physicians, and I cannot understand why you should summon me here."

Anne's face was pale with fear; he had never seen her so frightened for herself as she was for her son.

"My boy is ill," she said. "If anyone can save him, it is you."

Radcliffe went and examined the boy.

"He has scarlet fever," he said. "Good God, who bled him?"

The doctor who had done so admitted that he had.

"Then," said Radcliffe, "you may well have finished him. I can do nothing. You have destroyed him."

Anne listened as though in a trance. She let Radcliffe go and made no attempt to detain him.

She only muttered: "He is the best doctor in England and he says my boy is destroyed."

A future without this boy was something she could not face. She was numb with terror, yet bemused. Only a day or so ago he had stood before her bowing in his beautiful blue suit. It was not possible that he could be so ill.

She would nurse him. Dr. Radcliffe might say that they had destroyed him with the wrong treatment, but she would give him all that a mother could—perhaps what only a mother could.

She forgot her own maladies; there was only one thing that mattered to her. Her boy must live. She herself waited on him, nursed him, prepared the food which he could not eat. As she moved about the sick room, her lips moved in prayer.

"Oh, God, leave me my boy. You have taken all the others and this I accept. But this one is my own, my joy, my life. For eleven years I have cherished him, loved him, feared for him. You have taken the others; leave me this one."

He must improve. Such loving care must make him well.

"My boy . . . my boy . . ." she whispered as she looked at the hot little face that seemed so vulnerable without that white periwig, so childish and yet at times like that of an old man. "Do not leave me. I will give anything . . . anything in the world to keep you. My hopes of the crown . . . anything. . . ."

A fearful thought had struck her. Why did she suffer constant miscarriages? Why was she in danger of losing her best beloved boy?

Had her father once loved her and Mary as she loved this boy? Had he suffered through his children as she had been made to suffer through hers? Death and treachery . . . which was the harder to bear?

She shut out such thoughts. She called to her boy and to her God.

"Have pity on me. Have pity on this suffering mother."

But there was to be no pity. Five days after his birthday, William, Duke of Gloucester was dead.

THE LITTLE GENTLEMAN
IN BLACK VELVET

he Princess Anne remained in her apartments. She spoke to no one and no one could comfort her. She did not wish to see Mrs. Freeman, not that Sarah cared. She herself had suffered the loss of a son and she did not want to be reminded of that tragic time.

As Sarah said to Marlborough: "The death of Gloucester changes the position of Anne. That poor lump of woman ... how long will she last? And without an heir she is scarcely of any importance. You see how wise I was to link us with Godolphin, and it will be Sunderland before long."

Anne had not thought of her changed status. There was only her loss.

George came to her; they held hands and tried to speak of their lost child and then could not bear to.

They sat in silence crying quietly.

Anne said at length: "I keep seeing him, George, reviewing his soldiers, regarding us in his grave way. Do you remember his greeting to us? He wished us peace, unity, and concord. Peace ... how shall we ever know that again without him? I cannot believe it, George. Our little one. Never to see him again."

"Est-il possible?" murmured George brokenheartedly.

Anne wrote to her father. She wanted him to forgive her. She had been a wicked daughter to him and now she suffered a bitter penitence. Her great sorrow, she believed, was a punishment from heaven. Her heart was broken, but if he would forgive her she believed she could go on living.

When she had sent off that letter she felt a little happier; and when James replied forgiving her, asking her to use her utmost power to restore her brother to the throne if ever she came to it, and to accept it only in trust for him; she wept and said that her father's letter had comforted her as nothing else would.

William was growing weaker and Anne was the heir to the throne who could not shut herself away forever.

Sarah had become a little more insolent than before. She was determined to stress Anne's less powerful position even if Anne was unaware of it. She had succeeded in marrying her daughter Anne to Charles, Lord Spencer, and that little project had been carried through victoriously.

Sunderland, Godolphin, Marlborough. What a combination! In certain circumstances unbeatable. All that would be necessary for them to rule would be for Sarah to keep the flaccid Queen in leading strings; and that she could adequately do.

The death of one small boy had turned thousands of eyes toward the throne. The Whigs and the Tories were drawn closer together. The Tories wanted the old regime—a King such as they had been accustomed to; the Whigs preferred the Sovereigns they had made of William and Mary, whose power was governed by the Parliament. But they stood together on one point and passed the Act of Settlement which stipulated that the sovereign must be a member of the Anglican Church, must not leave the country without the consent of Parliament and must be advised by the entire Privy Council and not by counsellors who were secret.

This meant two things; there should be no return to that old Stuart love: The Divine Right of Kings; and James's son by his Catholic wife should be kept from the throne as long as he adhered to the Catholic faith. A constitutional Monarchy and a Protestant King.

William could not live long; Anne was not a healthy woman; in view of the Act of Settlement eyes were turned to the House of Hanover in which James I's granddaughter Sophia was Electress.

But William still lived and there was Anne, who was a young woman still. She was almost certain to become pregnant again soon and who knew what would happen? She had produced one child. Why should she not produce another?

It was hoped she would. What a lot of trouble that would save!

Death did not come singly to the royal family.

It had not been generally known that, early that year, James had had a stroke which left him partially paralysed. He lived on for a while but by September his condition had weakened and after a short illness he died at St. Germains.

In his last hours he reiterated that he forgave all his enemies and he mentioned specially his daughter Anne. He lovingly took farewell of Mary Beatrice, but he was not sorry to go; sickness and defeat had darkened his life, but what had hurt him most was the treachery of the daughters he had loved so dearly; that was something he would never forget. But the letter of Anne's, who herself was suffering through a beloved child, had given him some comfort. He was glad that she had asked forgiveness and he had given it before leaving the world.

Louis came to his deathbed and James made a dying request of him.

"Here is my son," he said. "In a few hours' time he will be King of England. Will you, my good friend, promise me that you will recognize him as such."

"I promise," answered Louis.

William knew that war was inevitable. Louis of France had proclaimed the son of James II and Mary Beatrice, King James III of England.

There was a new King over the Water for the Catholics to drink to.

Only such an act could rouse William from the physical disabilities which were overwhelming him. His body might be failing him, but his mind was as alert as ever. The proclamation of James' son as King of England was a minor issue. The question of the Spanish succession was involved; Charles II of Spain had named Louis' grandson Philip of Anjou as his successor. This could only mean that Louis would have a big control over Spain and the balance of power in Europe would be upset. A European war was brewing fast and Holland and England would have to stand together against France and Spain if they were to survive.

Such a project was such to put new life into a great war leader.

William rarely spent an evening drinking Holland's gin nowadays. He was in consultation with his most able ministers. Marlborough was a good soldier; William had seen enough of him in action to know that. There were Marlborough, Godolphin, and Sunderland . . . among others.

This was a time for unity. They would all see that.

And at such a time William ceased to be an irritable invalid.

The gateway of greatness was opening to Marlborough; Sarah knew it. And he would always remember whose had been the hand to unlock those gates. He would always remember what he owed to his wife.

She sat at her table in the anteroom to Anne's bedchamber drawing on her gloves, but she did not see the room; she saw Marlborough crowned with the laurels of success; her lovely daughters queens of their world; and young John, best beloved of all her children, who should have the grandest future of them all.

The door opened so silently that she was not aware that anyone had entered until a soft voice said: "Excuse me, my lady."

She looked up into the meek plain face of Abigail Hill.

"Good gracious, you startled me. I didn't hear you come."

"I am sorry, my lady. But you are wearing the Princess's gloves."

Sarah looked down at her hands. She thought they had seemed tight. Anne's hands were small, her fingers tapering; the only beauty she possessed.

Abigail was regarding her with such awe that she was first amused and then delighted. She supposed these women about Anne realized that she, Sarah Churchill, was of far more importance than their mistress.

She could not resist confirming this opinion or making sure that it existed in case it did not already.

She peeled them off turning up her nose as she did so. "Take them away at once. I do not care to wear something that has touched the *odious* hands of that disagreeable woman."

Abigail looked startled as Sarah had expected; Sarah flung the gloves at her; they fell to the floor and the woman meekly picked them up.

"Leave me, please. I am busy."

Sarah sat smiling as Abigail left. What she did not know was that Abigail had left the door open and that Anne in the adjoining room had heard Sarah's words, for Sarah had a loud penetrating voice.

She had said that to a serving woman! thought Anne. Mrs. Freeman had called her hands odious and her a disagreeable woman. Sarah was handsome, of course, and however disagreeable Sarah was, Anne could not help being fascinated by her. But to say such a thing to a serving woman! She would not have believed it if she had not heard it herself.

Sarah gave herself great airs since her daughters' marriages and since Marlborough was back in favor.

She didn't mean it perhaps. It was a joke. Yes, that was it. It was meant to be amusing. Sarah would never call her hands odious, herself disagreeable.

Abigail Hill brought the gloves to Anne.

"Can I help put them on, Your Highness."

Such a nice quiet voice, such a nice quiet woman! And she gave no sign of what must have been astonishing to her.

It couldn't be true. I imagined it, thought Anne. It was more comfortable that way; for in truth, although Mrs. Freeman was overbearing, although she was growing more and more inclined to bully, she was

Mrs. Morley's dear, dear friend and Mrs. Morley could not do without her, particularly now she was suffering so deeply from the loss of her beloved boy.

Abigail Hill was smiling shyly. Such a pleasant creature, but so quiet and self-effacing, one did not notice she was there until one wanted something.

Abigail made her think that she had imagined those words. How comforting! It was just what she wanted.

War! thought William.

The whole of Europe in conflict. But he would win; he was certain of it.

To be on the battlefield again! It was the life for him.

He pressed his heels into his horse's side. A good horse this, Sorrel, Fenwick's horse; the only good thing which had come out of that affair.

Before him was Hampton Court—his palace. How different he had made it since his arrival in England! It could be in Holland; there was the Dutch stamp on it—square and gracious and the gardens were a delight.

He was anxious to be there; he went into a gallop; but as he did so the horse plunged its forefoot into a molehill and William was rolling over and over on the grass.

His collarbone was fractured. It must be set and he must rest.

"Rest!" he cried. "With war imminent! I have to be at Kensington Palace this night to meet my Council!"

None dared dissuade him; and when he reached Kensington riding there in his carriage, the jolting he received had displaced the bones and they had to be reset. Moreover, his sickly body could not endure the strain and he was exhausted and forced to rest.

He lay tossing on his bed. He had no great desire to live, but this was not the time to die. There was so much to be done. War was threatening and he was a great war leader. He did not love England, nor did the

English love him; but his destiny, so clear at his birth, was the possession and retention of three crowns and he was not a man to evade his fate.

He must not allow a broken bone or two to deter him.

They said this King was immortal. They had been expecting him to die for years; yet he had outlived his wife; he had outlived James; and although a few days ago he had been believed to be near death he was recovering.

In the taverns the "Jacks" were secretly drinking to the Little Gentleman in Black Velvet—the mole who had made that hill which had brought down Fenwick's Sorrel. He had passed through many battles; he had been the victim of plots; he had faced death a hundred times and eluded it; could it be that the little mole had succeeded where his enemies had failed?

But it seemed as though it were not to be.

The Princess Anne and Prince George called on the King to congratulate him on his recovery and for a week or so William, although suffering more acutely than before, went about his business.

But it was true that the gentleman in black velvet had achieved what his enemies had failed to do.

The swollen legs grew larger; the asthma was worse; it was he himself who told those about his bed that the end had come.

Keppel was at his bedside; he was glad of that; but there was one other whom he wanted: Bentinck. The friend of the past. There must be one last touch of that once dearly beloved hand.

Bentinck came, sorrow in his eyes and in his heart.

The one who truly loved me, thought William—but there had been one other. There had been Mary.

On his arm was the bracelet of hair he had put there on her death. They would find it now and perhaps know that somewhere in his heart under the layers of ice there was a warmth for some. For loving Mary, for loyal Bentinck, for gay Keppel, for his dear Elizabeth.

He tried to speak to Bentinck. "I am near the end . . ." But there was no sound.

In her apartment Anne waited for news. Sarah was with her, too excited for speech.

To herself she spoke. It has come. This is the great day . . . the beginning of greatness. We shall be invincible. My entire dream is coming true.

She looked at the flaccid figure in the chair: the Queen of England.

Queen, thought Sarah, in name only. It shall be the Marlboroughs who rule.

People were coming into the apartment now. Oh, so respectful, so full of feigned sorrow, so full of suppressed excitement.

They knelt before Anne.

"Your Majesty," they said. And then there was a cry in the apartment. "Long Live Queen Anne."

Bibliography

Aubrey, William Hickman Smith *History of England*

Bathurst, Lt.-Col. The Hon. Benjamin *Letters of Two Queens*

Bray, William, ed. *Diary of John Evelyn*

Burnet, Bishop *History of His Own Time*, with notes by the Earls of Dartmouth and Hardwicke and Speaker Onslow, to which are added the cursory remarks of Swift

Chapman, Hester W. *Mary II, Queen of England*

Churchill, William S. *Marlborough, His Life and Times*

Dobrée, Bonamy *Three Eighteenth Century Figures*

Edwards, William *Notes on British History*

Kronenberger, Louis *Marlborough's Duchess*

Oman, Carola *Mary of Modena*

Pepys, Samuel *Diary and Correspondence* edited by Henry B. Wheatley

Renier, G.J. *William of Orange*

Sandars, Mary F. *Princess and Queen of England: Life of Mary II*

Sells, A. Lytton *The Memoirs of James II* (translated from the Bouillon manuscript, edited and collated with the Clarke Edition, with an introduction by Sir Arthur Bryant)

Stephen, Sir Leslie, and Sir Sidney Lee, eds. *The Dictionary of National Biography*

Strickland, Agnes *Lives of the Queens of England*

Traill, H.D. *William the Third*

Trevelyan, G. M. *England under the Stuarts*

Trevelyan, G. M. *English Social History*

Trevelyan, G. M. *History of England*

Wade, John *British History*

Macauley, Lord, edited by Lady Trevelyan *The History of England from the Accession of James II*

TURN THE PAGE TO READ AN EXCERPT FROM

JEAN PLAIDY'S SEVENTH AND FINAL BOOK IN

THE NOVELS OF THE STUARTS SERIES:

COURTING
HER HIGHNESS

978-0-307-71951-5

$16.00

ABIGAIL

HILL

When the attention of Lady Marlborough was called to her impecunious relations, the Hills, she looked upon the entire subject as a trivial inconvenience, although later—much later—she came to realize that it was one of the most—perhaps the most—important moments of her brilliant career.

In the first place it was meant to be an insult, but one which she had brushed aside as she would a tiresome gnat at a picnic party.

The occasion had been the birthday of the Princess Anne, and on that day Her Highness's complete attention had been given to her son, the young Duke of Gloucester. Anne's preoccupation with that boy, although understandable, for he was the only one of her children who had survived after countless pregnancies—at least Lady Marlborough had lost count, for there must have been a dozen to date—was a source of irritation. Before the boy's birth, Sarah Churchill, Lady Marlborough, had become accustomed to demanding the whole of the Princess's attention, and the friendship between them was the wonder and speculation of all at Court; when they were together Anne and Sarah were Mrs. Morley and Mrs. Freeman respectively, because Anne wished there to be no formality to mar their absolute intimacy. But since the boy had been born, although the friendship had not diminished, Anne's first love was for her son, and when she went on and on about "my boy" Sarah felt as though she could scream.

Thus it had been at the birthday celebrations; the boy was to have a formal introduction to the Court, and for the occasion Anne had ordered that a special costume be made for him; and she had had the absurd idea of decking him out in her own jewels. Anne herself did not greatly care for ceremonial occasions; she was far more comfortable reclining on her couch, with a cup of chocolate in her hand or a dish of sweetmeats beside her, entertaining herself with the cards or gossip. But she wanted "my boy" as she, to Sarah's exasperation, constantly referred to him, to look magnificent.

Poor little wretch! thought Sarah, who delighted in applying terms of contempt to persons in high places. He needed to be adorned. When she compared him with her own handsome son—John after his father—who was a few years older than the young Duke, she wanted to crow with triumph. In fact it was all she could do to prevent herself calling Anne's attention to the difference in the two boys. When she brought young John to Court, as she intended to quite soon, Anne would see for herself what a difference their was between the two.

But young Gloucester, in spite of his infirmity, was a bright boy. He was alert, extremely intelligent, and the doctors said that the fact that he suffered from water on the brain, far from harming his mind, made it more alert; and so it seemed. He was old for his years; sharp of wits, and to see him drilling the ninety boys in the park whom he called his army, was one of the sights of the Court. All the same, his head was too big for his body and he could not walk straight unless two attendants were close beside him. He was the delight and terror of his parents' life—and no wonder.

There he was on this occasion in a coat of blue velvet, the buttonholes of which were encrusted with diamonds; and about his small person were his mother's jewels. Over his shoulder was the blue ribbon of the Garter which Sarah could never look on without bitterness; she had so wanted the Garter for her dear Marl, her husband, who, she believed, was possessed of genius and could rule the country if he only had a chance. Therefore to see the small figure boasting that he was already a Knight of the Garter was a maddening sight; but when she looked at the white periwig, which added a touch of absurdity, and thought of that huge head beneath it, she was thankful that even if Marlborough had been denied the Garter, even if Dutch William was keeping him in the shadows, at least she had a healthy family; and it was only a matter of waiting for the end of William before, with Anne's coming to the throne, they were given what they deserved.

In the royal nursery young Gloucester had displayed the jewel which the King had given him; it was St. George on horseback set with diamonds, a magnificent piece; and it was certainly not William's custom to be so generous. But like everyone else at Court he had an affection for the little boy who, with his charming eccentricities, had even been able to break through the King's reserve.

"His Majesty gave me this," he said, "when he bestowed the Garter on me. He put on the Garter with his own hands which I assure you is most unusual. It is because he holds me in such regard. Am I not fortunate. But I shall repay His Majesty. Look here, Mama, this is the note I am sending him."

Anne had taken the note and Sarah, with the boy's governess, Lady Fitzharding, had looked over her shoulder as she read:

I, Your Majesty's most dutiful subject, had rather lose my life in Your Majesty's cause than in any man's else, and I hope it will not be long ere you conquer France. We, your Majesty's subjects, will stand by you while we have a drop of blood.

Gloucester

Anne had smiled and looked from Barbara Fitzharding to Sarah. Besottedly, thought Sarah. It was true the boy was precocious—but he was a child. And when he offered his soldiers—boys of his own age with toy muskets and swords to the King—it was a joke and nothing more. But even grim William gravely accepted these offers and came to Kensington to review the small troops. Perhaps, thought Sarah sardonically, this was not so foolish as it seemed; for it was only on such occasions, with the crowd looking on, that he managed to raise a cheer for himself.

"I am sure the King will be delighted," Anne had said.

"Doubtless he will think I am a little too fine," mused Gloucester thoughtfully. "But my loyalty may help to divert his impatience with my finery."

The Princess Anne had rolled her eyes in ecstasy. Was there ever such a boy! What wit! What observation! What a King he would make when his turn came!

When he had left them they had had to listen to accounts—heard many times before—of his wit and wisdom. Sarah was impatient, but Barbara Fitzharding was almost as besotted as the Princess; and there they had sat, like two old goodies, talking about this wonderful boy.

It was later when Sarah and Barbara were together, that Sarah gave way to her impatience.

"I do not think the King cared for all that display," she commented, a smile which was almost a sneer turning up a corner of her mouth.

"He is, I believe, truly fond of his nephew," Barbara replied. "And he is not fond of many people."

"There are his good friends, Bentinck and Keppel—Bentinck the faithful and Keppel the handsome—and of course his mistress."

Sarah looked slyly at Barbara, for it was her sister, Elizabeth Villiers, who had been William's mistress almost since the beginning of his marriage to the time of the Queen's death. The Queen had left a letter that had been opened after her death reproaching William and asking him to discontinue the liaison, and which had so shaken the King that he had left Elizabeth alone for a long time. Sarah believed, though, that the relationship had been resumed—very secretively; and Barbara, a spy reporting everything to her sister who passed it on to William, would know if this were so.

"He is so very ill these days," said Barbara. "I doubt whether he has the time or energy for diversions."

"His *gentlemen* friends remain at his side. I hear they enjoy themselves on Holland gin in the Hampton Banqueting House. He still finds time—and energy—to indulge his Dutchmen."

"But he is looking more frail every week."

"That is why it was a mistake to dress Gloucester up in all that finery. It was almost proclaiming him Prince of Wales before his mother is Queen."

"I wonder," said Barbara with a hint of sarcasm, "that you did not warn his mother since she would most assuredly listen to *you*."

"I did warn her."

"And she disobeyed?" Veiled insolence! Sarah had never liked Barbara Fitzharding since the days when as young Barbara Villiers she had lived with the circle of girls, Sarah among them, who had been brought up by Barbara's mother, with the young Princesses Anne and Mary in Richmond Palace.

"She is so besotted about that boy."

"He is her son."

"He is being pampered. I would not let one of mine be indulged as he is."

Was this a reflection on Barbara's governess-ship? Barbara disliked Sarah Churchill—who at Court did not?—and although she might rule the Princess Anne's household, Barbara was not going to allow her to interfere in that of the Duke of Gloucester.

"He is by no means indulged. He merely happens to be an extremely intelligent boy. In fact, I have never known one more intelligent."

"Have you not? I must invite you to St. Albans one day and you shall meet *my* children."

Barbara laughed. "Everything you have must naturally be better than other people's."

"*Must* always be? What do you mean by that? My children are strong, healthy, intelligent, which is not to be wondered at. Compare their father with that . . . oaf . . . I can call him nothing else . . . who goes around babbling 'Est-il possible?' to everything that is said to him! Prince George of Denmark! I call him Old Est-il-possible! And when I do everyone knows to whom I refer."

"One would think you were the royal Princess—Her Highness, your servant," said Barbara. "You ought to take care, Sarah Churchill. You should think back to the days when you first joined us at Richmond.

You were fortunate, were you not, to find a place there? It was the greatest good luck . . . for you. You must admit that you were not of the same social order as the rest of us. We were noble and you . . ."

"Your relative, Barbara Villiers—my lady Castlemaine as she became—put honors in your family's way because she was an expert performer in the King's bedchamber. We had no such ladies in our family."

"Your husband I believe did very well out of his relationship with my lady Castlemaine. She paid him for his services to her . . . in the bedchamber. Was it five thousand pounds with which he bought an annuity? You must find that very useful now that my lord Marlborough is out of favor and has no office at the Court."

If there was one person in the world whom Sarah truly loved it was her husband, John Churchill, Earl of Marlborough; and although he had had a reputation as a rake before their marriage, he had, she was certain, remained absolutely faithful to her since. This reference to past indiscretions aroused her fury.

She slapped Barbara Fitzharding's face.

Barbara, taken aback, stared at her, lifted her hand to retaliate and then remembered that there must be no brawling between women in positions such as theirs.

But her anger matched Sarah's.

"I'm not surprised at your mode of behavior," she said. "It is hardly to be wondered at. And besides being arrogant and ill-mannered you are also cruel. I should be ashamed, not to have poor relations, but to turn my back on them while they starve."

"What nonsense is this?"

"It is no nonsense. I heard only the other day the distressing story of the Hill family. I was interested . . . and so was my informant . . . because of their connection with the high and mighty Lady Marlborough! Your uncle, aunt, and cousins . . . dying of starvation! Two girls working as servants, I hear, two boys running about the streets, ragged and hungry."

"A pitiable story and one which does credit to your imagination, Lady Fitzharding."

"A pitiable story, Lady Marlborough, but it owes nothing to my imagination. Go and see for yourself. And let me tell you this, that I shall not feel it my duty to keep silent about this most shameful matter."

Sarah for once was speechless, and when Lady Fitzharding flounced out of the room she stared after her, murmuring: "Hill! Hill!" The name was familiar. Her grandfather Sir John Jennings, she had heard her own father say, had had twenty-two children and one of these, Mary, had married a Francis Hill who was a merchant of London.

Sarah had heard nothing of him since. One did not need to keep in touch with one's merchant connections—except of course when they were likely to bring disrepute.

Sarah made one of her prompt decisions.

Something must be done about the Hills.

Read all of Jean Plaidy's
Novels of the Stuarts
in historical order:

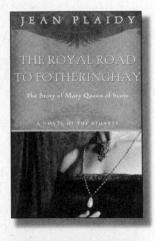

The Royal Road to Fotheringhay
The Story of Mary Queen of Scots
$15.00 PAPERBACK
978-0-609-81023-1

1

The Captive Queen of Scots
The Story of Queen Mary
$14.95 PAPERBACK
978-1-4000-8251-3

2

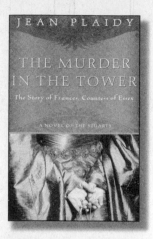

The Murder in the Tower
The Story of Frances,
Countess of Essex
$14.00 PAPERBACK
978-0-307-34621-6

The Loves of Charles II
The Stuart Saga
$16.00 PAPERBACK
978-1-4000-8248-3

previously published as
three separate volumes:
The Wandering Prince
Health Unto His Majesty
Here Lies Our Sovereign Lord

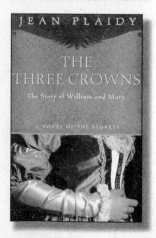

The Three Crowns
The Story of William and Mary
$14.00 PAPERBACK
978-0-307-34624-7

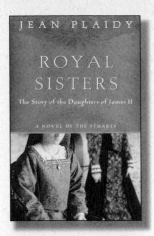

Royal Sisters
The Story of the
Daughters of James II
$15.00 PAPERBACK
978-0-307-71952-2

previously published
as *The Haunted Sisters*

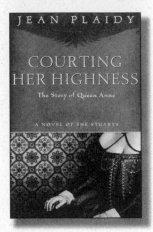

Courting Her Highness
The Story of Queen Anne
$16.00 PAPERBACK
978-0-307-71951-5

previously published as
The Queen's Favourites

COMING SUMMER 2011!

Available wherever books are sold

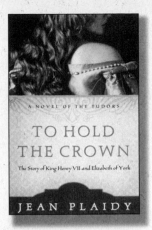

Read all of Jean Plaidy's
Novels of the Tudors
in historical order:

To Hold the Crown
The Story of King Henry VII
and Elizabeth of York
$14.95 PAPERBACK
978-0-307-34619-3

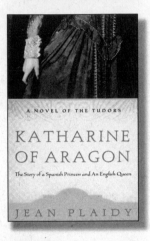

Katharine of Aragon
The Story of a Spanish Princess
and an English Queen
$16.00 PAPERBACK
978-0-609-81025-5

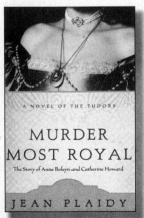

Murder Most Royal
The Story of Anne Boleyn
and Catherine Howard
$14.95 PAPERBACK
978-1-4000-8249-0

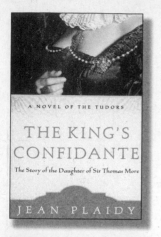

The King's Confidante
The Story of the Daughter
of Sir Thomas More
$13.95 PAPERBACK
978-0-307-34620-9

previously published as
St. Thomas's Eve

4

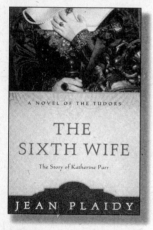

The Sixth Wife
The Story of Katherine Parr
$13.95 PAPERBACK
978-0-609-81026-2

5

The Thistle and the Rose
The Story of Margaret, Princess
of England, Queen of Scotland
$13.95 PAPERBACK
978-0-609-81022-4

6

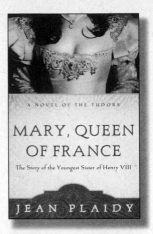

Mary, Queen of France
The Story of the Youngest Sister
of Henry VIII
$12.95 PAPERBACK
978-0-609-81021-7

For a Queen's Love
The Story of the Royal Wives
of Philip II
$14.00 PAPERBACK
978-0-307-34622-3

previously published as
The Spanish Bridegroom

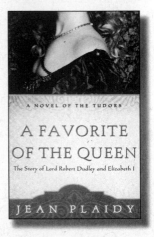

A Favorite of the Queen
The Story of Lord Robert Dudley
and Elizabeth I
$14.00 PAPERBACK
978-0-307-34623-0

previously published as
Gay Lord Robert

Available wherever books are sold